# FOREVER LOST, FOREVER GONE

# ABOUT THE CO-AUTHOR

Gerard Hunt covered the Birmingham pub bombings as a reporter in 1974 and then got to know the Birmingham Six personally while working for the *Birmingham Post* and *Mail*. He is currently Deputy Foreign Editor of the *Daily Mail*.

# FOREVER LOST, FOREVER GONE

Paddy Joe Hill
and
Gerard Hunt

BLOOMSBURY

First published 1995

This paperback edition published 1996

Copyright © 1995 by Paddy Joe Hill and Gerard Hunt

The moral right of the authors has been asserted

Bloomsbury Publishing Plc, 2 Soho Square, London W1V 6HB

A CIP catalogue record for this book is available from the British Library

ISBN 0 7475 2125 5

Typeset by Hewer Text Composition Services, Edinburgh
Printed in Great Britain by Cox & Wyman Ltd, Reading, Berkshire

To the victims of injustice in jails all over
the country, especially those whom I know personally.
May you all walk in freedom soon.
There is nothing in the world like it.

# CONTENTS

# Acknowledgements

In the long hot summer of 1975 I could count on two hands the number of people who believed in our innocence. On the day of our release, Thursday 14th March 1991, support in our innocence ran into millions throughout the world. I remain profoundly grateful to every individual who contributed in any small way to our eventual release and exoneration of all connection with the Birmingham Pub Bombings of November 1974.

I pay special tribute to the following: to the ordinary men, women and children from all over the world who wrote to me, put their pennies in collection boxes, and who raged and raised their voices against our injustice.

To Sarah Clark for all she has done from the beginning, not only for the Birmingham Six, the Guildford Four, the Maguire Seven and Judith Ward, but for all prisoners innocent and guilty. For the help, kindness and compassion she has shown to all of us and our families. We thank you – we are forever in your debt.

To Fr Denis Faul, Fr Raymond Murray and Fr Brady for their excellent work (1976). To 'The Birmingham Framework' for giving so much help and encouragement to me over the whole sixteen years of my wrongful imprisonment. To the (late) Cardinal O'Fiach and my very good friend Bishop Edward Daly (now retired). To the clergy in all the prisons we were incarcerated in and everything they did to make things easier for us.

To Chris Mullin, MP, for his brilliant, scholarly investigative work which produced the first TV documentary for World in Action that sparked the first significant public reaction. His book 'Error of Judgement' was a major breakthrough for the case of the Birmingham Six.

To Charles Tremayne, Ian McBride, Ray Fitzwalter and Leslie Udwin of Granada TV company for their great journalistic work in 'Who Bombed Birmingham' (1989).

To the MPs and TDs in England and Ireland who used their power and influence on our behalf. I would especially like to thank Jeremy Corbyn who continues to work tirelessly for all wrongfully convicted prisoners. To Dave Nellist, ex-MP for Coventry, and especially Sir John Farr, retired Conservative MP, who behaved so honourably towards me from the moment I made contact with him as my constituency MP in 1982.

There are some special and brave individuals whose evidence became so important. I pay tribute to the courage of PC Tom Clark, WPC Joyce Lynas and all other witnesses who came forward.

To all the entertainers who gave their services free and helped to raise thousands of pounds for our campaign, especially: Christy Moore, Jeremy Hardy, Kit Hollerbach, Conor Ryan, Billy Steven, Tom Robinson, Mary Black, Brush Shields and Sean Brady.

To trade union members of the NUM, UNISON, UCATT, MSF and the NUT who gave so generously to our cause.

To all the US Congressmen, Senators and other American politicians and Churchmen who helped to internationalise our case. To Fr Sean and Frank McManus, Sandy Boyer, Paul Dwyer, Governor William Bulger of Boston MA, and especially Dr Kathleen Lisowski who worked so tiredlessly on our behalf to get our case taken up by Congress. Kathleen, we owe you so much.

To our legal team: Lord Tony Gifford QC, Mike Mansfield QC, Richard Ferguson QC, Paddy O'Connor QC and all their staff for their friendship and brilliant advocacy on our behalf at the Appeal Courts.

To Dr Hugh Black who sadly passed away before it was proved that he had been right. I only wish he had lived to see it.

To solicitor Ivan Geffin for his courage in taking up our case immediately after our leave to appeal in 1976 failed. He showed so much bravery in championing our case for freedom.

To Michael Farrell, a Dublin-based lawyer and journalist who gave us his unstinting support. He never needed to be convinced of our innocence.

To Nulla Kelly, Maire Griffin, Joe Colgan, Tony Gregory TD,

Eithne ní Dhubbghaill, Peter and Muiread Green, Gay Nic Reamoinn and all those who organised the Parade of Innocence.

To Mrs Kathleen Doody and Mrs Margaret Zasbo and the other people who wrote to me regularly. You were all magnificent. It was the letters from you, the ordinary people, which gave us so much strength and determination to carry on our fight to prove our innocence.

When we first entered prison (Winson Green) in 1974 we suffered terrible batterings from the police and prison officers. The behaviour of those prison officers in that emotive time is not the normal way they behave. Due to the beating, a lot of people think all prison officers are bad. Far from it. From the very beginning there were those who were so good to us and our families.

The governor and staff at Lancaster were terrific towards us for the three months we were there. At Bristol, PO Turner and Officer Atkinson. Parkhurst – my first dispersal jail and the toughest jail in England – was the best jail I was in. I was never treated as others and the prisoners were great. They looked after me like a king. They there were always behind me and made sure that I had all the little comforts a jail can provide. My mother used to tell prison officers in the 1980s that no matter how well they treated her and the family, they could never treat her like the staff at Parkhurst. They couldn't have treated the Royal Family better. I say the same. They did so much to make it easier for me to adapt to life in prison and most of them believed we got a raw deal. I have many fond memories of staff and prisoners from every jail I was in. Whilst at Gartree Prison, where I was to remain the longest (nine years), I saw staff and prisoners come and go. When I was freed in 1991, I left a lot of good friends behind. PO Chester and SO Harrison and lots of others – to all of you my heartfelt thanks.

Up to this time we had been praying for a miracle, and while in Gartree I received an 'angel'– my solicitor Gareth Peirce. I extend my lifelong gratitude and affection. She continues to guide me and direct me.

To all the campaigners who set up support groups throughout the country. There are so many it would take a book for just your names alone. Here a just a few: Paul May, Sally Mulready, Felix Maguire, Bob Dawson (treasurer) who kept us all in stamps, Sue Milner, Joni Price, Anita Richards, Annie Blindell, Fr Pat Taaffe and the Birmingham group whose work in that city was particularly difficult.

To my good friend Ronnie McCartney who gave me so much help with the book and with my letter-writing campaign. He took over what Shane had started. Ronnie, I look forward to your long-awaited walk in freedom. Without you where would I be? Thanks mate, for everything.

To Dr McKeith and Dr Gudjonson for their patience and their time. They have been a great help to me since my release.

To Gerry Hunt, for his dedication and patience while we did this book.

To Mrs Ann Whelan and her husband Fred and for their inspiring work on behalf of the Bridgewater Four. To Michael Hickey (Ann's son), Vincent Hickey, Jimmy Robertson and Pat Molloy (RIP). We will continue to fight until you are free.

I pay a very special tribute to the six women who at that time were our wives. Traumatised and not knowing where to turn to, they kept our case alive in the early days when all doors were firmly shut against us. To Sandra Hunter for making sure the thousands of letters were posted. To Pat Hill, Eileen Callaghan and Nora Power who tramped the streets with petitions. To Teresa Walker and especially to the lady who was my inspiration, Kathleen McIlkenny. The six of us owe you so much.

To the twenty-seven children we left behind. They grew up without us but they never forgot us. Especially Maggie and Teresa McIlkenny and Paddy McIlkenny (Richard's brother) for their work on our behalf.

To my own family, especially my brother Billy. Thanks for everything.

To my five co-defendants for their support and good humour during the long hard years of our imprisonment. I wish you and your families all the happiness in the world.

Finally I pay a very special tribute to the most important person of all – my mother. Mum, you were always there for me when I needed you most. You're the best mum in the world. Thanks for everything. I love you.

# 1

## Prologue

I raised the glass of beer slowly to my lips and took a long, satisfying drink.

It was nearly midnight on a freezing cold Thursday in November 1974. Standing in the warmth of the bar on the *Duke of Lancaster* ferry as it prepared to pull out of the Lancashire port of Heysham, I thought about the weekend ahead.

In just a few hours I would be back in my home town of Belfast for the first time since leaving fourteen years earlier as a boy of fifteen. I had crossed the water to England on this same old boat, heading into the unknown with my family for a new life in the city of Birmingham. It was a very different Paddy Joe Hill making the return journey.

I had never wanted to leave Belfast, dragged away from my friends and relations, away from the streets I knew so well. But the yearning for home did not last long. In the cosmopolitan, comparatively affluent world of Birmingham I quickly realised what else I had left behind: the poverty, the religious discrimination, and the depression that comes of knowing that if, like me, you were a Catholic, you had little chance of ever getting a decent job. The streets of Birmingham were not exactly paved with gold in 1960, but there was work for all who wanted it, and they didn't ask your religion when you went for a job. As the years went by, Belfast became little more than a memory. I married a Birmingham girl, and by 1974 I had a young family of five daughters and a baby son to look after. I'd been out of work through illness, but was almost fully fit again and knew I'd have no trouble finding another job.

Yes, life was looking pretty good, and only one thing bothered me as I waited for the ferry to set sail. The reason I was making this

1

first trip home was that my Aunt Mary was seriously ill, and as she was in her eighties I feared the worst. I'd never had much reason to return before. But she had been like a second mother to me. As a kid I was forever at her house near ours in the Catholic enclave of Ardoyne. She had been in England earlier in 1974 and it was obvious then that she was dying. She had made me promise to go back to Belfast to see her one last time in that old house of hers.

I'd talked it over with my wife Pat who agreed that, despite our shortage of money because I was off work, I should make the effort to go. So I was toying with the idea when something completely unrelated occurred.

A young Belfast man called James McDade blew himself to bits planting a bomb for the Irish Republican Army in Coventry, a few miles down the road from Birmingham.

McDade was from the Ardoyne too. We had gone to the same school, but he was a few years younger than me so I'd not known him well, although I had been good friends with his elder brother Joe. I'd often been in their house and had had the occasional meal with the family. It was the way you lived in that tightly knit community, popping in and out of each other's homes. Years later, in the early 1970s, a younger McDade brother, Gerry, was shot dead by British soldiers. I didn't know it then, but his death led to James joining the ranks of the IRA.

McDade had moved to Birmingham in the late 1960s and I'd bumped into him once or twice, usually in pubs around the town where he was renowned as a great singer of country-and-western songs. I couldn't believe it when I heard how he had met his death. In the pubs I'd pictured him as another Jim Reeves, but never as a terrorist, an IRA bomber.

Some other Irish lads I knew in Birmingham who had also known McDade and his parents said they might go back to Belfast for the funeral. I told them that I'd been thinking of going back anyway to see my aunt, so I might join them. That I'd rather travel with someone than be on my own. But I said that if I couldn't raise the money for the fare I wouldn't bother. Then I got word that Aunt Mary had suffered a stroke, and I decided immediately I would have to find the cash to go. But it wasn't easy, and eventually I had to borrow it from the nuns at a convent near my home, promising to repay the loan with a bit of decorating for them on my return.

Five of us set off together from Birmingham on the boat train to Heysham that Thursday night. That was how I came to be standing at the bar on the *Duke of Lancaster*, idly reading a newspaper as I waited for the others. I was alone because I had drifted ahead of them as we got off the train and went through the security controls before boarding. The IRA had been bombing places around England for months, so checks on people travelling to and from Ireland had become routine. I was questioned for a time, but the policeman was happy with my answers and told me I was free to board.

As I walked up on to the boat a young crewman told me he'd heard that bombs had gone off somewhere earlier that night, although he didn't know where. That would explain why we were being questioned so closely as we got off the train. I presumed the others were being delayed by the checks and would soon join me. They certainly knew there was only one place to look for me – in the bar.

While I waited and sipped my pint I considered the brighter possibilities of what I expected would be a fairly gloomy weekend. Well, it was a great opportunity to see some of those old friends I had left behind years before. I'd only a few pounds in my pocket, but there were plenty of people back there who would look after me. And without the wife and kids to worry about I could have a good drink and enjoy the fun of what we Irish call the 'crack'.

But it didn't work out that way.

Within a few hours I was being battered around by policemen trying to get me to confess to planting bombs for the IRA.

Within days I was charged with five other men with the biggest mass murder in British history at that time, the Birmingham pub bombings in which 21 people died and more than 160 were injured.

And within months I was sent to jail. It was intended. I should stay there for the rest of my life. The judge told us we had been convicted 'on the clearest and most overwhelming evidence I have ever heard of the crime of murder'. I was one of the six most hated men in the country; my marriage fell apart; my children grew up never knowing me, nor I them; my father died as I languished in a prison cell; I suffered mental and physical abuse that will scar me until the day I die. I lost my freedom for 16 years, 3 months and 23 days.

But I was innocent.

# 2

# Early days

I was born on 20 December 1944 in a part of Belfast known as the Ardoyne, the second son of Robert and Anne Hill.

The Ardoyne was, and is, a close-knit, mainly Catholic community in the north of Belfast, a city which has become infamous around the world for its sectarian divide. Houses were always hard to come by, so for the first years after they got married my parents lived with my mother's mother, Grandma Johnston, at 141 Brompton Park. My mother and her family were originally from Armagh but had moved to Belfast before the war. It was there that she met my father, who had been born and raised in the rough Sailortown area around the docks.

My dad had joined the British Army in the 1930s as a professional soldier, like his dad before him, and was away serving in the Second World War as a sergeant when I was born and christened Patrick Joseph. The first of the family was my brother Bobby, who was two years older than me and, following family tradition, had been named after my dad. As the second son I was named after the patron saint of Ireland, Saint Patrick. Joseph seemed to be given as a second name to every other kid in Catholic Belfast. I would become known to one and all as Paddy Joe.

When I was about two we moved to a house in Beechmount, an area off the Falls Road, which is one of the two main roads through west Belfast and populated almost exclusively by Catholics. Dad had left the army after the war ended and took various jobs, usually as a driver. He also became a regular member of the part-time Territorial Army, working as a cook at its Henry Place base in Belfast two or three times a week.

Our house moves were usually related to my dad's work, in that he

4

would try to get a house fairly close to wherever he had a job. When I was three we moved again, this time to Spamount Street in the New Lodge area of north Belfast, and we stayed there till I was about seven. So it was of living here that I have my first memories.

The house was on a corner, and quite big by working-class Belfast standards. There were three bedrooms, a kitchen, a bathroom, and two rooms downstairs. But we needed the space because the family was growing. Three more brothers and a sister arrived over the years – Sammy, Billy, Frank and Josephine. My mum's full-time job was raising six children. We never had much money, but nor did any of the families around us, and the warmth and security of a loving home amply compensated for the lack of material wealth. We always seemed to have plenty of food in the house though, and I can't ever recall being desperately short of anything, or thinking of ourselves as being really poor. We never went away on holidays, but we had a great time on day trips during the summer to seaside places such as Bangor or Greencastle.

Dad used to run a little shop from the house selling second-hand books, and it was through that I developed a love of reading. By the time I started school at St Malachy's primary I was reading books well ahead of my age, having finished with comics because I didn't find them challenging enough. I was quickly into the schoolboy classics, such as *Tom Brown's Schooldays* and *Huckleberry Finn*. Later I graduated to Micky Spillane novels and gangster stories, which I found much more to my taste, far racier and evoking a world of action and excitement among the skyscrapers of New York.

But in its own way, Belfast was well able to satisfy the thirst for adventure of a little boy bursting with energy. In fact, life as a kid in that city then was pretty much one big – and usually happy – adventure. When I wasn't at school I would be out running in the streets with dozens of other youngsters, playing football, fighting, shouting at the girls and pinching sweets from the local shop. And forever wandering in and out of friends' houses. It may be a tired cliché to say the doors in the street were always open, but it really was like that. It was an upbringing that led you to meet a huge number of people, both young and old, but almost always from a similar background to yourself.

Like everybody else in my area I was a Catholic, and it was a simple fact of life that you went to Mass on Sundays and feast days, went to the funeral when somebody up the street died, and were expected to be married in a Catholic church. Both of my parents were Catholics, but I did not have an over-religious upbringing. Being a Catholic was not something you really thought about as a youngster. When I was a little older I became more aware of the divide between Catholics and Protestants in Northern Ireland. But as a kid there were too many other things to get on with, like playing soccer, or marbles, or cowboys and indians.

These days people forget there was a time when Belfast children had things to do other than throw stones at British soldiers. Not that we didn't find plenty of other ways to get into trouble. I always seemed to be getting into scrapes at school or on the streets, usually involving fights with other boys. I was small but I was determined not to be pushed around, and I was not averse to striking back at much bigger lads if they tried to bully me. If something like a piece of wood came to hand for me to use as a weapon, so much the better. There's no doubt that the streak of violence that has exploded within me frequently over the years was forged during my childhood on those hard streets.

At school I was forever getting the cane or the leather strap the teachers would wield with enthusiasm. Because I was advanced at reading compared to the boys around me I would get bored very quickly in class, and that was always a prelude to causing trouble. I would pull out my catapult and fire off rolled-up paper balls at some of the other kids. Inevitably it would end with the teacher shouting, 'Hill, step up here.'

I was seven when we moved house again because dad got a good job as a delivery driver at Mackies, an engineering works which was one of the biggest employers in Belfast. We went to West Circular Road, in north-west Belfast, and the new home was a sharp contrast to the back-to-back terraced houses of the Catholic ghettos. It even had front and back gardens! I switched schools, moving to Holy Cross primary in the Ardoyne, which meant most of my friends were from that area. It also meant I could see a lot more of my grandparents in Brompton Park, and my gran's sister, whom we called Aunt Mary, who lived next door. I used to love going to see them after school, often staying over at night or at weekends. Mum had a lot on her plate with six kids to bring up. Bobby was the apple of her eye, and with me always getting into trouble over one thing or another she was happy if she knew I was at her mother's. I was the special one with my gran and Aunt Mary, so it was a set-up that eased tensions all round.

At seven I still viewed life as one big adventure, and when I wasn't in Ardoyne I was out discovering that the area to which we had moved was ideally suited for a lad looking for fun. There was a big building site where new houses were being built; a sports ground; a little wood, which to us was a forest; a stream; a police shooting range; and allotments where people would grow fruit and vegetables. I was in a huge gang called the Apaches, and we would get up to all sorts of things. Sneaking into the shooting range was always exciting, and we would collect spent bullets and cartridge cases to throw on little fires we would build in the wood. The allotments were a regular target, with sometimes a dozen or more of us swarming over some poor gardener's prized carrots and potatoes or fruit trees.

I always had to be careful, though, because dad would lay down the law at home. He did so with all the firm discipline you would expect of an army man. And he was a big man. If I really stepped out of line he would take off his shiny leather army belt and use it to give me a good hiding across the backside. But he never made any of us feel resentful towards him. And unlike so many Belfast fathers, he would never come back to the house drunk after a session at the pub and start knocking his wife and kids around. He and mum had a good marriage, which stood the test of time.

I would often get a leathering from my dad for the sort of things that happen to every kid, such as splitting your shoes playing football in the street, or getting your shirt ripped in a fight. When your parents cannot afford to buy new shoes or a shirt every other day it is not surprising they lose their tempers and lash out, without causing any real harm. Another big source of trouble was the fact I always wanted to be out playing on the streets till all hours. Even as a kid of just five or six I would be out like a shot as soon as the door was open. I would regularly feel the power of my father's hand for staying out too late, but for me it was all part of the rough and tumble of growing up.

I do, though, remember vividly one occasion when dad went berserk and almost lost control with me. As usual, I deserved all I got. Mum used to keep a money box on a shelf in the house. She would put in an odd sixpence or shilling now and then, and liked to know she had a few pounds there for an emergency or for one of the kids' birthdays. One day, when I was about eight, I did the unthinkable and took the money box. I raced out of the house with it and went off with a gang of friends to some secret place where we forced it open.

There was about nine pounds in it which was an absolute fortune to us. In fact, it was pretty close to a fortune to my mother too. We headed straight for the shops, where I treated every kid in the area to sweets and pop. One of the kids had rescued an old pram from a rubbish tip and I was paraded around the streets in it for the rest of the day like a king. With, of course, frequent stops back at the sweet shop to top up, and then later in the day at the fish-and-chip shop.

It was an immense feeling of power. Whatever I said had to be obeyed by the other kids, my 'subjects'. I was enjoying myself so much I completely lost track of time and at 7 p.m. had still not gone home. By then my dad was home from work, and the theft of the money box had been reported to him by my outraged mum. He went out looking for me and found me a few streets away, still being pushed around in regal fashion while hanging on tightly to the money box. At that stage the contents were down to about three shillings.

My 'subjects' disappeared pretty rapidly at the sight of my dad in a raging temper and I was kicked practically all the way home, where I then got the biggest hiding of my young life.

Another memorable occasion, as it is for most Catholic children, was making my first Holy Communion at the age of seven. There were months of preparation at school and it was rated second only to Christmas as a day to look forward to. Not so much for the spiritual side, but more because you knew it was traditional for the first communicant to be showered with sixpences, shillings, and possibly even more by family friends and relations. Mum and dad saved up so that I would have a new short-trousers suit, crisp white shirt and blood-red tie for the big day.

I and the rest of the kids in my class made our first Holy Communion at Holy Cross Church in Ardoyne, a massive, awe-inspiring building. After the Mass we had family pictures taken outside the church with my dad's old box camera. And then indeed came the long-awaited pushing of silver into an ever-open little hand.

I remember getting half-crowns from both my gran and my Aunt Mary. I ended up with so much money I hardly knew what to do with it. While delighted with my riches, I can well recall the sense of disappointment at the end of the day that a first Holy Communion came around just once.

A few years later came another milestone in a Catholic childhood, confirmation, a sacrament that was administered by the local bishop, again at Holy Cross. On being confirmed you take on an additional name, usually chosen to signify devotion to a particular saint or for some such worthy reason. I took the name Aloysius, but cannot for the life of me remember why, unless it was to boast of having a name that defies most people's efforts to pronounce it correctly.

Many such celebrations as these revolved around the Church, with baptisms and weddings a regular feature. A regular feature too were deaths and funerals. I can particularly remember the death of my granddad Willy Johnston, my mother's father, in November 1953 shortly before my ninth birthday. He had been in a hospital for the terminally ill for some time, and I'd visited him there a lot with my mum. One day I was at home with mum when the window in the living room started rattling loudly for no apparent reason. My mum blessed herself and said to me, 'Your grandfather's gone.'

The next day came the news that he had indeed died. I couldn't stop crying. I went with my parents to my gran's house, where old Willy's body was in an open coffin in a bedroom up the stairs. I went up and people were saying prayers around the coffin. It was the first dead person I had seen, and I kept expecting him to wake up. I just sat there for a while, staring and crying. A day or so later we all went to Armagh for the funeral. It was the greatest sadness I'd known up to that age.

Nobody grows up in Belfast without being touched by sectarianism. There are two great tribes in that city – one Catholic, one Protestant; one green, one orange. You live in an enclosed, self-contained world in which virtually everybody you come into contact with is of the same tribe as yourself.

My family was Catholic and green, and nominally Republican, in as much as they wanted to see a united Ireland. The Catholic community had suffered terrible discrimination in housing and jobs at the hands of the dominant Protestant community which had ruled the

North of Ireland since the partition of Ireland in 1921. And Catholics believed they could seldom get a fair deal from the almost exclusively Protestant police force. People like my parents were aware that a united Ireland would put Catholics in the majority, which in a naïve way they felt would be the simple answer to all our problems. But Republicanism in our family stretched no further than that – and with a father and grandfather who had given some of the best years of their lives to the British Army that was no surprise. Nor was it a surprise that my elder brother Bobby joined the British Army when he was seventeen and served for nearly twenty-five years. There was no history of membership or support for the Irish Republican Army in our family, and indeed at that time the IRA was generally regarded across Belfast, if not most of the country, as a bit of a joke. It's true people often spoke and sang nostalgically of the Easter Rising of 1916 and IRA heroes of that era. But there was no real support for the remnants of the movement.

There was a brief resurgence of IRA activity in a border campaign which began in 1956 and fizzled out a few years later. But there was little impact in Belfast, far removed from the action along the border with the South. By any standards the campaign was a disaster. It failed to mobilise popular support, and the IRA had little influence through its political wing, Sinn Féin.

The Catholic/Protestant divide of Northern Ireland is epitomised by the annual Twelfth of July celebrations of the Protestants, when they mark a famous seventeenth-century victory over Catholics with colourful parades and marching bands. The Battle of the Boyne, in which the Protestant King William of Orange defeated the Catholic King James, may have happened in 1690, but its importance lives on as if it were yesterday in Protestant hearts.

You could feel the tension rising in the city in late June and early July. The Protestant bands would be reaching a peak in rehearsals, and the sounds of flutes and big drums would waft on the wind across into Catholic areas. In Protestant areas the kerbstones would be painted red, white and blue, and Union flags would flutter above the houses. There would be fights between Catholic and Protestant gangs on the dividing lines between different areas. And then came the big day.

The spectacle on the Twelfth was something to behold. Starting with huge bonfires as high as a house on the night before, many of us Catholics would watch it purely for its entertainment value. The marching bands in their uniforms, with the drum major hurling his baton way into the air and then catching it again without missing a step. The young lads on flutes rattling out tunes you couldn't resist tapping your feet to. The big fat man, always a big fat man, hammering out the rhythm on a big drum as he danced around like a man possessed. And the colourful, ornate banners denoting various Orange lodges, usually dominated by a huge tapestry of a victorious King Billy astride his white horse.

If it were not for the sectarian theme, such a march would surely prove one of Britain's biggest tourist attractions each year. I used to be fascinated by it but was always aware that as Catholics we were on the sidelines, that this was something alien to us. The bands would take hours to march by, going out to a field on the outskirts of town where a huge rally would be held. And afterwards, in the evening when the rally was over, there would always be trouble. There were youths gathered in the streets, and there was lots of drink. Protestant gangs would try to rampage through Catholic areas, and often succeed, smashing windows and terrifying the residents. Gangs of Catholic men would try to protect their areas, and there would be fights with bricks, and knives and broken bottles.

The sectarianism that infected every aspect of life really came home to me when I was eleven. Mackies, the engineering works at which my father had worked since I was seven, had a workforce that was almost exclusively Protestant. Quite how my father, a Catholic, got a job there I've never known. But perhaps his regular appearances in a British Army uniform as he went off to his Territorial Army duties in the evenings gave the impression he was a Protestant, and he did nothing to alter that view. He had a good job with good money and did not want to lose it.

One day I came home from school and knew from the sight of his discarded work clothes that dad was back early from work. I could feel a terrible atmosphere in the house. I asked mum why he was home and she told me bluntly, 'He's been sacked.' When I asked why she said, 'For being a Catholic.' Dad was upstairs in a bedroom and I sensed he would not welcome my questions. So nothing more was said.

It was years later before my father told me what had happened. Two days before he was sacked, he had loaded up his lorry with steel for delivery the following morning and was parking it in the yard with the help of another worker, who was a member of an Orange lodge, 'lodge' being the term used for a branch of the Protestant-supremacist Orange Order. Some of the steel was overhanging the back of the lorry, and as my dad reversed, it caught the other guy slightly. My dad jumped out of his cab and checked to see if the guy was all right, which he was. Dad said he should report the matter anyway in line with company policy. But the guy said not to bother as it was too minor to worry about. So dad parked his lorry and went home.

He made his delivery the next day, and when he got back to the works found a note on his clocking-on card telling him to report to the personnel office first thing the next morning. He did so, to be told he was being sacked for failing to report an accident. It turned out the Protestant worker had discovered my father was a Catholic and taken exception to him working at the firm. He had gone to the bosses and claimed my dad had refused to report the accident.

The loss of the job also meant the loss of our lovely house, as we could no longer afford the rent, so we moved back to the Ardoyne. I actually welcomed the move, because it meant being so much closer to my gran's and Aunt Mary's again, and closer to my schoolfriends. I had by now moved on to St Gabriel's secondary school, which was the automatic move for kids from Holy Cross.

I had a nice little sideline at this time which earned a few shillings each week. I would pinch wooden crates that had been left at the back of shops, and chop them up to make sticks. It was a lucrative little business, as everybody needed sticks for lighting the coal fires that were standard in our houses. I was chased once or twice by angry shopkeepers, but managed to keep clear of the police until I was thirteen. And then my first brush with the law was on a different matter altogether. Some older boys from school had broken into a sweet shop, and with what I and my pals took to be great generosity, dispensed their ill-gotten gains freely to us all. Unfortunately the police soon rounded us up and we were each fined five shillings for receiving stolen property.

School was viewed as a penance to be endured, and few of us gave much thought to education as a means to improve yourself, a route to a better life. Nobody from our area, where unemployment was the norm and prospects were nil, had real expectations of a brighter future. I had a natural grasp of mathematics and English, but with so little incentive to be successful, I could not be bothered with other subjects. I suppose our teachers at school did their best, but I can't recall any who provided much in the way of motivation. That meant I and the others in my class grew up in a world of school and the streets that was almost devoid of hope and ambition. Life revolved around day-to-day existence, and we looked no further. My parents encouraged me to go to school, but not so much because they could see the value of a good education. It was more to do with the fact that the authorities were rigorous in taking to court parents of children with bad attendance records. I don't blame my mum and dad for my childhood lack of dreams for the future; they knew no other world either.

Even when very young I was aware that the future seemed to offer only two possible paths to follow. One was to comply with the law of the land and stay at school until fifteen, and then get out at the first opportunity and try to get a job. You might just possibly succeed, but being a Catholic it was more likely you would spend your life unemployed or doing the most menial of jobs, like most of the people around you.

The other route was to do well at school with a view to going on to college and then getting a job away from Belfast. But that meant leaving behind your family and friends, and in our tight little community it was rarely considered a realistic option. Not only that, but access to higher education at that time was also limited by the blight of discrimination. The most famous seat of learning in Belfast is Queen's University. Even as a young teenager I was familiar with the old joke that the only way a Catholic could get there was by leaving his body to medical research.

In December 1959 I left school as soon as I reached fifteen, with no qualifications and a reputation as a little tearaway with a quick temper and ever-ready fists. Amazingly I managed to get a job almost straight away, at Ewart's linen mill on the Crumlin Road, in which the bulk of the workforce was female, and where I was one of just eight Catholics among the ninety men employed. I got the job thanks to brother Bobby, who had himself got in there through somebody he knew.

The work was dirty, oiling the spinning frames to keep them cool, but it meant a wage at the end of the week and I was glad to have it. Unfortunately it didn't last long.

I'd been there three months when two of the Catholic lads were attacked by a group of Protestant workers for being 'Papists'. They were badly beaten, and so the other six of us decided to be prepared for similar treatment, arming ourselves with a variety of weapons from around the mill. The police were called and we were fired.

I quickly got another job at another mill, this time Linsey's in Flax Street, which was predominantly Catholic. I was a rovedrawer, which meant I had to attach big spindles to machines as part of the linen-making process. Within a few weeks there I had picked up the characteristic that marks me to this day – a five-inch scar down my left cheek.

I was sitting outside the mill taking my lunch break when one of my mates and one of the girl workers appeared, having a real row over a bit of horseplay that had got out of hand. He said he was going to punch her and I jumped up to pull him away. I didn't realise it, but the girl had pulled out a knife she used in her job and had started to swing at him. I had come between them, and the blade went down my face. I felt the blood gush from the cut.

They took me into an office where one guy promptly fainted at the sight of the blood, but somebody had the sense to call an ambulance. I was taken to the Mater Hospital and had nineteen stitches put in the side of my face. I was told to lie on a bed and not move for a while, but when I saw two policemen enter the ward I was up and off. By then I had learned that a Catholic in Belfast doesn't spend time with the police if he can avoid it.

It was no good. I got home to be greeted by my mother screaming, 'What in God's name has happened to you?' With her were two policemen.

A few weeks later my pal, the girl and myself were all in court charged with affray and each fined £5. And because I refused to say who had used the knife, I was fined another £5 for contempt of court.

After some time off work because of the injury I returned to the mill. I was enjoying life. I would spend my spare time in snooker halls, at the cinema, and going to dances. I went out with one or two girls, but was not really interested in having a girlfriend. I was having too much fun with the lads I was running about with to let women complicate my life.

While I was out enjoying myself, events were taking place that would switch my life in a different direction altogether. My father had taken several odd jobs after being sacked from Mackies, finally setting up on his own as a chimney sweep. Eventually he told my mother he had had enough of Belfast and was going to break away, to see what life was like over the water in Birmingham. His brother had found work there and told my dad he could arrange a job for him too. When my dad told me he was going to England I was sad he would be leaving, but had seen it happen to so many other families I just accepted it as part of life. My elder brother Bobby succeeded in his application to join the British Army at about the same time, and they left together aboard the same boat in February 1960. Mum and I went to the docks to see them off, and we both shed a few tears before returning home.

I missed my dad, but he would ring the public telephone box at the end of our street at a prearranged time each week, and I would go down with mum and all the younger kids to speak to him. He would also write each week and send money, which was badly needed as I was the only one bringing a wage into the house, and that was just a few pounds.

Dad got a job in a factory in Birmingham almost immediately, and it was not long before my mum went over to join him and review the prospects for moving the whole family. She left me and the younger children in the care of her sister, who moved into our house to look after us while she was away. Mum wrote to us and phoned, using the same arrangement we had used with dad. She said things were much brighter there and that if she could organise some decent accommodation she would probably be back to take us all over. She had got a job too, and so there was a lot more money about.

But somehow what she was saying never really sunk in, and I didn't give much thought to the idea of moving to Birmingham. It all seemed unreal. And anyway, I was too busy having a good time with my mates in the Ardoyne, playing snooker and sneaking into pubs for an under-age drink, to worry about tomorrow.

Then on 1 August as I was leaving our house to go to work a taxi pulled up. Mum got out. I could hardly believe it was her. We kissed, and I told her how great it was to see her again, but said I was late for work and would have to go.

'No you don't,' she told me. 'You're all coming back to England with me tonight.'

# 3

## Second city

I didn't want to leave Belfast. I knew every street, every alleyway in my part of Ardoyne, and all my friends were there. It was the only life I'd known.

When mum and dad had gone to England I had just assumed they would return eventually. Anyway, at fifteen and a half I would soon be able to look after myself in Belfast. But mum was not in the mood to listen to my protests.

'You'll pack all your stuff and help the kids with theirs, so you will,' she ordered.

I stuffed the few things I had into an old bag and went off to say goodbye to my friends. Most of them did not have jobs, so were at home or on the street during the day. I explained what was happening, but there were no emotional farewells as if I were setting out for an exciting new life in a strange land. 'I'm off to England with my mum. But I'll be back soon,' I told them.

I got home to find an uncle had arrived with a van to take all our stuff to the docks. There wasn't a lot, just old suitcases and bags filled with clothes. We loaded them up and I went with him to the boat, where we were able to check in all the luggage before the ferry sailed that night. Then we went back to the house to say goodbye to my gran and Aunt Mary. Unlike us kids, they obviously knew we were going for good, because there were floods of tears as they kissed us and waved us off.

We all piled into the battered old van and set off for the ferry. It was the *Duke of Lancaster*, which sailed back and forth between Belfast and the port of Heysham in north-west England.

The boat was to sail at about 9.30 p.m., and I remember how shortly before that they rang a bell to warn people who were on

17

board but not travelling that they should leave. That was when it really came home to me that we were leaving for a trip into the unknown. The big boat's hooter sounded a few times, and then we slowly pulled away from the dock and headed out into the cold and dark of Belfast Lough, to England.

I stood alone on the deck watching the lights of the city fade away. In the blackness all I could hear was the rushing water of the ferry's wake. As I turned away to rejoin mum and the kids in the warmth of the lounge down below, I comforted myself with one thought. I would help the family settle down in this new city, and then when I turned sixteen, I'd get this same boat back the other way.

It was an uneventful journey, and early the following morning the big ferry eased its way into the docks at Heysham where we trooped off, mum carrying a big case and trailing little Frankie, and the rest of us struggling along with assorted bags and cases. A railway line came right into the port, almost up to the boat itself, and waiting there for us was the train for Birmingham. We all piled on, hurling bags into luggage racks and clambering on to seats. It seemed almost everybody who had been on the boat was catching the train too, and I remember thinking that Birmingham might not be such a bad place if so many people wanted to go there.

I didn't know much about Birmingham. I'd heard it was called England's Second City, because it was the second largest. Now it was to be my second city. I knew it was known as Brum. And I could recall from many years earlier that some relatives who had moved there had visited our house on one of their trips home. They told us, 'There's nothing for you here – get over to Birmingham where there are good jobs for everyone.'

They were right about that. At the time we arrived the city was the manufacturing heart of Britain, and with the booming 1960s underway there was full employment in a city of a million people. The industrial nature of Birmingham is symbolised by the city's coat of arms, which is topped by a raised arm wielding a hammer.

There were massive car factories employing thousands of men and women, dozens of medium-sized factories and engineering works, and literally hundreds of small workshops around the city, which were usually kept busy producing components for the larger works.

And with strong unions, the workers on the whole were some of the best-paid in the country.

The availability of well-paid work acted like a magnet for people from far beyond Birmingham's boundaries, those who were only too happy to leave their homes in Britain's depressed areas for the chance of a job in the Midlands. In 1960 there was already a massive Irish community in the city, and its impact could be seen most obviously in the large number of Catholic churches and schools in almost every district. There were Scots from the dying steel mills and coal mines of Lanarkshire and Ayrshire, Geordies from the dirty and dangerous pits of north-eastern England; and Welshmen from the valleys of south Wales.

In the late 1950s and 1960s the job prospects in Birmingham proved a great attraction for immigrants from even further afield. A great proportion of those who left the poverty of the West Indies, India and Pakistan and other corners of what had been Britain's empire to pursue dreams of wealth in the UK settled in and around the city.

On that bright August morning in 1960 our train pulled into Birmingham's New Street station at about midday. It was a blackened, grimy old station that had been built in the days of steam engines, very different to the modern station which replaced it seven years later to mark electrification of the railways. As we bashed open the doors and tumbled on to the platform I could feel I was now in a different environment, a different culture. A porter came to help us, the first Birmingham person I had met. He was friendly and kind, but his Brummie accent was so strong it was like a foreign language to me and I hardly understood a word he said.

We made our way to a taxi rank at the back of the station, in a street long since demolished called Jamaica Row. I remember the name well because under the street sign were two West Indian men talking. A black face was such a rare sight in Belfast I'd never seen more than one or two. Within minutes it had been driven home to me twice, by the porter's accent and these black faces, just what a different world I was now in.

We headed for Port Hope Road, a street of terraced houses off the main Stratford Road in Sparkbrook, a district south-east of the city centre which has long provided first homes to successive waves of immigrants. It was a three-storey house which my parents had part-rented from the Asian landlord. We had three bedrooms, a living room, a kitchen and a bathroom. The flat on the floor above us was rented by a young West Indian girl.

Dad was out at work in a local factory, so we made a cup of tea and unpacked, and waited for him to come home. We were all exhausted after the boat and train journeys. When he did it was great to see him again, for the first time in six months. He was kissing the younger kids and they were jumping all over him. After the excitement had died down I asked him what he really thought of Birmingham. He told me it was a tremendous city, with plenty of work and the religious troubles of Belfast nonexistent. He really loved it, and I could tell from that moment there was never going to be any prospect of us all returning to Belfast as a family. If I were to go back, it would have to be on my own. In fact, my dad did not set foot in Belfast again, and I never once heard him utter a word of regret at leaving. I went to bed that first night thinking that if dad rated the place so highly, it might not be so bad after all. I would have to give it a chance.

It did not take long for the wicked temper and ready recourse to violence that had begun to surface frequently in Belfast to show up again in Birmingham. The house was in a small side street, which meant it was safe enough for all the kids to play outside. In those days even the major roads had nothing like the traffic we see today. The morning after we arrived my little sister Josephine ran in from the street, crying her heart out. An older boy had made fun of her strong Belfast accent. I pulled her by the hand, dragging her back outside and, staring at the gang of lads standing around, asked her, 'Which one was it?'

She pointed him out and I strode over and beat him up, without any debate over the rights and wrongs of what might or might not have been said. In those days, and for many years after, I was far too prone to let my fists do the talking. I was not a lot over five feet tall, and the other lad was a lot bigger than me, but I was well used to having to defend myself and striking first whenever I thought it necessary. With big brother Bobby now away in the army I regarded it as my job to look after the younger ones in the family. To my way of thinking, that meant making my mark with the people around us, sending a clear message that I was not to be tangled with.

The boy's parents came to our house to complain to my dad. He questioned me about what had happened and I told him.

'I'm not going to let anybody make fun of us, or the way we talk,' I said.

'I understand that, son,' he replied. 'But you're not in Belfast now. People here won't stand for that sort of thing.'

He was right, of course, but it did not make much difference to me then and brawling, particularly after too much to drink, became part of life for me over the next few years. I'm not proud of that, but nor am I particularly ashamed because I seldom went looking for trouble. It's just I was never slow to take offence. I've always had a short fuse, and I still have to work hard at controlling my temper today.

A week after I arrived I began a job my mother had arranged for me at the factory where she worked, a company called Sercks which produced steel tubes. My job was as a tube drawer, which involved taking red-hot tubes as they came out of a furnace and feeding them through to a machine that would stretch them to order.

I was in a completely alien environment for my first few days. I was surrounded by English people, the 'old enemy' according to Irish folklore, who spoke a language I could barely understand. But it was not long before I realised these were people just like me, and that there were few real differences between us beneath the accents. I began to make friends with many of the English lads and the other young Irishmen working there. I also made friends outside work, mainly in the streets around our home. That helped prevent the homesickness I had feared, and I settled into life in Birmingham far more easily than I had expected. It was not long before I had left behind any thoughts of returning to Belfast.

My first wages were about £13 a week, which was an awful lot of money to me at that time. I would give mum about half for my board, and spend the rest pretty quickly. The thought of saving anything never occurred to me. I might have left Belfast behind, but not that mentality of day-to-day living and never looking to the future that had become ingrained in me. I would spend the money on clothes, on cigarettes, in snooker halls, and in pubs whenever I could sneak in without being spotted as an under-age drinker. Easy come, easy go, was the motto I lived by.

Life cruised along quite nicely until February 1961, six months after I had arrived, when we suddenly found ourselves thrown out on the street. Mum had been complaining to our landlord that she had occasionally seen a rat in the building or in the garden, but he had refused to do anything about it. Eventually she got in touch with the health officials at the local council, who came down heavily on the landlord. His response was to evict us.

We had nowhere to go, as homes suitable for a large family to rent were not easy to find. So mum had to move into a hostel in Acock's Green in the city with the four younger children, while me and dad had to take lodgings nearby. That lasted for a few months, and it was a strain on us all having the family split up in that way. Eventually, though, we got a place in Hockley, north-west of the city centre, where we stayed for two years. We then moved to another house in the same area. Mum and dad moved for the last time, in 1967, to a house off the main Chester Road, in Pype Hayes, north-east Birmingham.

I left Sercks in October 1961 because, having moved house, I found the travelling was becoming too much. The beauty of Birmingham in the 1960s was that it was a town where jobs were so plentiful you could walk out of a factory one afternoon and start a new job elsewhere the next morning. I went to a place called Fish and Atkinson, a plating and diecasting firm, and stayed there as a machine operator for two years, before doing another two-year stint at a plater's, Annertons. Next came eighteen months as a power press operator at a manufacturing firm, Garfields, followed by another eighteen months in the same job at a similar firm called Concentric.

It was at Garfields, in the late 1960s, that I had my first experience of trade union activity. The unions were very big at that time in the city, particularly at the massive car plants, but held less sway at the dozens of smaller engineering firms. There was no union at Garfields, so me and three or four others who all felt our conditions needed improving got together. We became part of the giant Amalgamated Union of Engineering Workers, with me as our shop steward, the local union representative. We put in a demand to the company for better pay and conditions, and eventually managed to get what we wanted without having to go on strike or take any action. I was really pleased, and impressed with the way we had achieved it.

I did go on strike though a couple of years later when working at

Concentric, where much of the work was in producing foot pedals for cars. I had been elected shop steward there and became involved in a dispute over bonuses. The management would not give way, so the lads voted to strike. We were all out for four days before the management called us in to say they would agree to our demands. It turned out the car industry was grinding to a halt because of the lack of foot pedals!

During those years I had been spending an increasing amount of time earning extra money by working with friends who ran commercial painting and decorating firms. By the end of the 1960s I had become bored with the routine of factory work and decided to go into painting full-time. I much preferred painting, because you were always in a different environment, meeting different people, tackling different jobs. Rather than stuck in a factory with nothing to hold your interest, you were out on the road travelling from job to job and seeing new places.

I was enjoying the work, but in the early 1970s I began to suffer from stomach ulcers, and at Christmas 1971 I had to go into East Birmingham Hospital for an operation. I was fine for a time after that, but in 1973 I began suffering gallstone trouble. It put me off work quite a lot through sickness and dizzy spells, and eventually at the end of 1973 the doctors, who were treating me with tablets and other medication, said I should finish work altogether for a time. I was then at a painting firm called Baxters and earning about £40 a week, which was pretty good money. After the doctor told me to stop work I was classed as being on sick leave and so still got paid, until August when I was made redundant and had to start claiming social security. When the events of November 1974 came around I was a lot better, and ready to start looking for a job again.

Outside of work, my socialising too often revolved around drink, and I was not keeping the best of company. It was not long before I was in trouble with the law, and over the next few years I built up a string of convictions for being drunk, for assaults, for burglary, and for other offences.

The first came in early 1961 when the gang of young lads I was with one night got into a fight with a rival gang. It was a vicious punch-up, in which as ever I played a leading part, and suddenly a lot of policemen were on the scene. We all ran off, scattering in every direction. I clambered over a nearby wall into an alleyway which ran beside some shops and decided to wait for the heat to die down. But a copper appeared, and when he challenged me I suggested, in the time-honoured language of the streets, that he go on his way.

He had other plans and arrested me. But far from being accused of taking part in a street brawl, I was charged with loitering with intent to break and enter the shops. I was fined £25 at Birmingham Magistrates' Court. Mum and dad went berserk. They had hoped a spin-off of the move to Birmingham would be a change in my behaviour, and were disappointed and angry that I was letting them down again.

Just weeks later I was in more trouble. I had been celebrating St Patrick's Night with some Irish friends and we were singing at the top of our voices on the way home when a policeman told us to tone it down. Abuse filled the air, and the result was a fine of a few pounds for being drunk and disorderly.

Not long after that, one of my younger brothers came home from school complaining that a teacher had hit him several times in the classroom. I went to the school the next day and thumped the teacher. I pleaded guilty to the inevitable assault charge, getting a hefty fine.

Over the next year or so I managed to stay out of trouble, although my success owed more to not being caught than to living a flawless existence. There were fights, and drunken behaviour and petty thieving.

My eighteenth birthday came at the end of 1962. It's an indication of the life I was leading that my only recollection of that landmark is that I got drunk celebrating the fact I could at last drink legally in pubs.

Then in 1963, when I was still only eighteen, came another conviction. I was with a group of lads who broke into a wholesaler's, having climbed on to the roof of the building and broken a skylight. We were caught red-handed and duly appeared in the magistrates' court.

I was given three months in a detention centre, which I was told would be one of those 'short, sharp shocks' so beloved of magistrates trying to straighten out wayward teenagers. In fact I loved it. The centre was like a farm, outside of Stoke-on-Trent in Staffordshire. For me, a city boy born and bred, it was a treat to be out in the countryside. I liked it so much that when it came time to leave I asked the governor if there was any chance of a job there.

The governor was a stern-looking man who I'm sure had spent his working life entirely in uniform of one sort or another. When I asked him about the possibility of a job, he peered at me through his gold-rimmed spectacles and said, 'Hill, it's not a job in a detention centre that you need. You need a few years in the army to put a bit of discipline into you.'

I left the detention centre towards the end of 1963 and again managed to avoid any convictions, this time for five years. But the police caught up with me eventually and in 1968 I got a sentence of nine months, suspended for two years, for breaking and entering at a factory. That meant I had to keep out of trouble at least for two years to avoid the sentence being imposed, and this time I made a genuine effort to keep on the straight and narrow. I was doing well, too, until the stag night for my younger brother, Sammy, in 1970, when I got into serious trouble through that usual combination of drink and my temper.

A big group of us had been drinking at various pubs around the town centre, one of which was the Tavern in the Town, a pub I would later be accused of bombing. We wanted to go on to a nightclub and chose a place called Rebecca's. There were about twenty of us and we decided to enter in groups of threes and fours rather than in one big gang. Eventually there was only a handful of us left and we walked up to the doors. The bouncers refused me entry because I was in a denim suit, which was not deemed smart enough.

I suppose a fight was the inevitable outcome of an argument in which I was involved, and sure enough one hell of a punch-up began. During it I pulled out a knife I habitually carried at that time and stabbed three of the bouncers. They were not hurt that badly, but I was charged with serious wounding. I was given a nine-month sentence, plus four months of my previous suspended sentence, to run concurrently.

I served most of my time in Winson Green Prison in Birmingham, which I now regard as a good experience in a perverse sort of way, preparing me in some respects for what was to happen a few years later. I was released on 25 June 1971, determined never to see the inside of a prison again, and made a great – and successful – effort to keep out of trouble. By then I was in my late twenties, married with a young family, and finally becoming mature enough to realise that the drink and the temper, and the lawbreaking, had to be curbed. By the time of that fateful arrest in November 1974 I had for three and a half years been living the life of your average, law-abiding citizen and family man.

Despite those brushes with the law, I enjoyed that amazing decade, the 1960s, in the same way as most Brummies of my age. I was a great soccer fan, and as a kid back in Belfast had always supported Liverpool. Now I had the chance to go and watch them frequently, playing at Aston Villa or Birmingham in the city itself, or at West Bromwich Albion only a few miles away. I also travelled a lot to Scotland to watch Glasgow Celtic, Britain's 'Catholic' team.

I played darts, dominoes, and cards for various pub teams, and that was a great way to get to know your way around a city and meet people. I went to the cinema to see the latest films, and of course I went to dances, which took on a new lease of life when the music explosion led by the Beatles and the Rolling Stones came along in 1963 – although personally I preferred the less trendy Searchers. I bought my flared trousers and multi-coloured shirts to keep up with the fashion, but unlike most lads I was never too interested in girls. I was always happier having a pint with my mates.

Until I met Pat, the Brummie girl who was to become my wife, I had had only one serious girlfriend. It was 1961 and I was sixteen. She was Lena, also sixteen, the daughter of a Greek guy who ran a coffee bar and chip shop. She was scared to tell him for quite some time that she was going out with me because he wanted her to marry a decent Greek lad. I was always in the coffee bar, and eventually her mother realised we were seeing each other.

She helped Lena break the news gently to her father, but he was as mad as we had expected him to be. After a time he insisted that if we were to continue dating the only decent thing to do was to become engaged. So I bought a cheap ring and we announced our engagement.

It didn't last long. We were always having rows, usually about my willingness to get involved in fights. One night in the coffee bar we got into a raging argument and she called me a 'stupid Irish bastard'. I didn't mind the 'stupid' or the 'bastard' too much, but I wasn't happy about how she had emphasised 'Irish'.

I smacked her across the face, and just at that point her father walked in. He went crazy and told me to get out of the coffee bar and never darken its doors again. Lena twisted the ring from her finger and with a dramatic flourish thrust it into my hand. I walked out and stood in the rain for a moment or two. Then I hurled the ring up over the rooftops and went for a drink with my mates.

It was a year or so later that I met Pat. I saw her for the first time in a pub called the Geech, where I played for the soccer and darts teams. She would occasionally pop into the pub with her parents, although she was only fifteen. I got to know her parents well in the bar, and that provided me with the opportunity to speak to her. One night she came into the pub with a friend to watch us playing darts and I overcame my nervousness and asked her out to see a film. She accepted, and we began courting, going out to pubs and clubs and the cinema.

Early in 1965 Pat, who by now had a job in a little factory, became pregnant, which was a shock to both of us with me only twenty and Pat eighteen. I certainly did not fancy the idea of fatherhood or settling down at a time when I was enjoying myself. The pressure of it all led to a big row between us and we split up. But when she had the baby in December I went to see them both in hospital. Pat looked great and our daughter, Tracey, was beautiful. I knew then I wanted to have a more serious relationship.

When they came out of hospital they came to live with me at my parents' house, and we married the following year at St Francis Roman Catholic Church, although Pat was not a Catholic. The rest of our family came along at almost yearly intervals – Michelle, Maxine, Sharon, and Nicola. Then, on Christmas Eve 1972, came the son we had longed for.

Years before, Pat had promised my uncle Sean on his deathbed that if we were blessed with a son, the boy would be named after him. And so he was. After five daughters, beautiful and loved as they all were, it was fabulous to be father of a little boy. Pat and I knew our family was complete.

By Christmas 1972 my eldest child was seven and I had four other little girls and a newborn son. My wild days were over and I was willingly taking on the responsibilities of a father. I would cook meals and change the babies' nappies, clean the house, and pick up the kids from school.

Of course, I still liked to go out for a pint with my pals, but more often than not a Saturday night would see me in front of the television set watching soccer on *Match of the Day* while Pat visited her mother.

I liked Birmingham – the town, the people, the mix of cultures, the way the place had been good to me. I was happy there. Now all I wanted was to head peacefully into middle age, watching my children grow up in the city I had adopted as my own. Unfortunately, that was not to be.

# 4

# The other five

Northern Ireland's civil rights movement was born in the late 1960s
– and not before time.

While I never cared much for politics, I saw the marches of
thousands of Catholics demanding jobs and better housing as a
turning point which would lead to something finally being done
to end the discrimination.

The national, and then international coverage of the campaign,
made it seem certain that Catholics would finally get a square deal
and be treated as equals, not continue to be regarded as second-class
citizens. Under the Special Powers Act of the Stormont government,
which ruled Ulster independently of the British parliament at
Westminster, the almost entirely Protestant police force was allowed
to operate various forms of policing that were illegal on the mainland.
It was no surprise that the South African Minister for Justice in 1963
remarked that he would exchange all of his apartheid legislation for
just one clause of Northern Ireland's Special Powers Act. Ulster was
an artificially created province, a British government idea to secure an
area of Protestant domination after it withdrew from most of Ireland
in the 1920s. Nine counties form the historic province of Ulster,
but three that are predominantly Catholic were excluded when the
boundary was drawn for the formation of Northern Ireland under
the deal which gave home rule to the South of Ireland. Within the
North of Ireland after that, local boundaries and voting qualifications
were manipulated to ensure continuing Protestant domination at all
levels of government.

The effect of that domination was clear to see when it came
to jobs at all levels. A survey taken shortly after I left school
in 1960 showed the extent of the discrimination. Catholics made

up one-third of the population and were in the majority in many parts of the North of Ireland. Yet in the senior grades of the civil service there were 209 Protestants and 13 Catholics. Of 84 legal officers, only 8 were Catholics; of 7 High Court judges, only 1 was a Catholic; and on public boards controlling housing and the health service only a handful of Catholic appointees sat alongside the hundreds of Protestants.

The civil rights marches began in August 1968 and quickly grew in strength and frequency. The Northern Ireland government, which for the forty-odd years of its existence had been in the hands of the predominantly Protestant Unionist Party, was not surprisingly unhappy with these protests, and sent in the police, the Royal Ulster Constabulary, to break them up. Television newscasts showed people, my people, being brutally battered and dragged away as they stood up for their rights. Then Protestant gangs began attacking Catholic areas, stoning and firebombing houses. In mixed or predominantly Protestant areas Catholics were burned out of their homes and told not to return. More often than not the loyalist gangs were working with the dreaded B Specials, an exclusively Protestant auxiliary police force which was so out of control it was eventually disbanded.

The Catholics had no means to fight back, and at that time the IRA simply didn't exist in an active sense. The handful of IRA men in Belfast were powerless, and the jibe at the time was that the three letters stood for 'I Ran Away'. The most they did was to take a role in the defence committees which were set up to protect Catholic areas.

Eventually the bloodshed and the mayhem became just too much and in August 1969 the British government in London ordered in troops to restore order. At first their main task was to protect Catholic areas, and they were welcomed as saviours. But that changed over the months. The Northern Ireland government was convinced the emergence of the civil rights movement was a Dublin-inspired plot orchestrated by the IRA, which it seemed to think was far more powerful than it actually was. The troops were ordered in to Catholic homes to look for suspected Republicans, and the honeymoon between the Catholic population and the troops was over.

Ironically, it was the raids and the harsh treatment of detained

Catholics that encouraged the growth of the IRA. But within the IRA itself splits developed over policy, and in late 1969 a group broke away and formed what was to be a 'provisional' leadership until the differences were ironed out. They never were, and today the IRA still has its two branches, the Officials and the Provisionals.

Harassment of Catholics by the army increased and relations plunged to a new low with the introduction of a curfew in the Catholic lower Falls area of west Belfast. Slowly the IRA was beginning to emerge as a force prepared to defend the Catholic community. Several Catholics had died in the violence. One was a boy of nine, Patrick Rooney, who had been asleep in bed when a bullet from an RUC machine gun ripped through a wall and struck him. Another was teenager Gerard McAuley, who was helping Catholics evacuate their homes which were being attacked by a Protestant mob when he was shot through the heart. While few people were staunch Republicans, it is not hard to understand that many were grateful for the appearance of a group ready to defend lives and homes against rampaging mobs of loyalists.

Riots became a way of life, and attacks on police and soldiers a regular occurrence. The Provisionals, who were always keener to resort to violence than the Officials, went more and more on the offensive. In February 1971 the first British soldier was killed, Gunner Robert Curtis, a twenty-year-old serving with the Royal Artillery.

Then came two events that were to prove to be of major significance, not just in their own right but particularly in the way they led to an upsurge in recruitment of young men and women to the ranks of the reborn IRA. In August 1971 the Northern Ireland government reintroduced internment, the detention without trial of suspected Republicans. The army swooped just before dawn one morning and took away hundreds of men to prison. The majority had no connections with the IRA, which had known internment was coming and had warned its members to leave their homes. Much of the information the army acted on was outdated or just false. The effect across Catholic communities in Belfast and other parts of the North of Ireland was immediate and devastating – an explosion of bombings, shootings and riots. The despised policy of internment continued for more than four years, with the last of the internees not released until December 1975.

The second event was without doubt a watershed in the history of the Northern Ireland state. One cold Sunday in January 1972 a civil rights march in Derry was suddenly disrupted by gunfire. Who fired first will always remain the subject of debate. What is not in doubt is that soldiers of the Parachute Regiment who were on duty then opened fire. They charged forward from behind their army vehicles and ran, firing, into the crowd. The men, women and children fled screaming in terror. After a few frenzied minutes thirteen people were dead and many more lay wounded.

The slaughter stunned the world and became infamous as Bloody Sunday. It also brought the biggest-ever boost to recruitment the IRA had known. During the years I was later to serve in prison I met many IRA men who pointed to that day as the moment they decided they wanted to hit back at Britain with more than just words or stones.

As with the early civil rights marches, I watched these later events unfold on television in the safety of my home in Birmingham, far removed from the blood and the bullets. I despaired over what was happening in my country to my people and prayed that change could be brought about without the violence and deaths and misery. But the thought of ever getting actively involved in any way never once crossed my mind; I had a wife and a big family to look after, and that was where my priorities lay. As I drank in the pubs and clubs of Birmingham I was not afraid to make my views known on what was happening in the North of Ireland, but even with my short temper I never once got into anything more serious than a heated discussion on the issue.

It was in those same pubs and clubs that I met the five other men from the North of Ireland with whom my own life would become inextricably linked. There is a common perception that the Birmingham Six were a tight-knit group of close friends, when in fact we were nothing of the sort. While I certainly regard them as friends now, after everything we have been through, I was not particularly close to any of them before our arrest. They were no more than acquaintances I knew from pubs I drank in.

I attended the same schools in Belfast as Gerry Hunter and Billy Power, who were both about the same age while I was about three years older. When you are kids three years is quite an age gap, so although I knew them I never regarded them as friends.

I don't particularly remember them after I left school, but I guess we saw each other from time to time on the street as we lived in the same area. After I moved to Birmingham in 1960, it was not until 1968 that I again met Gerry. I was walking along the road when I heard somebody shout my name. It was Gerry with some friends from Belfast. We had a chat, then went for a drink in a nearby pub and discussed old times. It turned out he had moved to Birmingham a few years earlier, when he was seventeen.

We parted and I didn't see him again until 1971, when again I met him and some of his friends by chance as they came out of a factory near my home where they had been working. Once more we had a drink, and that was it until about Christmas 1973. I had moved to the Kingstanding area of the city and used to use a pub called the Crossways, where I bumped into him again.

He lived near the pub and from then on I would see him quite frequently there, or at the Kingstanding Ex-servicemen's Club which we both used. We would have the odd drink together and play cards, but it was never a greater friendship than that. Like me, Gerry had married a Birmingham girl, Sandra, and they had two young boys and a little girl. He was a painter and worked fairly regularly.

The first I saw of Billy Power since Belfast was in the Crossways in early 1974. He and Gerry were good friends, and had gone to Birmingham together. After I was introduced to him in the pub we got chatting, and we realised we had something in common other than our Belfast background, which was that both our fathers had served in the British Army, Billy's as a sergeant major. But I seldom saw him after that, and I doubt whether he and I ever spent more than a few hours in each other's company. Billy had met an Irish girl from Cork, Nora, in Birmingham about two years after he arrived and they later married, with Gerry as best man. By 1974 they had four young children. He used to work on painting jobs, and in the evenings would normally drink in a works social club rather than the Crossways, which is why I saw him so rarely.

Hugh Callaghan was nearly fifteen years older than me, and whilst he was from Belfast I had never known him there. He also lived near the Crossways pub, and inevitably that was where I met him, seeing him in there from time to time. We did not become more than acquaintances until late in 1974 when we started to play snooker together once a week at the Kingstanding Ex-servicemen's club.

Hughie had come to England from Belfast in 1947, when he was seventeen, for the usual reason – to find work. He had had jobs around Birmingham for years, but had begun suffering badly from ulcers and that had kept him off work from 1971. He was married to Eileen, from County Mayo, and had a daughter. But that was about as much as I knew about him. He was never in my house, and I was never in his.

Richard McIlkenny was also older than me, by eleven years, and while he recalls knowing me as I grew up in Belfast, I have no recollection of him. He went to school with two of my uncles. Richard and his wife Kate were both from Ardoyne. He moved to Birmingham in 1956 to find a regular job, and was never out of work. He got a job as a millwright's mate at a firm in Witton in 1969 and was there until we were arrested. By that time he had four teenage children and two younger daughters. The first I knew of Richard was when I was living in the Hockley district of Birmingham in 1961 and he lived nearby. He and my father played darts together in the local pub, St Mathias's, and were quite good friends. They worked together for a time at a printing works in the city. I would see him quite a lot because I used the same pub frequently and played darts with them. We both later moved house and would see each other in the Crossways. I knew two of his brothers had been interned in Belfast and he was bitter about that, but he never expressed any stronger views than the rest of us. I liked Richard, and feel quite proud that he would say of me later, 'Paddy Joe is the sort of chap who gets on with everybody.'

John Walker was nearly ten years older than me and from Derry, so I did not know him over in Ireland. He came to England at seventeen in 1952, staying first in Reading but moving to Birmingham a year later. He married his Irish wife Theresa in the city in 1956 and they had seven children, six girls and a boy. John was always in work, and from 1969 had been working as a crane driver at the same firm in Witton as Richard McIlkenny. I never heard anybody say a bad word about John. Even a man who would later give damning evidence against him at our trial, a workmate called Tom Watt, was quoted years later as saying: 'John Walker was one of the kindest men I knew. He was always the first to help anyone in trouble. If a worker was off sick for a few weeks Walker would arrange a collection for him. And it made no difference whether the man was English, Irish, or any other nationality.'

I first met John at about Christmas 1972 in – surprise, surprise – the Crossways. Shortly after that, John and Gerry Hunter, who were friends, tried to organise a team from the Crossways to play don, an Irish card game. I was interested, and so was Richard McIlkenny. John and Gerry decided we should organise a weekly raffle to raise funds for the team. But then it was discovered that on the night the Birmingham Don League played their games there was no room available in the Crossways, so the idea of our pub team fell through. But it was decided to continue with the raffle, and send the money raised back to Ireland to help the families of people who were interned. The raffles went well and became a weekly feature at the pub. Gerry was treasurer for a time, but never sent the money anywhere, and then John took over. He knew an Irishman at his work called Michael Murray, who said he raised funds for dependants of internees and sent it to a charity in Dublin. He offered to send our money too, so John used to pass it on to him regularly. I only ever met Murray a couple of times, but knew he used to be able to get prizes on the cheap which he would give to John.

I used to help out selling tickets, and had a knack of getting people to part with their money for prizes which you could hardly class as highly desirable, such as cheap decorative clocks or table lamps. As Gerry was to recall later, 'Paddy Hill could sell more tickets than anyone else in the pub.'

I used to pass the money collected to John, although often when I was short of a few pounds I would borrow from it, so it was worth my while to sell a lot of tickets. If getting money from people was second nature to me, organising collections for good causes was second nature to John. A friend who visited him in jail in 1989 told me he was astonished to find John organising a collection among inmates – for Christmas presents for handicapped children.

The other man I knew at the time who changed the course of the lives of all six of us was James McDade. He had gone to school with both Gerry and Billy. I knew him as the younger brother of a friend of mine, Joe McDade, with whom I had regularly played snooker back in Belfast as a teenager.

The first that I knew Jamesie, as he was called, had moved to Birmingham was on that same day I met Gerry Hunter on the street in 1968. He was one of the guys with Gerry. Over the next few years I saw McDade occasionally – almost always in a pub, where he would get up to sing at the drop of a hat. He had an excellent voice, and would stand by the piano player in a pub or club and belt out Jim Reeves or Johnny Cash songs as good as the professionals. Wherever it was, the whole place would go quiet when he got up to sing.

He had lodged for a time with Gerry and Sandra, staying for a few months, but there were a lot of arguments and eventually they threw him out. Towards the end of 1973 McDade, who was by then married and had a child, asked Billy and Nora if they could move in with them for a while. Billy obliged, but the McDades only stayed a short time before moving on.

I didn't know McDade well at all, and so could not say what he was like as a person. But somebody who did know him once told me: 'He's all right, but a pig when he's drunk. He gives his wife a rotten time.'

McDade and I had no more than a nodding acquaintance, and certainly never discussed politics or the North of Ireland. I knew his younger brother Gerry had been shot dead by the British Army in Ardoyne at the end of 1970, and had been told that Gerry had been in the IRA. But I knew, or knew of, plenty of people in Belfast who had been shot or interned and it did not necessarily mean they were all in the IRA. Birmingham at that time had, and still has, a massive Irish population, many of whose members went home for holidays or funerals and when they returned they brought back all the news and gossip. When I heard of Gerry McDade's death I had no reason to think his brother Jamesie, who had been in Birmingham for years, was in the IRA, and I can't recall even having considered it.

Unlike many of my Irish friends, I had never been back to Ireland, north or south, until the summer of 1974. Lack of money was one reason of course, but it was not the overriding factor. I just never had any great desire to return once I was settled in Birmingham. My parents were in Brum, my wife was English with no links to Ireland, and my children were as Brummie as the kids next door. But in that summer came an opportunity I thought was too good to miss. Every June Ireland holds its commemmoration of the eighteenth-century republican hero Wolfe Tone, whose remains are believed to be buried at Bodenstown in County Kildare. Sinn Féin, the political wing of the

IRA, was organising a cheap trip to the event and I heard that a few of the lads from the Crossways, including John and Gerry, were going on one of the coaches.

Both Sinn Féin and the IRA were legal organisations at the time in Britain. In hindsight I can see that going on such a trip looks bad, as though we were all at least IRA supporters, if not actual members. But I and several others like me saw it simply as the means to a cheap weekend in Dublin, costing only about £12 for the coach trip and two nights in a hotel. Even that amount was out of my reach at the time, so I solved the problem by keeping the proceeds from raffling three watches I had got from John for our Crossways draws.

I didn't even go to the Bodenstown ceremonies. I spent most of the Saturday and Sunday getting inebriated in a friend's bar, the Twanghan, in Dublin, and came home on the Monday.

But also on the Crossways coach were a number of guys who, unknown to me, were in the Birmingham IRA. They included Mick Murray, the man who worked with John Walker and used to take the raffle money, and Martin Coughlin, who it turned out was head of the IRA in Birmingham at the time. Among the other IRA men from the city who went were Jimmy Ashe, Gerry Young and Seamus McLoughlin. I knew Coughlin from around the pubs and different painting jobs I'd been on. I had watched Ashe grow up in Birmingham, as I was friends with his parents. I'd seen Young playing guitar at Irish functions around Birmingham. I knew McLoughlin vaguely from back home in Belfast and had seen him a few times in Birmingham. It may seem naïve now, but at the time I didn't have a clue that any of them were in the IRA. I didn't know any of them well enough to have any suspicions.

Within weeks of our return from that trip several of them were arrested. What had been for me an innocent weekend drinking trip would later be portrayed in a far more sinister way.

# 5

# IRA bombers

The IRA first took its modern campaign against British rule to England itself in February 1972. The Official IRA planted a bomb outside the officers' mess at the headquarters of the Parachute Regiment in Aldershot in reprisal for Bloody Sunday. Seven people died – five women cleaners, a Catholic chaplain, and a gardener.

It was a dreadful attack and I was horrified. I supported the aim of a united Ireland, but could never justify the use of bombings or shootings to achieve that end.

The appalling result of the bomb and the outrage it caused must have made the leaderships of both Officials and Provisionals reconsider their tactics. For there was then a lengthy lull in attacks, the Officials having called a ceasefire, until March 1973 when the Provisionals planted four car bombs in the heart of London. Two were defused, but two went off. One was outside the Central Criminal Court, the Old Bailey, and the other was at the Metropolitan Police headquarters at New Scotland Yard. More than two hundred people needed hospital treatment for their injuries, and one man died shortly after leaving hospital. Most of the IRA team were arrested.

The car bombs were followed by a wave of letter bomb attacks in London, and incendiary devices went off in department stores around the capital.

Also in March 1973, a Catholic priest, Father Patrick Fell, and six other men were arrested in Coventry and charged with conspiracy to cause explosions in that city, which had been well acquainted with IRA violence in the past. In 1939, during an IRA campaign across Britain, a bomb had gone off in the busy shopping centre, killing five people and injuring a dozen or more. Two Irishmen, James McCormack and Peter Barnes, were convicted of the bombing and hanged, although until his death Barnes proclaimed his innocence. Thirty-five years later the shadow of the IRA once more hovered over the city and Father Fell, who had been born an English Protestant, was eventually jailed for twelve years. One of those jailed with him, Frank Stagg, later died on hunger strike.

The focus of IRA attacks at the time was on London, but the Fell arrests made it clear that other parts of the country were viewed by the IRA as potential targets. The Midlands remained free of any incident until the end of August 1973. On 27 August Scotland Yard put out a warning to all provincial police forces that the next wave of terrorist attacks was expected to be outside the capital.

Two days later bombs went off within minutes of each other outside a bank and a building society in Solihull, a prosperous town between Coventry and Birmingham. The explosions were at about 10.30 at night, and with the streets fairly empty at that time nobody was hurt. The next day, incendiary devices went off in shops in Birmingham's city centre, causing panic and terror. It was the first time the bombers had struck in the heart of England's second city.

An assistant at a shoe shop in New Street had found a plastic bag outside the store as she arrived for work. Thinking it must have been left by one of her colleagues who had arrived earlier, she brought it in. The fire which subsequently gutted the shop also caused damage to the four floors of offices above. The two other incendiaries which went off that day caused less damage, but just as much fear and confusion.

The Birmingham police created a bomb squad to investigate each incident, while the Special Branch concentrated on watching IRA suspects and sympathisers. To deal with suspect packages the police joined forces with the army's bomb disposal squad based at Hereford. The army unit attached to the Birmingham police was under the command of a young captain, Ron Wilkinson, and he was in action almost immediately. On 2 September he and his colleagues had to defuse a bomb in Birmingham city centre. The following day they had to deal with a bomb found by a group of children. A week later they were at Sutton Coldfield, north of the city, where a bomb went off causing minor injuries.

There were other attacks in and around the city over the next two weeks, all without serious casualties. Then, on 17 September, just after midnight, a bomb exploded in a factory in the Witton area of the city. At about 7 a.m. there was a report of a device in the suburb of Edgbaston. The police and Captain Wilkinson got there to find a postman had noticed a plastic bucket with a polythene cover over it in the doorway of an office block. A quick check confirmed it was indeed a bomb. The captain, who had served in the North of Ireland where many of his colleagues had been killed, went through normal procedure. The area was evacuated, and then he waited to see if the bomb would go off. After an hour he decided he would have to go in to try to defuse it. He did not have the benefit of the sophisticated technology available today. He walked in alone, with only his training and his courage to help him. Minutes later there was a blinding flash and a huge bang. Captain Wilkinson died from his injuries six days later.

The death caused massive public outrage and the police came under intense pressure to get results and put the bombers behind bars. Dozens of houses across the city were raided and scores of Irishmen were pulled in for questioning. But only one man was charged – Patrick Dowling of Selly Oak in the city. He was thirty-eight years old and got four years for conspiracy to cause explosions after being found with bomb-making instructions. I'd never heard of him.

After the death of Captain Wilkinson there was a lull in IRA attacks in Birmingham which lasted until the night of 2 January 1974, when a bomb went off at an office in the city centre. It was followed minutes later by a big explosion at New Street station. Both caused a lot of damage, but luckily no injuries.

The focus switched again to London with Madame Tussaud's, the Boat Show, and two army generals among the targets. At the end of January a letter bomb campaign began. It was a particularly vicious form of attack in which many people, often not the target, lost fingers, hands or eyesight when a small device exploded as they opened a package.

Then in February 1974 came the M62 bombing. A coach carrying soldiers and their families from Manchester to their army base at Catterick was blown apart on the M62 motorway. Twelve people died and many suffered awful injuries. I could relate to that tragedy more than to any of the others, for I was the son of a soldier, the grandson of a soldier, the brother of a soldier. There were a few more bombs in Birmingham in April, and then a break again until July when the city was subjected to an intense, determined wave of attacks. Bombs and incendiaries went off all over the place: at New Street station, at shops, cinemas and timber yards. A favourite target was the circular skyscraper office block called the Rotunda, which dominates the Birmingham skyline. The IRA was also busy in other parts of the country, hitting a variety of targets in London, Manchester, Hertfordshire, Lancashire and Surrey. Bombings were now so commonplace that they had to wreak particular havoc to gain the national publicity the bombers were seeking. One that did was the bombing of the White Tower of the Tower of London on 17 July. Fifty people, mainly tourists and schoolchildren, were inside the tightly confined space when the bomb exploded. Amazingly, only one person was killed, a woman from south London, but everybody else there was injured.

In Birmingham the police finally got a breakthrough, which came through a stroke of luck rather than brilliant detective work. An IRA man in the city, Patrick Christie, had found a girlfriend with whom he wanted to settle down, and he told his colleagues he was leaving the organisation. They were not happy at that and kidnapped him. Christie had told his girl that if anything were to happen to him she should tell the police he had probably been taken to an IRA house in the Sparkbrook area of the city, 232 Clifton Road. She did so, and the police put the house under close surveillance. By watching people coming to and from the house they identified two other addresses as suspect. On the night of Friday 2 August they moved in on the three homes. At two of them police found clocks, batteries, weedkiller and detonators – all items indicative of a bomb factory. Four men were arrested, including Tip Guilfoyle and Gerry Small. They had been in the IRA in Manchester, but had fled in April that year after Guilfoyle had, somewhat carelessly, lit a cigarette while preparing a bomb. The resulting explosion had set the house alight, but they had managed to get away and escaped to Birmingham. After their arrest, the police continued surveillance and the next day arrested two men who rolled up to one of the homes. They were Martin Coughlin and Gerry Young, who proved to be the top two men in the Birmingham IRA at the time. Shortly afterwards police picked up two more members of the gang, Jimmy Ashe and Tony Madigan. Several of them had been on the trip to Bodenstown in June of that year. I knew three of them. But I had never had a clue that any of them were anything to do with the IRA. The arrests brought a dramatic reduction in IRA attacks in the Midlands, and almost all of the few incidents that occurred in the next few months involved devices that failed to go off, suggesting that the men with experience had been arrested. But around the rest of England bomb attacks were continuing.

Then came two horrific attacks, both in the south of England. The first was in the town of Guildford, Surrey. On 5 October bombs went off in two pubs popular with off-duty soldiers, the Horse and Groom and the Seven Stars. They left five people dead and more than fifty injured. At the beginning of November, in Woolwich, another pub used by soldiers, the King's Arms, was bombed. Two died and more than thirty were injured.

Throughout all of this period my reaction to the attacks was that of the Brummies' around me – one of shock and horror, and contempt for the people planting the bombs. It seemed nowhere was safe. Clearly the IRA was bringing its murder and mayhem to the city in which I lived, and like anybody else in Birmingham I was worried that I, my wife or my kids might become victims of the bombing campaign. Shops began searching your bags as you went in; sometimes pubs would give you a quick check; and at New Street station there were regular announcements on the loudspeakers warning passengers not to leave bags unattended.

The thought would occasionally cross my mind that the bombers could be among the crowds of Irishmen who packed the pubs I drank in. But how on earth could you tell who was an IRA man? Although the organisation was not illegal in Britain at that time, it was a secret society. Some naïve people seem to think that if you were Irish and went to Irish pubs in Birmingham at that time you must have known who was in the IRA. Do they believe the IRA were going around planting bombs and then popping back to pubs to broadcast what they had done? It just didn't happen like that.

From time to time I would get word from Belfast of somebody I knew having been shot or arrested by soldiers, and that would make me angry. But I knew that what was happening in England would prove no solution to the problem. I think that like most of my friends and neighbours I despaired at what was going on. There was a feeling of helplessness, that nothing ordinary people could do would change anything. You prayed that neither you nor your family would get caught up in it all, and tried to get on with living life as normal.

It was in November 1974 that the IRA in Birmingham became active again, bombing Conservative Party offices in the city, a tax office in Wolverhampton, and various other targets in the region. Each time I heard on the news that yet another bomb had gone off my reaction was a muttered prayer of thanks that I'd not been affected.

But before long I would be.

People often say they can remember just where they were and what they were doing when they heard some news of earth-shattering importance. All of us beyond a certain age seem able to recall exactly how we heard the news that President John Kennedy had been assassinated in November 1963. I certainly can. I had gone into hospital in Birmingham to have work done on my facial scar and was in bed when I heard a newsflash on the radio saying Kennedy had been shot. That moment is imprinted on my memory. So considering it was claimed at my trial that I had carried out the worst atrocity in British criminal history to avenge the death of my alleged friend and 'comrade' James McDade, you would think I would remember vividly the moment I heard of his death on an IRA bombing mission. I don't, for the simple reason the incident meant nothing to me at the time.

McDade was the guy who I'd known as a kid three years younger than me at school in Belfast; who I'd known casually when I went drinking around Birmingham; who I'd known as the pub singer with the wonderful voice.

What I didn't know was that he was in the IRA.

On Thursday 14 November 1974 McDade and another IRA man, Raymond McLaughlin, travelled from Birmingham to Coventry to plant a bomb at the new telephone exchange in the city centre, not far from the central police station. They probably didn't realise it, but 14 November had long been a significant date in Coventry's history. It was on that night in 1940 that Coventry was blitzed by Hitler's air force, the first major attack of the Second World War on a provincial city. The bombing raid left 554 people dead and thousands injured. On the thirty-fourth anniversary of that raid came another bomb attack on Coventry. But this time it was the bomber who died.

McDade was the planter and McLaughlin was to be the look-out. It did not come out at the time, but I've learned since that a third man went with them, a driver who took them to Coventry in a van. Exactly what happened that night will never be known. But the bomb exploded and McDade was literally blasted to bits. Parts of his body were scattered across a wide area of the city centre. He was in his late twenties, and his wife, a Protestant English girl called Jackie, was left with a child aged two and a baby on the way.

McDade would not have known it on the night he set off for Coventry, but the police were closing in on him. Eight days earlier, on the morning of Wednesday 6 November 1974, police had been called to the premises of Guidex Ltd, a firm of office equipment manufacturers in Constitution Hill, Birmingham, where an incendiary device had exploded. Detective Chief Inspector Bernard Brook went along in his role as head of the West Midlands Police scenes-of-crime department.

Near the window through which the device had been put into the building he found a paper bag. He took the bag back to the force headquarters at Lloyd House in Birmingham and treated it with the chemicals of his trade. The impression of a fingerprint emerged on it. He took a photograph of the impression and sent it to the force fingerprinting bureau. A few days later Brook was working late at a murder scene in West Bromwich where a postmistress and her husband had been shot by the killer who became infamous as the Black Panther. The following morning, 12 November he got to his office in Lloyd House to find a note on his desk. It said that the print on the paper bag found at Guidex had been identified as that of the left thumb of James McDade. His prints were on record because he had committed a minor criminal offence a few years earlier. Two days later Brook was called to the scene at Coventry where a man had blown himself to pieces. The only complete part of his body to be recovered was a thumb. An impression was taken from it and rushed to the fingerprint bureau for an immediate check. The word came back that it was a thumbprint of James McDade.

His accomplice, McLaughlin, had been held by a group of pub drinkers as he ran from the scene, having thrown away a pistol which was later recovered from a flowerbed. He was handed over to the police and was subsequently jailed. The third man, the driver, headed back to Birmingham in a state of shock.

I think it was on the television news that night that I heard a bomb had gone off in Coventry and somebody had been killed, but I can't be sure. Bombs were going off all over the country, and indeed on 14 November itself there had been other explosions earlier in the day. There were two in Birmingham, one in Wolverhampton, one in Solihull and one in Northampton.

I do recall hearing the next day on the news that the dead man had been named as Jamie McDade, because I remember remarking to my wife Pat that the name suggested he was a Scotsman. It may seem odd now, but at the time I never for one minute thought the guy involved was Jamesie McDade the pub singer. Had he died in Birmingham perhaps I would have made the connection.

The first I knew of his involvement was when I went to the Crossways pub on the following Saturday lunchtime, where I came across Gerry Hunter, John Walker, and Richard McIlkenny.

Gerry asked me, 'What do you think about Jamesie McDade?'

I thought from Gerry's voice McDade must have left his wife or something. 'What about him?' I said.

'It was Jamesie blew himself up in Coventry.'

'What? I never knew he was in the IRA.' I was astonished.

'Nor did we,' said Gerry.

Although Gerry had much earlier thrown McDade out of his house, they had remained on speaking terms. Gerry had last seen him about six weeks before he died.

In the pub we talked about whether funeral arrangements had been made, and Gerry said he thought it would be on the following Friday in Belfast. He was keen to go if he could get the money, but he had been out of work since the end of September. It would mean travelling on the boat train from Birmingham on the Thursday night. John had met McDade through Gerry, and said he would try to get to the funeral. Richard knew McDade too, but his reason for wanting to go was that he had known McDade's parents back in Belfast and felt sorry for them.

I told them that I had been thinking of going back to Belfast anyway because of my promise to my Aunt Mary, my grandmother's sister, who was in her eighties and had been ill for some time, that I would try to get back to see her in Belfast before she died. I saw that if I went now, I could travel with the other lads and as well as see Aunt Mary I could pay my respects to McDade's parents and go to the funeral.

Our decision to go to McDade's funeral has been viewed by many English people with great suspicion. Why should we want to go the funeral of a bomber? Indeed, it was claimed at our trial that in going we were honouring a known bomber as an IRA hero. But it's a simple fact that Catholics from Belfast, indeed the Irish Catholic community generally, see funerals very differently from people in England.

In Ireland everybody goes to funerals of people they know, and even those they don't know, irrespective of the kind of life led by the person who has died. One of the major reasons is to show support for the family left behind. It's just an Irish way of life, or rather, death. I've been to plenty of funerals where the church has been packed out, even though the late unlamented was a real villain. You can argue that it's sheer hypocrisy; but whether or not that's the case, you have to accept it's the way things have been done in Ireland for centuries.

And, of course, there is another side to it. It's a great opportunity to see old friends and catch up on the news, and yes, have a good drink. An Irish funeral is far more than a church service – it's a social occasion.

In the Crossways I told John, Gerry and Richard that I'd like to go with them, but as I was living on social security I doubted whether I would be able to afford the fare. I finished my drink and went home, where Pat was as shocked as me to hear about McDade. Like me, Pat could not see how I would be able to afford to go back with the other lads, and I pretty much dropped the idea. In the meantime, but unknown to me, Billy Power told Gerry he would like to go with him to the funeral if he could raise the cash.

On the following Tuesday Pat came home from my mother's and said mum had got word from Belfast that Aunt Mary had suffered a stroke. That was it. I told Pat that I would have to get the money somehow. The fare for the boat train from Birmingham to Heysham and the ferry across was only about £13 for a return and £7 for a single. But that was a lot of money at that time when you were on the dole with a wife and six children to feed. I spent the Wednesday trying to think of ways to get it, without success, and went to bed that night feeling pretty depressed.

If only I'd abandoned the idea there and then.

# 6

## A helping hand

On the morning of Thursday 21 November 1974, the torrential rain we'd had all week was still pouring down. As I lay in bed with the rain battering against the windows, a thought struck me. Perhaps Johnny Walker would loan me a few pounds from the Crossways raffle money. Or, as he had a job, he might even be prepared to lend me some money of his own. I had still not paid him the raffle money which I had used to pay my way to Bodenstown a few months earlier, so he might not be too keen to lend me anything. But it was worth a try.

I thought Johnny would be at work until late afternoon. I knew there were two boat trains, leaving at about 7 p.m. and 8 p.m. So I reckoned I could get to his house, get the money, get home to say goodbye to Pat and the kids, and still have plenty of time to get to New Street station in the city centre.

At lunchtime I went to the Crossways for a drink and phoned John's house from there. I was told he hadn't gone to work, but was out and would be back later. I had another pint and a chat, then went off to pick some of the kids up from school and take them home.

At about 3.30 p.m. I set off for John's house, which was in Perry Common, two bus rides from my home in Kilburn Road, Kingstanding. I took my little boy Sean, who was then nearly two.

John was in, but I was out of luck. He had already sent the raffle money back to Ireland, and the little money he had spare of his own he was lending to Gerry Hunter, because he hadn't got the fare either. He told me they were catching the later train.

I had a cup of tea, left the house and went to a phone box on the corner to tell Pat I would not be going. Pat knew how badly I wanted to see Aunt Mary, and she now came to the rescue. She used to keep

47

a money box in the house in which she saved odd bits of change, but she kept the key to it at a friend's house. I suppose she suspected I would get into it if I was short of the price of a pint. She told me to call round to see the friend, Rose Murphy, and collect the key.

Then she told me she would also try to get some money from the nuns at the Convent of the Little Sisters of the Assumption near our house. We knew the nuns well, particularly Sister Bridget, as they gave religious instruction to our children, who went to a non-Catholic school, and they had taken the kids away on holiday in the past. They were always lending a helping hand. In return I had done odd painting and decorating jobs around the convent for them. I'd borrowed money from them before, always paying it back either in cash or in kind.

When I got home Pat opened the money box and gave me £2 and told me she had arranged for me to get £15 from the convent. I got washed and changed, put a few clothes in a blue suitcase, said goodbye to the family and went off to the convent. Sister Bridget was there and I started explaining to her all about my aunt being ill. But she held up her hands and said, 'Paddy, you'd bring tears to a glass eye. You don't have to explain anything to me.'

She handed me the money, wished me all the best and promised to say a prayer for my aunt, and I left. I had told John that if I was able to get the money to go I would see him in the Crossways at about 6 p.m., so I headed for the pub. I got there at about 6.30, but he was not there and when I phoned his house they told me he had gone to Gerry Hunter's. I nipped into the library next door to return a book and the young assistant charged me a sixpence fine because it was a fortnight overdue. I phoned Pat from there to say I'd got the money from Sister Bridget. Then I went back into the Crossways and had a drink. The landlord, Noel Walsh, came into the bar briefly at one stage and I joked with him about lending me twenty or thirty pounds because I was going back to Ireland. I asked one of the lads I knew in the bar, Tommy Jolly, if he would give me a lift into town. He said he couldn't because he was in his company's lorry and he was not allowed to use if for private purposes.

I left the pub at about 7.15 p.m. and saw two men I knew, Brian Craven and Arthur Southall, driving into the car park and asked them for a lift. I can't recall who was driving, but whoever it was told me he'd had a couple of drinks and did not want to go into town where there were more police patrols and he would run a greater risk of being stopped for drink-driving.

'Fair play to you,' I said, and walked off over the road to catch the bus to town and New Street station.

During that Thursday the other lads had been making their own arrangements to get to Belfast.

John, who had a good job as a crane driver at a factory, had taken the day off, but was going in to work to pick up his wages. Gerry and Billy, who had borrowed his fare from a brother-in-law, called at John's house in the morning with some Mass cards which had been signed by others who knew McDade. Mass cards are a traditional Catholic symbol of sympathy for the family of the bereaved. You buy a card and ask a priest to say a Mass for the soul of the person who has died, and then the cards are usually placed on the coffin at the wake.

The three of them set off to St Margaret Mary's Church on Perry Common Road to ask the priest there, Father Ryan, to sign the cards. He was not in, so they left the cards with the housekeeper and John said he would collect them later.

John left the other two, telling Gerry he would call for him at about 6.15 p.m. to go to the station. He then went to the Crossways where he met Richard, and they went to the factory where they worked, Forging and Pressings in Witton, to collect their wages. Then they went home, arranging to meet at John's house later before picking up Gerry.

Billy and Gerry, after leaving John that morning, had bumped into Hugh Callaghan in the street and explained they were hoping to go back for the funeral. The two of them left Hughie and went for a drink, and then on to some betting shops where Billy, who was mad on gambling, had a couple of good wins on the dogs. They split up at about 4 p.m., agreeing to meet at New Street station at 6.30 p.m. in time for the first of the two boat trains, which would leave just before 7 p.m.

Hughie had collected his social security money that morning and gone for a drink at the Crossways, meeting Gerry and Billy on his way there. Then he went to the Kingstanding Ex-servicemen's Club to continue drinking, leaving there at about 4.15 p.m. He called in at Richard's house to repay a pound he had borrowed, and Richard told him that he was going to McDade's funeral with John, Gerry and Billy. Clearly none of them thought I would be able to come up with the money to go. Hughie said he would see them off from the station. He should have been back at his own house hours earlier to hand over the social security money to his wife Eileen for housekeeping. By going to the station he could delay a little longer the moment at which he would have to face the music at home.

At about 6 p.m. Richard and Hugh went around to John's house, and the three of them caught a bus to Gerry's. Just before 6.30 all four caught a bus into the city centre and walked the short distance to the station. Gerry urged them to hurry as he had promised to meet Billy at 6.30. Richard clearly recalls the station clock changing to 6.57 as they arrived.

Billy had got to the station at 6.35 and waited. He got annoyed that Gerry had not turned up, and when he saw the first of the boat trains leaving he decided to go home. He was on his way out of the station when the others arrived. He told them, 'You're late, we've missed the train.'

But the others said there was no rush and that the 8 p.m train would be fine. They bought tickets and talked about having a drink, and Hughie suggested going to the Mulberry Bush pub nearby where drinks were cheaper. But they decided to stay in the station and go to the Taurus Bar on the concourse.

Meanwhile, though we were not aware of it in all our toing and froing, over in Coventry that day hundreds of police were on duty as the remains of McDade were released to the family and then transported to Birmingham airport on a flight to Belfast.

After McDade had killed himself, I had seen funeral notices circulating which read:

On November 21 at 3.30 the remains of our comrade James McDade will be escorted from Coventry to Birmingham and on to Belfast. We consider it the duty of all Irish people to be present at Coventry mortuary. The coffin will be draped in the tricolour that covered the coffin of Michael Gaughan.

Gaughan was an IRA man who had died in jail on hunger strike earlier that year.

I knew from the papers that week that Sinn Féin was determined to give McDade a hero's send-off by escorting the coffin all twelve miles to the airport. The authorities were equally determined that there should be no ceremonial procession in honour of a man who was clearly a bomber. The police applied to Birmingham City Council for a banning order on the grounds that existing powers 'will not be sufficient to prevent serious public disorder being occasioned by the holding of any public procession in connection with the death of James McDade'. It was granted unanimously at a four-minute, specially convened meeting of the council, and Coventry and Solihull councils made similar orders.

I didn't know it at the time, but all police leave was cancelled, and extra police were drafted in. The police were already stretched to the limit, having earlier that day mounted a massive security operation as the Birmingham IRA men arrested in the summer made their weekly remand appearance at the city's magistrates' court. That Thursday morning on the radio news Birmingham MP Jill Knight demanded that the IRA be made illegal in Britain.

According to the newspaper reports of the events in Coventry, several hundred Sinn Féin members from around the country turned up at the mortuary. In the chapel two priests conducted a short service in defiance of a ban by the Catholic Archbishop of Birmingham.

Among the mourners were Brendan McGill, the national organiser of Sinn Féin, and George Lynch, who headed the Birmingham branch of the organisation. McGill spoke to the crowd through a loudhailer, urging everyone to stay calm and orderly as he did not want to see any trouble.

There was a rival demonstration by the National Front, and as the coffin appeared they sang 'Go Home You Bums' and chanted 'IRA out'. At the same time a bagpiper in a kilt stepped forward and played a funeral lament. A few missiles were thrown and there was a bit of scuffling, but the massive police presence prevented any major trouble as the hearse, escorted by police cars, set off for the airport.

The coffin was loaded aboard a British Airways plane and the twenty-two mourners with it settled into their seats. It was due to take off at 6.30 p.m., but word came through that airport workers in Belfast had refused to unload the remains. Protestant paramilitary groups in Belfast had apparently warned they would take 'action' against anybody involved in unloading the coffin. Eventually the coffin was taken off and those with it were told to wait in a passenger lounge. After much discussion, the pilot of an Aer Lingus flight to Dublin agreed to take the coffin and mourners. It would be 9.15 p.m. before the plane finally got into the air.

I didn't know anything of what was going on in Coventry. After leaving the Crossways I caught a bus into the city centre and made my way to New Street station. As I walked in I saw the clock near the ticket office showing 7.45. I went across to the Taurus bar in the station to see if John or Gerry was there, and found them having a drink with Richard, Billy and Hughie. I had known Richard had spoken of going, but I was surprised to see Billy and Hughie.

That was the first time all six of us had ever been together as a group.

They were all surprised to see me. John said, 'Where do you think you're going?'

'Off to Belfast with you lads,' I replied, not yet realising that Hugh had only come to see the others off.

'And where did you get the money from?' John asked.

'I borrowed it off the nuns at the convent.'

John gave me a dirty look and said I was wrong taking the money from the sisters. That got me angry because I'd gone to a lot of trouble to get the money, which John had refused to lend me. And he knew how ill my aunt was.

'Look John, it's none of your business how I got it. But anyway, I've always paid it back before and I will this time, or I'll do a bit of decorating for them,' I told him.

John knew he'd hit a raw nerve and apologised, slapping me on the back and giving his big grin. The flashpoint was over and I went to the bar to get a drink, but Richard shouted that there was no time as the train would shortly be leaving. So I just bought twenty Park Drive cigarettes. Billy said he did not want to rush his pint and so gave it to me to finish off. We all left the bar together and I went to the ticket office. The others had already got their tickets. I bought a single rather than a return, because I wanted to have some money with me for a drink on the way. My unemployment cheque was to arrive the next morning and Pat was going to cash it and send a few pounds across to Belfast straight away for me. Even if I didn't get that, I knew I'd be able to borrow some money in Belfast to get back. Hughie had to buy a platform ticket to come down to the train and wave goodbye. We were all in great form, having a laugh and a joke, and looking forward to going home. It was at five minutes to eight that the train, the *Ulster Express*, pulled slowly away from platform 9.

# 7

# The Birmingham pub bombs

Minutes after we left the station, at 8.11 p.m. precisely, a telephonist at the *Birmingham Post* and *Mail* newspapers answered a call.

It was a man with an Irish accent. He said: 'The codeword is Double X. There is a bomb planted in the Rotunda and there is a bomb in New Street . . . at the tax office.'

He rang off.

At 8.17 a massive explosion rocked the Mulberry Bush, a pub at the base of the Rotunda.

I was on the train to Heysham and knew nothing of what was happening in the city I'd just left. But official statements and newspaper reports give a terrifyingly graphic account of the horror that unfolded.

Maureen Carlin, aged twenty-two, had just walked through the door of the Mulberry Bush with her fiancé and had not even had time to buy a drink when the blast came. 'The lights just sort of flickered and then went out, and I was being carried through the air,' she recalled later.

Another engaged couple in the pub were Derek Blake aged thirty, and twenty-year-old Pam Palmer, who had gone there to discuss their wedding plans. Derek said: 'I was buying some drinks when the bomb went off. Pam was only ten feet from me and I reckon she must have been on top of it. I felt my legs go. Everything went black and the whole place seemed to come in on me as the ceiling collapsed. I tried to get to Pam to see if she was all right. I could not move and I could not hear my own voice, even though I was shouting. It was not until three days afterwards that I was told Pam had died. There we were, going to talk about our future together, and the next second there was no future. Everything was over. I wanted to die too.'

54

Derek lost a leg and suffered other awful injuries.

PC Rodney Hazelwood was one of the first policemen on the scene. He was not prepared for what he found at what was left of the pub. He said: 'The ceiling had collapsed and the remainder of the building had been devastated. A lot of people were lying injured on the floor and people were running about screaming.'

The Mulberry Bush customers were a mixed crowd: late shoppers and workers having a drink before going home, as well as young people on a night out. Among the dead were John Rowlands, a forty-six-year-old electrician, and Stan Bodman and John Jones, both in their fifties. Hours later, as rescue workers cleared the rubble outside the pub, they found the bodies of two young men. The pair had been walking past when the building was blown apart.

Anthony Gaynor was driving a number 90 bus past the Rotunda into New Street when he heard the huge bang.

'I thought at first someone had hit the bus in the back, but when I looked around I realised that a lot of the windows had been blown in,' he said.

'I realised then it had been an explosion. I got out of the bus and went to see how the passengers were. There were some suffering from cuts, and we were treating those that were hurt when we suddenly heard another explosion.'

It was another bomb, a few hundred yards away at the Tavern in the Town underground bar in New Street, in a building generally known as the tax office.

Barman John Boyle was working in the Tavern when he heard the Mulberry Bush blast, but had no idea what had happened. Then everything went black in his own bar.

'There was an almighty blast and there were screams and shouts from everywhere,' he said. 'The ceiling fell in and the bar blew back at me. It was just a screaming mass of people.'

PC Brian Yates had been clearing people out of New Street after the Mulberry Bush blast and was just yards from the doorway to the Tavern when the bomb left there exploded. He was caught in the blast from the explosion and thrown bodily back into a bus shelter. He picked himself up and went with a colleague, Inspector Baden Skitt, down the stairs into what was left of the bar.

They found the dead piled in heaps and the survivors, their clothing torn to shreds, trampling over bodies as they tried to get out.

'It was in total darkness with dust and smoke everywhere,' said the inspector. 'We could hear the sound of crying out and screaming. We had to feel our way downstairs. We could feel people reaching out, trying to touch us as we stood there, but we weren't able to see them.'

Many of the people lying on the floor had the most terrible injuries. PC Yates shone his torch and could see people staggering around in a daze.

'There was screaming and people calling to each other in the blackness. There was utter chaos, people were trampling on people on the floor, staggering about burned with their clothes blasted from their bodies. I stayed in the Tavern until the last of the retrievable dead had been removed. This was a man with his skull and legs blown off. He was carried up by me and three others in a blanket. I can only say the scene was utter carnage. There were no words in the English language to describe it.'

Among the bodies on the floor was that of Paula Nash, a dark-haired girl of twenty-two who had gone to the pub with some friends after finishing work at a fashionable boutique in the city centre. It was payday, and she felt she deserved to relax in the Tavern after a hard day's work in the shop. Maureen Roberts went there with a girlfriend. She had been looking forward to her twenty-first birthday in a few months' time. Maxine Hamilton was just eighteen and about to start a new job as a secretary. She had planned a party to celebrate and went to the Tavern to meet several of her friends to invite them along. Also in the Tavern was the youngest person to die, Jane Davis, who was just seventeen.

And there was the agony of the injured. Anne Sanders was a pretty young mother of twenty-two who walked into the Tavern for a drink and left in an ambulance with severe eye injuries. It was her first night out since being badly hurt in a car crash. 'I was laughing and chatting and the next thing I knew I was in an ambulance. People were shining torches in my face and asking if I could see, and I couldn't. I thought I was going to be blind for life.'

The death and destruction at both pubs was horrendous. At the Mulberry Bush, 10 people died and 40 were injured. At the Tavern, 11 died and more than 120 were wounded. Of the injured, many were disfigured for life.

The majority of the victims were young people, men and women in their teens and early twenties who were out enjoying a night on the town. The pubs had no connections with the army or any other arm of the military.

The city's hospitals took on the sickening air of war zones that night as the dead and injured were ferried in by ambulance and private car for treatment by overstretched medical staff. James Inglis was head of the intensive care unit of Birmingham General, where fifty doctors and nearly two hundred nurses battled to save lives. He saw in more detail than most the full horror of what the bombers had done.

'What was contained in these bombs was inhuman and sadistic,' he said. 'I've seen all types of burns in the past, but these were particularly horrible. The sights in the operating theatres were just horrific.' The hospital matron, Anne Hirons, said tearfully that it was the worst night she had known in twenty-three years of nursing.

Later came the task for parents and next of kin of identifying their loved ones. It was a dreadful experience for everybody, but for one father the heartbreak must have been unbearable. John Reilly, an Irish Catholic from Donegal, had two sons: Eugene, aged twenty-three and Desmond, aged twenty-one. The younger son had been working as a pipefitter two hundred miles away from Birmingham in Durham. Mr Reilly was called by police to identify Eugene, but was shown first the body of another man. It was Desmond. He had finished the Durham job earlier than expected and, unknown to his parents, had met his brother Eugene for a quick drink in the Tavern. The distraught dad was then shown the body of his other boy. Four months after the bombing Desmond's young widow gave birth to their son.

Not surprisingly, in the hours after the blasts fear gripped the city centre, with people terrified that another bomb could go off at any time. And indeed others had been planted.

Alf Meeks, a caretaker for an insurance company, was returning at about 9.15 p.m. to his home in Hagley Road, Ladywood, a couple of miles from the city centre, when he noticed two white plastic carrier bags at the back of the nearby Barclay's bank. His first thought was to have a look inside them, so he bent down and touched one. It felt hard. He thought again, and rang the police.

Each bag was found to contain explosives and a detonator, and forensic evidence would later show the bombs were similar in construction to those that went off in the pubs. The Hagley Road bombs were destroyed by the army in a controlled explosion.

The pub bombings were at the time the biggest mass murder in British history. Public revulsion led to a wave of bitter, anti-Irish feeling that led to attacks on Irish people and property. In Birmingham a petrol bomb was thrown at the Irish Community Centre in Digbeth, and another at the College Arms in Kingstanding, which was known as an Irish pub. A fire was started at St Gerard's Catholic school on the city's Castle Vale estate. There were abusive and threatening phone calls to Irish clubs and Catholic churches, and walkouts at factories as workers downed tools to go on anti-IRA marches. Irish workers were punched and kicked at their jobs. The management of the huge British Leyland car plants across the Midlands warned they would send home troublemakers stirring up anti-Irish feeling. Trade union leaders appealed to members 'not to take it out on the Irish'. Churchmen called for calm.

There were demands for the immediate reinstatement of hanging for bombers. The day after the bombings the Labour Home Secretary, Roy Jenkins, told MPs that emergency legislation would be brought in within a week to combat terrorism. A few days later Parliament passed the Prevention of Terrorism Act after a seventeen-hour sitting. It outlawed the IRA and gave police extensive new powers, allowing them to hold suspects for up to a week without charge, as opposed to the existing forty-eight hours. Immigration authorities were given the power to turn back 'undesirables' travelling from Southern or Northern Ireland.

Two days after the bombings the Provisional IRA issued a statement in Dublin which said in part: 'It has never been and is not the policy of the IRA to bomb non-military targets without giving adequate warnings to ensure the safety of civilians.' It said a detailed investigation was in progress to determine the extent, if any, of IRA involvement in the bombings. The general interpretation of this was that even the hierarchy of the IRA, normally quick to claim responsibility for murders it committed were so shocked at what had happened they wanted to distance themselves from it. Ireland's foreign minister, Dr Garret FitzGerald, certainly read the statement as a denial of involvement, saying: 'We know how often in the past such repudiations have been made. They have never hesitated to lie.' It would be many years before the IRA would finally accept the atrocity had been carried out by its members in Birmingham, operating without the approval of leaders in Ireland.

Shortly after the bombs went off, ports and airports around the country were flashed messages warning them to be on the alert for any suspicious passengers travelling from Birmingham. That night police officers from all across the force area flocked to the West Midlands Police headquarters in the Lloyd House skyscraper block near the city centre. Statements given by officers who were involved describe how late in the night Detective Chief Superintendent Harry Robinson, the head of CID, held a briefing in the conference room on the top floor. The police officers there were split into groups of seven or eight, each with a firearms man, a dog handler, a Special Branch officer, and a policewoman. Shortly before midnight they were despatched to dozens of addresses of IRA suspects or sympathisers across the city.

Very little was found. And the police statements make clear that much of the information they were working on was out of date. One place said to be an IRA 'safe house' had long been turned into a motor repair shop. The home of a 'definite IRA man' was full of West Indians, who had lived there for months since the Irish occupant had moved out. One elderly Irishman whose home was raided clearly had nothing to do with the IRA or bombs, but he was arrested for theft when the police found some brass fittings he admitted taking from the factory where he worked.

According to newspaper reports, the police received information that the bombers could be aboard a train heading for Euston station in London, which had left just before the bombs went off. When it arrived in London, passengers were kept on board and policemen with sniffer dogs searched every compartment. The dogs, trained to detect explosives, were let off their leads and allowed to roam freely throughout the train. Passengers had to prove their identity and luggage was searched. But at the end of it all police drew a blank and the travellers were allowed to go on their way.

That night, security was stepped up in Whitehall and Westminster. Unattended cars were watched, and drivers were questioned when they returned to their vehicles. Then a booking clerk at New Street station in Birmingham reported selling tickets for the Belfast boat train to a group of Irishmen not long before the blasts.

Transport police at Heysham, the train's destination, were informed and they got ready to meet it.

# 8

## Held at Heysham

We were like a bunch of kids on that train ride to Heysham. There we were, five men off back home together with hardly a care in the world, laughing, playing cards, telling jokes, recalling stories from our Belfast days, talking of who we would see when we arrived. The crack was fierce. There were a lot of other people on the train and I think they viewed us as entertainment because we were having such a laugh together.

We changed at Crewe, where I bought some teas for the lads in the station buffet bar and a meat pie for myself, and got to Heysham just before 11 p.m. I got off the train just ahead of the others and moved with the crowd towards the boat, joining the queue to go through the single door for the security checks before boarding. There was a little girl beside me who had been on the train with us, and I could see her parents were ahead of us in the queue, loaded down with bags and other children. She was beginning to get upset at not being with her mum and dad, so I picked her up and asked the people in front of me to let me through so I could get her back to her parents. Then I stayed with the family in the queue. That meant I was separated from the other lads, but as we were all getting the same boat it didn't matter.

The security checks were being carried out at little tables. As I stepped up, a policeman I later learned was Detective Constable Fred Willoughby asked me to go into a small office with him. He asked me a few routine questions about who I was, where I was going and so forth, and asked me to open my suitcase.

I told him I was going to see my Aunt Mary and showed him the case, which contained just a few things: a shirt, some socks, and shaving gear. He asked if I owed the courts any money.

I told him I didn't, saying that any money I had owed in the past had been paid, and at that he started to chuckle.

When I asked what it was he found so funny he said: 'Because I've caught you out there. Now I know you've been in trouble with the police.'

Then it was my turn to laugh and his to ask what was so funny. I told him: 'I'm laughing at you. You must think all us Irish are stupid. The only thing that's green over there is the grass. You haven't caught me out, because I haven't tried to fool you. I know damn well you can pick up that phone and call the police criminal records and have my life story in front of you in less than five minutes. And then you can call my wife to see if I've been telling you the truth.'

He was laughing again, holding his hands in front of him, and saying: 'All right, all right. There's no need to go that far, you can go.'

I had not been nervous about his questions because I knew I had done nothing wrong and had nothing to hide. In the light of what happened later at the hands of the police I want to make one thing clear: Willoughby's behaviour was impeccable. He was doing his job properly and getting the information he needed, but I could not have been better treated if I had been one of the Royal Family.

We came out of the office, back to the security tables and through to the boat where Willoughby said, 'I hope your aunt gets better, all the best son,' and went back to his job.

I looked around but couldn't see the other four and presumed they were either on the boat already or would be soon. So I walked up on to the *Duke of Lancaster* ferry, the very boat on which I had travelled to England fourteen years earlier. As I did so I could see two crew members staring at me. One was a kid of about seventeen or eighteen, but the other was about my age, nearly thirty, and while I knew the face I couldn't think of his name.

As I reached them the older man put his hand out and said, 'Long time no see, Paddy Joe.'

He grabbed me and threw his arms around me, and as he did so the young lad said, 'Who's this, Whiskey?'

The mention of his name brought the memories flooding back. It was Whiskey McGill, an old friend I'd grown up with in the Ardoyne but hadn't seen for about fifteen years, since he went off to join the Merchant Navy. We just stood there firing questions at each other. Then Whiskey said he had work to do, and that I should go downstairs to the bar for a drink and he would join me in about an hour.

I told him who I was travelling with, and as he knew Gerry and Billy too he said he would direct them to the bar if he saw them. I said, 'You won't need to tell them, Whiskey, they'll know where to find me!'

As I left them the young lad said he had heard something on the news about bombs going off in England, but he didn't know where. I didn't give it much thought.

I went down to the bar, got a drink, and stood there thinking about the weekend ahead. I glanced at the door from time to time for any sign of the other lads, and continued reading the *Birmingham Evening Mail* I had brought with me. There was a big report about McDade's body being released from the mortuary at Coventry, and all the security surrounding it. But I was more interested in the piece on the back page about the England–Portugal soccer match the night before which had been a 0–0 draw. There was a journalists' strike at the time which kept some of the usual features out of the paper. I was annoyed that there was no crossword as I had thought I would do that while waiting. The boat was due to sail at 11.45 p.m., and with just five or six minutes to go I began to be really puzzled at what was keeping the others.

Then I saw DC Willoughby come into the bar with a uniformed policeman leading a dog. Willoughby explained that a Sergeant Bell of the port security police wanted a word with me in connection with inquiries he was making, and he asked if I would mind going with them. He said he was sorry I would have to miss the boat, but I could catch another the next day. I said I didn't mind at all and went to move off straight away, but Willoughby said there was no rush and that I could finish my pint.

People have asked me since why I didn't kick up a fuss with the police at that point, particularly about missing the boat. But my philosophy had developed over the years from my experiences of brushes with the law. If you've nothing to hide, just go along with what they want. Whatever the inconvenience, they can make it a lot worse if you create a stink.

So we walked off the boat and into one of the security offices, where there was another uniformed officer, and Willoughby and the dog handler left me saying they would be back soon. After they left, the cop in the room began speaking to me in the Irish language but I told him I did not understand Gaelic. 'How do you know it's Gaelic then?' he snapped.

'I can't speak it, but I can recognise it,' I snapped back.

He scowled and never said another word. It was the first of what were to be many bizarre 'conversations' with policemen over the coming days, one of the catalogue of incidents I've never been able to explain.

Willoughby came back with Sergeant Bell who told me he was sorry for the inconvenience, but they had had a phone call to say that bombs had gone off in pubs in Birmingham city centre. 'The Birmingham police want to speak to anybody who has been in the area tonight,' he said. 'They're talking about thirteen or fourteen dead and hundreds injured at the moment. Excuse the pun, but you know how these things can get blown up out of all proportion and it may turn out to be not so bad.'

And that was the first I ever knew of the Birmingham pub bombs.

I was shocked at the news, and said I would be happy to return to Birmingham to see the police, but he told me cops from there were on the way. After they had seen me I would be able to get the ferry to Belfast the next day.

It was then that I realised why the other lads had not made it on to the boat to join me. They must have been held for questioning too. It was only later that I was to learn exactly what had happened.

When they had reached the security check after getting off the train, they had stood together and said they were all travelling from Birmingham. After they had given their names and addresses the routine questioning continued while another officer checked their details with Special Branch in Birmingham. The word came back that Special Branch had never heard of any of them. They were about to be freed to board the boat when a call came through from the head of Lancashire CID who was told four men from Birmingham had been detained. He told the police to take the men to Morecambe police station for forensic tests.

As they were being put in a van, Gerry Hunter turned and asked one of them, 'What about our mate?'

The cop replied, 'What mate?'

'Our mate Paddy,' said Gerry. 'He's travelling with us but we got split up. He's probably in the bar on the boat. Can you let him know what's happening?'

That was how Willoughby and his colleague were dispatched to bring me back off the ferry as the others were driven away. What great friends, eh? I've really given Gerry some stick over the years for landing me in it!

If one, solitary incident in this whole affair epitomised our innocence, this was surely it. Can anybody believe that a gang of hardened IRA bombers, making their getaway from a horrendous attack, would happily volunteer that another gang member was still free? And tell the police where to find him?

Back in the security office, Bell told me the Birmingham cops would be going to Morecambe and they would see me there. I said I was happy to go if they would tell me the way, but DC Willoughby and one of his mates said they would take me there. They were not clear until about 2 a.m., so I just sat around waiting until they were ready to go. We set off in the car, and the atmosphere couldn't have been friendlier. We were cracking jokes and talking about soccer, particularly the England game of the night before. They were giving me some friendly ribbing about how it was so many Irishmen with little money could travel back to Belfast so often to see their families. They were used to seeing guys arriving for the ferry with no more than a small bag of belongings, or a fair-sized case like mine containing little more than a pair of socks and a clean shirt.

'Because we're not like you – we don't need lots of money and a suitcase full of clothes to go home to see our mothers,' I told him. 'All we need is the fare to get from A to B, and the rest is taken care of.'

We'd not been on the road long when one of them said, 'Here we are,' and we pulled up outside a gleaming new police station which, I later discovered, had only recently been opened. We got out into a driving wind, with bitter, icy rain lashing down, and walked up a few steps to the doors.

The only person around inside was a desk sergeant and I was told to take a seat and wait. For the next forty minutes I sat there, and on a couple of occasions even the sergeant left. I could have just got up and walked out, but I thought I had no reason to fear.

Willoughby reappeared and told me, 'Come into the back, Paddy, it's freezing tonight and it's warmer back here.' He took me through to the cells area and left me sitting on a bench by a desk. I was reading the paper and chatting to different cops about all sorts of things when Willoughby returned at about 4 a.m. and asked if I would be happy to make a statement about my movements. It could then be given to the Birmingham cops when they arrived to speed things up.

So I went into an office and gave a detailed, truthful statement of every single thing I had done, every penny I had spent, since getting up on Thursday morning. When it was completed they asked me to wait again on the bench in the cell area and I asked a cop if there was anything to read. He opened a cupboard and gave me a copy of Alistair MacLean's *Bear Island*.

At one point I asked to use the toilet and was taken along a corridor. Opposite the toilet was a room with the door slightly ajar, and as I passed I could see the bottom half of a man sitting on a chair. I was pretty sure it was John Walker, so I figured then that all the others must also be in the station. Willoughby later came back again and told me they had been checking details of what I had said in the statement. Everything had proved to be correct, except for a shortfall of two or three pence in the way I had accounted for my money.

'I must have been short-changed by those bastards in the BR buffet at Crewe,' I told him, and we all had a good laugh.

It was 6 a.m. when I asked Willoughby if I could get some cigarettes as I had run out, but he said the local shop didn't open until 9. He pulled a tobacco tin out of his pocket, threw it to me and told me to roll a few of my own. I did four or five, handed the tin back and thanked him. Willoughby walked off saying his shift finished at 6.30, and that was the last contact I ever had with him.

Shortly after that I got alarmed for the first time when a door facing me opened and I saw a plainclothes policeman standing there with a gun strapped to his hip. He waved two other cops into the area and they dumped a bundle of clothes behind the door. They were all giving me dirty looks, especially the guy with the gun. As they left I thought to myself, Jesus, somebody's in trouble, something heavy must have happened.

But I was still confident I had nothing to fear. Now they

knew that my statement checked out I'd probably soon be on my way.

Then at about 7.40, as I was sitting on the bench reading the book, a shadow loomed over me. I looked up and saw a cop staring at me with pure hatred in his eyes.

He was rubbing his hands and he snarled; 'Soon, you little Irish bastard, you dirty little murdering pig.'

'What the fuck are you talking about?' I asked, astonished.

'You'll find out soon, you little Irish bastard.' He spat in my face and walked away.

It was my introduction to the West Midlands Serious Crime Squad.

# 9

# Tested and beaten

Shortly after 8 a.m. a big cop whom I later learned was Det. Sgt Ray Bennett took me to a room where there were two men behind a table. One was forensic scientist Dr Frank Skuse, the other his assistant, Mr Peyton, who never said a word throughout.

Skuse asked if I had any objections to his taking swabs of my hands. Thrusting them out, I answered, 'None at all, take whatever tests you want.'

He mentioned my hands were greasy, and I told him it must have been the meat pie I had bought when we changed trains at Crewe. It had broken apart spilling gravy all over my fingers. He wiped my hands with small pieces of damp cotton wool and used a small tool to scrape under my nails. He put what he had got into little vials and told me I could go.

Skuse used an instant version of what is known as the Griess Test on the samples he had taken. This was a two-step procedure to detect a group of nitro-compounds named after a discovery by the 19th century scientist, Dr Johann P. Griess. By 1974 Dr Skuse had developed his own modification of the Griess test which he was convinced could actually identify nitroglycerine on the spot. The majority of scientific opinion believed that a positive result to the Griess test would indicate nothing more than a possibility that nitroglycerine might be present. To eliminate other non-explosive compounds (such as nitrocellulose) it had to be followed by more sophisticated testing in the laboratory before any absolute conclusion could be drawn. In simple terms caustic soda is added to the sample, and then a chemical called Griess Reagent. According to Dr Skuse, if nitroglycerine was present in the sample, it should turn pink within ten seconds. When Skuse tested the sample from my right hand he recorded a 'positive'.

That, he later testified, made him '99 per cent certain' I had been handling explosives although the other much more accurate laboratory tests that Dr Skuse carried out a few days later on that same sample proved *negative*.

In all, my time with Skuse took no more than fifteen minutes and I was then taken back to my bench in the cell area.

Almost as soon as I walked out, barefoot, from that room, Bennett told me I had to go back to Dr Skuse for some more tests. I had no idea what they were for, but discovered later they were to check for the presence of ammonium and nitrate ions. Ammonium nitrate is a constituent of explosives. But on their own the presence of the individual ions would indicate nothing suspicious as they also occur in many everyday substances. Dr Skuse claimed that if they occurred together this confirmed the presence of ammonium nitrate and, coupled with a positive Griess test for nitroglycerine, it would be conclusive proof that the person had handled explosives. At least, that was Skuse's opinion. Very few other scientists would agree with that line of reasoning. The tests on my hands showed positive for the separate ammonium and nitrate ions. I didn't realise it, but now I was in deep, deep trouble.

Minutes later Bennett returned and took me to another room where there were a few policemen and a pile of plastic bags. One of the men told me his name was Ingram and that he was from the Serious Crime Squad that had travelled up from Birmingham. He asked if I had any objection to all my clothes and property being sent for forensic examination and I said no. Then he told me, 'Don't fuck about, get stripped.'

I had to take each piece of clothing off, put it into a bag and tell Ingram what it was so that he could make a note on a ticket which also went into the bag, and which was then sealed. Finally all the small plastic bags were put into one large bag. Ingram pointed to a pile of clothes, telling me to take some. There were five sets of shirts, trousers and jackets, but no underwear, socks or shoes. The number of sets confirmed to me that all the other lads were in the station.

After these tests I was taken out of the room. From that point onwards, there are two very different versions about what happened to me over the next few days. There is my account, which I described to the court at my trial. Then there is the version of Bennett and other officers, which the jury chose to believe. I and the officers all swore on oath that what we were saying was true. I will recount here what I said in evidence, but I will also give later the police version of events.

I told the court that after being told to leave the room after Skuse's tests I was confronted in the corridor by Bennett and one of his colleagues, Det. Con. John Brand. Bennett told me to stand against the wall, facing it, and then came up behind me and grabbed my arm, forcing it up between my shoulder blades.

I screamed in pain and shouted, 'What's the rough stuff for:'

'You'll find out in a minute, you little Irish fuck pig,' he replied.

Just after that Skuse and his assistant came out of their room and walked off. Bennett told me to go back into it. As I walked in, Bennett punched me on the back of the head and I went flying. I'm only 5ft 3in. Bennett must have been well over 6ft and weighing 15 stone. They shut the door and then he and Brand ran at me and started punching and kicking me. Bennett shouted to Brand not to mark my face.

They just went completely berserk. They were screaming at me and calling me a murdering bastard. Bennett told me that I was covered in gelignite from head to toe. I said I had never even seen the stuff. He kicked me.

'You've more gelly on you than Judith Ward,' he said. (She was the woman convicted of the M62 bombing of February 1974.)

He called me an Irish bastard, while slapping me and kicking me on the shins. They asked where the gelignite came from and I told them I didn't know. They were shouting questions about gelignite: how was it sent to England, who sent it, how did it get to Birmingham? To every question I shouted back: I don't know.

Bennett kept grabbing me by the hair, pulling it, and yelling that I was a 'lying bastard' and an 'Irish fuck pig'. At one point they told me to sit in a chair. Bennett told me bluntly, 'You're covered in gelignite.'

I told him that was impossible as I'd never seen explosives, let alone ever touched any. He told me it was not him that was saying so but Dr Skuse. When I said it was not true he said, 'Are you calling the doctor a liar?'

Bennett slapped me in the face, and Brand kicked me on the back of the head. I fell off the chair on to the floor. Bennett grabbed me by the hair and started dragging me around the floor, screaming at me.

Not once throughout all this did they ask me any question that was actually about the pub bombs. They didn't ask me who had made the bombs, or who had planted them, or how it had been done. They just went on asking over and over again where the ammo dumps were and how explosives got into the country, and saying I would have to make a statement about it. And all the time there was abuse about my wife and family. Bennett was determined he was going to get a statement.

'You are going to make a statement admitting you planted those bombs in Birmingham,' he said.

I told them I wasn't. I said I would make a statement about how I had been in the Crossways and gone to the station. They started laughing. They said that if I didn't make their statement, they would kick one out of me. They said I shouldn't bother asking to see anybody, because if I didn't give them their statement I might never see anybody but these two again. I would not be allowed to see a solicitor because I had no rights. I was just a 'little Irish murdering bastard.'

It went on for ages. Most of the time they were both with me in the room, but occasionally one or other would leave for a while. I was never allowed out or given any food, but I was told that if I admitted planting the bombs I could get something to eat and drink, have a smoke, and the beating would stop. I do remember at some stage, I think the early afternoon, somebody putting their head around the door and telling the cops to keep the noise down for a little while because there were visitors in the station. I discovered later that a group of local dignitaries were being shown around the newly opened station. If only they could have seen what was happening to me in their precious new building.

At that point Bennett again left the room for a while, and when he returned after about fifteen minutes he said they now had more information. He said I had gone to Walker's house with another man at about 4 p.m. on the Thursday. He said we had gone to make sure the bombs had arrived for that night. I told him it was true I had gone to Walker's, but that I had been with my two-year-old son and that I knew nothing about bombs. That set the two of them off again; the punching and the kicking and the abuse, and all the while I was shouting that I knew nothing. Bennett said it didn't really matter what I said – he couldn't care less. They had plenty of experience, and that if I didn't make a statement they would get me thirty years anyway, whichever way they did it.

I told them I knew nothing and was signing nothing.

The Bennett and Brand version of what happened that day at Morecambe could hardly be more different to mine. They both told identical stories, supporting each other's evidence in every detail. I will give their descriptions of what occurred later, but the crux of their version is that they acted perfectly properly, that there was no abuse and there was no violence whatsoever.

Throughout much of my ordeal I could hear the other lads screaming in other rooms, and chairs and tables being knocked over. In a perverse sort of way that helped. It was difficult explaining this to the others in later years, but the fact that I knew I was not on my own, that the others were getting the same treatment, somehow made it more bearable for me. And they certainly were getting similar treatment.

All had had their hands tested by Skuse. Richard and Gerry had proved negative to all the tests. Billy had shown a positive to the Griess test, and both he and John had shown positives for the ammonium and nitrate ions tests. These results, given to the police by a scientific expert using his own instant test, obviously convinced them they had the right men. They were in no mood to listen to protestations of innocence.

Billy says he was taken to a room by two cops who started beating him and telling him the scientist had said that he was covered in gelignite. One of the cops put a pair of handcuffs over his own hand like a knuckleduster and kept whacking the back of Billy's hands with it. They gave him the same terrible time my two had given me. They even said there was a mob outside his house waiting to lynch his wife and kids, and only the police were holding them back. If he didn't make a statement admitting to planting the bombs, they would call the police off and leave his family to the mob.

Then he was taken to another, darkened room where there were about six cops who laid into him mercilessly. Eventually he was spreadeagled against a wall and a voice shouted 'stretch his balls'. He was told he would never have sex with his wife again.

At that point Billy caved in. As he put it, 'I screamed OK, OK. I had to say something to stop them because I couldn't take any more.'

He was then dragged back into another room, at which point somebody shouted 'Who was the sixth man?' Billy hadn't a clue what they meant and said so. He was punched again and was told 'The man who stayed behind'. He said 'Oh, you mean Hughie?' They demanded Hughie's second name, which Billy couldn't give them because he hardly knew him. Then they threatened to hurl him out of a plate glass window and started dragging him towards it. After what had already happened, Billy believed they were quite capable of throwing him out. So he shouted in desperation, 'Don't, don't! I'll say anything you want.'

The cops who had interviewed Billy said that within a short time of beginning some gentle questioning he had admitted his involvement in the pub bombings. He made a 'confession' statement in which he said he knew Gerry and John were in the IRA. He said he arrived at New Street Station where he met the other five of us. We were all carrying plastic bags which he knew had bombs in them. He was given two bags which he was told to take to the Mulberry Bush pub. He left them beside the juke box in the pub and returned to the station.

This was the briefest of statements, lacking any detail, and ended with Billy supposedly saying, 'Jesus, I am sorry. I wish this day had never come.' Then he signed it.

John says he was beaten up by two cops who at one stage took out a gun and discussed whether they should 'shoot the bastard'. They put a blanket over his head and pushed the gun against it. There was a clap, and for a second John thought he'd been shot. He also had a larger blister on his right big toe, caused by new shoes, and one of the cops took pleasure in pushing a lighted cigarette into it. The beating continued for hours until eventually he passed out, waking up later in a cell.

Gerry was one of the last to be interviewed. He recalls sitting in his cell and hearing me shouting and screaming while I was being beaten, and the cops screaming at me. The cops who dealt with him were Supt George Reade, the leader of the Birmingham detectives, and his deputy Inspector John Moore. Gerry says he was knocked about badly, and that they took particular pleasure in dragging him around by his very long hair. As with each of us, they told him he would have to make a statement admitting to planting the pub bombs.

Richard had one of the shortest 'interviews', but says it was not without brutality. He had been sitting in his cell, terrified as he listened to my screams, when they came for him. He was slapped around and then kicked in the chest. When he was on the floor one of the cops put a blanket over him and held it tight, making it difficult for him to breathe. Eventually Richard went limp. They then took the blanket off him and left him alone.

All the police officers involved in interviewing John, Gerry and Richard strenuously denied that any violence or abuse took place at any time, except in the case of Gerry whom they said had to be subdued at one point when he became violent towards the officers.

Back in my 'interview', I kept thinking every now and then it must all be a bad dream, that I would soon wake up and find I was in bed with my wife, with the only shouting coming from the kids. I didn't think it was possible what they were doing to me. I said to myself, 'Just hold on Paddy, there's got to be some decent policemen in this police station. Somebody is going to put a stop to this.'

But nobody ever did. And I defy anybody who was in that station that day to tell their Maker on Judgement Day they did not know what was happening. They would have to have been deaf not to have heard those screams – not just ours but those of the police too as they went at us like men possessed.

I lost all track of time, but I discovered later the beating stopped at about 5 p.m. Bennett left the room briefly and returned to say he was taking me back to Birmingham, to his own 'patch'.

I was just so relieved that I would be spending a couple of hours in a car on the motorway, away from the battering and abuse.

# 10

## Motorway madness

I was wrong again. Handcuffs were put on me and I was led out to a corridor where we stood around for a few minutes. They said we would be going in a convoy of cars to Birmingham, but because there was a big group of reporters and photographers outside the station we would have to wait a while. Clearly word of the police "success" in catching the bombers so quickly had been leaked to the media. I learned later that the police had organised a dummy convoy to fool the waiting press. It was made up of policemen and cadets with blankets over their heads who were loaded into vans which sped off.

Then a jacket was put over my head and I was taken out into a yard, still barefoot, and bundled into the rear seat of a car. The handcuff on my left hand was taken off and snapped around the passenger grip above the door. Brand was in the driver's seat and told me to keep quiet while Bennett went off somewhere. Up to the car came another cop who I'd not seen before. He turned out to be Insp. Moore, the second-in-command of the police team.

Moore asked Brand who he'd got in the car and after being told it was me walked off. Minutes later Bennett and Moore returned together. Bennett uncuffed me from the passenger grip, pushed me across the back seat, cuffed my left arm to the grip on that side and got in beside me. Moore got into the passenger seat in front of me. The car started – and so did Bennett.

Minutes after leaving the police station, the jacket was pulled off my head and he started punching me around the ears, screaming at me that I was going to make a statement admitting I had planted the bombs. I just kept repeating what I'd been telling them all day – that I'd done nothing and so had no intention of signing any statement.

Bennett kept laughing. Then he told me to sit forward on the seat and to keep my legs wide open. He produced a truncheon and started ramming it into my testicles, all the time screaming and shouting abuse. There was a leather thong on one end of the truncheon and he began whipping me across my privates with it, yelling, 'You'll make no more Irish bastards when I'm finished with you.'

Every now and then Moore would turn around from his front passenger seat and punch me on the head or in the chest. They were smoking as the car sped southwards in a convoy down the outside lane of the M6 motorway. Each time Bennett neared the end of his cigarette he would start to stub it out on my right foot, just by the toes. The pain was excruciating. Bennett told me that when we got to Birmingham I would be back on his home patch and that when we got there things would either get rougher or the violence would stop. It was all up to me. I was going to make a statement confessing to the pub bombs. And I would also sign a form saying I had been well treated at the hands of the Birmingham police, that I had not been harmed in any way, and that I had been fed and well looked after.

It cooled down for a while after that but not for long. Moore suddenly turned around and drew out a gun, a revolver. The sight of it in his hand terrified me. The punching and abuse and beating with the truncheon was bad enough, but this was putting things on a different level altogether. Something that Bennett and Brand had said back at Morecambe immediately flashed into my mind. They had told me that on the way back to Birmingham they might just shoot me and throw me out on the motorway. Nobody would know they had done it, because nobody knew that I was in police custody. Despite the beating I was taking when they had said that, it had seemed like an idle threat just to frighten me. Now I wasn't so sure.

Moore hit me on the head with the gun, looked me straight in the face and told me to open my mouth. I did so, and he rammed the muzzle of the gun between my teeth and started rattling it around.

'I'm going to blow your fucking head off,' he said.

How can anybody describe in words just how you feel in a situation like that? Everything seemed to stop and I just stared in terror at the gun inches below my eyes. He pulled the trigger. There was a click.

Moore started laughing, and told the others there was something wrong with the ammunition.

'We must have been given duds,' he said, then shook the gun in front of my face and said, 'I'll try again.'

He pushed the gun back into my mouth and again pulled the trigger. Again there was just a click. He pulled the gun out and waved it.

'You must have a charmed life,' he said, then put the gun against my eye and spoke quietly. 'Third time lucky.'

He said the gun had not been loaded on the first and second time he had put it in my mouth. But, he asked, how was I to know whether it was loaded this time? He pulled the trigger and for a third time there was just a click.

Bennett, Brand and Moore would later all testify that there was not one word of conversation with me during the two-hour trip in the car from Morecambe to Birmingham; that my head remained covered with a jacket throughout; and that I was not subjected to any form of violence or ill-treatment. They all agreed that while Moore was carrying a revolver, it was never produced at any stage of the journey.

# 11

## Queen's Road

We arrived at Queen's Road police station in Aston, Birmingham, to find the place packed with police officers, guns and dogs. Brand and Bennett led me to a cell, took the handcuffs off and threw me in. The cell door slammed shut. I'd lost track of time, but I've since learned this was shortly after 8 p.m. Soon after the cops left another group of three or four arrived. One had a shotgun, one had a hand gun, and a third had an alsatian dog on a lead. One was carrying a plate with a little slice of pork pie on it.

The guy with the dog came forward, took the pie slice and said, 'Watch this.'

He threw the slice into the air and as it came down the dog went mad for it.

'As you can see, he hasn't been fed yet,' said the cop. 'If I hear any of you lot trying to talk to each other through the walls I'll let this dog in here, and it won't be on a lead. It will eat the balls off you. Do you understand?'

Off they went muttering more abuse about how if they had their way there wouldn't be a trial, they'd just shoot us and that would be the end of it. I went and sat down on a bench in the cell and thought, 'What the hell is happening to us?' Although I was in a daze, I can remember thinking that if they are doing this to us, what is happening to our wives and children and our homes?

Suddenly the flap on the cell door opened, a shotgun was poked through it and a voice screamed, 'Who the fuck told you to sit down you murdering little bastard?'

I jumped up and he said I should be grateful I had legs to stand on. There were young people in those pubs who no longer had legs because of me. He wanted me in the middle of the cell with my legs

apart and my arms raised from my sides. I did so, and he told me that
if he returned to find me sitting down, he would shoot me. The gun
was withdrawn, the flap closed, and then I heard him going through
the same routine at a cell nearby.

Some time later he returned, the gun came through, and he
shouted, 'sit up in that corner. I don't want to see you!'

He left and after ten minutes he was back. 'I told you to stand up.
Get in the middle of the floor.'

This went on all Friday night and the early hours of Saturday. It
was the same routine over and over again, the flap being opened ever
ten minutes, the gun poked through, the barked orders. All the time
this was accompanied with screaming abuse.

- Stand up! Who said you could sit?
- Sit down! Who said you could stand?
- Get those arms up you Irish bastard!
- Put those arms down you Irish bastard!
- They're bringing back hanging for you.
- We should give you to that mob outside.
- I should shoot you myself and get it over with.

The entire night rang to the sounds of cops shouting and swearing,
guns clanging against cell doors, and dogs barking. It went on and
on, hour after hour. I'd had no sleep on Thursday, and clearly
there would be no chance of a rest with this treatment. Eventually
exhaustion seemed to blot out the fear of the cell door flap flying
open and the shouted instructions. I just began acting like a robot,
jumping up and down to whatever orders they gave.

While I was getting this treatment, a delighted Maurice Buck,
an Assistant Chief Constable of the West Midlands, was telling a
crowded press conference a mile or two away in Birmingham city
centre, 'I am satisfied that we have captured the men primarily
responsible.'

At some time on early Saturday morning I heard footsteps
approaching. You knew that they were coming for you, but you
just hoped and prayed they would go past. By now I realised these
people could do whatever they wanted with you, and I was terrified.
I dreaded the door opening. I wanted that door to stay shut and keep
far away from me the outside world and furthest of all the Serious

Crime Squad. But the steps stopped outside my cell, as I knew they would, and I sat there absolutely petrified. I'd been in dodgy situations before, violent situations where I would be frightened. But now I knew the meaning of total, absolute fear.

The keys jangled, the door flew open and a group of cops came in, grabbed me and took me to an office where I was fingerprinted, and then frogmarched back to the cell. Brand told me to pick up the cell blanket and put it over my head and then he took me through the station. It was like walking a gauntlet. My head was covered but I was looking at the floor and could see the legs and feet of policemen and policewomen. As I was walked by I was kicked and punched and abused. Yet what I remember most clearly of all now seems quite bizarre.

As I was being taken up a staircase I heard the sound of milk crates being moved, the distinctive tinkle of milk bottles being knocked against each other. I've no idea why, but I have never forgotten that sound.

Then I was pushed into a room. Bennett was there. He told me to sit down in a chair. He said I'd had all night to think about it, and asked if I was now going to make a statement. I told him I wasn't.

'You can have it the easy way or the hard way,' he said. 'If you don't make a statement, you are going to go around the walls again.'

Another cop came into the room at that point and told me he was Det. Con. Michael French. He put one hand on my shoulder and said quietly that they had been late leaving Morecambe the night before because Power had been finishing off his statement. He said he had promised Billy that if he signed the statement the police would take his wife and children to a safe place, because his house had been surrounded by a mob who wanted to get them. Billy had signed, and French had been at his house that morning to take the family to safety. He said there was now a crowd outside my house, screaming for my wife and kids' blood, but if I signed a statement he would do for me what he had done for Billy.

'Think about it a minute,' he said. 'We have police officers at your house guarding it. If you don't make a statement, fuck you, we'll take them off and the crowd can have your kids.'

How can you possible explain to anybody what goes through your mind over something like that? I'd done nothing wrong, but maybe there really was a mob outside my house. What was happening to Pat, to my little girls, and to baby Sean? Should I just give them what they want and try to sort it all out later? But by then it might be too late. I had nothing to confess, so why should I, despite the fears I held for my family?

I told him I was signing nothing about planting bombs. French punched me in the back of the head, kicked me and walked out of the room. He later denied he had ever seen me that day. With French gone, I was left alone with Bennett and Brand.

'Around the walls again,' said Bennet.

I was kicked and punched all around the room. They kept telling me that I would make a statement or they would kick me to death. They said they would take me to court and say I had admitted being part of the IRA, that I had virtually admitted planting the bombs but would not make a statement. I would get done anyway. And they said that even if I got off, they would tell the IRA that I had been squealing, and so the IRA would shoot me. Then they said they were going to eat and I was taken back to the cell.

I sat there worrying about my family, and wondering how something like this could happen in England in 1974. The government was always complaining about human rights in other countries, but this was happening to us right here in Birmingham.

They came back for me in mid-afternoon. Bennett was holding some papers which he said was Billy Power's statement. He read out bits about plastic bags. He didn't let me see it, but said Billy had implicated me in the bombings up to my neck. All the others were now confessing, all saying that I was the brains of the organisation and that I had made the bombs. Bennett said I should get my bit in now and put the blame on them. He said I should get it off my conscience like the rest of them and I would feel a lot better.

Bennett said he had statements from my wife Pat in which she had told them I was in the IRA and used to attend meetings. He showed me a paper she had signed, but would not let me see what it said. He claimed she'd said in it that I was always beating her up and the kids, and that I called them all English bastards. I told them I didn't believe them and that I was signing nothing. He started calling Pat an IRA whore and my kids IRA bastards. My daughters would grow up to be IRA whores. The insults got me really angry and it must have shown in my eyes, for Brand said,

'Go on, you're getting mad now, take a dig at me.' I put my hands behind my back.

I was taken back to the cell, and then later on the Saturday they came back for a third time. Once more I was asked if I would make a statement and when I again refused I was slapped and kicked. At some stage Bennett told me that Hughie had been arrested and had made a statement confessing his role. It was the first I knew that poor old Hughie had been dragged into this mess. Bennett and Brand later denied any violence or abuse had taken place at any interview, and firmly rejected the suggestion that there were three interviews that day, saying there had only been two.

Back in my cell once more I was given half a cup of water and a pork pie. It was the first food I had been offered. But I don't like pork pies and couldn't eat it, despite not having eaten since that meat pie at Crewe station on the Thursday night. As I sat there I would hear a commotion now and then, with abuse and shouting and cell doors being opened and closed. It was obvious the others were getting the same treatment. For the first time, I started to think to myself something that had never occurred to me before. Was it possible, could it be, that these others lads actually were in the IRA? Maybe they really had planted the bombs in those pubs. I didn't know them that well. And I had been the last to arrive at the station. Could they have planted the bombs before I got there?

This was the only point in our whole ordeal at which I ever contemplated the possibility. However that train of thought came to an abrupt end when suddenly everything went quiet, and I heard a faint noise in the next cell. I went to the corner of my cell and put my ear up against the wall. I could hear somebody moving in there. I sat for a while wondering who it was, and whether I should try to make contact, before deciding to take a chance.

I got up against the wall in the corner and said in a low voice, 'Who's that, who's in there?'

It was Billy Power's voice that replied.

'It's me Paddy Joe, it's me. They've been battering and torturing me.'

I told him I'd been battered too, and that they'd told me he had signed a statement. 'Is that true Billy?' I asked.

'Yes.'

82

'What in God's name did you do that for? Did you plant the bombs, or any of the other lads?'

'No.'

'So what the fuck did you sign for?'

'I couldn't take any more Paddy Joe, I just couldn't take any more.'

I knew Billy was telling the truth and any doubts about him or the others disappeared for ever. I just sat there, looking at the wall, telling Billy it was O.K. and not to worry. 'We've got witnesses, we'll be all right. It will all get straightened out.'

Despite this, in my own mind I knew we were going to jail.

That night there was a repeat of Friday night's performance, their way of ensuring I didn't get any sleep so that I would be too exhausted to hold out any longer. Guns through the flap, get up, sit down, abuse, insults, threats, dogs barking. As they yelled and screamed, I could feel the anger and hatred coming off them in waves.

I still have nightmares about those Friday and Saturday nights. In them I'm sitting or standing and desperate to go to sleep. I've been awake since Thursday morning and it's now gone midnight on Saturday. I can hardly keep my eyes open and every part of my body is aching from tiredness and pain. My arms are that sore I can hardly lift them. My chest is so sore I have to remember not to take deep breaths. And my mind? One minute it's just not operating and the next it's running riot thinking about myself, the family, the other lads, and the cops coming back.

Early on the Sunday morning the cell was opened, I was given a plastic cup of water and told I was to be charged that day. The cell door slammed shut again, but this time I was behind it with a seed of hope. If I was to be charged, that would surely mean an end to all this; the brutality, the abuse and the torture sessions that would later be described in court as 'interviews'.

Later I was taken to a room and a cop introduced himself as Det. Sgt. Roy Bunn. He noticed I was barefoot. He told the cops with him to get me some footwear and I was given a pair of slippers.

Bunn was fiddling with a typewriter and asked if I wanted a cup of tea. I said I'd love one, so he gave the other guy some money and sent him out for three teas. When he returned, and as we drank, Bunn told me he had a copy of Hughie's statement and asked if I wanted to read it. I did so, and when I finished it I told Bunn it was all nonsense.

'That's not my statement,' Bunn replied.

'That's the statement Callaghan made. Are you going to make a statement?' He said everybody else had made statements, but I said I could not because I knew nothing about bombs.

Then an amazing change came over Det. Sgt. Bunn. He lost his temper, leaned across the table and grabbed me by the jacket I was wearing, twisting it around his big fists and pulled me up off the chair a few inches.

'If you tell me again you don't know anything about the bombings I'll kick fuck out of you,' he said.

He put me back in my chair and said he didn't believe in beating prisoners and so would not beat me up as the others had done.

'If you're going to make a statement say "Yes". If you're not going to make a statement say "No", and we can all get on with the antecedent forms,' he said.

I told him there would be no statement, and he said, 'Fair enough.'

Then he started typing up the antecedents form, a list of my previous convictions, but he and his mate were called away. I was taken off to be photographed and then put in my cell. Bunn later gave a very different version of this interview, denying any threats and saying I had made a free admission of my part in the bombings, which we will come to later.

Billy had signed a 'confession' at Morecambe police station. John and Richard both eventually signed 'confessions' at Queen's Road. John says he finally agreed to sign some typed papers that were put in front of him. 'I just wanted to stop the beating,' he later told the court. His hand was shaking so much one of the cops had to hold it to steady his signature. Richard says he was beaten up too, and at one stage got the sort of treatment with a gun I had experienced in the car on the motorway. Gerry, despite what he says was dreadful treatment, never signed anything.

Hughie had been arrested at his home at about 11 p.m. on the Friday night. Quite how he came to get involved has never been properly explained, but I believe the key to it was the demand put to Billy at Morecambe, 'Who was the sixth man?'

When the others had first met at New Street Station on the Thursday, Gerry had mentioned he thought a man had been watching them. He later discovered the man was a Special Branch officer.

Special Branch had obviously, and reasonably, been conducting surveillance on the house where McDade's widow and friends had been on the Thursday morning. It seems quite likely they had kept watch on Gerry and Billy who had popped into the house earlier that day to see their wives. Sandra and Nora had known Jackie McDade and had gone around to console her. The Special Branch man Gerry saw at the station presumably passed on the information that six of us had been together but that only five had boarded the train.

Hughie was first taken to Queen's Road Station, but was later transferred to Sutton Coldfield because of a shortage of room. He was not badly beaten, but for a man of nervous disposition the threats and browbeating over a period of hours were enough. As he put it, 'I was in a state of shock. They said things to me, I agreed and they wrote it down.'

During the police interviews with Hughie, the novel element of our 'ranks' within the IRA was introduced. He was asked who was the brigadier and who was the captain, and gave them the first names that came into his head. He said John was the brigadier, Gerry the captain, and the rest of us were all lieutenants. Even those with just a passing knowledge of the IRA know there are no such ranks as brigadiers and captains within their structure. Also lieutenant tends to be a title bestowed only on members who have died.

The so-called confessions are remarkable documents. They are all incredibly brief, and the actual planting of the bombs is skipped over in each case in just a few sentences. There is no mention anywhere in any of the confessions about who made the bombs, where they were made, or of how and where the bombs were primed. There are numerous contradictions in regard to the number of bombs involved and who did the planting in each of the pubs. According to Richard, I went with him to put bombs in the Tavern in the Town. John says it was he and Gerry who planted bombs there. Billy says he went alone to put a bomb in the Mulberry Bush. But Hughie says it was he and Gerry who went to the Mulberry Bush, and he states the bombs were left outside the pub.

All of the 'confessions' refer to the bombs being in white plastic bags. Yet the forensic scientists who sifted through the wreckage of the pubs would later tell the trial that the bombs had been placed inside the pubs, and had been in a small suitcase or briefcase. How odd that four men who had been kept apart should make confessions that talked only of white plastic bags, without a briefcase or suitcase in sight. Of course, another bomb had been found in Birmingham that night, the one that failed to go off in the Hagley Road and was discovered before the Birmingham police set off for Heysham. It had indeed been in a white plastic bag. We didn't know that. But the police did.

# 12

## Charged and in court

On the Sunday I was taken from my cell at five to two in the afternoon and charged with the murder of Jane Davis, a young girl of seventeen who had died in the Tavern in the Town. It was a holding charge. It was weeks later before the accusation of murdering the other twenty people who died was added. The words were read out to me, but by then my mind had almost closed down and what they were saying didn't mean a lot to me. I was returned to my cell and sat there in a daze. About thirty minutes later I heard a lot of noise outside. The door flew open and a large group of cops came in, although I recognised only Bennett, Moore and Brand. Out of the crowd came a smaller guy who I discovered later was Chief Superintendent Harry Robinson, the head of the CID.

'Listen Hill, you're going to court tomorrow and I want to know if you'll recognise it,' he said. 'I don't want any outbursts or performance in the court like other IRA men have done.'

I told him I would recognise the court, that there would be no outbursts from me, that I wasn't in the IRA, that he knew it, and that I was innocent.

'Do I have your word that you'll recognise the court with no outbursts?' he asked.

I said yes. Then he put his arm out and shook my hand.

Those who were present all later denied this ever took place. As Robinson told the court, the last thing he would ever dream of doing would be to shake hands with an IRA bomber. That may be true, for I was no IRA bomber. But he did shake hands with me that day.

They all trooped out and I was left alone in the cell once more. But not for long. There was a huge commotion in the cell area and I could hear doors being opened, one at a time, followed by shouting of insults and abuse.

The commotion was getting closer and closer, and suddenly my door was opened and I was told to get out. I walked through the door to find myself surrounded by police, dozens of them. Some had shotguns, some were holding handguns, and some had guns in holsters. I was handcuffed and taken out to a car. Once inside, I was told to bend forward with my head on my knees, and then a coat was thrown over me. After a while the car set off.

It had not gone far, perhaps a ten-minute drive, when I was bundled out and taken down a flight of stairs to a cell. I was in Steelhouse Lane police station and court in the city centre. We were put one to a cell, each with the adjacent cells left empty so that we could not communicate. The police station was packed; apparently a lot of officers had stayed around just to see us. The cop in charge of the station later testified about the state we were in on arrival. 'They were absolutely terrified. I have never seen men so frightened,' he said.

There was a lot of abuse again, and guns being poked through the flaps, but it was not as bad as before. Alone in the cell, I decided to take a good look at my body to see what evidence there was of the beatings I had suffered. I could feel my left ear was badly swollen. It was cut on the back and bleeding a little inside. There were bumps on the back of my head. All over my chest and upper arms there were black and blue bruises. I had a big bruise on my right hip where I had been kicked. There were red lines around my privates where I had been whipped with the leather strap of a truncheon on the motorway ride. I had lots of cuts and bruises on both legs. And there were marks and a blister where cigarettes had been stubbed out on my feet.

I lay down on the bed in the cell, completely exhausted, and began to think about the court appearance the next day. Would anyone I knew be there? Would Pat be in court, or any friendly face? The thinking didn't last long, because without the disruptions of Friday and Saturday night at Queen's Road I was at last able to drift off into a sleep, my first since Thursday morning.

I don't know how long I slept for, but I woke with a jolt when I heard the key jangling in the cell lock. It was Monday morning. They brought me a cup of tea in an old plastic cup and some sort of sandwich. I took a mouthful of tea and immediately spat it out. Somebody had urinated in it.

A little later the cell door opened again and a cop told me to go and wash the congealed blood away from around my face because I was going into court soon. As I used the washbasin in the corner, he stood beside me waving a little noose he had made from a piece of string.

Shortly after that the door opened to reveal a young man in a suit standing in the doorway. He said he was Ian Gold, a duty solicitor, and asked if I wanted him to represent me in court. Yes, oh yes please, I told him. It seemed as though at last my prayers had been answered; now this could be sorted out.

He said I looked as if I'd been having a hard time, and I told him I certainly had. I lifted up my shirt to show him the marks on my chest, and then the words came out in a torrent. I told him how the police had battered me, how they had been beating me since Friday morning, how they were trying to get me to make a confession, how they wanted me to admit to planting the pub bombs, how I needed his help, how I was innocent, innocent, innocent.

He cut me off, saying he hadn't got much time. He had to get me to fill in some legal forms quickly as we would be going up to court soon. He said we would be remanded in custody to Winson Green Prison, to not even think of applying for bail, and that he would try to arrange for a doctor to see us that afternoon at the prison. And then he walked out.

Gold had qualified as a solicitor only three years earlier, and although he had his own practice I think he was way out of his depth in dealing with a matter as serious as ours. He was more used to representing small-time, petty criminals, not people charged with mass murder. Had he spent more time with me, examined the marks on my body and noted them down, the outcome could have been so different.

He was also assigned to Billy and Hugh. He later told the court he had glanced briefly when I lifted my shirt. 'I did see, I think upon his chest, what I can only describe as discolouration. I can't be any more precise.' He said he had been concerned that we should be seen by an independent doctor, and that he spoke to four or five by phone before he could find one willing to inspect us. It would be another three days before that happened. Gold was asked in court if he had done anything to encourage us to show other parts of our bodies. 'No, quite the contrary', he replied. 'I regret I discouraged them showing any further parts of the body because I was more concerned about the business in hand.'

Not long after Gold left the cell the door opened again and I was taken out, handcuffed to a cop, and brought along to a corridor where I saw the rest of the lads lined up against a wall at the bottom of a flight of stairs. It was the first time I had seen them since I'd got off the train. John seemed to be in a trance, and the rest of them all looked dreadful. Each of them was handcuffed to a cop, and all around us were policemen waving shotguns and handguns, and dogs on leads. We were warned in very clear terms not to consider making a scene in court.

I heard some noise in what was obviously a courtroom at the top of the stairs. Then a voice shouted, 'Send the first one up.' I can't recall who went up first, but he was only away for thirty or forty seconds before he was pushed back down the stairs and the voice shouted, 'Next.'

I was about third or fourth up. I desperately tried to look about to see if there was anyone I knew, but my eyes seemed to glaze over. My name was read out and Gold was asked if there was an application for bail. 'No sir,' he said, and then I was bundled back down the stairs.

When the last one was dealt with we were all taken together to await transport to Winson Green Prison where we were to be held on remand. Policemen were swarming around shouting abuse. Then one stepped forward with a big grin on his face.

He told us they had laid on a special reception for us at the Green.

# 13

## Welcome to Winson

We were taken out into the loading yard and dragged into a big van in which each of us was locked inside individual little cubicles where we sat handcuffed and facing the front.

To my left side was a window which I could just see through. After sitting there for a few minutes I saw the big steel door of the Steelhouse Lane Compound roll up, and as the van drew out into the road I saw a massive crowd. They surged forward, banging on the sides of the van and spitting, shouting every name imaginable, and screaming for us to be hanged. I saw placards with gallows drawn on them, and others which read 'HANG THE IRA BASTARDS'. I could see the faces of people in the crowd, and every one was contorted with hatred. All I could think of was how they had got it so wrong.

Then we were through the crowd and were off at top speed with the van's lights flashing and sirens blaring as it raced along in the middle of a convoy of marked police cars, unmarked cars full of armed detectives, and half a dozen motorcycle outriders.

Within minutes we were at Winson Green Prison, pulling up at the reception block. Peering through my window I could see nothing but prison officers, cops with shotguns shouting out orders, and dogs barking and snarling. The door to my cubicle was unlocked and the cuffs were taken off. A big cop pulled me up from the seat by my shirt collar, and with a hefty push and a kick up the backside I was sent flying down the narrow little corridor along the middle of the van. I stumbled out of the back door and down the van steps. I was grabbed by the arms and frogmarched into the prison reception area. I was slammed against a wall and told to stay there, not moving a muscle, with my nose touching the brickwork.

One of the prison officers on duty who saw us arrive, Ivor Vincent, later said: 'There was a permanent banter from the police, clearly trying to frighten or intimidate the men. All of them appeared stiff and awkward and ungainly as they moved to the bottom of the van's steps as though they had been beaten about the body and/or legs. As they came out of the van they were visibly petrified to a man.'

He watched us being taken up a set of steps and through a door into the prison. He later recalled that as one of us went in he heard a noise 'which I immediately recognised as being similar to a head hitting a wall very hard indeed'.

Another prison officer, Patrick Murtagh, was later to describe our arrival in the reception area. 'They were petrified, like zombies. Walker ran blindly across in front of the desk and straight into a wall. He even kept running after he had run into the wall, as though trying to run up it.' Murtagh knew me from my previous stay in the Green. With a snarl of contempt he told me: 'The IRA must be pretty hard up for recruits to have picked you.'

The other lads were lined up against the wall alongside me and the cops started shouting to the screws (prison officers, that is) to come and look at us and discover who was who. John Walker was next to me. They said he was the brigadier, that he was in charge of us all. They pulled him back a foot or two, and then hurled him straight into the wall. I was next. They said that I was the explosives expert, that I had made the bombs, and that there was enough gelignite in our homes to blow up half of Birmingham. Because I hadn't signed a statement they told the screws I should be given extra special treatment, and a cop gave me a sharp kick between the legs as an example. They went along the line with each of the others, spouting all this nonsense about them holding various ranks in the IRA. When they got to the end of the line there was a cry of 'you bastards' and a general free-for-all began, with the cops and the screws laying into us, all kicking and punching and screaming.

After a few minutes the cops left and we were told to sit on some benches before being called into another room one at a time. I went in to find several screws who started hurling a stream of verbal abuse. They told me to remove all my clothes and gave me some prison gear to put on. I was given a number. From now on I was no longer Paddy Joe Hill, but Prisoner 509496.

The others were dragged in to join me and had their clothes taken.

As the last of us changed, the screws, loads of them by now, just went completely crazy attacking us. I was punched and kicked across the room and ended up supporting myself against a small swing door which led into the bath area. It was made of wood, and only about four feet high, like a shower screen. Somebody grabbed me by the hair and smashed my face down on top of the door. My nose burst apart and the blood ran from it like a tap. There was blood everywhere, all over my shirt and soaking my chest and stomach. A screw told me to keep my head up because the blood was making a mess on the floor. My eyes were beginning to close because I had been punched so much and my whole face was puffing up.

I remember old Hughie collapsing on to the ground and Richard and I trying to help him up. But the screws told us to get away and started kicking him and screaming at him to get up. They told him there were poor kids who would never be able to get up after what he had done. Hughie struggled across to the guy shouting loudest at him, and he was crying and begging not to be beaten any more. But they carried on.

Prison officer Brian Sharp knew it was out of control. He admitted later that while he had not taken part in the violence he had turned to one of his colleagues and said, 'Let's get these blokes away before they get killed.'

They told us to get up to a cell on the first-floor landing and as we made our way up the stairs we were punched and kicked. They threw us all in one cell and slammed the door shut. Nobody said a word as we sat trying to take in what was happening to us. I remember looking at each one of the others, horrified at the state of them. And I realised I must have looked the same. My shirt was saturated in blood and my face was swollen up like a balloon. John looked like a zombie, as if his mind had closed down altogether. Richard's chin was split and he had a hollow look in his eyes. Gerry and Hughie and Billy were the same – cut, blood-spattered and stunned. Gerry was the first to break the silence.

'Much more of this fucking stuff and I'm going to top myself,' he said. 'I just can't take any more.'

He'd put into words what we were all feeling. We sat there together for maybe fifteen minutes, mumbling that if we didn't commit suicide we would end up being killed. Over and over we kept asking each other how this could be happening to us. Whatever happened to being innocent until proved guilty?

Then came the sound of boots in the corridor and the jangling of keys as the cell door was unlocked. A bunch of screws told us we would have to get our kit. We staggered off somewhere with them to be given a bedroll, a chamber pot and some other bits and pieces. Then we were thrown into separate cells on D-wing, with an empty cell between each of us so that we could not communicate. We'd been there some time when I heard one of the cells being opened and a bellow that seemed to bounce off the cell doors as it echoed along the wing: 'Send the first one down.'

Seconds later I heard screams and shouts and swearing and knew that one of the others must be getting beaten again. The screws sounded as though they were working themselves into a real frenzy once more. The screams of whichever of the lads they had got trailed off, and I realised he was being taken off the wing. Then after a while the noise and commotion increased again as he was brought back to his cell. There was a brief pause after the cell door was slammed shut. Then came a shout. 'Next.' And it started all over again. This time I heard them shouting something about 'washing you dirty bastards' and knew we were being sent down to the bath.

Each time somebody was brought back the shouting got nearer to my cell, and I knew my turn was coming. It's impossible for words to describe the sheer terror I felt, cowering in a corner of my cell. I knew with every passing second that the moment when my door would be opened was growing closer. What the hell was going on out there?

I heard a cell door slam again, and then the footsteps coming towards me. I went absolutely cold. Frozen. I was rooted to the spot with fear, terrified about what they might have in store for me now. The terror was well founded. A screw later recalled that during the bathing one of us had pleaded: 'All I want to do is die. Let me die. Just let me alone.'

My cell door was flung open and I saw a screw I recognised from my previous stay at Winson. I'm sure he remembered me, but he just fixed me with a cold stare and whispered, 'Down the stairs for a bath.'

I could hardly get up because I was so frightened, so he and another screw dragged me out and pulled me along the landing to the staircase which was lined with their mates. I got to the top of the stairs where they shouted, 'Down you go you Irish bastard', and started punching and kicking.

I could only get down the first step or two because they were falling over each other to have a go at me, but the next thing I knew I had been flung down the iron stairs. There were another two flights to go, so I scrambled to my feet and half ran, half stumbled the rest of the way. From the bottom of the stairs to the bath house was a gauntlet of screws and I rushed through, being kicked and punched and spat on as I went. As I got to the bath some screws grabbed me and started to pull my clothes off, shouting: 'Get a fucking bath, you dirty animal.' Then before my clothes were all off they just picked me up and tipped me in. Gordon Willingham was one of the screws at the bath. In a statement later he said, 'I lost my temper as soon as the first one came down because the very sight of them confirmed my opinion that they were fucking animals.'

The water was icy cold, and red because there was so much blood in there. Big clumps of hair were floating around. There was blood in the water, blood down the side of the bath, blood down the walls, blood on the floor and blood on the clothes dumped by the others.

They grabbed me by the hair and forced my head under the water again and again until I was sure I would drown. I had to struggle to get my head up so that I could breathe, but the more I struggled the more they beat me. They screamed at me to take the rest of my clothes off, so with them pulling at me I somehow got out and stripped. Then they told me to get back in and wash all the blood off myself. I got in again but it was impossible to get clean because there was just so much blood in the water. They told me to get out and get back up the stairs and threw me a towel. I staggered and stumbled back through the gauntlet of kicks and punches and practically crawled back up the stairs to my cell. I dried off, then sat there shivering and trembling in the cold.

After a while alone in my cell with just the towel, a screw came and threw some clothes in and told me to get dressed, saying the prison doctor would be coming soon to examine me. For a fleeting moment I thought this might be the chance to put an end to the nightmare. But the screw must have caught a glimmer of hope in my eyes, for he warned, 'And if you say a fucking word we'll be back.'

Thirty minutes later I again heard the sound of boots outside the door. It was flung open, and there stood the screw with the doctor, Kenneth Harwood.

'Right Hill, on your feet. Name and number to the doctor.'

'My name is Hill, but I don't know my number.'

Not knowing your number is sacrilege in prison. 'What do you mean you don't know your number?' barked the screw. 'Don't think you're going to be like the rest of this IRA scum in here who think they're political prisoners. You're all criminals, murdering scumbags. You're 509496 Hill and you'd better remember it.'

As the doctor began checking me I was too terrified to mention a word of what had happened, but it was so obvious I'd been beaten up I didn't think I would need to say anything. I doubt whether anything I might have said would have made any difference. He just wasn't interested. He asked what had happened to me to cause the cuts, the bruises and the blood. I said I'd fallen getting out of the police van, and I'd fallen in the prison while going up the stairs, and I'd fallen again going down the stairs.

After a cursory examination in which he jotted down notes of a few of the more trivial injuries on a pad, he said, 'Well Hill, you'll have to be more careful how you get out of police vans and walk down stairs in future.' Then he walked out and the door slammed behind him.

I was alone again.

# 14

## First days in the Green

The rest of that Monday is pretty much a blur.

We continued to get a lot of verbal abuse from the screws as they came to our doors, and then a fresh session started when the night shift came on later. But at least the worst of the beatings was over. What I remember most about that evening is the dreadful pain from my teeth. They had been knocked around badly by Moore sticking the gun in my mouth on the motorway ride, and after everything else that had happened it now felt there was not a tooth in my mouth that was not chipped, broken or loose. I couldn't eat any of the food they brought us, and even sipping a cup of water was agony.

Eventually the screws told us we could get undressed and go to bed, and although they switched on a red light in the cell which stayed on all night, I was soon asleep. But within a few hours it was back to awful reality as I was woken by banging on the doors and lights being switched on and off. I had no way of keeping track of time and it was only when we were able to get watches a week or so later we realised the screws were getting us up at about 4.30 a.m., hours before any other prisoners.

I was allowed out of the cell for a short time to 'slop out' which is the prison term for emptying your chamber pot and getting some water for a wash, and then they brought breakfast, but I couldn't eat. I sat in the cell for hours and at one stage it was opened to reveal the Governor or some senior figure standing in the doorway.

'Are you all right?' he asked with a smile before striding off as I mumbled something about being fine.

Was I all right? I'd been beaten to a pulp, as anyone could see, and there was this fool asking if I was all right.

I was hoping for a visit that day, but thought it would be unlikely they would let anybody into the prison to see us in the state we were in. I was desperate to see Pat, because after the hatred we had faced I knew things must have been rough for her and the other wives too.

Just how rough I only learned much later.

On the Thursday night, after I had gone to the station, Pat had arranged a babysitter and gone to the Crossways for a drink. As she said later: 'I was playing a game of darts when a chap came in and said that bombs had gone off in two pubs in the town, and lots of people were dead and injured.

'I came off the dartboard and sat down. An old lady asked me what was wrong because I had gone as white as a sheet. I told her that my husband had gone into town to catch a train, and that he might have gone into one of the pubs because he liked a drink. I went home and turned on the television, and it was all about the bombings. I rang one of Paddy's brothers and told him I was worried that Paddy might have been caught up in it.

'He said he would ring around the hospitals, and quite a bit later he phoned back to say Paddy had not been admitted, and he was sure Paddy would have got the train and now be on his way to Belfast.

'I felt a lot better after that, and so went to bed. At about 3 a.m. on the Friday morning I was woken by our Michelle, who was seven, who said somebody was banging on the front door. I told her to go back to sleep as I thought she was dreaming.

'Then I heard an almighty bang on the door and nearly fell out of bed. I looked out of the window and saw loads of people in the garden with torches. I got the fright of my life. I shouted down, asking who it was, and they said the police.

'I told the kids to stay in bed and went down to let the police in. They said they had a warrant to search the house, and started going through every room. They were firing questions at me about Paddy, asking about the IRA, but I didn't know what they were on about. They wanted to know what he was wearing and what had been in his case, whether or not there'd been any plastic bags. I said I didn't know as my daughter Tracey had helped him pack. They made me get her out of bed and then they questioned her, a little girl of eight.

'They saw the phone and asked if the IRA had put it in, and I told them no, it was the GPO. They thought I was trying to be funny and got quite nasty. When I asked what they were looking for they wouldn't answer, and eventually they left, leaving the house like a tip.'

The police kept a watch on the house all day, and came back in the evening to ask Pat if I'd known McDade. She said I had and it was likely I would have gone to his funeral. Then one of them asked, 'What would you say if I said your husband is in the IRA?'

'I don't know.'

'That's not the answer I want.'

'Well, I'm not as brainy as you.'

They left.

That night my mother called Pat to ask what was going on, because she had heard my house had been raided, and Pat said she would see her in the Crossways that night at about 10 p.m. Shortly after they met, two policemen and two policewomen walked into the pub and ordered Pat out. They put her in a car where one of the cops told her I'd been picked up, and that my hands were covered in gelignite. She told them that was impossible. They took her to Sutton Coldfield police station to make a statement.

At the station she told them it was ridiculous to suggest I was in the IRA. She was asked if she knew the other five lads and she told them she knew only John Walker. In fact she did know some of the others vaguely, but only by first names and so didn't recognise the full names the police gave her. When they said she could go, one of the cops told her, 'He's going down for thirty years.'

They wouldn't tell her where I was or what was happening. It was not until about 6 p.m. on the Sunday night when our names were read out on the television news that the horror of it all really sunk in.

'I just couldn't take it in when I heard Paddy's name read out,' Pat said later. 'I just sat there stunned, staring at the television set and crying.'

That night a big metal coat hook was thrown through our living-room window, just missing our son Sean who was asleep in his pram. On the Monday Pat was too fearful to go to the Steelhouse Lane court for our first appearance, and that was probably just as well. Not knowing what else to do, she tried to continue as normal, taking the kids to school. But a gang of youngsters surrounded our Tracey, and started calling her an 'IRA bastard' and hitting her.

Pat was called to the school and took our kids away. They never went back.

On the Tuesday, in desperation, Pat called in the welfare people from the local council and asked them to take the five girls into care because she was frightened for their safety. She kept Sean, and moved out of the house, going to stay with a friend.

All the other wives were interviewed by the police, but none of them was told what was happening to us. After the names came out, some of the wives had a dreadful time. The homes of John and Gerry were looted and wrecked and the families went to stay with relatives in Ireland. All the wives eventually moved from their homes.

Back at Winson Green, we were allowed out of our cells for exercise on the Tuesday morning. None of us was in a fit state to exercise, but they took us anyway. Five of us were standing in an alcove by the door leading out to the yard when John came around the corner, hobbling and limping. He looked at me and with watery blue eyes said, 'They beat me up Paddy Joe, they beat me up.'

I didn't know whether to laugh or cry. 'They beat *you* up,' I said. 'What the hell do you think they did to me?'

I think Richard was in the worst shape physically at that time, with all the cuts and gashes on his face. But mentally I would say Hughie was lowest. At forty-four he was the oldest of us, a gentle man who had seldom known even minor violence. Gerry had blood matting his long, straggly hair. Billy looked shell-shocked. All six of us were complete wrecks.

We were taken out into the yard and told to walk around in single file with a gap of a few yards between us. And there was to be no talking. As I walked I realised what a bad state my legs were in. The sores from where the cops had stubbed their cigarettes out on me days earlier were beginning to fester, yet it would be a week before I would get any treatment.

After the exercise we were taken back to our cells. I perked up a little when I was told later I would be having my first visit. I was warned to be careful about what I said and not to say anything about my treatment, and told that if I spoke out of turn the visit would be terminated. A group of officers with dogs took me to the visiting area. On the way, one of them told me that a large sum of money was on offer to any of the 'ordinary' prisoners who could get to one of us and try to kill us.

They had constructed a special visiting room for us which consisted of a few cubicles, separated by pieces of plywood from floor to ceiling. I was told to sit on the wooden bench in the cubicle. In front of me was a wooden partition a few feet high, and on top of that a clear plastic screen with holes cut into it, and wire mesh over the holes. That was so you could speak to your visitor, but with any other kind of contact prevented. I sat there for a while, expecting to see Pat or my mother, before being jolted with a cry of 'Visitors for Hill.'

Suddenly in front of me were my dad and elder brother Bobby. My brother was serving in the British Army in Germany at the time and had flown home on special leave when he heard I'd been arrested. We'd never been that close as adults. But as he walked into the cubicle I felt so proud of him, standing there looking great in his uniform.

The two of them looked at me and I could see from their faces they were stunned at the sight they saw. Gone was the cheeky grin and cocky swagger of the son and brother they knew. In their place was the shell of a man. I wanted to grab hold of my dad, to hug him and tell him to take me home. I wanted him to put his arms around me and tell me everything would be all right. I was twenty-nine, but I wanted to be his little boy again back in Belfast.

Dad went to say something, and I knew he was going to ask what had happened to me, so I motioned to him not to and he sat down. What a moment it must have been for him. I'd broken his heart so many times in the past by getting into trouble. Now here he was, a man who had given years of devoted service to the British Army facing a son accused of such an atrocious crime against the system he had proudly upheld. He had brought his family away from Belfast to leave the bitterness and hatred there behind. He and mum had worked hard to bring up a big family as best they could. And it had come to this.

He looked through the screen at me, staring into my eyes in silence for minutes. Then he said quietly, 'Son, did you have anything to do with that business that happened up in the town?'

I looked him straight in the eyes and told him: 'No dad, nothing. I know absolutely nothing about it, and nor do any of the other fellas. We're innocent.'

Dad looked at me and said, 'That's good enough for me.'

I would love to be able to say that my word was indeed good enough for him, that afterwards he never once doubted my innocence. But I know he was troubled in the years that followed. He knew I had never lied to him when I had been accused of offences in the past, and so felt he must accept what I told him had happened. But at the same time he simply could not conceive that the police were capable of doing what I told him they had done to me. The police and the courts were part of a system of which he was proud. As a kid I can recall him telling people, 'British justice is the finest in the world.' How was he to reconcile that lifelong belief with my claim of innocence?

The visit didn't last long. They asked if I needed anything and I told them I wanted a watch, a radio and some clothes. I asked about Pat and the kids and mum, and they said everybody was fine and that Pat would be up to see me the next day. Then it was over. I was taken back to my cell.

The next afternoon I had my first visit from Pat, who brought Sean, just two, along with her. It was not a happy visit. Pat nearly collapsed when she saw me, and Sean kept crying. Pat told me she had had to move in with Rose Murphy, the friend who kept the key to the money box, and that the girls had been put into care. It was terrible news for a father to hear.

Pat still remembers those minutes vividly.

'They called my name and I went into this cubicle, and when I saw Paddy I just went into a state of shock. I could not believe what I was seeing. His face was all swollen, and he had two big black eyes. He could not talk properly because his teeth were broken and his jaw was so swollen. My friend who had gone up to the prison with me asked who had done this to him, but he shook his head to make it clear we were not to discuss it.

'Sean didn't recognise his daddy at first. Then when he did he started to scream and cry, and tried to get through the screen between us to get to Paddy. There was hardly anything we could say, and after about fifteen minutes the visit was over. I went home in a daze.

'That night Sean began screaming in his sleep, shouting for his daddy. He was in such a state the next day I had to take him to the doctor for some medication. It was a long time before I ever took him to the prison to see Paddy again.'

The visit, something I had looked forward to, was heartbreaking. The pain of the beatings during the previous few days had been awful, but this was agony on a different level altogether. Not to be able to reach out and pick up your little boy and give him a hug when he cries is unbearable. And what on earth do you say to your wife in those circumstances? I felt so helpless. The pain from my shattered teeth meant I suffered searing pain whenever I tried to speak, but really there was nothing meaningful I could say. Pat was in tears and I mumbled over and over again about how everything was all right and would be sorted out. But Pat could see from the state of the husband in front of her that everything was far from all right. We were both in such a bad way, but we weren't allowed to talk about how I had come to be there. She didn't have to ask about the bombings; she knew I could never have done anything like that. I'd not done a thing, and yet this was happening to me and my family. But for once in my life I was so shattered, so completely drained, I had not even the strength to be angry. And then the visit was over.

After they left I was taken back to my cell in a terrible state. I lay on the bed and I began to cry, and the tears would not stop. I cried for Pat and everything she was going through; I cried for Sean, too young to know anything of what was happening; and I cried for myself. But most of all I cried for my little girls, five little smashers who were now all in care. The memories came flooding into my mind; their births, their first steps, their first words. And now they were in council care. I'd heard some terrible stories about kids being badly treated in care. What would happen to my girls? When there were no tears left, I began pacing the cell, around and around for hour after hour, thinking of nothing, just stumbling around in a trance. The screws brought my tea, but I told them I couldn't eat. They turned the main light out as it got late, and switched on that red bulb in the ceiling. And as I walked in the night silence, a thought eventually began to form in the emptiness of my head, at first swirling around, but then getting clearer and clearer. There was a way to end all this. I looked at the bars across the window, and then at the chair beside the table. I went to the bed and checked the sheet. Yes, I could make a noose out of that. I sat on the bed twisting the sheet into a rope. I pictured the sheet with one end around the bars and the other around my neck as I stood on the chair. My mind drifted off into what would happen when they found my body. Would the screws be blamed for not checking me, or be rewarded for letting me do it? Would the public think again? Would anybody come to my funeral?

But as I sat there the tears suddenly came again, jerking me back to reality. This was not the answer. How would it help Pat, or my girls, or Sean? Paddy Joe, I thought, you have to fight. Not quit.

I finally got off to sleep and on the Thursday morning was wakened early and told to get ready to go to court again. The security was the same as on the journey to prison the previous Monday; a convoy of armed cops in cars and on motorbikes rode shotgun as we sat locked in our little cubicles in the van. We still got plenty of verbal abuse from the cops and screws, but the physical violence was reduced to the odd push and kick. At Steelhouse Lane we went through the same procedure as before. Each cuffed to a cop, we were whisked up the stairs one at a time, remanded in custody and taken away, all within seconds. But it was long enough to let people see we had been beaten.

There were gasps of astonishment from some of those in court when men who had been in the custody of the prison service appeared with cuts, bruises, black eyes and swollen faces. Journalists who had been in court for our first appearance and failed to see any injuries could not miss them this time. The television and radio news reports and the newspapers were full of it.

Even at that early stage I could see a major problem looming for us over the prison assaults. Yes, the screws had battered us, but it was the beating from the police that made four of the lads sign confessions. The real damage caused by the prison violence was that the Winson Green injuries covered up the crucial ones – those we had received at the hands of the police. I could see we would have a hell of a job trying to prove what had really happened.

We were taken back to the prison under the same heavy security, and that afternoon my solicitor, Gold, finally managed to track down an independent doctor who was willing to see us. But now, with the menacing atmosphere of threats in the prison, I did not want to see him. I felt it would only bring me more trouble. The doctor, a general practitioner called Dharm Adlakha, came to my cell and asked to examine me.

'I'm all right, sir,' I told him, and refused to let him look at me. It was not until 3 December, twelve days after I had been taken off the ferry, that I was persuaded by Gold to have a proper examination. Much of the damage was fading by that time. Even so, Dr Adlakha found large bruises under each eye; bruises on my arms and shoulders; a bruise on the left side of my chest; and bruises on my loins. He also found two septic wounds on my right leg, one on the calf and one above the ankle.

On the first Saturday night in Winson Green, a screw came to my door and told me that one of the senior prison officers wanted to see me. It turned out to be Jim Higginbotham, a man I had met when in the Green years before. He knew my father quite well, and an auntie of mine who lived near him.

I was taken to an office where he sat me down and threw me a packet of cigarettes. He cupped his chin in his hands and said: 'What in the name of God have you got yourself into, mister? What the hell am I going to tell your father when I see him?'

I told him I was innocent, and so were the others.

He said: 'I'd like to think you're innocent. If I knew for one second you were guilty I'd string you and your mates up myself and proudly plead guilty to it. Now what happened?'

I told him everything, and also about what had happened when we arrived at the prison. He told me that if he'd been on duty it wouldn't have happened, and I believe he meant it.

I think he believed me. I can't be sure, but what I do know is that after that chat things got a little easier for me in prison.

On the outside though, things were very different. We were the six most hated men in Britain, and it would be a very long time before there was any change in that charged atmosphere of hatred towards us.

# 15

## On remand

During our first few days in Winson Green we were the only prisoners on D-wing. Then they brought over from another wing the men who had been arrested in August for the Birmingham and Manchester bombing campaign earlier that year. That was to keep all the 'Irish prisoners', as all alleged or convicted IRA men are called in jail, together in isolation on that wing.

I had been in prison before, but as an 'ordinary' criminal and not as an alleged top terrorist. This time the regime was completely different, with stringent security measures surrounding my every move. Even while I was just stuck in the cell there was a check every fifteen minutes or so. And if I left the cell, several screws went with me. They noted where I went, at what time, and how long for in a book they carried with them.

I started to settle into a routine. Being locked up for most of each twenty-four hours meant my cell was pretty much my world. It was quite large, about 12 feet by 8 feet. The window was about 8 feet off the ground, with bars on the inside and a metal grille on the outside. The glass was mostly broken, so I used to stuff newspapers between the bars to keep the cold out. Between the grille and the glass, old bits of food and other rubbish had collected, which produced a permanent stink in the cell. The bed was bolted to the floor, with a heavily stained thin mattress. There was a small, plastic-topped little table, and a tubular frame chair with a wooden seat. To the side of the cell door was a three-cornered wooden washstand in which was a plastic washing bowl and water jug. Underneath was a chamber pot.

The day began at 7 a.m. with slopping-out, followed by breakfast. The food was brought from the canteen to the wing on a heated trolley, and dished out to each of us on a tray as we came out of

106

our cells one at a time. Breakfast was normally a hard-boiled egg, a dollop of porridge, some bread and a cup of tea. Then we would slop out again and be locked up until exercise. I would spend my time reading the papers or listening to the radio.

After exercise of about an hour we would have lunch, which would consist of a wafer-thin slice of ham or corned beef, some mashed potatoes, boiled cabbage and a pudding. In the afternoon there might be a family or legal visit. Prisoners on remand, that is awaiting tria were allowed daily visits, as opposed to convicted men, who were far more restricted.

After visits would be tea (slice of ham, bread, cup of tea), before the last slop-out of the day at about 6 p.m., after which we would be locked up until the following morning, with lights out at about 9.30.

Our families had to suffer terrible degradation and humiliation every time they came to see us. When Pat arrived at the prison she would be put into a waiting room with the families of all other prisoners. Then a screw would bellow: 'Visitors for the bombers,' and Pat and the children would have to get up and make their way through the staring crowd. But she took it all and used to get up to see me several times a week throughout the six months I was on remand at Winson. Mum used to visit a couple of times a week, and made a point of writing me a letter every single week throughout my entire imprisonment. The visits were awful for churning up your emotions, but they were an escape from the prison routine and a chance to see the faces of loved ones instead of the hate-filled faces of the screws. And they were a chance too for the smallest of things to brighten up your life. Nobody will ever know the pleasure I got from the fresh pair of socks Pat would bring on each visit. My feet were in a terrible state from the cigarette burns, and the clean socks were a real luxury.

But the whole atmosphere on visits was an evil mixture of depression and oppression. In the visiting cubicles there would be two screws with me and one with the visitor. They relished their power to invade your privacy. Other screws stomped up and down behind us listening to every word, so conversation was inevitably stilted and awkward.

'How are you?'

'I'm fine. How are you?'

'O.K. Are you sure you're all right?'
'Yes I'm fine. How are the kids?'
'They're fine.'
'Good.'

One day shortly after our arrival we were out in the exercise yard when three new prisoners appeared. We hadn't a clue what they were in for, yet they would later stand alongside us in the dock. They were Mick Murray, Mick Sheehan and James Kelly.

Murray, the man to whom John Walker would pass the money raised in raffles for the families of internees, was in his late thirties, originally from Dublin, and a staunch Republican who had been involved in the IRA border campaign of 1956–62. He lived with his wife and children in Erdington, an area of Birmingham near my home. I had seen him a few times in the Crossways with John but the extent of our relationship was limited to the occasional nod of recognition when we saw each other. Apparently at the firm where he and John worked Murray made no secret of his views about Ireland.

He had been arrested in the early hours of the Monday after the bombings. The police claimed they got his name from me, but that was nonsense. I think it more likely his name was passed to the police as a suspect by workmates, who knew him as 'Big Mick', or neighbours. After the pub bombs the police were inundated with calls from people suggesting suspects, although often the callers were just harbouring grudges or settling old scores. Under questioning, Murray admitted to being a member of the IRA, but nothing else.

A remarkable thing happened concerning Murray after his arrest. Maurice Buck, the assistant chief constable who'd held a triumphant press conference on our first night at Queen's Road, personally called a leading solicitor in Birmingham to ask if he would be willing to represent Murray. Quite why an officer of that rank should be bothered with such a mundane task as organising a lawyer for an arrested man has always puzzled me. I certainly never had the benefit of such courtesy.

When the police raided Murray's house they found a receipt for payment of a £41 fine made out to a Mrs Sheehan, of Kingstanding. It turned out Murray had loaned the money to pay a fine for her husband, Mick. I had first met Sheehan when he fixed a car for a lodger at my house, and I saw him in the pub a few times after that.

He was in his thirties, from Kilkenny, and had come to Birmingham when he was fifteen. Police arrested him eight days after the bombings. I don't know whether Sheehan was in the IRA and involved with bombs or not, but he told me later he was not and I believed him. Certainly the IRA never claimed him as one of their men.

On the same day as Sheehan's arrest the police picked up Kelly, who I'd never heard of or seen in my life. He had been born an Ulster Protestant with the name Woods and joined the British Army in 1963. A year later he deserted and settled in England under his new name. His story was that he had worked alongside Sheehan, who eventually confided he was in the IRA. Kelly then decided to infiltrate and spy on the group, but never got around to telling the police what he was doing until he was arrested. A very strange man.

Shortly before Christmas 1974 I was called from my cell to see an important visitor. It was an assistant chief constable of Lincolnshire, Davis Owen, who had been appointed to conduct an inquiry into the beatings we had suffered on admission to Winson Green.

After we had made our second court appearance in Birmingham, battered and bruised for all to see, there had been comment around the country. It was not exactly a public outcry over our being attacked, more a murmuring that the great judicial pillar of 'innocent until proven guilty' appeared to have been undermined. The general belief was that we had got what we deserved from the other prisoners in the Green, a view the prison authorities were happy to encourage. The prison officers had, it seemed, been guilty of no more than looking the other way when the assaults took place. But then a prisoner who had witnessed it all was released and told his story to the papers. It didn't look good, so something had to be done.

That something took the form of an inquiry led by Mr Owen. I saw it as another opportunity to proclaim the full story of what had happened to us. Owen told me he was conducting an investigation into allegations we had been beaten while in custody and asked me to detail what had happened to me. I told him I was delighted to get the chance to explain every-thing, and began to tell him about how it had all started, in Morecambe police station. I'd only got a few words out when

Owen jumped up from his seat opposite me and banged his fist on the table.

'I'm not here to listen to any of that,' he said. 'All I want to know about is what happened when you got to Winson Green. That's all I'm empowered to do. I don't want to hear all this stuff about the police. Now let's get on with it from when you arrived here.'

I was livid, and only calmed down when he assured me there was likely to be an investigation into the police later. So I gave my statement, but at the end said I'd no intention of signing it unless he added a paragraph at the bottom. I was determined to make it clear somewhere that many of my injuries had been caused at Morecambe and Queen's Road police stations by Birmingham policemen trying to get me to sign a confession to the pub bombings. After a bit of a row, Owen agreed and I signed the statement.

Owen's report went to the Director of Public Prosecutions in May 1975, shortly before our trial began. It would be a long time before any action was taken.

Each week we were taken under the usual heavy police escort from the prison to the magistrates' court in Birmingham for the regular remand hearing on the single charge of murdering Jane Davis. The court procedure was the same every time. We would go into the dock, the prosecution would request a remand for a week, and it would be granted. The hearing rarely lasted more than a minute. We had made fifteen of these appearances when, in March 1975, we were charged with the murders of the other twenty people who had died in the pubs. Murray, Sheehan, and Kelly were taken to court with us each time, to be remanded on charges of conspiracy to cause explosions, but there was never any suggestion they were being linked with us. Obviously our main concern during the time on remand was to get our lawyers doing all they could to prove our innocence. But they were relatively inexperienced and not up to climbing the mountain we were going to have to scale. They were not helped by the public feeling of revulsion towards us.

In my own case I knew I had witnesses who could prove that at the time I was supposedly planting bombs I was doing other things. For a start there were the guys I had spoken to in the Crossways where I had had a drink on the Thursday evening; the guys I'd met in the car park coming out; and the bus driver who took me into the city centre. On top of that there were surely other customers in the pub, passengers on the bus, and people at New Street station who might remember seeing me. I told my solicitor, Gold, I wanted him to track them down and get them to give statements.

But he was defeated by the scale of public revulsion towards us. I was in prison, but I got the daily papers and listened to the radio. I knew how strong the feelings were outside. Screws would tell me how customers in their local pub were starting a petition to bring back hanging just for us. Pat or mum in their visits or letters would let drop something which indicated how ordinary people felt about us. The fact that no friends were coming to visit me spoke for itself. I was under no illusions about the public hostility towards us six.

Nobody wanted to help us, and certainly nobody wanted to be seen to be helping us. The customers at the Crossways did not want to get involved, and the bus drivers' union would not let Gold speak to the drivers. I wanted the local papers and radio to carry appeals for witnesses but they would not consider it. Our wives contacted everybody they could think of to help – priests, councillors, MPs. Every door was slammed shut. The usual response they got was, 'If your husband really is innocent, it will be proved in court, so you've nothing to fear.'

Pat got a hard time from most people she knew. But she had a few good friends, and having gone to stay with one, Rose Murphy, after the kids were put in care, she moved on to others each time after a few days as the people around discovered who she was. She would get terrible abuse in the street, being called a 'bomber's wife' and an 'IRA whore'. Some of the other lads' wives went back to Ireland for a while, taking the kids with them. But Pat was a Birmingham girl, with her family in the city, and she could not contemplate leaving.

After a few weeks of moving from friend to friend she decided to go back to our home. She got the girls out of care and tried to make life normal for them, but it was impossible. One day she sent Tracey, who was just nine, to the corner shop for a packet of tea. My little girl came back in tears. The guy in the shop had asked one of the assistants to pass a packet of tea for her and shouted, so everybody could hear, 'And make sure it doesn't blow up.'

Pat had to deal with obscene, threatening phone calls to our home, and eventually got the council to rehouse herself and the kids. But very quickly the new neighbours discovered who they were, and the same harassment began all over again. This happened several times, and at one house the neighbours actually raised a petition, demanding the council move my family out. Pat was sure she was being watched by the police, and stopped talking to any of our friends who were Irish in case they were pulled in for questioning.

With all the worry, her weight dropped from more than eight stone to less than six in a matter of weeks. There she was, having to make visits to the prison each week, trying to raise a young family as best she could, and being subject to all the abuse. It was no surprise she started drinking quite heavily, and then had to be put on tablets by the doctor for her nerves. Years later she was still taking nerve pills as a result of what she went through then.

All this put a terrible strain on our relationship. If you are an ordinary couple living together at home, you can talk over your problems with each other. You can have rows and clear the air, sort things out. But what can you discuss of real importance when you are seeing each other for just a few minutes each week under the conditions I've described? Pat needed to talk to me about the problems she and the kids were facing: the trouble with neighbours, the problems at school, the fact one or other of the kids was ill. But she did not want to burden me with it all. And to be honest, I did not want to hear about it while I was stuck inside and unable to change anything. She never doubted my innocence, but the fact remained that she was having a terrible time because I was in jail. The word 'blame' was rarely spoken, but after a while it seemed to be always hanging in the air. Sometimes the tension would get to us both and would explode into a row. Occasionally she would storm out of a visit, at other times I would jump up and demand to be taken back to my cell. The pressure was beginning to prove just too much.

The only public proclamation of our innocence throughout all of this came from a source that was of little use – the IRA. In an interview published in an Irish paper on 1 December 1974 the IRA said an investigation had not yet determined whether one of its units had carried out the bombings. But it had established that the six men being held were not members of any known Republican organisation. It was absolutely true, but the British public was hardly in the mood to accept the word of the IRA.

Then as the months went by the lawyers finally came up with a bit of good news. They had found a scientist, Dr Hugh Black, who believed the conclusion Skuse had drawn from his tests on our hands was completely wrong. Not only did Dr Black think so, but he was prepared to come to court on our behalf and say so. It was great news and lifted our spirits tremendously. But it was soon cancelled out by a major setback. We were informed that when we went to trial we would not be on our own in the dock. Joining us would be three others: Murray, Sheehan and Kelly. Yet they were not being charged with the pub bombings. The main accusation against them was conspiracy to cause explosions.

We were livid, particularly as Murray was by now a convicted IRA man. He had just been given a twelve-year jail term for conspiracy to cause explosions in the trial of the eight men arrested in August 1974 who clearly were part of the Birmingham IRA. How would it look having him standing alongside us in the dock? And he was sure to repeat the then IRA tactic of refusing to recognise the court.

We demanded to be tried on our own and went to court with an application for what is known as 'severance' to get the other three dealt with separately. Our request was thrown out.

We were committed for trial, to be held in Lancaster at the request of defence lawyers on the grounds that we would not get a fair hearing in Birmingham. Although it was our lawyers who asked for this, I was unhappy about it because I believed that the local knowledge of a Birmingham jury would help us when it came to talk about pubs and bus routes and so on. It was yet another in the string of setbacks.

Another disappointment – possibly the worst of all – was not long in coming. This was the introduction to my barrister, the man to whom I was entrusting my chance of freedom, Mr John Field Evans QC. I had been badgering Gold for months about who was going to represent us. Gold did not say as much, but I got the impression he was finding it difficult to get anybody willing to take us on. Eventually he said he had got Field Evans, whom he regarded as a 'great catch' because he had experience of bombing cases. At that time in Britain bomb trials were quite a rarity. Our barrister's expertise, said Gold, particularly with regard to forensic matters, would prove a real advantage. I was delighted, as were Hughie and Billy whom Gold also represented. I told Gold to try to arrange a meeting as quickly as possible as our trial was not far off.

The introduction was fixed for the last week of May, little more

113

than a week before the trial was due to begin. I was in my cell on the third floor of D-wing, reading a book one afternoon, when I heard boots approaching. A screw opened the door and said I was wanted in cell number 6, which was one of the empty ones along the landing from mine. I was escorted down to the door, where Gold was waiting. He shook hands and took me inside where two men were sitting at a table reading some notes. They were Field Evans and his assistant. The barrister was a tall, distinguished-looking man, smartly dressed and exuding authority. He shook my hand, introducing himself and his colleague, and indicated I should sit down opposite him at the table.

'Mr Hill, you do realise you're going to get a life sentence with a thirty-year recommendation for this?' he said.

I leaned back in the chair, stunned and speechless.

There were a few seconds of silence as his words sank in, and then the anger erupted.

'What the fuck do you mean?' I screamed. 'I'm innocent. We're all innocent. Don't you understand that? We didn't do it, and it's your job to make sure the jury realises that.' I pushed the table towards him, got up and stormed out of the door. Out on the landing Gold, red with embarrassment, caught up with me and pleaded for me to go back.

'He thinks I'm guilty,' I raged. 'He thinks we're just going up to court to be sentenced. Where the hell did you get him from?'

Gold spoke quickly, trying to calm me down, saying all Field Evans was doing was making me aware of the worst scenario. He wanted me to appreciate just how serious the charges were. As if I didn't realise. How more serious can it get than twenty-one murder charges?

Gold kept rattling on, saying that we were so close to the trial it would be madness to change barristers now. Field Evans was one of the best around, and it would be a big mistake to lose him. Eventually I relented and agreed to return.

I went back in and sat down. There were no apologies; no protest that I had gained the wrong impression; no declaration of faith in my innocence. Field Evans just picked up his pen and in a businesslike manner asked a few questions and made a few notes. He spoke briefly about the procedure to expect at the trial, and then said he was finished. I got up and went back to my cell.

As the trial approached I tried to be more optimistic when Pat came to visit. This would be the end of it all, I told her. We would finally be freed. But I said that I did not want her to attend the case. She had to look after the children, and besides, we had no money to pay for her to stay anywhere in Lancaster. I also knew I would have enough to concentrate on during the trial without having to worry about Pat and the kids as well.

On 31 May we were told we were to be moved that day to Lancaster. The attitude of many of the screws in Winson Green towards us had changed dramatically by then. We still had a few problems with some of them, but most knew at that stage we were innocent. They had lived with us every day for six months. They had watched the way we behaved and had listened to us continually proclaim our innocence. They had seen the startling contrast between our behaviour and that of the other Irish prisoners in the jail who really were in the IRA. They knew, even if they could not or would not say anything publicly. Several of them wished us well that day.

As I was led to the van to head up the M6 motorway one of the screws who had assaulted us when we first entered the prison shook my hand.

'Good luck. I hope you walk,' he said.

# 16

## On trial

Our arrival at Lancaster Prison was so different to that at Winson Green six months earlier.

If only the screws at the Green had dealt with us in the same manner as those at Lancaster, I've no doubt we would have been able to prove our innocence. We got out of the van, to be greeted by a prison officer who told us, 'Don't worry, this isn't Winson Green, nobody will lay a finger on you here.'

The governor told us that we would be examined from head to toe by a doctor and that if we had any complaints we should speak out without fear. It was a comforting assurance that I believe was genuine. Then we were taken off to the cells to await our trial. It was to have started at the beginning of June, but was delayed a week for some administrative reason.

And so it was on the beautiful sunny morning of Monday 9 June 1975 that we found ourselves preparing to go into court, each to face twenty-one charges of murder in the biggest trial of its kind in British history. I was a bundle of nerves as I woke up from an uncomfortable night's sleep. I had a cup of tea, but did not bother with breakfast. A screw came and told me it was time to go, and I was escorted through the tunnel from the prison to the court, which together make up the 900-year-old Lancaster Castle complex. The security precautions were enormous. Parking was banned within a quarter-mile radius of the castle. Armed policemen were everywhere. The identity of the judge was not revealed until that morning. A specially constructed dock had to be built to accommodate us. The administrative and security expenses of the trial were expected to be so high, at more than £100,000, that Lancashire County Council asked the Home

Office to ease the burden by taking on more than the usual half-cost. The atmosphere was electric and I felt just the same as the other lads, nervous and apprehensive, as we waited silently with our guards on a staircase below the court. Because we knew we were innocent the other five were convinced that we would walk free, that this would be our moment and the nightmare would be brought to an end. I wasn't so sure. I had felt since that moment in the cells in Queen's Road police station when Billy told me he had signed a confession that we were going to end up in jail. But whatever our private thoughts, none of us imagined the scale of the bitterness and hatred that was in store at the top of those stairs.

The silence was broken by a shout for us to be brought up, and we climbed the steep staircase to enter the dock. The courtroom was every Hollywood director's idea of what an English court should look like. It was a huge, cavernous place, with a high ceiling and wood panelling around the walls. The judge, fifty-eight-year-old, Mr Justice Bridge, sat in all his majesty high up above the rest of the court, with the lawyers in their gowns and wigs down below him at their rows of desks. We six, plus Murray, Sheehan and Kelly, sat in a long dock, opposite the jury. The press desk and the public gallery were packed.

The prosecution was led by Harry Skinner QC, who was forty-eight and the man who two years earlier had successfully prosecuted Father Fell and five others from Coventry for running an IRA cell there. Field Evans represented Billy, Hughie and me, while John, Gerry and Richard were represented by Michael Underhill QC.

Mr Skinner's case boiled down to a few simple points. We were all members of an IRA team in Birmingham and had set out to avenge the death of our friend and fellow Republican James McDade by blowing up two pubs in Birmingham.

'Although his death was by his own hand, the accused six were both grieved and outraged and from then till November 21 they made their plans to avenge and commemorate his death,' he said. Five of us caught a train to Heysham to escape to Belfast and to honour McDade at his funeral, while the sixth saw us off and then went drinking. An alert at the port led to us being held and taken for forensic tests. The tests showed that I and Billy Power had handled nitroglycerine and that John Walker may have done.

Mr Skinner singled me out on the grounds I had been particularly devious in claiming to Sister Bridget, the nun from whom I'd borrowed the £15, that I had wanted money to get back to see a dying aunt. 'That was a plain lie as Hill was going to bury McDade,' he said.

Murray, Sheehan and Kelly were each charged with possessing explosives and conspiracy to cause explosions. Mr Skinner said there was no evidence to link them to any particular bombing, but they were part of the same IRA unit as ourselves.

'Everyone in the dock was a member of the team, and the first six undoubtedly planted the bombs,' he said. 'We are not charging these people with being Irish nationalists or being members of the IRA. We are charging them with murder and conspiracy to cause explosions.'

Our defence was that we had planned to go to McDade's funeral as men who knew him and his family, not to honour a terrorist. We were not members of the IRA and had nothing to do with it. We had not planted those bombs and knew nothing about them. The forensic evidence was flawed in that the Griess test did not prove we had handled nitroglycerine. Many innocuous substances could produce the same result.

After the opening speeches came a series of witness statements from people whose evidence was not in question. The first important witness in person was Ian Cropper, the telephonist at the *Birmingham Post* and *Mail* papers who had taken the phone warning about the bombs. He said it had been from a public call box (he could tell by the sound of the pips before money was put in) at 8.11 p.m. The voice was that of an Irishman who gave a codeword, although Mr Cropper did not recognise it as such, and then the vague warning before ringing off. Mr Cropper immediately called the police and then told his news desk.

He was followed by Clifford Godwin, the booking office clerk at New Street station who had sold us the tickets to Belfast; by a woman who had been in a cinema and seen a man acting suspiciously before the bombs went off; and by a man who had seen two young men acting suspiciously near the Mulberry Bush before the explosion. Rab Nawaz, the guard on the train we caught, told how he had checked our tickets and thought the five of us 'were in a jolly mood'. Linda Jones, a passenger, remembered a small man (me) having difficulty putting his case in the overhead luggage rack, and then the five of us playing cards.

Noel Walsh, the landlord of the Crossways pub, was called. He said he knew myself and a few of the others from the pub, and that he regarded John as the leader of our group. Mr Skinner had referred in his opening address to my visit to the Crossways on the Thursday night when I had been carrying a suitcase. 'You can be pretty certain there was one bomb in that suitcase,' he told the jury. 'When arrested at Heysham, Hill had just a small amount of clothing in the case. Not enough to justify carrying a case of that type.' Mr Skinner no doubt had the luxury of owning a variety of suitcases, using large or small ones as appropriate. In my house there was no question of choice – we had only the one case.

Walsh was asked about my visit.

Q: Was anything said about his suitcase?
A: He said 'If I leave this here you would be sorry,' and he smiled like, laughed about it.
Q: Has he made that joke before?
A: Yes, quite a few times.

Walsh must have heard such jokes in his pub in the past, and quite possibly be me. It was the sort of joke made all over the country at the time by people in pubs and clubs and shops. I didn't make any such joke that night though, because I had only one brief chat with him, when I asked him to lend me some money, before he disappeared from the bar. The implication of his comment to the jury was clear. I had not been joking – I really had got a bomb in the case. Walsh may just have been confused, although I don't know why he described John as our 'leader', which was just not true. But many years later he was to confess that while waiting to give evidence he had been approached by some policemen outside the courtroom. He told them that in giving evidence he was going to say a word on our behalf, particularly for John whom he liked. The policemen told him Walker was without doubt a high-ranking IRA officer.

'That threw me,' said Walsh in 1990. 'I felt disillusioned. You think you know a person and want to try and help, and then you are told something like that. I was in a daze. I just wanted to get out of that court.'

The court was read a statement from Sister Bridget, who confirmed she had known our family for a couple of years, had helped us out in the past, and had been told by me that I needed the money to go and see my aunt, who was dying.

One of the strangest witnesses of the case was a chap called Tom Watt, whose damning testimony was aimed mainly at John Walker, but by implication was bad for all of us. Watt lived in Alum Rock, Birmingham, and worked at the same factory as John, Richard, and Murray. He said that he knew they were IRA sympathisers and that John had been on an IRA training session in Ireland. He claimed John had often told him not to go out on particular nights, and on each occasion bombs had gone off around the city. On the Thursday of the pub bombings, he said, John had told him: 'Don't be going out for a drink tonight.'

He said John had been very bitter at McDade's death, and shortly after it had asked Watt if he knew where he could get some cheap alarm clocks. Watt said he had told John, 'I thought you usually used pocket watches,' and John had replied, 'These are going to be big bastards.' He claimed John had drawn a sketch for him of how to make a bomb. All in all it was pretty devastating testimony, which must have had enormous influence on the jury.

Watt said that he had gone to the police in June 1974, five months before the pub bombings, to make them aware of his suspicions about John and the others, and that the police had been in regular contact with him for information about them. Yet the police themselves admitted that their Special Branch files never made any mention of John or Richard. And then Watt stunned everybody with another strange revelation.

He admitted under cross-examination that on the night of the pub bombings a man called Kenneth Littlejohn had stayed at his house. Littlejohn was a character who in March 1974 had escaped with his brother Keith from Mountjoy Prison in Dublin. Littlejohn had been sentenced to twenty years' imprisonment and his brother to fifteen for robbing the Allied Irish Bank in Dublin of £67,000 in 1972. At that time they were already wanted by the West Midlands Police for a £38,000 robbery in Birmingham in 1970.

They made headlines at their trial in Ireland when they claimed they had been working for British intelligence. Littlejohn said he had infiltrated the IRA on behalf of the MI6 intelligence service, which had ordered him to carry out the Dublin robbery. The idea was to discredit the IRA and encourage the Irish government to introduce stronger anti-IRA legislation. The British government admitted the brothers had been seen by the then Army Minister, Mr Geoffrey Johnson-Smith, in 1971 when they had offered to supply information about the IRA. That, of course, was while they were wanted by the police for the Birmingham robbery. The British government refused to give further details about their dealings with the pair, except for denying they were on the payroll of the intelligence services. Whatever the facts of the case, there is no doubt that while a 'wanted man', Littlejohn had been able to make regular trips between Britain and Ireland. At his Dublin trial Littlejohn claimed he had been promised by MI6 that if he escaped to England after the bank robbery he would not be extradited. He also claimed he had been cleared by MI6 to murder 'certain targets'.

At our trial, Tom Watt said that he had harboured Littlejohn, while knowing the police were after him, until early December when Littlejohn was arrested at his home. 'When the police came to arrest him they arrested my son and my wife,' he told the court. 'They took them off to the police station for a couple of hours, until I came home from work and it was all sorted out.'

Unfortunately, Watt didn't volunteer to the court, and was never questioned on, just what he meant by 'it was all sorted out'. The worst he had to put up with was a brief exchange with John's barrister, Mr Underhill, which went as follows:

Q: You knew the authorities were looking for him when he was staying in your house?

A: Yes.

Q: And you thought, and you think now, you may get into trouble over it?

A: No.

Q: And you hope to ingratiate yourself with the authorities by telling these lies today?

A: I have not told any lies about Mr Walker, and I have no fears about getting into trouble over it.

After his arrest at Watt's house Littlejohn was extradited and returned to prison in Dublin, where he was reunited with his brother

Keith, who had been caught shortly after the break-out. Both were unexpectedly released in September 1981, Kenneth Littlejohn having served only eight years of his twenty-year sentence. The Irish government said they had been given their freedom on 'humanitarian grounds' and on condition they stayed away from Ireland.

It was because of the importance of the so-called confessions in our case that within a short time of the trial opening the judge dismissed the jury for eight days to hold a 'trial within a trial' to determine whether or not they could be admitted as evidence.

The mini-trial was a straightforward affair. Either we were lying or the police were. There was no middle ground. Our problem was that we had no evidence to show the liars were the police. Nearly all the medical evidence was unsatisfactory because it was so difficult to differentiate between the injuries we had received from the police and those inflicted at Winson Green. In our fleeting, first court appearance in Birmingham there were few facial injuries to be observed because the police had ensured most of the violence took place below the neck. All that was obvious was a black eye on John Walker. That came from the beating he took while being interrogated at Morecambe. But it was explained away as having been caused accidentally when he bumped his head while being put into a police car.

Dr Kenneth Harwood, the prison doctor who saw us shortly after admission to the Green, seemed so desperate to clear the prison officers of any blame whatsoever that his evidence was patently ridiculous. He said he was sure all the injuries he had seen had occurred in police custody or, repeating the lame excuses we had given when we first saw him, genuinely resulted from us falling up or down stairs. He steadfastly refused to accept that any violence could have occurred after we were admitted to prison. But following our second court appearance in Birmingham, the whole country knew that we had been beaten up in prison, and indeed a police inquiry had been completed into what had happened. What he said was so ludicrous it destroyed his credibility altogether in the eyes of the jury. And it sank our hope of proving we had been assaulted by the police. For we had banked on Harwood differentiating between the injuries we received before and after entering the Green. I'm sure we would have had a better chance of persuading the jury about police violence if our lawyers had called as witnesses some of the prison

officers who had seen us on admission. Several had made statements
to the police inquiry. Those statements made it clear we already had
various injuries, which could only have been caused while in police
custody. I've always felt this was a major failure on the part of our
legal team.

The 'trial within a trial' was effectively a parade of the policemen
who had dealt with us, who gave their version of events, and then
of us six, who gave ours. As nearly eight months had passed, the
officers were allowed to refresh their memories with the notes they
had taken and written up during and after the 'interviews'. Of
course, where two or more officers had been involved, their notes
were always identical. Detective Sergeant Raymond Bennett said he
had interviewed me, with Detective Constable John Brand taking
notes as the interviews went along. At some stages, he claimed,
Detective Inspector Moore was also involved. What follows is
Bennett's version of what happened.

On first meeting me at Morecambe police station he had introduced
himself and his colleague Brand and told me: 'We are making
inquiries into incidents which occurred at Birmingham last evening
and I intend asking you certain questions. You are not obliged to say
anything unless you wish to do so, but what you say will be put into
writing and may be given in evidence.'

I told him I was going to Belfast to visit my sick aunt and had
loaned the money from the nuns. I had travelled alone and did not
know any of the other men now being held at the police station. I was
asked whether I had ever handled explosives, or fertiliser, or guns,
and had said no to each question. I denied that I was a member of
the IRA. When asked what I had thought about McDade's death, I
replied: 'I was very upset. I've known him all my life, we went to
school together.'

Bennett suggested that because of that it was likely I was going
to McDade's funeral, but I had been adamant I was only going to
see my aunt. When asked about IRA meetings, I allegedly said that I
knew they met at a pub called the White Horse and that I sometimes
made collections for them.

There was then a break for ninety minutes before Bennett returned
with Detective Inspector Moore to tell me that Dr Skuse's tests had
shown I had handled explosives. I had replied: 'I don't believe what
you say, you're trying to trap me.' I again denied knowing any of the

other lads until Moore said they knew I had been at Walker's house and that I had travelled with them. I then admitted knowing them, but said I knew nothing about bombs. Later I was told I was being arrested for the pub bombings and would be taken to Birmingham. Bennett told the court, 'He put his head in his hands and made what appeared to be a crying noise, a whimpering and general moaning.'

We travelled to Queen's Road police station by car in an uneventful journey. The following morning, Saturday, when interviewed again by Bennett I said I had thought things over during the night and wanted to help. I knew the others were all in the IRA, but I was not, although I had helped with collections. Then I suddenly blurted out: 'Oh my God, oh my God. We've had it, we've had it. If I tell you the truth, what will you do for me?'

Bennett told me he could make no promises, but said it was best I tell the whole truth. I told him the explosives had been at Walker's house, and the plan was to put the bombs in the pubs shortly before we caught the train. Walker and Hunter were in charge of the planting. Bennett said he believed I had planted a bomb, to which I replied: 'Jesus, Mary, I don't know what to say. I've told you everything I can, just leave me alone. I've got enough on my mind.'

They left me and returned later to read a statement by McIlkenny which said I had planted a bomb in the Tavern. I told them: 'He's told you the truth there, I never thought he'd make a statement. He's a hard bastard like Hunter. You don't cross them. We left them in the downstairs bar. I was that scared all I wanted to do was get out and get away on the train.'

I was asked why, if I was not in the IRA, I had carried out the bombing. I replied: 'It's obvious, isn't it. I am in the IRA. We all are, and this was because of Jamie and everything he died for, the cause and everything. But you wouldn't understand. But I never thought it would come to this. There was supposed to be a warning.'

When asked to make a written statement I replied: 'I've told you what I know. Surely you have enough? Dick has said it all and I just want to forget it. For God's sake just leave me alone, leave me alone. I don't want to say any more. Just leave me. I've got nothing more to say.'

According to Bennett, that was the end of his interview and I was returned to my cell.

Then Detective Sergeant Roy Bunn gave his version of his dealings with me on the Sunday morning. He told the court that our conversation began with me telling him: 'There is no point in telling any more lies. I couldn't sleep last night through thinking about it.'

Then I was supposed to have given a lot of names of people I said were in the IRA, including several of those who had already been dealt with for IRA bombings, and a 'Big Mick' and another man called Mick. I said I had never been back to Ireland since 1960 and was reminded of the Bodenstown trip in June 1974. I replied: 'Yes sir, you are right. I'd forgotten about that. I went to the celebrations to represent the Birmingham branch of the IRA.' The court was told that the descriptions I gave of the men called Mick matched those of Murray and Sheehan. When asked about the Hagley Road bomb that didn't go off I was said to have replied: 'Honest to God, I don't know nothing about that one. All I did was the one in the town.'

Some of the stuff at the beginning of Bennett's evidence, about why I was going to Belfast, and about not understanding how I could have traces of explosives on my hands, was true. But not all the important stuff, the admissions of IRA links and the planting of the bombs. My barrister, Field Evans, cross-examined each of them.

Q: Mr Bennett, quite early that Friday morning you and your colleague Mr Brand pushed Hill into the room where Skuse had been doing the tests and began to ill-treat him straight away.

A: No sir, it is not true.

Q: And your ill-treatment of him continued throughout Friday and until you started that journey back to Birmingham in the car.

A: There was no ill-treatment of Hill at any time.

Q: You sat beside him in the car, did you not?

A: I did sir.

Q: Did you not attack him yourself in the car?

A: Certainly not sir.

Q: Both with some sort of truncheon and a cigarette or cigar end?

A: No sir.

Q: Nothing of that sort at all?

A: Definitely not.

Inspector Moore was quizzed about my nightmare journey down the motorway.

> Q: You hit him with the gun, did you not?
> A: No sir.
> Q: You twice put the muzzle of the gun in his mouth and pulled the trigger, did you not?
> A: Completely untrue sir.
> Q: You put it in his eye and did the same.
> A: No sir.

Detective Sergeant Bunn was asked about our Sunday morning meeting.

> Q: I suggest that up to the time of your interview, Hill had made no confession of any description.
> A: That is not true.
> Q: You were going to have a try to see what you could do in that respect.
> A: No.
> Q: And you told him first of all that you were not going to hit him. Isn't that right?
> A: No.
> Q: And then you leaned over the table and grabbed him by the coat.
> A: No.
> Q: And threatened him if he didn't make a statement?
> A: I didn't threaten Hill at any time.
> Q: In effect saying that if he kept on saying that he didn't know anything about it – which is what he was saying – you would kick the fuck out of him?
> A: No, my Lord.

The officers of the West Midlands Serious Crime Squad went on one after another testifying how everything had been done by the book, that nobody had raised a hand in anger to any of us, and that there had been no verbal misbehaviour. There was, they said, only one occasion of any violence, and that was when Gerry Hunter made an unprovoked assault on Superintendent Reade and had to be restrained. Walker's black eye was of course due to bumping his head getting into the car at Morecambe.

I thought their claims of lilywhite behaviour might actually work against them. After all, here was a group of policemen who had come from the scene of the worst atrocity Britain had known, dealing with a suspected IRA gang who a scientist said had been handling explosives. Surely a bit of rough behaviour would have been understandable?

The defence case began with Billy and Hughie first up for us, but they got fairly short shrift from Skinner. I was next and believe I handled myself well. A combination of knowing you are innocent and having previous experience in the witness box helps a great deal. My problem was, as somebody put it later, I looked as though I might have done it. A tough, stocky Irishman with a scar down one cheek can appear intimidating.

Field Evans took me through my evidence, and I told the whole story from start to finish. Then I was cross-examined by Skinner, who tried to catch me out, or to find chinks in my story at every opportunity.

Q: You were at Walker's house at 4 p.m.?
A: That is correct.
Q: That is where you got the nitroglycerine on your hands?
A: No sir.
Q: Because he had some bombs there?
A: No, he had not.
Q: That is when the plans were made, at 4 p.m. that afternoon?
A: There were no plans made.

Skinner asked about my relationship with McDade. I said that while I hadn't known him well, he had seemed all right as a person. I had been shocked when I heard he had been planting a bomb.

Q: All of you going to Belfast were going to his funeral to pay your last respects?
A: No sir. I was going to see my aunt, and as I have admitted, I would have gone to his funeral while I was in Ireland.
Q: That is absolute nonsense.
A: It is not nonsense, it is absolutely true.

Q: He was a fellow soldier of yours?

A: No sir, I am a soldier of nothing.

Q: You did not really think McDade had done something wrong?

A: He had done something wrong.

Q: You thought he was a brave man who was worthy of respect?

A: No sir.

Q: You planted those bombs before you went in honour of his memory, because of Jamie, the cause and all he died for?

A: Completely untrue.

I was cross-examined for little more than an hour. Then came Gerry, who was given a hard time for being unable to explain why it was that if he had been beaten so badly, a police picture of his face showed few injuries. Richard was impressive, but after him came John who had only vague recollections of his 'interviews'. Great play was made of the fact he did not seem to be able to remember very much. Nobody pointed out that his poor memory was just possibly a result of having been so badly treated.

At the end of the eight days of the 'trial within a trial' the judge had no difficulty in deciding we were the liars. I'm only surprised it took him so long, as he had made it clear where his sympathies lay from the start.

In allowing the confessions to be admitted as evidence he said: 'I have come to the conclusion that there is no reason to entertain any doubt on the soundness of my impression produced by the police officers who gave evidence. I am satisfied those witnesses were giving honest and accurate evidence.'

He told Reade that the allegations against his men were so grotesque that if ever any of them were shown to be true, Reade would have to suffer the consequences. Reade assured him his men had operated with utmost propriety and to the highest standard.

The jury was brought back and the trial proper continued.

# 17

## Forensics and confessions

Right up to the moment we entered the courtroom I thought the prosecution might have been bluffing about the forensic evidence. I knew that I had never touched explosives, so how could there possibly have been any trace on my hands? The alleged presence of explosives was the second crucial plank of the prosecution case against us, and so took up a good deal of time. But before we got to that there was some very interesting evidence on another matter.

The prosecution called two eminent scientists who had sifted through the wreckage of the two pubs. Donald Lidstone, who had examined the Tavern in the Town, said that among the rubble he and his team had found parts of two alarm clocks, a battery and a Phillips-head screw. He felt the presence of two clocks indicated either two bombs with a clock each, or a single bomb with, for whatever reason, two clocks. Similar material had been recovered at the scene of other explosions in the weeks before the pub bombs, including the Coventry bomb which killed McDade. His conclusion was that all had been made by the same hand.

But Mr Lidstone also found what remained of two sets of D-shackles, the sort used in the handles of carrying cases or briefcases. He told the court: 'Such a case could have been used to contain a high-explosive bomb. The presence of two sets of shackles suggests the involvement of two separate, but similar, cases.'

Douglas Higgs had examined the debris of the Mulberry Bush and had also found parts of clocks, batteries, and screws. He too had found part of a D-shackle, and part of a small lock of the type used on briefcases. He was adamant the explosives had been in such a case, and was quizzed on the matter by Field Evans.

Q: You have no doubt, have you, that the device or devices were contained in some sort of suitcase, briefcase or holdall?
A: That is my opinion.
Q: A confidently held opinion?
A: Yes.

Now that was odd. For in each of the four 'confessions' made in the hours after the bombings the lads had referred only to the bombs being in plastic bags. There was no mention of cases or holdalls. It was much, much later that the scientists who examined the wreckage were able to tell the police just what the bombs had really been in.

After those two scientists came the man who held the key to the whole affair – Dr Frank Skuse. On the fateful night he had been called to Morecambe police station from his home in Wigan. He normally worked at the government's forensic science laboratory in Chorley, which covered north-west England.

The simple little test that Dr Skuse conducted on us at Morecambe, the Griess test, was explained to the jury in layman's terms. He described how he had carried it out on each of us, and how he had gained a 'strong' positive from my right hand and a positive from my left hand. He had got a positive from Billy's right hand, but tests on the other lads had proved negative. He then described his results from the test for ammonium or nitrate ions, which could also indicate contact with explosives. My left hand had proved positive for the ions test, as had Billy's right hand, and both of John's.

Skuse went on to explain how he had taken away the samples from us three for more sophisticated laboratory testing to detect the presence of nitroglycerine, involving two different processes; gas chromotography/mass spectrometry (GCMS) and thin-layer chromotography (TLC). These should be able to detect the tiniest trace of nitroglycerine, being far more sensitive than the rather basic Griess test. The sample from Billy's right hand was negative to both GCMS and TLC. The samples from John's hands were negative to both. The 'strong positive' sample from my right hand was negative to GCMS and TLC. The sample from my left hand was negative to TLC. But, said Skuse, it showed positive under the GCMS test, although he could not present the court with any documentation to prove what he was saying had occurred.

Looking perfectly confident in the witness box, he declared that the Griess tests had made him 'quite happy' that Billy and I had been handling explosives. When asked what he meant by that, he replied firmly, 'Ninety-nine per cent certain.'

My barrister said he was puzzled that while the TLC and GCMS tests were far more sensitive and sophisticated than the Griess test, all the samples had proved negative to these except the one GCMS test on the sample from my left hand. How could this be? he asked.

Dr Skuse was not at all ruffled. 'Evaporation,' he replied.

Field Evans got Skuse to confirm there was no documentary proof of the alleged positive GCMS test on my left hand, and then asked:

Q: I take it there is a possibility of human error?
A: I would not agree with you there.
Q: Not even the possibility?
A: No.

Dr Skuse accepted that ammonium and nitrate ions could come from a variety of innocent sources. But when asked if there were any other substances which might give a positive result to the Griess test, he was confident. There was only one other substance that could possibly give a positive result, and it too was a constituent of explosives.

It was his confidence that had led Sergeant Bennett to tell me that I was covered in gelignite from head to toe, and that it was 'the scientist' who said so.

Our response to Skuse was Dr Hugh Black, who had for many years been a chief inspector of explosives for the Home Office. He told the court that Skuse had simply got it wrong in relying on the Griess test results so strongly. He said that his view, and the view of most other scientists, was that Griess was only an indicator. It was the result of the laboratory tests which were crucial. He said that a sample might turn pink in the Griess test because of the presence of nitrocellulose rather than nitroglycerine. Nitrocellulose was present in a range of everyday products, such as lacquers, varnishes and paints.

He argued that my one positive result under the laboratory test should be ignored because Skuse had taken only one reading from the equipment when he should have taken three. And he said that if we had got nitroglycerine on our hands, he would have expected traces to have shown up on the clothes we were wearing at the time. All the tests on the clothes had proved negative.

I thought things were looking good for us until the judge, who had clearly taken a dislike to Dr Black, asked whether he had ever actually conducted tests to see if what he was saying could be proved. To be fair to the judge, which I believe he wasn't to us, it was a reasonable question. And with the answer, our defence on the forensics fell apart. No, Dr Black had never tested his theory that nitrocellulose could give positive results to a Griess test. Furthermore, he had never swabbed anyone's hands, had never been in a forensic science lab, and had never carried out a GCMS test.

I never held anything against Dr Black. It was our defence team I was fuming with for not having covered such points. Dr Black said years later that he had met my lawyers and suggested that tests should be conducted to support his theory, but that they had not acted on his advice. He felt they either did not appreciate the importance of his theory, or feared the results might prove him wrong.

Field Evans said later he could not recall the suggestion ever being put forward at the meeting, which was held at his chambers in Birmingham on 6 June – just three days before our trial began. He did accept that the 'possibility and wisdom of doing so might have been discussed'. It was years before Dr Black was vindicated. When his views were finally put to the test and showed he was right it was a turning point in our fight for freedom. Sadly, he died before seeing us released and having his reputation restored.

When we got on to the confessions in front of the jury it was just like a rerun of the mini-trial, with the police sticking rigidly to their script. In many ways the mini-trial had been a bonus for them, something of a dress rehearsal. As I sat in the dock and listened to them I found it hard to believe that the twelve men and women in the jury box could accept what the police were saying at face value. Here we were being portrayed on the one hand as a bunch of ruthless, highly skilled terrorists, giving crafty answers to fox the police as a result of our counter-interrogation training. On the other hand, we are all supposed to have broken down within a short time of gentle questioning and confessed to one of the worst crimes in recent British history. Billy, author of the first 'confession', was said to have wept and freely offered the full story after just forty minutes, without the police laying a finger on him.

Outside of the forensics and the confessions, the prosecution had nothing in the way of solid evidence. There were no witnesses who saw us making our way to the city centre with white plastic bags, or who saw any of us in the pubs. There was no evidence of fingerprints or any other incriminating evidence against us found in the pubs. There was no evidence of explosives at our homes or on our clothes.

There was, of course, circumstantial evidence. That alone in the eyes of many people was enough to condemn. Little credibility was given to our argument that attending the funeral of somebody we knew was the done thing, that it was tradition. Then there was the trip to Bodenstown. What I had seen as a cheap drinking trip to Dublin came across as though it were an IRA training session. There were the clocks found at John's house, just about the only thing the police could come up with from the rigorous searches of our homes. We all knew John was forever getting clocks on the cheap for use as raffle prizes. Yet the unspoken word association in the courtroom was. 'clock equals bombs'. It cut no ice that John's clocks were the decorative sort you would put on a mantelpiece rather than the alarm clocks that the scientist Lidstone had referred to.

Our side was short on witnesses because of the reluctance of people to come forward. The only one to speak on my behalf was Arthur Southall, one of the men who drove into the car park of the Crossways as I was leaving that night. He did all I would have asked of anyone, simply telling the truth about what time he had seen me, and how I had asked for a lift into town.

There was further circumstantial evidence from witnesses which, while being meaningless in isolation, was sinister in the overall picture being painted by the prosecution. People were wheeled on to say how at various times they had heard us discussing the situation in Northern Ireland; how John was seen late at night taking 'bags' from the back of a car into his house; how Hughie had arrived home on the Thursday night apparently nervous and shook up. One such example was the evidence of Mrs Kathleen Hannon, who worked in the kitchen of the New Street station restaurant. She told how in the early evening she saw a group of men sitting in the restaurant, one of whom was carrying a parcel. That was the sum total of her evidence. But later in the trial one of the cops claimed John had kept referring to bombs as 'parcels', and that John had described how we had been at the station with our 'parcels'. Who knows what effect that kind of rubbish has on a jury.

As the days rolled by, the partiality of the judge became more and more obvious. But it was not just him, it was the whole atmosphere of the place. I remember sitting in the dock thinking that even if Jesus Christ and the Queen were suddenly to turn up and give evidence on our behalf they would be laughed out of court. Mr Justice Bridge even stepped in at the one and only point that a chink appeared in the police version of events. Each officer, whether from the West Midland or the Lancashire force, had sworn that the Birmingham cops had not gone near us at Morecambe until 9.30 on the Friday morning. Our efforts to show the interviews started much earlier were fruitless. If we could only show the police were lying about the times, the jury just might begin to question their overall credibility. They might start to look at the confessions in a different light.

Then out of the blue came Sergeant Ron Buckley, who was in charge of the cells at Morecambe on the night we were brought in. He had been called to confirm a few minor points about his being in the station at the time. He said he had come on duty at 7 a.m. and agreed that we would have had access to toilets. But this was of more than academic interest, because the Birmingham cops had said Billy Power had fouled his trousers before they got to interview him. Buckley was asked whether it would have been his duty to see that a prisoner got to use a toilet if he wished.

'Not necessarily, because of the Birmingham officers that were with the prisoners,' he replied.

When pressed, Buckley was adamant that Birmingham cops had been with some of us from the time he came on duty, just as we had said, and just as the cops involved had denied on oath. With each follow-up question Buckley was stronger and stronger in his conviction. I was getting really excited, thinking this could be the golden key to our freedom.

But then Mr Justice Bridge stepped in. He interrupted the flow of questions to stress earnestly to Buckley how vital it was that times were fixed accurately. He looked down on him benevolently, saying in sympathetic tones that if he were not certain, absolutely certain, of the times, he should not be afraid to say so. Buckley got the message. The judge spoke kindly to him again.

> Q: Are you able to fix with accuracy the time when Birmingham officers, as opposed to Lancashire officers, were first engaged in interviewing prisoners at Morecambe police station?
> A: No sir.

As in the mini-trial, Billy and Hughie went into the witness box first. Both are softly spoken men, and they were constantly berated by the judge for not speaking up in the cavernous courtroom. Eventually he ordered that a microphone be brought in so they could be heard. Then on Thursday 10 July came the time for me to go into the witness box and give my version of events. As I walked over to take the oath I heard one of the prosecution team say, 'I don't think we'll be needing the microphone for this one.' It's true that I could never be described as softly spoken. As Kate McIlkenny, Richard's wife, once said of me: 'You hear him before you see him.'

In the days before we were to give evidence I had been coaching the other lads in how to behave in the box, much to the amusement of the prison officers with whom we had become quite friendly. They were keen to see how the 'expert' himself would perform. I believe I did rather well in the day and a half I spent giving evidence and being cross-examined. Knowing you are telling the truth is the most powerful of weapons in those situations. I held a bible in my right hand and promised to 'tell the truth, the whole truth, and nothing but the truth'. As I handed the book back to the usher I was praying inside. Please God, please let them believe the truth.

Most of my time in the witness box revolved around my activities in Birmingham before the bombings and the confessions. I began, as in the mini-trial, by outlining everything that had happened from start to finish. Then I was cross-examined, mainly by Mr Skinner, who I knew from our earlier skirmishes in the mini-trial would be out to trip me up. He asked me about McDade, who I explained was an acquaintance rather than a friend. I'd seen him in pubs, but I'd never bought him a drink and he'd never bought me one.

Q: The truth is that he was a friend of yours and you knew he was Lieutenant McDade.
A: No sir.
Q: And you were going to give him an IRA funeral.
A: No sir.
Q: Along with other members of your unit.
A: No sir.
Q: And you decided to put on a special show for McDade.
A: No sir.
Q: And that is how you got nitroglycerine on your hands, by putting bombs in the pubs.
A: No sir.

I was quizzed on the Bodenstown trip, which was presented as though I was going as a representative of the Birmingham branch of the IRA.

Q: You must have had a lot of nationalist slogans and so on being carried on that party about a united Ireland?
A: I didn't carry any.
Q: I did not say you did. But you must have seen them?
A: I saw some banners.
Q: They were all talking about a united Ireland, were they not?
A: Some people were, some people weren't. I spent most of the time in the pub.

Mr Skinner questioned me about my arrival at New Street station.

Q: And you had a bomb in your bag, did you not?
A: No sir, I did not.
Q: And you joined with the others in a little five or six-minute tour to the Mulberry Bush and the Tavern in the Town to plant those bombs?
A: No sir.

He was unhappy with my explanation of why I had bought only a single ticket to Belfast.

Q: Were you intending to go into hiding?

A: Hiding from what?

Q: Hiding from the men who were trying to trace the men who had planted bombs in Birmingham?

A: No sir.

Q: Hiding because you thought you might have nitroglycerine on your hands?

A: Completely untrue.

It was suggested that I had split from the other lads at Heysham because I was scared at the sight of security checks, and that I had constantly denied knowing any of them during several interviews. I was asked about Inspector Moore, who had told the court he had joined Bennett and Brand while they were questioning me at Morecambe. I said that was not true, and that he had also been lying when he said he had been present at an interview at Queen's Road.

Q: Is he right about that?

A: No sir, he was never with me other than on the car journey.

Q: He is lying about that?

A: Yes sir.

Q: And when Mr Bennett and Mr Brand said that he was present on both days, they are lying as well?

A: Yes sir.

Obviously it did not look too good stating that every single police officer who had dealt with me had gone into the witness box and lied on oath. Neither did it look too good when I was asked about the marks on my legs that had been made by Bennett and the others with cigarettes. Here Mr Skinner cleverly returned to the Bodenstown trip, getting me to agree readily that one of those on it was Jimmy Ashe. By the time of our trial Ashe had been jailed for conspiracy to cause explosions.

Q: Do you remember that when Mr Ashe pleaded guilty he admitted that he had put cigarette burns on his own arms after his arrest?

A: No sir.

Q: And had initially tried to suggest that the police had caused those burns?

A: No sir.

Q: And then admitted that he had done it himself?

A: No sir I didn't. It's the first I've heard of it.

Q: That is something that IRA men frequently do, is it not, inflict wounds on themselves like that?

A: I wouldn't know.

It was a skilful bit of cross-examination which, if I had been on the jury, would have made quite an impact on me. There was little questioning over the forensic evidence, as most of that was dealt with by the respective scientists. I was just asked about the procedure Skuse had gone through, and whether I could explain his findings that I had handled explosives. I said I had not got a clue. I had never touched explosives.

Q: So he must be wrong?

A: He must be wrong.

Q: Or you are lying?

A: Or I'm lying. I say he's wrong.

Eventually it was all over and I returned to my seat in the dock. The whole session in the witness box was quite an ordeal, but it was my opportunity to state my case, and I felt I handled it reasonably well. Apparently others did too. I was given a message later that prosecutor Skinner had said if we were cleared he was going to buy me a drink, as I was one of the best witnesses he'd seen in all his years at the Bar. Sadly, due to his prosecuting zeal, I was unable to take him up on it.

One of the things that impressed many people over the years is the way we six have never changed our story from the time we were first held. What we told our lawyers then was the same as what we told the court, and what we have told everybody ever since. If you are telling lies it is difficult to repeat the detail of the same story accurately over and over again. If six of you are telling lies, the potential for being tripped up through mistakes and contradictions is enormous. The only sure way to be consistent is to rely on the truth.

Admittedly the numerous policemen against us were also consistent to a great extent. But every one of them was allowed to use a notebook in which their version was recorded. What a difference it would have been if the judge had refused to let them refer to their notebooks and had made them give their evidence in the way we had to do – from memory alone.

The case dragged on through the summer and the hot sticky days of July and August. The case had opened with a fanfare of publicity and the press and public benches overflowing. But after the first few days the interest dwindled. My wife Pat came up for two or three days of the trial, but I did not really want her there, and asked her to stay away. I thought it would all be too much for her. And for me too. When you are in that situation you have enough to do trying to keep yourself together. I don't think I could have handled seeing Pat each day in court, knowing as I did what the result was going to be.

There were numerous stoppages. After just two days the trial was adjourned so that a 400-year-old ceremony could be carried out. The new High Sheriff of Lancashire handed over to Lord Derby, the Constable of the Castle, his personal shield so that it could be hung alongside the 400 others on the walls. I was locked away in a cell deep in the castle while this was going on, reflecting on how up above me people were enjoying this traditional ceremony while my whole future lay in the balance.

There were interruptions due to the health problems of the judge, Mr Justice Bridge. We stopped once so that he could see a dentist. In July there was an adjournment for a week when he was taken to hospital with a stomach complaint. After that the daily proceedings were shortened.

But eventually the evidence drew to a close and the prosecution and defence prepared to sum up.

# 18

## Jailed for life

Mr Skinner did not pull any punches as he described us in his final speech to the jury.

'Every one of the six has been unreliable, shifty and dishonest in the witness box,' he said. 'Have you any doubt that these men were determined to get to the funeral to make sure McDade had a hero's funeral, and have you any doubt that they would have had a hero's welcome themselves for planting bombs on the way?'

We had been caught, he said, in a superb police operation, but had tried to blacken the names of the decent men who had brought us to justice. 'They have told you a pack of lies about a fine body of dedicated and hard-working policemen. The truth is that the six men were caught red-handed. Three were caught gelly-handed. They are not only liars, but they have been amply proved to be bombers and murderers.'

Mr Skinner turned to each of us individually, saying Gerry was 'the most fanatical and unbalanced', and that John was quite clearly our leader – 'an evil man whose malevolence erupted in the witness box'. 'Paddy Hill,' he said, 'is a cocky, aggressive little liar.'

I watched the jury as he spoke to them. One or two nodded their heads in agreement as he denigrated us, and all twelve appeared to be listening closely. When it was time for our lawyers to make their final speeches, the men and women of the jury looked bored. It was as though they were tired of hearing claims that the police had forced confessions, and that the test for nitroglycerine was not infallible.

Then it was time for Mr Justice Bridge to sum up.

The judge made his position clear from the start.

'I do not think any of us can be detached. We all see things differently, but I have naturally formed an impression of the conclusions to which the evidence leads, as I daresay some of you already have. I think, however hard a judge tries to be impartial, inevitably his presentation of the case, his summary of the evidence, is bound to be coloured by his own views.

'So I am of the opinion, not shared by all my brothers on the Bench, that if a judge has formed a clear view it is much better to let the jury see that and say so, and not pretend to be a kind of Olympian detached observer.'

He certainly kept to his word. He spent some time going through the evidence of the forensic scientists Higgs and Lidstone; our backgrounds and links with each other and McDade; our movements on the day of the bombings; and the damning evidence of Tom Watt against John Walker. Then he told the jury: 'We move on now to what are two absolutely critical chapters in this story, that is to say in my summing-up of the murder case against the first six defendants. The chapters are headed Forensic Evidence and Police Evidence.'

On the forensics, he said there was no dispute between Skuse and Black over which tests were conducted, how they were carried out and the results obtained. 'But there is a violent conflict of scientific opinion between Dr Skuse and Dr Black as to the significance of the results these tests yielded.'

It did not take him long to begin denigrating Dr Black. Our scientist had listed several categories of substances which could give the same results which Skuse had obtained from the Griess test, although he stressed that only one – nitrocellulose – was commonplace. When pressed, Black had said that one of the other substances was used in a rare form of tablet for high blood pressure. Now the judge asked: 'Do you really think, members of the jury, that it could have come from capsules prescribed for high blood pressure? Or do you think that Dr Black in introducing that matter was wasting your time?'

After detailing the complicated technicalities of the chemistry involved, Bridge told the jury it was so complicated they would probably have to rely on the impression they had gained of each of the two scientists, and by comparing their relative experience.

'Dr Skuse is a Bachelor of Science, a Doctor of Philosophy, and a forensic scientist employed as such at the Home Office forensic science laboratory,' he said.

'He is a man whose working life is spent detecting the evidential value of such samples as can be found by swabbing a man's hands to see if they have been in contact with explosives. The evaluation of the significance of samples of the kind he took in this case is part of his everyday work. He has given evidence in many similar cases.

'Let us just look at Dr Black's qualifications for a moment. He has had a very distinguished career in the world of explosives. He is a Bachelor of Science, a Doctor of Philosophy, a Fellow of the Royal Institute of Chemists and he has spent most of his working life in the explosives industry. He finished up as chief inspector of explosives at the Home Office.

'I have no doubt that if you were the manager of an explosives factory and you wanted to know the most efficient precautions to be taken against accidents, you could not consult a better authority than Dr Black.

'What is his experience, however, in the very different field of forensic science? I hope I am not being unfair to Dr Black, but we do not need to look beyond his own admissions to see how very limited his experience in that field is.

'He has never been into a forensic science laboratory in his life. He has never taken swabs from any human body in his life, let alone subjected them to a Griess or any other test. He has only once in his life ever carried out the Griess test, and that was on a piece of rag which he had been given in advance and which had been soaked in nitroglycerine. His practical experience as a forensic expert has been limited to giving evidence in three or four previous explosives cases for the defence.'

Black had put particular emphasis on the fact that the varnish and lacquers used on many bars in pubs contained nitrocellulose, and so a hand that had been in contact with such a bar could conceivably give a positive Griess test. But of course our lawyers had never asked him to put his theory to the test. Bridge told the jury: 'He could to his heart's content have gone round all the public houses in the country rubbing his hands on bar counters which had been lacquered and soaked in that way. Did he do any such test? No, ladies and gentlemen, he did not.

'Please do not think I am trying to pre-empt your decision on this

142

very important issue. I am afraid that I have made my views on this issue between Dr Skuse and Dr Black pretty plain. If you think that in what I have been saying I have been talking rubbish, just disregard everything I have said and arrive at your own independent conclusions.'

But, he said, if Black were right, Skuse had spent most of his professional life wasting his time. 'Do you think Dr Skuse has been wasting most of his time?', he asked the jury. 'It is a matter entirely for you.'

That brought Bridge to the end of the 'forensic chapter', but he then had to abandon his summing-up for the day because he had lost his voice. With our future lives at stake he seemed to think it appropriate to introduce a little light-heartedness into affairs, and revealed that a throat spray prescribed by a doctor that morning was of the sort 'given to pop stars'. With his voice reduced to a croak, he apologised to the court saying, 'This trial has been beset by my ailments.'

When he resumed the next morning, 13 August, ('I believe my voice is much better today') he turned to the alleged confessions. After the way he had torn Black's evidence apart I could see no hope of him putting a fair case to the jury on this. He had already decided for himself who was telling the truth when he ruled weeks earlier at the 'trial within a trial' that the confessions were admissible evidence. Now he said: 'In this part of the case we are concerned with a conflict of evidence of a totally different kind from that as between Dr Skuse and Dr Black. This is no difference of opinion. This is an absolute conflict as to the circumstances in which the defendants were interviewed.'

The four who had made statements had said they did so because they could suffer no more. 'Hill and Hunter were made of sterner stuff, so they tell you,' he said.

He recalled that Mr Skinner in his final speech had likened the police behaviour we had alleged to that of Hitler's Gestapo. 'In my recollection, Hitler's Gestapo did not bother about confessions,' he said. 'They were going to execute you whatever you said. But my mind went even further back in history. It seems to me that the kind of treatment to which, as they say, these defendants were subjected was reminiscent of the days of the Star Chamber, the rack and the thumbscrew under the Tudor monarchs of this country.

'One thing is clear beyond all doubt, is it not, that this is a conflict of evidence which is completely irreconcilable? There is manifestly gross perjury being committed on one side or the other.'

I sat waiting impatiently to hear how Bridge could possibly explain away the glaring inconsistencies that were scattered throughout the 'confessions'. He could not possibly ignore them. And he didn't. Bridge told the jury: 'Of course, it is inescapable that these statements are not accurate in detail. But do they necessarily show that the statements are not genuine? It is common experience for those of us who are in court day in, day out, that men often seek relief from their inner tensions by making confessions.' The discrepancies could be explained, he suggested, by the desire of criminals to minimise their own role. 'They are often anxious to show that somebody else has really induced them against their better judgment to do what they have done, to shift the main responsibility on to someone else's shoulders. Read through, if you will, the statements of Power and Walker in particular to see whether you cannot detect that psychological process at work.'

He went through the evidence of each of us six in turn. After reminding the jury of the police version of their dealings with me he told the jury: 'Hill's account differs from that quite radically. You will remember Hill very vividly as a witness. He was very forthright in the manner in which he gave his evidence. Some might have said that he was perhaps a little arrogant in the manner in which he gave his evidence. But that is a matter entirely for you.'

He told the jury how both Richard and Gerry had said in their evidence that they had heard somebody shouting at me: 'You're covered in gelignite, there's more on you than there was on Judith Ward.' This had been Detective Sergeant Bennett, referring to the woman convicted (wrongly) earlier of another IRA bombing.

'Is this a genuine recollection on the part of these three defendants?' Bridge asked. 'Or is it something they have concocted together in order to corroborate each other? It is entirely a matter for you.'

Finally, in going over my evidence, Bridge recalled how I had told of the incident in which Chief Superintendent Harry Robinson had shook my hand before we first went into court in Birmingham. Bridge said: 'Do you believe that the most senior officer in the Birmingham CID would go round asking if they were going to behave in court? And when he got an assurance that they were, that he would go around shaking hands with them? Does that have the ring of truth about it?

'Members of the jury, it is entirely a matter for you.'

Bridge capped his support for the police by telling the jury that if what we had alleged were true, the officers were involved in a massive conspiracy 'unprecedented in the annals of British criminal history'. He said that the confessions, if bogus, would have taken a great deal of invention on the part of the police. 'Consider the artistry that has gone into the preparation of these statements, if indeed they are works of fiction,' he said. 'If the evidence of the defendants is true, it shows the police not only to be masters of the vile techniques of cruelty and brutality to suspects. It shows them to have a very lively and inventive imagination in making up stories to put into suspects' mouths.'

But the fact is that most of what was in the statements was true, namely the sections involving our movements up to the critical time of the bombing. They didn't need 'artistry'. The crucial matter of the planting of the bombs is skipped over incredibly quickly in each statement. Richard tells how he planted a bomb in the Tavern in just 55 words. John describes planting bombs in the Tavern in 48 words. Billy takes 69 words to explain how he put bombs in the Mulberry Bush. And Hughie described leaving a bomb outside the Mulberry Bush in only 34 words. Not much artistry there. Nor is there anywhere in the statements any description of the preparation and priming of the bombs, which would surely have formed a vital part of freely given confessions.

And what of the invention that would have been necessary for us to have concocted our version of events? Bridge didn't ask the jury to consider the artistry that would be needed for six fairly uneducated Irishmen to fabricate a story that was similar in almost every detail, and which withstood the fiercest cross-examination from some of the greatest legal brains in the country. Now that would have taken some doing.

The only witness to suffer more from Bridge's tongue in the summing-up than Dr Black was the hapless Kenneth Harwood, the Winson Green prison doctor who brought condemnation upon himself by insisting none of us had been injured by prison officers. Bridge spent considerable time on what he described as the 'blatant nonsense' of Harwood's testimony that every injury he found was so old it must have been inflicted in police custody. There were many questions over inconsistencies in his evidence, the judge said, and he asked the jury. 'In the light of those questions, can you believe one single word of what Dr Harwood says?

'There are on one side or the other inescapably many perjurers who have given evidence from that witness box. If Dr Harwood is one of them, is he not one of the worst?

'If this gentleman has come to this court deliberately to give you false evidence to protect his cronies in the prison service, then not only is he not fit to be in the prison service, but he is certainly not fit to be a member of the honourable profession upon which, if he has perjured himself, he has brought terrible shame.'

Finally, towards the end of his summing-up, Bridge dealt briefly with the case against Murray, Sheehan and Kelly on conspiracy charges. For the last named two, it revolved around an incident in which Sheehan and John Walker had taken to Kelly's house a bag which was said to contain detonators, guns and ammunition, although both John and Sheehan had maintained they had not known what was in the bag. Kelly had claimed that while he knew what was in the bag, he was infiltrating the IRA and had planned to pass on the information to the police.

Bridge said he viewed Murray as 'a mysterious figure, an isolated figure'. He was a self-confessed member of the IRA, although at the time of his arrest membership had not been illegal. He was the only one of the nine in the dock not to give evidence, ignoring the proceedings throughout. Bridge said he felt the case against Murray was so thin 'I had to consider at the close of the Crown case whether there was enough evidence to allow the case to proceed against him at all.' That seemed odd, especially as Mr Skinner in his final speech had told the jury, 'You may think Mr Murray was the organiser behind the scenes.'

Bridge said a forensic test on Murray's hands had proved positive for ammonium and nitrate ions, but he reminded the jury such contamination could have a perfectly innocent cause.

'You may think his conduct in this trial has shown a certain measure of dignity which is totally absent from the conduct of some of his co-defendants,' he said. 'You may find yourself in difficulty in withhholding from Murray a certain grudging measure of respect.

'Murray's conduct has been consistent with what you might expect of a member of the IRA. It comes near to not recognising the court. I do not mean of course that Murray has been discourteous to me. He has not. He has been perfectly polite. He has stood; he has not turned his back on me; he has behaved perfectly throughout. He has behaved as one would expect a member of another army to behave.'

He spoke of how, like a captured soldier, Murray had given only his name, and remained silent during the case. And he suggested it might be that the other eight defendants knew Murray was the one man who would stand by the IRA's code of silence. 'Knowing that they had sitting beside them an admitted IRA member who would be silent throughout the trial, what better whipping boy could they have found upon whom to shuffle the blame?' he asked.

'Those are all matters for you, members of the jury.'

Mr Justice Bridge finished his summing-up at 3.33 p.m. on Thursday 14 August. It had taken him three days, and when typed up his words would cover 289 pages. The jury retired to consider their verdicts.

We trooped silently and sullenly out of the dock on that warm summer afternoon, knowing it was a lost cause and that we could do nothing but hope for some miracle. We hardly had a word to say to each other as the prison officers escorted us back to our cells. There was none of the banter now, the nervous joking and chattering of those early days in June when we had bounced up the steps into the dock, looking for the truth finally to come out. I stayed up all that night in my cell, unable to sleep as I went over the case again and again in my mind. There were so many things I felt I should have shouted from the witness box, so many points I should have told our lawyers to challenge. It was too late now. I sat restlessly on the flimsy bed of the cell, staring at the blank walls, ripping loose threads from my shirt as my mood swung between deep depression and raging anger. I was going to be found guilty of something I hadn't done.

The jury came back at 12.28 in the afternoon of the next day, Friday 15 August. There was absolute silence in the courtroom as the Clerk of the Court rose and told the foreman of the jury to stand. He asked, 'Have you reached verdicts upon which you are all agreed in respect of all the counts upon this indictment?'

'We have.'

'In respect of the first count, do you find the defendant William Power guilty or not guilty?'

'Guilty.'

'Do you find Hugh Callaghan guilty or not guilty?'

'Guilty'

'Do you find Patrick Joseph Hill guilty or not guilty?'

'Guilty.'

That single word hit me like a sledgehammer in the stomach. My legs began trembling and my insides were turning over. My mouth was dry, and when I tried to raise a shout of protest the words wouldn't come out. I stood there dumbfounded.

And so it went on, through the first count against Gerry, Richard and John, and then back to Billy again for the second of the twenty-one counts of murder. The jury foreman said 'guilty' 126 times. When he finished, I looked across the court at the policemen who had tortured and abused us. They stood grinning and shaking hands.

The judge then addressed us. 'You stand convicted on each of twenty-one counts, on the clearest and most overwhelming evidence I have ever heard, of the crime of murder. The sentence for that crime is not determined by me. It is determined by the law of England. Accordingly, in respect of each count, each one of you is now sentenced to imprisonment for life. Let them be taken down.'

If this was the clearest evidence he had ever heard, how many other innocent men had that judge sent to jail? We were taken away as he sentenced the other three. The Jury was now told that Murray had been sentenced three months previously at Birmingham Crown Court to twelve years in jail for conspiracy to cause explosions, and to ten years for causing an explosion, to run concurrently. Bridge gave him another nine years, also concurrent. So in real terms he didn't get one extra day's penalty as a result of the trial he'd just been through. Sheehan got nine years. Kelly managed the only 'not guilty' verdict of the trial, on the conspiracy charge. He was found guilty of possessing explosives and got one year, but because of time spent in custody awaiting trial he was freed a week later.

The judge then called before him the senior police officers involved to be congratulated. He told Chief Superintendent Robinson, 'I am entirely satisfied, and the jury by their verdicts have shown, that these investigations both at Morecambe and Birmingham were carried out with scrupulous propriety by all your officers.'

The six of us were taken back to the wing of the prison, and when we got there one of the senior members of the prison staff stood in front of us with tears in his eyes. He said it was the biggest miscarriage of justice he had ever seen. Then he shook hands with us one by one. By the time he reached me the sense of despair I had felt as the verdicts were announced was starting to be replaced by anger. As the officer gripped my hand I told him now the fight would really begin. The police and the screws and the lawyers and the court and the judge were not going to do what they had done to me and get away with it. I was going to prove my innocence.

And one day I would walk free.

# 19

# Bristol Jail

They did not keep us at Lancaster for long. We were taken back to our cells and Hughie, Richard and I were told to get our stuff together, ready for a move. When they came for me I asked if I could say goodbye to Gerry, Billy and John who were still locked up. The screws allowed me to go to each door to say a few words. 'I'll be in touch. Keep fighting,' I told them. There was not a lot more to say.

I was handcuffed and taken out to a van with six or seven screws in it. I shouted my goodbyes to Hughie and Richard and we wished each other luck. There were half a dozen police cars, and a helicopter was flying overhead. As we pulled out of the prison I could see through the window the road ahead. It was packed with people and photographers and TV cameras. As we swept by them I could hear the crowd yelling abuse and see them shaking their fists.

The van made its way through the town and eventually to a motorway where we raced along in convoy. I didn't want to talk to the screws, so I sat there pretending to read a newspaper. But the words were just a blur.

I don't know how long the journey took, or which route we followed, but eventually, in the early evening, we arrived at Bristol Prison. As the van stopped and I was marched into the reception area, I became more and more nervous. Would there be another 'welcoming committee' for me? One thing was certain. Never again would I take the treatment we had had in the past, whether it was from screws, or cops, or cons. If they started on me here, I would take some of them out and they would have to kill me to stop me. I knew I would have to make that clear from the start.

The cuffs were removed and the screws began the procedure for processing me into the prison system. Thankfully there was no violence, and the worst I had to put up with was their sniggering and snide remarks. 'You know that when you're released you won't be able to possess a shotgun for five years?' said one. 'Still, you don't need to worry. You won't be getting released.'

While I in reception I was surprised to see Richard and Hughie arrive. They had been brought to Bristol together, while the other three lads were sent elsewhere. At least there would be two friendly faces here. We three were to be held in Bristol for a few months for psychological and medical assessment so that the authorities could decide which maximum security prison we should be sent to.

I was told to take a shower, and then went for my prison clothes. The clothes were being handed out by another con. He rummaged through some large brown boxes and pulled out a ripped, striped shirt, old stained underpants, a pair of rough grey trousers which clearly wouldn't fit, socks with holes, and a pair of shoes about two sizes too big. I looked at the clothes, and then at him. He was smirking, and glancing across at the screws as if to say he was on their side. It was the first big test.

I rolled up the clothes into a ball and threw them back at him, yelling for all to hear: 'Listen you scumbag, I'm not an animal, I'm an innocent man. I want decent clothes and decent treatment. If you or anybody else messes me about I'll take your head off.'

There was absolute silence. Then a screw stepped forward and quietly told the cowering con to give me some proper clothes. It was a crucial moment. Word would spread throughout the prison that I was prepared to fight, and that was important.

I gathered my clothes, collected my bedroll and chamber pot, and then a screw called Atkinson arrived to take us away to the top-security A-wing. I'll never forget him, for he immediately cut through the tension with his kindness and easy-going manner. 'You don't need to worry, nothing like what happened at the Green will happen here,' he said. 'For what it's worth, a lot of us here think you got a really raw deal. If you need anything, give me a shout.'

I decided to take him at his word straightaway. I asked if he could get me another newspaper and he gave me one from his own pocket. He took us to our cells, but shortly after locking me up he returned. 'Here's a few books for you, Paddy. I hope they're OK.' Just a small act of kindness, but in a system as brutal as prison it meant a great deal.

A little later we were given something to eat, and after that we were 'banged up' (locked in our cells) for the night. I tried to read the paper and then the books, but it was pointless. I couldn't concentrate. I sat on the bed having a smoke, thinking once more about Pat and the girls and Sean. How were they, what would they do, how would they cope? I thought of the other lads and their young families. I wondered what was to happen to me. And through it all rang the faint echo of Bennett's words: 'We can just shoot you and nobody will ask questions.'

I decided to try to write to Pat. I'd been given a free letter, already stamped, and so I sat at the table struggling to put some words on paper. I was in Bristol, I was all right, I would send her a VO (a visiting order). I told her lies about how I was sure everything would be sorted out soon. What else could I tell her? It took me an age to scribble out ten lines.

I stuck the letter in the envelope and sat there again with the thoughts tumbling around in my head, always ending up in the same words of despair: What can I do? And then slowly, over the next hour or so, a hazy idea began to take shape. The courts had failed us. The press and MPs had failed us. But our families had by now contacted one or two people who were willing to listen. In particular there were two priests from Northern Ireland, fathers Dennis Faul and Raymond Murray. They had taken statements from us while we were on remand. And they believed us! Maybe, just maybe, they could get a ball rolling, spread the word, make people listen to the truth.

I wasn't sure exactly what I had in mind, but I knew there was something in my head. It wasn't anything as clear as a plan, or an outline of a course of action. Certainly nothing as grand as a campaign. But whatever it was, it gave me the one thing I needed most that night. Hope.

I was woken early the next morning by the sound of the prison coming to life. I looked at the walls and the bars and thought, Oh, shit.

I got up to slop out, waiting for that characteristic jangling of the keys as the screw approached your door. As I went along the corridor I passed a group of screws and heard one of them grumble:

'There's one of those Birmingham lot. They cost me twenty quid.' I was puzzled, but walked on. Maybe he meant taxpayers were having to pay to keep us in prison for years, whereas hanging would have been the end of the matter. But then I heard another saying we'd cost him a tenner. I decided to ask what they were on about. It turned out they had been convinced we would be acquitted at the trial, and had been betting with prisoners on the outcome.

We were locked up for twenty-three hours a day at first. For an hour each day the three of us had to exercise on our own in the exercise yard, so we did not get to meet many of the other cons. But we could hear them. Word of our innocence had not yet got through to most of them, and as they went past our cells some would batter on the door, screaming abuse and threats. Although by then we had heard every possible insult in the book, it was unsettling and left us in a permanent state of high tension. The assaults dished out at the Green still made us all nervous. Being jailed on an IRA charge carried a mark of particular danger. I know some of the lads in other prisons were singled out for brutal treatment, from screws and cons alike, in the early years. I was lucky never to suffer that.

Being a Catholic – although not exactly devout – I expected to go to Mass in the prison chapel on our first Sunday at 9.30 a.m. About an hour beforehand the cell was opened and the priest came in, an elderly Englishman with grey hair. He was quite nervous, and gradually it became clear he did not want me, or Richard or Hughie, to attend his Mass. He said he knew that some of the other prisoners would not be happy about it, and he thought it would be better all round if we did not show up. I could not believe this was coming from a priest.

'But father, I'm innocent,' I told him.

'No, you are not, you are guilty and you've been found guilty in the courts.'

I screamed at him to get out, telling him that if he ever came back to my cell I would rip his collar off and ram it somewhere. The three of us went to Mass anyway, on that Sunday and in the weeks that followed, and there was never any hint of trouble.

After about a week Hughie, Richard and myself were allowed to go together to the prison library. On the way we passed the cell occupied by Big Alex, a Scotsman in for armed robbery. He said he wanted a word with us, and the escort screws, knowing he was a power in the prison, allowed us to stop and chat to him for a while. He told us he had heard we were innocent and asked if it was true. We told him what had happened to us. Then he asked if we had had any trouble in the prison and we told him about the banging and shouting at the cell doors. He said he would fix it. The next morning at slopping out we heard the alarm bells go off and watched as screws came running from everywhere. In the recess where you got your water a con was lying half-conscious with a bloody nose. Big Alex was putting the word out that we were not to be touched. The harassment ended.

Shortly after our trial we made an application for leave to appeal against the convictions. The grounds were that the judge had declared his own views so strongly it had been impossible for the jury to take an independent view; that he had overstepped the mark in denigrating defence witnesses; and that he had failed to remind the jury at all or sufficiently of vital parts of our case. This point specifically referred to the impossibility of being able to pack sixty pounds of gelignite (the amount the scientists had maintained was used), batteries, switching, wiring, clocks, the alleged plastic bags which contained the bombs, and the various items of clothing into the two small cases we were carrying. Unfortunately, the forensic evidence, which was later to be so comprehensively demolished, did not form part of our grounds of appeal.

While the lawyers were handling the appeal application the hazy idea that had been in my head like a seed that first night in Bristol had started to grow, but only slowly. I'd written a few letters to people proclaiming our innocence. There was no response. Until somebody began to take an interest in us we would have to continue with the legal process, even though I had no faith in it.

I began to get used to life as a convicted prisoner. There are two classes of Category A prisoner, described as being 'on' or 'off' the book. Being 'Cat. A, on the book', as I was for most of my sentence, is the highest level of security classification, and correspondingly the restrictions are tightest. The 'book' is the document that must be filled in every time you leave your cell, detailing what time you left the cell, where you were going, who was your prison officer escort, and when you were returned.

My early spell under this top-security classification was effectively solitary confinement; I was locked in my cell twenty-three hours a day and allowed out only to slop-out, to exercise, to take a bath or visit the library. A Cat. A prisoner doesn't share a cell. Having one to yourself works two ways, of course. It means you don't have to share with a con you may not like. But it also means hours of loneliness with nobody to talk to. I was allowed to receive only one letter a week, and could send only two or three. All mail coming in and going out was heavily censored. I was allowed far fewer visits than when on remand, and they were for just thirty minutes each. The visitor was rigorously screened, and screws would sit in on the visit, which was held in a more secure room than that used by other prisoners. Anybody not in my immediate family who wished to visit me would have to fill in various forms, and would then be interviewed by Special Branch officers who would recommend whether or not that person should be allowed to see me. Those turned down were never given a reason.

Pat had visited me frequently while I was in the Green, but at Bristol it became much more difficult. It meant a round journey of hundreds of miles, usually with some of the kids in tow. And, of course, it was expensive. Prisoners' wives are entitled to travel warrants to cover the costs, which are issued by the government at the local office of the Department of Health and Social Security. But often Pat was given the runaround by some assistant behind a counter who was not going to be sympathetic to a 'bomber's wife'. When she finally got to the prison our half-hour would be taken up with me talking about my efforts to win my freedom. At Winson I had gone on and on about how the trial was the key to our freedom. Now I would tell her the appeal was the answer. She would have to sit and listen, and would rarely let on about the hardship she was enduring outside.

Despite being locked up for so much of the day, money was still vital, for you needed it to buy the little things that take on such importance when you are deprived of easy access to them. Tobacco, soap, shampoo, toothpaste, a battery for your radio. We got a nominal sum of less than one pound a week in place of any wages, because as we were there only for assessment we did no prison work. I had always smoked, so it was an extra punishment to be deprived of a ready supply of fags. Richard used to joke that I did not need toothpaste, as I'd eventually had all my teeth removed because of the damage caused when the gun was smashed around in my mouth during that motorway ride. He said the time I'd had them out was the only time he'd ever known me to be quiet.

I needed his little jokes and the crack to keep me going, for two emotions were to dictate my behaviour during every single day of my life for the next fifteen and a half years. Anger. And bitterness. There were few moments when I could forget I was in prison for something that was nothing to do with me. I had been in prison before, but I had been guilty then and so just got on with serving my time. This was different. The rage and the hatred inside me was to boil over many times.

In those first days at Bristol I made the decision that led to me having countless clashes with the authorities over the years. They resulted in so many punishments that I spent about one-third of my entire time in jail in solitary confinement on the punishment block. I decided that as I was an innocent man and prisons were for the guilty, there was no reason why I should obey their rules. I would stick to my own. Rule number one was that I would not co-operate with the system. I told governors and screws as I moved from prison to prison that this was my philosophy, and not surprisingly it did not go down too well. I imagine every jail I went to regarded me as a disruptive influence, but I make no apologies for that.

Two main forms of control operate in prison. One is being sent to the punishment block, where you are locked up for twenty-three hours a day in solitary confinement. When you are 'on the block' you can be deprived of privileges such as a radio, or have your bedding taken away during the day. The other main sanction to use on a disruptive prisoner is for the governor to make an order under Circular Instruction 10/74. We simply called it a 'lie-down'. The procedure allows a prison governor to move a con from one prison to another where he is kept on the block for twenty-eight days. It's called a lie-down because being locked in your cell all day leaves you with nothing else to do. I got quite used to them.

But what I could never get used to was being in prison at night, for it was then I would sink to my lowest ebb. You are locked up with no human contact and the prison falls silent. No wonder so many cons get drunk on 'hooch', the illegal booze made inside, or high on grass (cannabis) smuggled in. And I was no different. If you can get stoned or drunk when you're behind that door you don't have to think too much.

I would sit or lie there knowing my life, my world had crumbled around me; there were few nights in prison when I didn't shed tears. Sometimes I would become so wound up I would drift off into a form of madness. I'd get up, put on my jacket and tell myself I was off home to the wife and kids, and turn to walk out of that cell. Then all I would see ahead of me would be that big, dirty steel door, and I'd throw myself at it and claw at it with my nails until my fingers began to bleed. I'd find myself on the floor in a heap, crying with frustration and rage as I came back to reality.

And I'd tell myself I would have to channel that anger into my fight for justice.

# 20

# Parkhurst

Shortly before the first anniversary of the pub bombings, in November 1975, my cell door was thrown open at about 11.30 in the morning.

'Right Hill, get your gear together, you're on the move.'

I got up and did the prison equivalent of packing my suitcase – dumping all my belongings into an empty pillowcase. There was not a lot to take, just a few pictures, some letters, and a radio. I had got a little tobacco left, so as I was taken down to reception I stopped at Big Alex's cell and called him to the door. 'I'm on the move,' I told him. 'I want you to take this. Thanks for everything.'

He argued but finally took the tobacco, and wished me well, saying he was sure I'd soon be out. I walked on along the landing. Word of a prisoner on the move spreads like wildfire through a prison, and all the cons knew within minutes I was leaving. As I passed the cells they began banging on the doors. Many of them were prisoners who had shouted abuse and kicked my door when I first arrived. This 'banging out' was their way of saying goodbye and good luck, a sign that I had been accepted.

Down in reception I was joined by a wide-eyed Hughie. We were being moved together. We both knew we were off to a long-term prison, but as usual the screws would give us no clues. I hoped it would be in the Midlands, which would make it far easier for Pat and the kids to visit.

Hughie and I were both handcuffed to screws and we were taken out into the prison yard and put in the back of different vans with half a dozen more screws. I could look out of the windows, but people could not see in. I heard some sirens and then we were off. I could see around us all the usual nonsense – armed police, motorbikes,

158

police cars. I thought then, and I've wondered since, just how much money from taxpayers' pockets went on transporting us innocent men around Britain over all those years.

We finally reached Southampton, which meant we were heading for one of the two big prisons on the Isle of Wight, either Albany or Parkhurst. We were too early for the ferry, so we were taken to the secure area under the city's combined police station and court. A few of the cops had stayed behind after their shift, having heard that two of the ruthless Birmingham pub bombers were coming in. They must have been disappointed when they saw old Hughie and little me.

A police sergeant in the station told the screws to take the handcuffs off, but they refused. He told them: 'I'm in charge here. They're not in prison, they're in my custody. Now get those cuffs off.'

It was so nice to be treated with a little humanity. And it got even better. The sergeant made us a really strong cup of tea, totally different from what we'd been drinking in Bristol. He even let us take a little exercise after sitting in the prison van for hours, walking up and down a corridor while the screws were getting their own tea.

'I've heard all about you lads,' he told us. 'I reckon you were hard done by.'

Eventually the screws returned and we drove down to the ferry, which had been delayed coming into port because of stormy weather. As we stepped on to the deck the waves came crashing over us. I turned to the screw cuffed to me and said, 'If the boat starts sinking, will you take these cuffs off?'

'I'll take mine off and lock it to that rail,' he said.

'Are you joking?' I asked.

'Do I look as if I'm joking?'

He didn't, so I prayed for a smooth crossing.

We got to the island without incident. I was dropped at Parkhurst, while Hughie continued on, being taken to Albany. When I arrived in the late afternoon it was cold, wet, windy and dark. Even on a good day, Parkhurst is one hell of an eerie place. It's as if you can feel evil oozing from its walls. It made me shiver. I conjured up visions of the prisoners of years gone by awaiting transportation to Australia for stealing a loaf of bread. When I got there it was home to the infamous Kray twins and the cop-killer Harry Roberts. For the next three years it would be my home too.

I dumped my pillowcase on the counter at reception and was processed. Then the screw in charge told me: 'Listen Hill, we have received information that the prisoners are going to do you. So we're putting you on Rule 43.'

I went crazy. Rule 43 usually means being put in solitary confinement in a separate block of the prison for your own protection. It usually applies automatically to sex offenders or informants, people who will always be a target in prison. I told them I had no intention of going on to a wing with prisoners despised by everyone else in the jail. When they told me it was on the governor's orders, I told them they had better get him.

'Hill, we can't guarantee your safety,' he said.

'Governor, you worry about your own safety. I can look after myself.'

They took me off to a regular wing and put me in my cell. A little later a screw let me out, and told me I could go along the landing to the water urn to get a cup of tea to take back to my cell. I thought it was unusually kind of him. While getting the tea he stood twenty yards away, and I saw him talking to two guys, one black and the other white.

The next morning the black guy, Eugene, told me that the night before the screw had said to him and his mate: 'There's one of the Birmingham bombers. Go and give him some stick and I won't be watching.' Luckily Eugene and his mate told the screw to get stuffed. But he told me there was a lot of bad feeling towards me from other prisoners and he wanted to know the truth. I explained what had happened and was obviously convincing because he said he would spread the word. Cons are quick to recognise when somebody is a fraud and when somebody is genuine. The hostility quickly evaporated.

I began to get on well with the other prisoners on the wing. But not long after my arrival an anonymous note was dropped in the post box which each wing has for prisoners to send letters. The box's contents are collected every day and passed to the prison censor for checking. The note, allegedly from a con wanting to protect me, said that other cons were preparing to attack me and that I would be stabbed. The censor immediately called the governor, who ordered the prison staff to take me forcibly to the punishment block, allegedly for my own protection. I spent four weeks in solitary confinement under Rule 43. But finally a delegation of some of the toughest cons in the prison went to the governor. They made it clear I was in no danger, and that if I was not back on the wing quickly, there would be no wing for me to come back to. I was returned within an hour. I've never had any doubts that it was a screw, and not a con, who was responsible for the note.

After the endless days of Bristol where I was locked up for twenty-three hours a day it was a relief when I soon got into the same routine as the rest of the prison population. Breakfast would normally be followed by work, which for me was usually in workshops making mailbags or prison clothes, or in the laundry. You would be paid a pittance each week. In the afternoons there would be exercise, either walking around the yard, playing soccer or working out in the gym. The evenings were for association, when you were allowed to mix with other prisoners, going in and out of cells on your wing. There were also education classes, which I never attended, and hobby classes, in which I used to make soft toys for the kids and friends. And, of course, at night you could watch television.

The prison system has an amazingly effective grapevine and with all this mixing it was not long before cons and screws alike got the message that there had been a grave miscarriage of justice. None of us six acted like IRA prisoners and, certainly in later days, we were not treated as such. For me the change came quite early on. Even before my first year was up I was no longer being strictly treated as a 'Cat. A, on the book' prisoner. By contrast, the rules were rigorously enforced at all times for the real IRA men who were in the same prison.

My relationship with the IRA prisoners I met in jail was complex. I was bitter towards the IRA itself, because if it had not blown up those pubs I would not have been in prison. I had never supported its policy of violence, and now was even more strongly against it. But in each jail I went to, the individual IRA men would make it clear from the start they were sorry I was there. They, more than anybody, knew I was innocent. They would also make that fact perfectly clear to all the other cons and screws, and left people in no doubt I should not be touched. It was their way of trying to make up in part for the harm their organisation had caused me. And it was a protective shield I was glad to know existed.

I was never asked to join them, and despite my anger at what the British system had done to me, I never once considered seeking membership as a way of hitting back. But I did become friendly with several of the IRA men as individuals. The common thread of an Irish, or particularly a Belfast, background would often draw us together. I might not have known them back in Belfast, but I often knew somebody in their families, or their friends. And while I could never condone the things they did on behalf of the IRA, the fact that I had grown up in the same town meant I could easily understand how they had been sucked into the movement.

The IRA has a strong command structure in prison based on army-like discipline. Nobody would go near them when they were holding meetings in exercise yards. Where ordinary criminals would tend to look out for just themselves, there was a solidarity among the IRA men which was clear for all to see. They were different too in that most of them got involved in education, particularly history and politics, and in their own classes on the Irish language and culture. I, on the other hand, had no time for anything other than working to get out.

As well as the IRA prisoners I also met other Irishmen in prison who, like ourselves, were wrongly convicted of being bombers, including Paul Hill, Gerry Conlon and Paddy Armstrong of the Guildford Four. Everybody in the prisons could see that we and those three neither acted like IRA men nor were treated as such. The real IRA men made no secret of why they were in prison. They would be openly listed in the IRA's own newspaper as 'prisoners of war' in British jails. We were always listed as innocent Irish people being held.

I spent my first Christmas as a convicted bomber in Parkhurst and it was awful.

No prisoner enjoys Christmas, the greatest family time of the year. He just wants to get it over with quickly and get into a new year of his sentence. When you are innocent it is so much worse. Visits are always double-edged. It's great to see the people you love, people from outside the prison walls. But too often the visit breaks your heart. And never more so than at Christmas.

My mother and my sister Josephine came to see me and it was dreadful. They were in tears and I was in tears. It was sheer torture for all of us. Hardly any words were spoken. When time was up the two of them grabbed an arm each and tried to march me to the door. They were both screaming: 'You're not staying here. You haven't done anything. You're coming home with us.'

I told them in a letter afterwards that it was probably better for us all if they and the rest of the family did not come too often. Mum, Josie and my brothers rarely came again. Far from feeling abandoned, I was happier that way. I knew I was better off not getting visits at all than trying to cope with the agony of such scenes. Each time I would have to try to put on an act, making out that things were not too bad. Finding the strength to get through each visit took a huge toll emotionally.

I felt the same way about visits from Pat, although because of the distance to the Isle of Wight she was only able to make two or three visits a year. The separation and the hardship we were enduring began to really pull our relationship apart. Neither of us would mention it on a visit, but we both knew that our marriage was dying a little day by day.

She was still suffering dreadfully outside. As well as the house moves because of the harassment for being a 'bomber's wife', she was having to cope with the problems the kids had through constantly changing schools. Their education in those formative years was completely disrupted. Pat suffered continual verbal abuse, and several times much worse. She was attacked by one man, and had a table thrown at her by another. Windows were smashed at the various houses she lived in. Once, as she collected one of the girls from school, a middle-aged couple approached Pat; the woman tried to hit her with a milk bottle. There were abusive phone calls, and several death threats. Pat reported many of the incidents to the police, but not surprisingly there was not a lot of help from that direction.

Most of this she would never tell me about, for fear of upsetting me further and knowing there was nothing I could do. But I was not stupid and I knew Pat too well. I could fill in the gaps between the bits she did tell me.

She always brought some of the kids with her on visits. The agony of being an innocent man and having the only contact with your young children within prison walls is impossible to describe. I remember one visit when Pat brought my son Sean. He was only three or four at the time, bouncing up and down on my knee. Then he looked up into my face.

'When are you coming home daddy?' he asked.

Pat and I just sat there looking at each other with tears rolling down our cheeks.

Shortly after the depression of Christmas 1975 came a surprise announcement which gave me a lift. On New Year's Eve the Director of Public Prosecutions announced that fourteen Winson Green screws were to go on trial charged with assaulting us.

Bloody marvellous, isn't it? I thought as I listened to the news on the radio. This lot are being done, but the cops are still getting away with it.

At least a trial meant there would be another opportunity for the truth to come out. I knew I would be called as a witness, so I would have to make sure I stayed in one piece.

Despite the interventions of Eugene and others, that was not the easiest thing to do in Parkhurst. It was a tough, violent jail, holding probably the hardest men in Britain. They tended to be older cons who had been through wilder young days and now knew they had to get on and serve their time. In a sense they ran the jail, not the authorities. The control was based on the premiss that if the screws didn't bother them too much, they wouldn't bother the screws, and everybody would have an easier life. If such a word can be used I would say I 'enjoyed' my time at Parkhurst more than anywhere else inside, and certainly made some great friends. Those guys were supposed to be evil, but I had experienced real evil at the hands of the other side of the law. I knew which side had been worst towards me.

Violence is a part of everyday life in all prisons. I was no stranger to punch-ups and brawls, but the violence in a maximum security prison is on a different level altogether. Self-preservation is the number one rule for every con, so almost everybody has a weapon concealed somewhere close to hand, usually on their person or in their cell. The ingenuity that goes into crafting something that has the sole aim of inflicting awful injury is remarkable. Something as innocuous as a plastic toothbrush presents several possibilities. I've

The Birmingham Six before the arrest. *Clockwise from top left:* Paddy, Hugh Callaghan, John Walker, Billy Power, Gerry Hunter, Richard McIlkenny.

The Birmingham Six after two or three days in police custody. *Clockwise from top left:* Paddy, Hugh Callaghan, John Walker, Billy Power, Gerry Hunter, Richard McIlkenny

The Birmingham Six three days after their admission to Birmingham's Winson Green Prison. *Left to right from the top:* Hugh Callaghan, Paddy, John Walker, Gerry Hunter, Billy Power, Richard McIlkenny.

I only wish that Dr Hugh Black, the forensic scientist for our defence, had lived long enough to see his 1975 trial evidence proved right.

My daughters Michelle *(left)* and Maxine at their First Communion in June 1976 with my son Sean.

All my kids on holiday in 1978. *Left to right:* Nicola, Sharon, Tracey, Michelle, Maxine, Sean.

My father with his great granddaughter Charmaine in 1984.

My daughter Sharon *(front row, third from left)* in London with a group of supporters in 1987.

On the way to the Old Bailey for the final appeal in March 1991.

Free at last on Thursday 14 March 1991.

*From left to right:* Billy Power, Richard McIlkenny, John Walker, Gerry Hunter, Paddy, Hugh Callaghan.

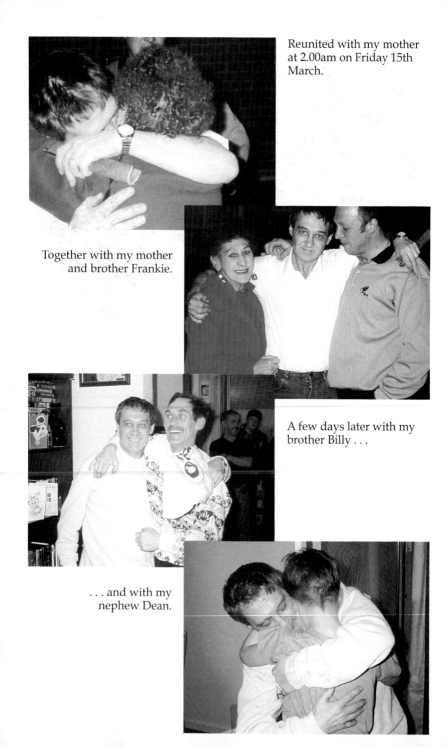

Reunited with my mother at 2.00am on Friday 15th March.

Together with my mother and brother Frankie.

A few days later with my brother Billy . . .

. . . and with my nephew Dean.

Meeting Irish President Dr Mary Robinson in June 1991.

With US Campaigner Kathleen Lisowski *(on my right)* and the Governor of Massachusetts William Bulger *(on my left)* in Boston, June 1991.

In Jerusalem, August 1991.

Adjusting to normal life again with my grandson in Bushy Park, West London.

seen guys heat up the end of a toothbrush until it was soft enough to have a razor blade inserted, which would be held in place as the plastic cooled and hardened. I've watched a con spend hours filing down a toothbrush until it was like a stiletto. Wooden broom handles have a hefty, four-inch nail embedded in the end; scissors are prised apart to provide not one, but two handy knives; jugs of boiling water are often used for purposes other than washing dishes. The commonplace PP9 battery, normally used in radios, is a favourite weapon when concealed in a sock. It has even given rise to a verb in the prison vocabulary – to PP9, as in 'he PP-nined him'.

Prison is a dangerous place in which anybody seen to be weak becomes a potential target. And when the violence happens it happens quickly, brutally and without warning. I've seen people slashed, scalded, stabbed and knocked unconscious. I've been in the semi-darkness of the television room and heard the distinctive dull thud of a PP9 striking a head, to be followed by the sound of a body slumping to the floor. Or, even more unsettling, the high-pitched squeal that comes from a man whose back has been pierced by a blade. I once saw a con go after another guy who was taking a bath, and who had ensured the six-feet high screen around the bath was locked for privacy. The con simply climbed the screen and let fly with a 'harpoon' made of a knife lashed to the end of a broomstick.

You have to be constantly on your guard in prison. Much of the violence is due to the fact that in maximum security jails you have some of the hardest cons around, people who put very little value on life. But the violence also arises because of the large number of cons who are mentally unstable, who should never really be in a prison at all. You go to slop out and say 'good morning' to a guy. Next thing you know he's got you by the neck demanding to know what's good about it. The following morning you decide it's best to say nothing to him. So he grabs you by the neck demanding to know why you're ignoring him.

I knew one guy called Psycho Willie. I heard how he gained his name when two new cons came to Parkhurst. They told me that he had initially got a five-year sentence, then got another five years and nine months added for attacking another con. Somebody told Willie that a certain guy was a grass. Later Willie went to the cell the guy shared and slashed the man inside over and over again. It didn't bother him when he was told he'd got the wrong man. On another occasion I heard him telling a con he'd been asked to kill a guy when he got out.

'How much will you get paid?' asked the con.

'Paid? I do it for pleasure,' he replied. And he meant it.

Our application to appeal against our convictions was heard by the Lord Chief Justice, Lord Widgery, and two other appeal judges. The line-up gave me little confidence, Widgery having produced the whitewash report into the events of Bloody Sunday in Derry in 1972. They announced their decision on 30 March 1976. Widgery opened the proceedings by reviewing much of the evidence heard at the trial but within minutes made the first of several quite stunning comments.

Even though the forensic evidence was not part of our submission, he went over how we had been tested by Skuse. 'A positive reaction was obtained in the case of Hill and Power,' said the judge. 'This is not a point, as we see it, of great importance in the case because there was no trace of explosives found on the other hands, and even in the case of Hill and Power a subsequent and more precise and accurate test failed to confirm the original one.' He then said that although the Skuse tests were 'not an important item at the trial', they did ensure the police kept us in custody. Not important? Our trial judge, Bridge, had been clear in his summing-up that the forensic tests were one of the two 'absolutely critical chapters' in the story.

Widgery said Bridge had not gone beyond reasonable limits in making his own views clear to the jury, because he had consistently made the point that it was 'entirely a matter for them'. Widgery said: 'The judge must not do this so often and so much as really to deprive the jury of any free choice. Having examined the instances of which complaint has been made we do not find that the judge pre-empted the jury's views.'

Widgery did accept that Bridge had gone too far in denigrating Dr Harwood, the Winsor Green prison doctor who had maintained we had not been injured in prison but by the police. He said Bridge's suggestion to the jury that Harwood might have committed perjury and was not fit to be a doctor 'was not called for in the circumstances'. But he claimed that Harwood had never qualified for consideration as a truthful witness. Because 'no reasonable jury could have given any credence to Dr Harwood' Widgery concluded that Bridge's denigration of him had in no way undermined our convictions.

Widgery and his colleagues were dismissive of the claims of police beatings. He said that when we had appeared in the magistrates' court in Birmingham for the first time, the only obvious injury was Walker's black eye. For the rest of us, there was no evidence to indicate 'they had experienced damage or knocking about beyond the ordinary'. Unfortunately the good judges failed to enlighten us as to their view of what constituted 'the ordinary'. And I would have been grateful if Widgery had gone on to say just when it was that the police were given permission to knock people about so long as it was not 'beyond the ordinary'.

As for the matter of whether two massive bombs and everything else could have been crammed into two relatively small suitcases, the appeal judges felt this was such an unimportant matter it was not worth addressing. It was no surprise to find our application to appeal against conviction was rejected.

The decision was another low point, and I took refuge for a few days in drink and drugs. I made use of both to blank out the pain of everyday life in prison, but would go overboard at times of particular stress. The amount of illegal booze and weed (cannabis) sloshing around in jail is phenomenal. An outsider's surprise at just how much is available would be matched only by his amazement at the ingenuity involved in the smuggling and manufacturing that goes on. Every now and then, to make a point, a prison governor will order a sweep of cells in search of drink and drugs, but in routine prison life both are tolerated at the highest level because they keep the lid on these human cauldrons. I haven't the slightest doubt that there would be a riot at every jail in the country if the authorities really tried to clamp down. Drink is brewed from a variety of ingredients, such as fruit and potatoes, along with the magic additive, yeast. Having a good brewer on your wing is a real bonus in prison. But of course everything is relative. What you would class as a good drink inside would be enough to make you sue the distillery outside. It was prison hooch that eventually put me off alcohol for good.

At first I used to enjoy it, or at least getting drunk on it. The first few sips always tasted dreadful, but once you were over that you were raring to go. A con known as Phil the Brewer once invited me and a friend of mine, Henry, over to a party in his cell. Phil was from Dublin, and was in for armed robbery and other offences. He was mad for the drink. He had a shaven head and penetrating eyes, and he used to strip naked in the middle of the exercise yard and do all sorts of Kung Fu exercises.

Henry was from Lancashire, and was also in for armed robbery. He had been in Hull prison with John Walker before coming to Parkhurst, so he knew all about us six. We hit it off as soon as we met. You don't let too many of your true feelings slip to another prisoner, as cons can be so fickle. But Henry was one of the closest friends I had in prison. We shared everything – food, tobacco, grass. It was the kindness and support of Henry and all the other cons like him that helped me to survive.

On the night we went to Phil the Brewer's cell we found the booze had already been strained into the basin in the cell, ready for the half-dozen of us there. Phil handed out small cups to each of us, but was himself dipping into the booze with a big jug. He poured it down his throat at an incredible rate, one jugful after another. After a while Henry, who really enjoyed a drink, got angry at Phil's apparent greed and shouted at him, 'You invited us over for a drink, but the way you're going at it like a madman there'll be none left for us.'

'Don't be daft,' said Phil. 'There's another seven buckets of it under the bed.'

'And there were. Phil eventually passed out, so we pushed him under the bed, now cleared of buckets, and left him there when we staggered back to our own cells. Apparently he woke up in the early hours screaming in terror, convinced he was in a coffin.

The booze provided some great laughs, but it would put me into terrible black depressions, as if I didn't have enough to cope with already. And it inevitably made me more aggressive than I already was. I would smash up everything in the cell, even pictures of my family, and then try to set fire to the place. On one occasion in 1977 I drank too much hooch and ran amok attacking every screw in sight. They eventually overpowered me and I was put in a straitjacket for a couple of days and given thirty-five days on the block. I had to see the prison doctor, a guy whom I respected a lot, and we had a heart-to-heart.

'I'm telling you, Paddy,' he said, 'if you keep on like this you are going to end up killing somebody, and then you will be in for life for something you really have done. You'll not get yourself out of here if you carry on with the hooch.'

He was right, and I knew it. I gave up drink there and then, and lapsed only once, in the mid-1980s when I was at the end of my tether. It sent me haywire for a few days. But that doctor's words came back, and I never touched a drink in prison after that.

Weed has to be smuggled into prison either by visitors or by screws themselves. I knew a London gangster, John, who had sweetened a screw with some nice payoffs for bringing in tobacco for him. As you would expect, bribes in prison go up on a sliding scale in line with the risk. The payoff for smuggling cannabis is considerably more than that for smuggling tobacco. This John was granted a weekend home leave, and arranged to send to the screw's home address a shoe box full of pouches of loose tobacco, which was later to be discreetly handed over to John inside. For a fee, of course. When John returned after the weekend he told me happily he was expecting a delivery from the screw soon. But later that day I met the screw and he was fuming.

He told me to get John to meet him immediately in a particular empty cell. I stood outside, desperate to hear what was happening, as the two had a blazing row. Then John popped his head around the door and told me to rush off and get a friend of his 'and tell him to bring plenty of cash'. I did so and the friend, complete with a huge wad of notes, joined them in the cell.

Minutes later the screw emerged looking considerably happier, to be followed by John and his mate looking relieved. They explained that John had spent most of his weekend leave opening the pouches of tobacco and removing half of their contents. He replaced the missing tobacco with weed, and then carefully resealed the pouches before sending them off in the shoe box to the screw. But the screw checked inside the box and found one packet had not been sealed properly. He looked at it and realised it contained weed. He was understandably angry to discover he was smuggling cannabis into the prison. Not because it was an offence – but because John was only paying him the rate for smuggling tobacco!

After our application for leave to appeal against conviction was refused, I dispensed with the services of Mr Gold and Mr Field Evans as my legal team. Billy's family had by then arranged for him to be represented by a battling young lawyer, Brian Rose-Smith. They were impressed by Rose-Smith and told me of his interest, so I asked him to represent me too.

The summer of 1976 was one of the hottest on record, and it coincided with a prison officers' strike. One of the effects was that we had no work to do, and so spent most of the long hot days out in the exercise yard or on the football pitch sunbathing for hours on end. I ended up with the best suntan I'd ever had. In June jockey Lester Piggott won the Derby on Empery. I was always keen on the horses, and being in prison didn't change that. Lester's victory was memorable because it was his seventh success in the race, a record. But something far more important for me happened that month. The Winson Green prison officers went on trial. It was a remarkable case in that the public can never have been more supportive of a group of defendants facing serious assault charges.

Hughie and I were both taken from our Isle of Wight prisons to be held at jails closer to Birmingham, the venue for the trial. I was taken to Gartree in Leicestershire. Gerry was there too, and it was great to see him again. I was also reunited briefly with Billy, who was at nearby Leicester jail. One morning when we were both to be witnesses he was in the prison van that arrived to take me to court. But I didn't see anything of John or Richard.

Despite being separated, the six of us had kept in touch through letters and through visitors who would pass on messages for us. We knew there wasn't the slightest chance of the screws being convicted, but that didn't bother us greatly. We saw it as another platform on which publicly to proclaim our innocence, and relished getting into the witness box. At every opportunity we pointed out that, yes, we had been beaten by the screws, but only after being beaten by the police. And what a change in the performance of the rest of the lads there was compared with the meek showing at Lancaster!

Billy and Hughie particularly were apparently transformed in the box. They didn't need microphones or coaching from me this time. At one point Hughie shouted across the courtroom while giving evidence, 'We're six innocent men who were wrongly convicted.' Then he pointed at the press bench and told the reporters, 'And I want that published – it hasn't been yet.'

Billy interrupted a barrister who had said we had carried bombs in plastic bags to the pubs, saying, 'But the forensic report said the bombs were in briefcases or attaché cases.' When the lawyer ploughed on, referring to Billy's 'confession' to planting a bomb beside a jukebox, Billy again pulled him up, saying, 'But the forensic report clearly stated the seat of the explosion was nowhere near the jukebox.'

As a defence barrister cross-examined Gerry, dismissively referring to him as a 'bomber', Gerry interjected, 'Excuse me, sir, we're no bombers.'

I was really proud of us all.

Nineteen of the cops who had taken part in our 'interviews' or had escorted us to prison told the court that, apart from John's black eye, none of us had a mark. The screws themselves all refused to go into the witness box, preferring instead to make from the dock unsworn statements of denial on which they could not be cross-examined. But their defence team did provide us with some startling new evidence. They called Dr David Paul, a consultant in clinical forensic medicine, who specialised in spotting and interpreting injuries from photographs. He had studied the police pictures taken of us at Queen's Road station after being in police hands for three days and found injuries on each one of us which he said would never be noticed by the casual observer. He told the court he had no doubt the injuries had been caused while in police custody.

The result was a foregone conclusion and at the end of five weeks all the screws were cleared. After the verdict a leading article appeared in the *Guardian* newspaper under the headline 'Who Beat up the Bombers?'. Part of it read:

The view that the bombers got what was coming to them is understandable. But the jury [in the prison officers' trial] were unanimous in their verdicts, so unless the verdicts are to be regarded as perverse, it follows that the men who carried out the beatings have yet to be found and charged. The concern does not arise from any misplaced sympathy with the bombers. But the judicial process requires for its proper working that from the moment of arrest until the completion of sentence prisoners shall not be abused. Any weakness at any point undermines the process and the confidence in it.

Obviously I was disappointed these brutal men had got off, but

171

shortly afterwards I received a big morale booster when an eighty-two-page booklet called *The Birmingham Framework* was published. It was put together by the Northern Ireland priests Father Faul and Father Murray, who had become involved with us before our convictions. Our families had contacted them because of their reputations for taking on cases of injustice. Each of us six gave them statements about what had happened to us, and they researched other material such as details of the trial and press cuttings. The result was a very persuasive account of our innocence, but *The Birmingham Framework* had a limited circulation and caused barely a ripple in circles that mattered.

At least, though, we now had a campaign of sorts underway. But a great dark shadow increasingly hovered over our fight for freedom, and still hangs over us today. It was the firm belief held by so many people that, although we might not have actually planted those pub bombs, we were part of the IRA in Birmingham. If we had not personally blown up those two pubs, we had probably known about the operation and carried out other bombings for which we had not been charged. So it was right that we were in prison and we should stay there. People could not understand, or perhaps didn't want to face the fact, that what had happened to us took place even though we had absolutely nothing to do with the IRA or any bombings. The suspicion that we were at least guilty by association caused our supporters to be dismissed as being pro–IRA.

Many who took that view believed our campaign did not start until the mid-1980s, years after our conviction, when we began to gain publicity as a national and then an international issue. But we and our families had proclaimed our innocence right from the start. It was not our fault that for years almost nobody in the media wanted to listen to us. The lack of publicity meant nobody knew that we and our families were battling away for our freedom, week in, week out, year after year. So it was no surprise, yet galling all the same, to hear a senior West Midlands police officer saying cynically in the late 1980s when we were in the headlines: 'Why has it taken all these years for them to claim they are innocent? Why are they suddenly going on about it now?'

In the early days the only ones who wanted to know were our families and some close friends. Richard McIlkenny's wife Kate had a friend, Sue Milner, who was a tremendous supporter, as was Anita

Richards, a trade unionist in Birmingham. But practically every door knocked at by our tiny band of supporters was slammed in their faces. A handy excuse for an MP or priest feeling uneasy at the sight on the doorstep of a distraught wife and her young children proclaiming her husband's innocence was to say the matter was *sub judice*. That meant it was before the courts and they could not interfere in the legal process. They weren't being asked to interfere, just to listen, but the magic phrase '*sub judice*' provided a wonderful escape route for years.

There had been a few minor rumblings in the aftermath of our trial. The odd article appeared now and then in small-circulation, usually left-wing publications and in the Irish press. In the mainstream British press, the few stories that did get into print were about how wrong it was that while we had undeniably been beaten, nobody had been brought to account. That was fine, a worthy subject for discussion. But such stories seldom dwelt on our crucial complaint – we were innocent.

Those early years were so lonely for our wives as they took on the hardship of bringing up big families on their own as well as fighting to clear our names. They were all saints, but outstanding among them was Kate McIlkenny. She was an absolute diamond, battling away so hard on behalf of us all and never accepting defeat, despite the numerous setbacks. I'll never forget what she did for us.

While I was in Parkhurst I wrote a few letters each week to anybody I thought might help, but to little effect. When it was clear that the British politicians I'd written to had no intention of getting involved I wrote politicians in Ireland, on the grounds that any Irishman, born north or south of the border, is an Irish citizen under Irish law. The response was just as disappointing.

The most important development in our case by the end of 1976 had been the evidence of Dr Paul in the prison officers' trial about injuries which could be seen on pictures of us taken while we were in police custody. Now, armed with his testimony, we were ready for the next step in our tortuous legal battle. Rose-Smith and the lawyers for the other men decided that the best course of action would be to start a civil action against the Lancashire and West Midlands police forces and the Home Office for injuries received in police and prison custody. Of course, we were not looking for damages. But it would be another opportunity to try to prove to a court that we had been beaten by the police. If we won, it would blow things wide open.

Because of the time and expense involved, the lawyers decided to launch the action on behalf of just one of us, although any victory would obviously apply to us all. One thing had been perfectly clear at our trial; either we were all completely innocent, or we were all guilty. There was no question of some of us being guilty but not the others. The lawyers decided to go ahead in Gerry's name, as he was 'cleanest' of all. Only he and I had never made confessions. But, in addition, Gerry had never had any forensic evidence against him.

In January 1977 an American guy called Gary Gilmore was executed by firing squad for murder, the first execution in the United States for ten years. It brought home to me the fact that we would certainly have been hanged if capital punishment had still been in force in Britain. It was not the sort of news I wanted to see, but I was determined to maintain an interest in what was happening in the world outside, if only to stop the feeling closing in on me that nothing beyond the prison walls mattered. For me that mostly meant keeping up to date with the big sporting events. In April I was cheering as loudly as anyone outside when Irish jockey Tommy Stack rode Red Rum to an historic third victory in the Grand National. The following month I was cheering again as Liverpool, the soccer team I'd always followed, won the European Cup for the first time. But what a difference it was to go from in front of the television to your cell, rather than down the pub to sink a few pints in celebration. I didn't cheer when the TV in June was full of the activities marking the Queen's silver jubilee, the anniversary of her twenty-five years as monarch. As a victim of the so-called justice being carried out in her name, I had nothing to celebrate.

The civil action was launched in November 1977. It was not just the new evidence which gave us hope. Our legal team was now more experienced and, we felt, more committed to our cause. The Home Office, despite the acquittal of the prison officers, admitted liability, but the police were determined to fight.

Before the civil action could even begin they applied to have it thrown out on the grounds that Dr Paul's evidence could have been presented at the original trial, and that the matter of police beatings had been aired and decided in favour of the police at that trial. This meant a separate court case on the police action. The wheels of legal machinery move incredibly slowly and month after month passed without a decision. I was stuck in the constant depression of Parkhurst, with only a few sporting highlights to brighten my days. In May 1978 Liverpool won the European Cup for a second successive year, and in June Argentina won the World Cup.

In October I got some bad news from Belfast. My Aunt Mary had died, at the age of eighty-six. She had been in a bad state ever since the stroke she suffered in 1974 which had led me to take that fateful journey. I'm not sure if she ever knew that I was on my way to see her on the night I was stopped.

Then, in November, there was at long last some good news. Amazingly, we had found a judge on our side. Mr Justice Cantley dismissed the police application and said our case could go ahead. He ruled: 'It seems to me that if further evidence is tendered and it appears genuine and not from a suspect source, and it also appears capable of belief, it must go into the scales in deciding whether the plaintiffs should be shut out altogether from proceeding with their case.' His point was that it was not up to him to decide whether another court might accept the new evidence or not. His job was simply to say whether another court should be given the opportunity to consider such evidence.

Four long years had passed since that night they took me off the *Duke of Lancaster* ferry. Now it looked as though the truth would come out at last.

# 21

# 'An appalling vista'

The Cantley judgment was a real shot in the arm. My fifth Christmas in custody was approaching, but for once there was good reason to be optimistic.

The decision would make my thirty-fourth birthday in December a happier occasion too. I had had precious little to celebrate on the previous four. I was missing what should have been the best years of my life, watching my children grow up. The first of my daughters to become a teenager, Tracey, would have her thirteenth birthday the week before my thirty-fourth. Perhaps this would be the last birthday of hers I would miss. I stuck a note on my cell wall to make sure I remembered to get her a card in time to send it over to Belfast where she was now living with my grandmother. Adding to the upbeat feeling was the knowledge that for the first time in prison I would be getting an edible Christmas dinner. I had become good friends in Parkhurst with a young lad from Trinidad, Nizamodeen Hosein, who had been serving life since 1970 for the kidnapping and murder of the wife of a newspaper executive. He always maintained that he was innocent, and that his elder brother, who was jailed with him, had been responsible. Nizamodeen was renowned on our wing as a great cook, and he had promised to cook a Christmas chicken with all the trimmings for me and a few other lads.

But then came two blows in quick succession. The first was that the West Midlands Police announced they would be appealing against the Cantley ruling. My high hopes disappeared. Not only would this mean the case dragging on, but it also meant we would have to be extremely lucky to find another judge of the calibre of Cantley to give us any chance of success. My view of the judiciary was that there were very few Cantleys around.

176

The second blow came a few days before Tracey's birthday in mid-December when my cell door was flung open one morning before 6 a.m. Alec the Burglar, a screw so named because of his skills in searching cells, told me to get ready for a move. I couldn't believe it. And as I became more awake I became more angry. I erupted, screaming at Alec to get out of the cell and yelling that they would have to drag me out if they wanted to move me.

Alec beat a hasty retreat and closed the door as I threw my table, chair and chamber pot after him. He left me ranting and raving like a lunatic and went to get help. A few minutes later a group of screws returned, led by a Principal Officer who was a tremendous guy. He had shown me a lot of kindness in the past. I was cursing and smashing the bed up when he knocked on the door and said: 'Paddy, I'm coming in on my own, and I don't want you to start getting violent with me.'

He opened the door and took a few steps inside. Had it been anyone else I would have taken a chair leg to him, but even in a rage I knew this was a screw who deserved the respect he had shown me. I sat back on what was left of the bed and told him they couldn't move me because my Christmas was planned. I had ordered a birthday card for Tracey from the prison shop, and I was having Christmas dinner cooked by Nizamodeen. They were things that would be dismissed as trivial outside the prison walls. But inside, such minor matters take on massive importance. This PO knew how I felt. He waited until I had finished, then said: 'Look Paddy, this is all off the record, because you know I can't talk about movements. But I spoke to your mother and father last night, and they are expecting to speak to you at your new place tonight. There's a VO already waiting for them there, and they'll visit you in a couple of days. You are going nearer home for your parents' sake and your kids' sake. I'll make sure there's a birthday card there for you to send to Tracey. The van's waiting out in the yard to take you. Now get your stuff and go.'

He was not a screw who would bullshit you. So I grabbed my pillowcase and tossed in my few belongings.

I was off to Long Lartin Prison in the Worcestershire countryside, a low-level modern jail which was a stark contrast to the Victorian hulks of Winson, Bristol and Parkhurst. I checked at reception whether there was a VO for my parents. There was. I spoke to my mother by phone that night. And there was a birthday card waiting for me in the prison shop the next morning.

The birthday card had special significance. It was not just something to mark Tracey becoming a teenager. It was vital to me to keep a link with my children because I knew now my marriage was unlikely to survive. The strain was proving just too much for Pat. Her visits and letters were by now infrequent, and I knew she was having to resort more and more to nerve pills to cope. In the same way as I was blotting out the reality of life with grass, Pat was using drink as the only way to escape the daily hardship she was facing. I was losing my wife, but I was determined to keep in touch with my children.

John was in Long Lartin when I arrived, and it was great to see him – for the first time since the day we had been convicted, more than three years earlier. He had a reputation as one of the finest brewers of hooch in the jail. That – and his own warm personality – meant he had a lot of friends there. Gerry Hunter arrived in May 1979. It was about the time Margaret Thatcher was elected Conservative Prime Minister of Britain. I watched on television as she said in her victory speech, 'Where there is despair, may we bring hope.' Somehow I didn't think she had me in mind.

Although John, Gerry and I had our own friends in prison, it was good to know that three of us in the same boat were there together. We made a point of trying to boost each other whenever one of us felt down.

The police appeal against the Cantley decision was eventually heard by the civil division of the Court of Appeal in November 1979. The ruling came a month later, in January 1980, from the Master of the Rolls, Lord Denning.

'Just consider the course of events if this action were to proceed to trial. It will not be tried for eighteen months or two years. The evidence about violence and threats will be given all over again, but this time six or seven years after the event, instead of one year. If the six men fail, it will mean that much time and money and worry will have been expended by many people for no good purpose.

'If the six men win, it will mean that the police were guilty of perjury, that they were guilty of violence and threats, that the confessions were involuntary and were improperly admitted in evidence and that the convictions were erroneous. That would mean the Home Secretary would either have to recommend they be pardoned, or he would have to remit the case to the Court of Appeal.

'This is such an appalling vista that every sensible person in the land would say "It cannot be right these actions should go any further." They should be struck out.

'This case shows what a civilised country we are. Here are six men who have been proved guilty of the most wicked murder of twenty-one innocent people. They have no money. Yet the state lavished large sums on their defence. They were convicted of murder and sentenced to imprisonment for life. In their evidence they were guilty of gross perjury. Yet the state continued to lavish large sums on them in their actions against the police. It is high time that it stopped. It is really an attempt to set aside the convictions by a sidewind.'

Denning's ruling left me absolutely flattened. It was not just what he had decided, but the justification for his decision. It was a blatant admission that the truth of the case didn't really matter. It was far more important that public confidence in the police and judiciary be maintained than that six wrongly imprisoned men receive justice.

Denning's colleague on the bench, Sir George Baker, was in complete agreement. It would be 'grossly unfair' if the police officers we had accused of beating us and lying on oath had to go through it all again. 'The morale of the police force and the confidence of the public in it and in the judicial system is every bit as precious to society as an anxiety to allow a murderer to present his case twice,' he said.

We appealed, which meant the next stop would be the House of Lords, but the ruling knocked me into a depression which lasted for weeks. Rose-Smith told me he was switching into another branch of law, so would no longer be able to represent me. The appeal would continue, because technically it was in Gerry's name and his lawyers would see it through.

I bounced back from this low spot when the *Guardian* newspaper printed a report on a scientist who had conducted research, unrelated to our case, into the Griess test. He had discovered that substances other than nitroglycerine could give a positive result to Griess. Skuse had claimed in court that only one other substance could possibly give a positive, and that was also a form of explosive. Now, five years later, here was a scientist saying hands could give a positive for Griess if they had been in contact with, of all things, cigarette smoke! Dr Black had not suggested that in his theory, but he was certain there was a wide range of substances which could produce the same result as nitroglycerine.

It's easy to look back now and ask why we didn't get scientists to test Black's theory straight after our trial. But we were a bunch of ordinary Irishmen, not scientists. All that we knew for certain was that the police had beaten us up, and we felt proving that fact would be our key to freedom. Black and his theory were denigrated so much in court it seemed pointless to pursue it. Our lawyers did not even list the possibility in our original grounds of appeal.

The latest revelation did not provoke any public interest, but it led to fathers Faul and Murray putting out a supplement to their booklet *The Birmingham Framework*. By now we had a support group, made up of family and a few friends, working on our behalf, and they put a package together on the whole case. They could get no response from British or Irish politicians, so they sent it to an American Congressman, Hamilton Fish, who began to take an interest. Slowly the small-scale campaign was beginning to move forward.

But the progress was far too slow for me, and I became increasingly disruptive at Long Lartin. By the end of my three years at Parkhurst I had been relatively settled, but the disruption of moving and the fact that I did not get on well with the Long Lartin deputy governor and a few of the screws meant I was never going to fit in there. Added to that was the belief in my heart that my marriage was over. Pat had made few visits, even though Long Lartin was fairly close to Birmingham. She came in December 1980 and we found we had little to say to each other. Seeing your marriage fall apart and not being able to do anything about it causes immense strain.

The way I was feeling wasn't helped by the fact that they were tightening up the regime. The Tories had announced a new prison policy and lots of new rules came in. Added to that, the food at this time was terrible. The jail became very tense.

Things came to a head one day in February 1981. There was fish for tea and it smelled rotten. That was the last straw – we told the screws none too politely to leave the wing and they did. We were left on our own and a few of us made it clear to everyone that there was to be no smashing up, this was to be a peaceful protest. Over the weekend everything returned to normal, and on the Monday I went to work at the laundry. But later that day some of the lads were nicked and taken to the block, and on the Tuesday I was stopped on my way to work and taken there too.

I was shipped out on a twenty-eight-day lie-down. We headed north through the Worcestershire countryside, and then I began to notice I was going through familiar territory. We passed the West Bromwich Albion football ground, which I'd often gone to for matches. Then we passed the Concentric factory where I had worked in my early days in Birmingham. Surely, I thought, they can't be taking me back to Winson Green?

I started to squirm in my seat and began sweating. Then the familiar sight of the Green came into view. 'You must be joking,' I told the screws.

But it was no joke. The van turned into the same yard we'd pulled into more than seven years earlier. My heart was racing and I was panting as I sat wondering what would happen now. The Lartin screws took me into reception, removed the cuffs and left to go for a cup of tea, saying they would pick me up in a month's time. I looked around and there was not a screw in sight. Everything looked exactly the same as it had done on that day we were brought in. But there were no screws, no armed cops, no swearing and screaming. And there was no blood.

I had never been in a reception area without screws. The sweat began pouring off me. I was convinced they were all suddenly going to come running, kicking and shouting. I picked up a tea tray that was lying on a chair. I remembered I had a pen in my pocket. Both could be handy when the trouble started. I wouldn't go down this time without one hell of a fight. Then I jumped as I heard a voice cry out behind me, 'Bloody hell, Paddy, what are you doing here?' It was another con from Long Lartin, on his way back after his own lie-down. 'Are you all right? You look as white as a sheet.'

'You would too,' I told him 'if you'd gone through what I did here.'

He was with some Winson screws who I didn't recognise, and we stood chatting for a while. I began to unwind. Then there was another shout.

'Mr Hill, could you come in here please.'

It was a screw, and I presumed he was talking to one of his colleagues. I'd never been called 'Mr Hill' in prison. But it was me he wanted. He brought me into an office where we went through the processing quickly and efficiently. Then I was taken up to a wing and put in the cell where as part of the lie-down punishment I was to be locked up for twenty-three hours a day.

I sat on the bed wondering just how much had changed here in seven years. The memory of what had happened was still crystal clear and I had to fight to keep those images of flailing fists and boots out of my mind. But it was difficult to focus on anything else in an empty cell. Then, thankfully, I was interrupted when I was told one of the assistant governors wanted to see me. As I walked into his office I came face to face with one of those screws who had beaten us up. He was standing beside the assistant governor, the AG, and turned away when I tried to look him in the eye. The AG was brief and to the point.

'Look Hill, what happened has happened. It's all in the past. I wasn't here then, so it's nothing to do with me. And most of the officers who were here are no longer with us. Try to put it behind you.'

That's easy for you to say, I thought, as I was marched out of his office by the screw I had recognised. We walked back to my cell in silence. But as he locked me up he told me: 'There won't be any repeats of what happened before. We were used as well, you know.'

I wasn't there for long. Other cons were doing everything to make life comfortable for me, passing me food, extra fruit and tobacco. It was as though they knew what I had gone through at the prison previously, and were determined to make sure I wanted for nothing. I was supposed to be on punishment, but was living like a king. Clearly the authorities were not happy at the way I was being treated, and after less than a week I was whisked away from Winson at fifteen minutes' notice and with the explanation that some of the screws thought I might attack them!

The next destination was Bristol, where I'd spent my first few months after conviction. It was while I was there I met another prisoner who was to become a close friend. He was Ronnie McCartney, an IRA man who had been jailed for shooting and wounding a policeman in Southampton. He was by then beginning to question the IRA's use of violence, and within a few years was to break from the organisation altogether. Like all IRA prisoners, he knew better than anybody that I was innocent and felt some guilt that I was inside for something his organisation had done. He had been on a wing with Hughie Callaghan in Albany and so knew all about us six. He was very easy to get along with, and like me enjoyed playing and talking about soccer, so we quickly hit it off. As he didn't smoke he usually had more money than me, and often gave me what he had so that I could buy little extras, particularly stamps. I was still writing away to people proclaiming our innocence. And still getting no response.

The first six months of 1981 were spent on a series of consecutive lie-downs. I was shunted around between Long Lartin, Winson, Bristol and Lincoln jails, refusing to toe the line at each. The worst aspect of a lie-down is never knowing where you will be from one day to the next, so trying to arrange visits is a nightmare. The result was that I did not have one visit in that entire six months. Whilst I was not conscious of any long-term harm the lie-downs were causing, I'm sure the psychological stress of long spells in solitary and the disruption of the moves took their toll.

Trivial matters took on an importance way out of proportion, but so too did small acts of kindness become especially memorable . . . the gift of a bit of tobacco from another con when you were dying for a smoke, or a piece of fruit, or a bar of chocolate. Screws could sometimes be capable of kindess too. I once went berserk in my cell in Bristol, smashing it up and screaming abuse because I had no battery for my radio. I had ordered a new one, but because of a strike by the prison administrative staff it had not come through. Locked up on your own for twenty-three hours a day with no radio for company was bad enough. Being told I would not get a battery in time to listen to the commentary on the Cup Final the following day pushed me over the edge. An officer called George arrived as I broke up the cell furniture. He asked what was wrong and I explained about the battery. Other screws had maintained there was nothing that could be done until the admin. strike was over. George had a battery for me within thirty minutes.

The series of lie-downs ended when I was moved to Albany in late June 1981. A few days after I arrived I was told one of the assistant governors wanted to see me and I was taken to his office.

'How are you settling in?' he asked.

'How would you settle in if you were doing twenty-one life sentences for something you knew nothing about?'

'Not very well, I suppose.'

'No, and nor am I.'

We started discussing my innocence, and I said I had known of prison governors who had made representations on behalf of prisoners they believed to be innocent.

'I know you are innocent, but when the shit hits the fan I don't want to be anywhere near your case,' he said. 'It says on your file you are to die in prison. So if you don't prove your innocence, you will never be released. I'll do all I can to help you here and I wish you luck. But I can't do any more than that, and this conversation never took place.'

It was the first time it had really sunk in that I could actually be in prison until the day I died.

At the end of July 1981 Prince Charles married Lady Diana Spencer and the television and papers were full of it. Inevitably I thought of the state of my own marriage, if the word can be applied to such a devastated relationship. I didn't want to dwell on it.

At about that time, my daughter Tracey, who had recently returned with her sister Michelle from Belfast to live with Pat, wrote to me saying that she planned to join the British Army as soon as she was old enough. I couldn't believe it. I saw the army as part and parcel of the Establishment that had locked me away. I wrote back to her saying, 'If you go ahead you'll have to change your name, because you'll no longer be any daughter of mine.' Michelle then wrote to me, saying her mum had decided that if I was disowning Tracey I was disowning them all. I had felt for some time Pat had been seeking a reason to call it a day, and had seized on my letter to Tracey as the excuse she needed. On 3 September 1981 I knew without question the marriage was over. Pat had religiously ensured every year I received a card on that day – our wedding anniversary. That year there was no card.

A few days later, on Tuesday 8 September, I finally received a visit from a member of staff of the Irish embassy in London. I had been writing to them for six years and been consistently ignored, but I had kept on writing anyway. Perhaps now they were willing to get involved, and I was quite excited at the prospect. The guy came into the visiting room and it was immediately clear the aim was just to put in an appearance so they could not be accused of never having visited me. I began to explain the whole story but gave up after a few minutes because of his obvious lack of interest. I got up and walked out saying, 'I can see that I'm just an embarrassment to you.'

Shortly after that the House of Lords upheld Denning's ruling. It was seven years after we had first been held, and a month before my thirty-seventh birthday. So far as the legal process was concerned we had come to the end of the road.

# 22

# On hunger strike

There are few ways for a maximum security prisoner to bring public attention to his case. I had earlier suggested to the other lads through indirect contacts that if the House of Lords ruled against us we should stage a hunger strike. I believed it would gain us a lot of publicity which, with the legal avenues exhausted, was the only hope we had left. I assumed the other lads had agreed to go along with it, so one week after the Lords ruling I simply announced to a screw I would no longer be taking food and told him to tell the authorities.

Lots of the cons told me it was a stupid idea. Ronnie McCartney, who was then also in Albany, said it would be counter-productive because hunger striking was seen as an IRA form of protest. Earlier that year Bobby Sands and nine other IRA men had died on a hunger strike. The British government under Margaret Thatcher had steadfastly refused to cave in to their demands. They were not going to back down to me, said Ronnie. They would just let me die too. And even if I did get publicity, the public would see it as no more than confirmation that I was indeed a member of the IRA.

But I didn't see things that way. Other figures in history had used hunger strikes as a form of protest, not just the IRA. And I was at the end of my tether. I had spent seven years proclaiming my innocence and trying to get people to do something about it, but everything had failed. I hadn't really got a step further forward from the day we were first held. I reasoned that if I was going to die in prison, I would die fighting in a manner that would make people take notice. My marriage was practically over and my kids hardly knew who I was. There was no further legal course open to me. What else was there left to lose?

For the first few days I went about my normal daily prison life, except for not eating. I drank plenty of water and didn't feel too bad. Ronnie told me he had heard that the other lads had not gone on hunger strike and that I had misunderstood when I thought we had all agreed to take part. But I felt he was just telling me that to make me stop. After about a week I was moved to the prison's hospital wing, which was really just a few cells set aside for sick prisoners. I lay in bed all day, reading and listening to the radio, with two screws alongside me. I took twenty pints of water each day, one with salt in it which somebody had told me was vital. After a while I suffered from stomach cramps and hunger pains. But although I began to lose weight, the symptoms were not as bad as I had expected.

I got to see most of the papers each day, and my protest was not exactly making headline news. The most it received was the odd paragraph at the bottom of a page in some of the quality papers. Whenever something did appear, it referred only to me, and not to the six of us. I presumed this was the hand of the authorities making sure we did not get any comfort from knowing we were all making the protest together.

After nearly three weeks I felt a lot weaker, having lost more than a stone in weight, and I asked if a visit by my kids could be arranged. I had not seen Pat for nearly a year, and did not think it would do either of us any good if she were to come now. But I wanted to see the children. A probation officer agreed to bring four of the girls and Sean, who was then eight. Tracey didn't come, as relations were still soured by that letter I had sent her. I ordered a lot of sweets for the kids through the prison shop. When they all tumbled into the room they seemed to give me an injection of energy. Only the older girls had any idea of what was going on; the younger kids just thought dad was poorly and they were there to cheer him up. They certainly did that, playing around and climbing over the bed and laughing. They went off to spend the night at a guesthouse on the island, and returned again in the morning. They were still full of fun, but it was very different for me. I knew there was a chance this might be the last time I would see them. When it was time for them to go I was determined not to let them see me upset. But as I kissed each of them goodbye it was impossible to hold back the tears.

Shortly after that I was moved from Albany to the hospital wing at Parkhurst, which had better medical facilities. I began receiving letters from a lot of our small band of supporters outside, urging me to call off the hunger strike and stressing it was pointless. One was an emotional letter from Richard's wife Kate, in which she said Richard had been seriously ill with stomach ulcers and had needed an operation. She told me he was not on hunger strike and nor were any of the other lads, and it was pointless for me to go on. My protest was not causing a ripple of interest outside. Another letter came from a long-time supporter of our case, a nun called Sister Sarah Clarke, who said I had been doing a great job in sending out letters about our case. I should give up the strike and get back to writing, which would be the only route to freedom.

I was convinced the others were taking part, and that those who were telling me I was on my own were doing so just to make me give up. It strengthened my resolve to keep going. But on the forty-first day, when my weight was down from more than 11 stone to below 8 stone, I had a long chat with Dr Cooper, the same prison doctor who had warned me about the dangers of prison hooch. He told me I was getting to the critical stage. Apart from the weight loss and a few problems with my eyesight, I did not think I was too bad. But he made it clear in no uncertain terms that I was not in a position to judge. After six weeks without food it was impossible for my mind to operate properly. Dr Cooper said he was going to call his counterpart at Long Lartin, Dr Green, whom I also knew, who would get Gerry Hunter on the phone. He made the call and passed me the phone when Dr Green came on the line. I asked if Gerry was on hunger strike. He said: 'He's not, and nor are any of the others. I don't know where you got the idea from that they were. But don't take my word for it. Give me half an hour and I'll call you back, and I'll have Hunter here on the phone to tell you himself.'

I told him not to bother. I knew that if he was prepared to do that he must be telling me the truth. I hung up and lay back in the bed. I could not understand how I'd got it all wrong. What I'd thought was a joint plan had been arranged indirectly, through people who were visiting each of us and through cryptic notes in letters over a period of months. In my depression and desperation I'd clearly misread their responses. I'd wanted it to be a hunger strike by us all and so had stubbornly convinced myself that everybody had agreed.

Now there was no point in continuing. I lay there for a few hours, trying to decide what to do. Dr Cooper had explained in gruesome detail what was ahead if I continued: convulsions, blindness, and an agonising death. I felt I had the inner strength to go through with it, but what was the point? I was on my own, and the strike's aim of getting widespread publicity had clearly been a massive failure. It was all over, and I knew it. Eventually I turned to the screw in my room and told him, 'Chief, I'm off the hunger strike.'

He asked if I wanted some food straight away. I said I did, and when he told me what was available I said I'd have a chicken and mushroom pie, mashed potato, carrots and cabbage. The screws and Dr Cooper all laughed.

'You can't have that – you'll kill yourself,' they said.

'Listen,' I told them. 'I'm bloody starving. Now get me some food and make it quick.'

Despite their fears, I wolfed down the meal and suffered no ill effects. I regained my strength quite quickly, although I never put back all the weight I had lost. I was kept in the hospital wing for a week for observation, and was planning to string it out for longer if possible. The food was better than back at Albany, and it was generally a cushier life. But at the end of the week I was out in the exercise yard when something happened that made me decide to get back to the 'normal' cons as soon as possible.

I was walking around the yard when I saw two guys having a go at each other by an empty pond. Beside the pond stood an old, dead tree. The pond had once contained goldfish and had been meant as an attractive diversion for those in the hospital wing. But prison folklore had it that the infamous poisoner Graham Young had put something in the water while he had been there. All the fish had died, and after that the pond was drained, never to be refilled.

I went over to the two guys and one, pointing to the other in a rage, told me: 'He's trying to talk to my fish, Paddy Joe. Look at it, it's a lovely fish and I don't want him talking to it.'

I looked into the empty pond and felt it diplomatic to agree it was indeed a lovely fish. As I did so the other guy grabbed me and, pointing to the old tree, shouted: 'Well, he's trying to talk to my bird up there. He shouldn't do that.'

I looked at the old tree, which didn't boast a leaf, never mind a bird, and agreed the other guy shouldn't really talk to it. Then I quickly went back inside and told the doctor I was well enough to return to my own wing.

Not long after ending the hunger strike I was told unofficially I would probably be moved back closer to my parents and kids. In the first week of February 1982 I was moved to Gartree Prison in Leicestershire.

The anger and bitterness I felt each and every day in prison had always caused me to kick against the system, but I moved into a different phase altogether in Gartree. The legal process had run its course, and our campaign was getting nowhere. I had stopped writing letters about our case because nobody was taking any notice. Hope was the one thing that had kept me going for the past eight long years, but now there was very little left. I had no incentive to be a well-behaved prisoner serving his time, because no time would be taken off my sentence for good behaviour. I was never going to get parole, because you cannot be considered until you have admitted your guilt and I was never going to do that. I'd been told bluntly that I was going to die in prison. This all combined to leave me in a permanent state of rebellion. I had nothing to lose by letting my frustration boil over in moments of madness every now and then.

There was one spectacular occasion when I went on the rampage and smashed up a workshop. I used to work sewing mailbags and at the time the wages were about £3 a week. The governor withheld my wages one week as a fine for some breach of prison pettiness. So the following day when I went to the workshop I knew exactly what I was going to do. I got hold of a big hammer and went berserk. I started at the bottom of the shop smashing the sewing machines to pieces, one after another, as I worked my way forward. The other cons just stood aside, cheering and egging me on. The screws in the workshop were terrified. They sounded the alarm and fled to await reinforcements. Each time I battered the hammer down on a machine I felt a burst of relief, as though the frustration and desperation coiled up inside me were being released a little at a time.

Eventually a squad of screws in riot gear rushed in. The first one in saw me swinging away with the hammer and shouted in despair, 'Oh no, it's Hill.'

There wasn't a lot they could do by then, and after demolishing the last machine I handed over the hammer saying, 'Tell the governor this lot's going to cost a lot more than £3.' The consequences never bothered me. If you're already serving twenty-one life sentences, what more can they do?

There is a catch-all section of Rule 43, the one entitled 'Good Order and Discipline', which can be applied to just about any activity the prison authorities dislike. There were wide-ranging penalties under this section such as being sent to the block, being fined, being banned from smoking, and losing remission. That last one of course meant nothing to me. I fell foul of Rule 43 on countless occasions. Once we were given meat pies for dinner and they were clearly bad, resulting in many of the lads being sick. I held on to mine after the first bite and let it be known I was going to send it off to the public health people to see if it was fit for human consumption. Result? Twenty-eight days on the block on 'good order and discipline'. On another occasion I was watching a couple of cons having a fight when some screws arrived to break it up. But one of them decided to take a swing at one of the lads involved. I made a dive for him and had to be held back by other screws. Result? Up before the governor next day on Rule 43 and given fourteen days on the block.

While I was always prepared to buck the system by giving prison officers a hard time, I was not averse to using it for my own ends. One such case occurred when I sued the governor of Gartree for loss of earnings.

I was influenced by the spectacular success of another con who had sued the governor for 50p, the price of a piece of salami he had ordered at the prison shop. He did not receive it, but found the 50p had been deducted from his account. When he complained he was told somebody else must have used his name to obtain the salami, and that there was nothing he could do. But he was not prepared to accept that, and sued the governor for return of the 50p. Amazingly he won – and the icing on the cake was that he got a small award of damages too.

Encouraged by such audacity I decided to sue the governor when he docked my wages by £2.16. My job at the time was cleaning machines in the workshop. The lads working the machines had a row with the screws over something or other, and the result was they went on strike for a couple of days, leaving me with nothing to do through no fault of my own. So when I realised I had been penalised I decided to write to the local court for the relevant papers to sue. I was then able to have served on the governor a summons which read as follows:

> Breach of contract resulting in financial loss of £2.16. The plaintiff's claim against you is that Mr Hill works five days per week for a wage of £4.58. In the week in question Mr Hill attended his place of work in accordance with his employment obligations as a maintenance man. In view of there being no reason directly relating to Mr Hill for having his wages reduced, the said reduction was illegal since it is a breach of contract. In the event of the court giving Mr Hill judgment he asks for redress, plus whatever damages the court deems right.

The case was heard in Leicester Magistrates' Court, and on the day I had to be taken there with all the usual rigmarole surrounding the transportation of a top-security prisoner: screws, cops and police outriders on motorbikes. God knows what the magistrate thought when he found himself confronted by one of the infamous Birmingham pub bombers suing the prison governor for the mighty sum of £2.16. It was not a long hearing and proved to be yet another in the string of court actions that went against me. The magistrate was not impressed with my argument. I lost the case – but it was a wonderful day out!

It was in April 1982 that Pat finally told me she wanted a divorce. I had not seen her since December 1980 and she had not written, but I had kept in touch through the kids. Tracey had quickly dropped the idea of joining the army and we soon healed our little rift. I would send a letter to her and to Michelle regularly, and each time insert two other letters in each of their envelopes, for Maxine, Sharon, Nicola and Sean. As well as the letters, I would see them on occasional visits. During one of those one of the older girls told me that Pat wanted to come in and see me, but did not explain why. They had already broken the news to me that she was seeing another man. That hurt, but it had not come as a great surprise. From my first days in prison I had seen other men crack up on being told their wife was seeing somebody else. I had decided long beforehand that I would condition myself to make sure I did not fall apart when the moment came for me.

The visit was in a small room with Pat and I sitting at a table with a couple of the kids, and a screw sitting in the corner listening to everything. We were trying to make conversation, but it was difficult as Pat was nervous and obviously had something important to say, but did not know how to begin. Eventually I just told her to come out with whatever was bothering her.

'I want a divorce,' she said.

I had known for years this day was coming, but it was no less of a blow for all that. I just sat rigid in my chair. The screw gave a cough, then got up and left the room, saying he would be back in a while. When I eventually recovered I told her there was nothing I could do if that was what she wanted, and that I would not stand in her way. But I told her to tell her new man that the children were mine, and he was always to remember that.

There was not much else to say after that, and Pat and the kids left. I went back to my cell and fell further into depression. Most of that summer passed in a blur, which I spent almost entirely on the block for causing trouble. Argentina invaded the Falklands and was then forced to surrender to the British Task Force; Israel invaded the Lebanon; the IRA murdered two guardsmen and seven of their horses in a bombing in London's Hyde Park; and Italy beat West Germany 3–1 in the World Cup final. It all meant very little to me.

Then on 3 September, our sixteenth wedding anniversary, Pat came to visit again. She brought a beautiful card, and told me she had changed her mind and did not want a divorce after all. I was delighted, but at the back of my mind was a feeling that it didn't make sense. I knew she must have gone through a lot of turmoil before deciding to ask for a divorce, and suspected this might just be a gesture of a mixed-up mind. A month or so later the kids came to see me and told me Pat would not be coming again.

One day shortly after that, just after midday, a screw came to my cell door and handed me a long brown envelope which had been opened and read by the prison censor. As he gave it to me the screw had a look of genuine sadness and said: 'I'm sorry Paddy. As if you don't have enough to cope with.'

He left and I stood in the middle of the cell, pulling out the contents of the package. It was the divorce papers, with Pat's statement explaining how her husband was serving twenty-one life sentences for murder and she wanted to remarry. As I read through it the tears splashed down and smeared the ink of the signatures. I went cold inside and the warmth has never returned.

Towards the end of 1982 I was at my lowest point in the eight years in which I had been locked up. I was considering another hunger strike. There seemed to be nothing left to live for, so this time I would go all the way and finally leave prison in a style that would stick two fingers up to the world.

Then I met a young guy in the jail from Derry called Shane Doherty. He had been jailed for life at the Old Bailey in 1976 for masterminding the IRA's letter-bombing campaign in the early 1970s. By the time I met him he had left the IRA and renouncing its violence with the words 'I was a hypocrite. In injuring human beings I did not cure injustices, I created new ones.'

He had studied a great deal in prison and was a great one for writing. He knew the depression I was in, but ridiculed the hunger strike idea and said I had to pick up my pen and start writing again. Not just a few letters a week, but dozens. He drafted out a letter for me, explaining I was unlikely to get anywhere by simply scrawling that I was innocent and littering the note with obscenities about the police and the courts. It had to be clear and brief, but with enough detail to attract the attention of the person receiving it. I didn't feel like starting up again, but he was insistent. I wrote out my first, to one of the papers, and showed it to him. He made a few corrections and suggested a few changes. I rewrote it and sent it off. It wasn't published, but Shane's enthusiasm for my cause was infectious. With his help I began firing off letters to all sorts of people and to papers, magazines, radio and television stations.

I started to feel I had something to keep me going once more. But I knew from the experience of the previous eight years I would need a person on the outside with more expertise than our little campaign group to champion the cause. Then Shane told me about his solicitor, a woman called Gareth Peirce. She had worked in the media, had dealt with unpopular cases, and had a lot of contacts.

'And there's another thing,' said Shane. 'She's the best lawyer in the country.'

# 23

# The campaign

One winter's afternoon at the end of 1982 I was escorted to the visiting room at Gartree to meet a timid-looking woman dressed in a heavy, dark coat and carrying a bulky briefcase stuffed with papers. She was Gareth Peirce. I had written to her after Shane had told her about me. I had asked her to come to see me and she had fixed a visit within weeks, which impressed me enormously. But without even thanking her for that I came straight to the point.

'I don't need your legal skills,' were my first words to her. 'What I need is somebody out there who knows how things work, who knows about getting publicity as well as legal matters. You might be a great lawyer, but I need you to be a lot more than that.'

She knew what I meant, that a high-profile campaign would have to go hand in hand with legal work on the road to freedom. She had clearly done her homework. She knew all about the case, but nevertheless wanted to hear about it right from the start in my own words. She didn't waste any time on sympathy, but was brisk and businesslike, knowing that in a mere two-hour visit there is little time for pleasantries.

I explained everything I had done over the years, showing her all the papers and records I had kept. I had a book in which I had recorded the details of every letter I had sent – to whom, the date, the contents and what reply, if any, there had been. She could see there were a lot of blank spaces in the replies column.

'It's hard trying to get people involved when you're writing from a prison cell,' I told her. 'It makes it too easy for people just to ignore you or fob you off. That's why I need the right sort of person on the outside.' I asked her what she had done in the past, and she explained she had spent the 1960s in America as a journalist on a New York newspaper. She had got actively involved in the civil rights campaign there, and had finally decided she wanted to become a defence lawyer. So she returned to Britain to train as a solicitor, and shortly afterwards became involved with a landmark legal case. Two men, Cooper and McMahon, had been wrongly jailed for a post office robbery. The case was referred back to the Appeal Court over and over again, but every time the judges refused to accept the new evidence. Eventually the Home Secretary overruled the judges and ordered the men to be freed. After going through all of this Gareth said she hoped I realised the enormity of the task ahead, and I sat back in my chair and laughed. I told her I was under no illusions – eight years of battering my head against brick walls had seen to that. Then she said she would be willing to work for me. It was not a spectacular moment. I had known from the first few minutes with her that this was a woman who relished the challenge of fighting injustice, that she would not just walk away. But there was something else I had to make clear.

'I hope you realise that it's not just me,' I said. 'If you take me on, you're really acting for all six of us. We all stand or fall together.'

She understood that. And, of course, the fact that as I had no sort of appeal pending, there was no way of obtaining legal aid to pay for her services. She would be working for nothing. After a few words of encouragement to continue with my letter writing she was gone. I was taken back to my wing by the screws, and as I walked along I felt like skipping with joy. This, I thought, is a woman who is going to get things done.

Back in my cell I launched, with renewed vigour, into a phenomenal letters campaign. I wrote to everybody I could think of who might be able to help in any way. I fired letters off to practically every MP and lord in the country, to the media, to human rights bodies, to churchmen. By now Hughie was in Gartree with me, and I badgered him into writing too. I got in touch with the other lads at their various jails and urged them to join in, but by then they had pretty much given up hope. I religiously kept my log of letters sent, so that there would be no duplication and so that I could keep track of any responses. On some days I was sending a dozen letters, complete with photocopies of relevant material on the case. It cost a lot of money, and I have to thank my family and friends for providing it, as well as my friends in prison who often helped out.

Once again, few people had the decency to reply. Those who did normally fell into two categories, saying either that there was nothing they could do, or that I should write to the MP whose constituency covered Gartree. He was Sir John Farr, who I believed to be an ultra-conservative member of the Tory party, so I had little in the way of hope or expectation when I stuck the stamp on the envelope addressed to him.

I wrote to the Prison Reform Trust and received a reply from the director, Dr Stephen Shaw. The first of the two paragraphs of his brief response read thus:

I have been aware for some time of the dubious nature of the convictions following the Birmingham pub bombings, although I suspect you and your colleagues did have close links with an IRA cell and I suspect too that you are actually aware of who carried out this most appalling crime.

That view had a familiar ring to it. He suggested I write to Justice, the British section of the International Commission of Jurists. They said there was nothing they could do. They replied: 'In a case like yours, so many reputations are at stake that the obstacles to be overcome are insuperable.' Very encouraging.

I wrote to Edward Daly, the Catholic Bishop of Derry, who I had admired since Bloody Sunday in 1972 when television news reports had shown him waving a white handkerchief as he tried to help the dying. He wrote back:

I must confess that at the time I was convinced of your guilt. Now that you have written to me I will take a further interest in it. I would ask you not to build up too many hopes. As you say yourself, it will take a miracle.

I wrote to the Birmingham MP Jill Knight, and was horrified to read in the papers a few days later that a bomb had been discovered under her car. She probably read my letter while still shaking from the shock of that. No wonder she did not reply.

But then came my first real success, when one of my letters was printed in *Tribune*, a publication of the left wing of the Labour Party, which had carried some fairly positive articles over the years about our case and that of the Guildford Four. The editor was a guy called Chris Mullin, who as well as printing the letter wrote back to me saying: 'I regard these cases as probably the most serious miscarriages of justice for many years.' He said he would be willing to see what he could do to help and I put him in touch with Gareth Peirce. A short time later another of my letters was printed in the influential Irish magazine *Magill*. Things were looking up.

And then I heard back from Sir John Farr, the Leicestershire MP whose constituent I now was. He said he wanted to come to see me to discuss the case. He actually sounded as if he was interested. I couldn't believe it. He came in March 1983, but as he walked into the visiting room my heart sank. He was the very picture of a country squire, a stout man with a florid face. I half expected to see a couple of servants follow him in. When he introduced himself he spoke with the accent of a class way above mine. I couldn't see him being much help to a bunch of ordinary men. I wondered whether I had wasted my time in bringing along all my papers on our case. But as he was the first member of what I would call the Establishment who had had the decency to come and see me I was determined not to let my initial impressions colour my judgement of him. I dumped the papers on the table between us and pushed them towards him, saying: 'I don't expect you to believe me just because I say I am innocent. But I would like you to take away all this stuff and read it. When you read it try to put out of your mind any prejudice you may have against convicted men. And after you have read it, if you think I am guilty come back here and tell me so.'

He said he would read it, but pointed out that it was a huge pile of documents and would take time. He wanted to spend a few days going through it all in one go, rather than stopping and starting, so it might be some time before he got back in touch. That was reasonable, and we then went on to talk for some time about my case and my vain struggle for justice. He impressed me as a good, honest man, and by the time he left I had a strong feeling that this was a man who cared.

Shortly after that, Shane was moved to another prison. I missed him and the inspiration he gave me, but we kept in touch through letters. He was a classic example of a decent young man who had got into trouble because of the injustice he had witnessed. He was genuinely sorry for the pain and suffering he had caused, and I was delighted when he finally got his freedom in 1990.

Weeks passed, and then months, without a word from Farr. I decided that my normally sharp sensors for detecting the genuine from frauds had let me down. He was just like the rest. A Tory MP was not going to risk his position by making waves with his own government for a bunch of Irishmen; he was part of the Establishment and its members' first rule was to protect it at all costs.

But there were other developments to make up for the disappointment. Within a month or so of Farr's visit I received a second letter from Bishop Daly, saying he would like to visit me. He had been to see John Walker, who being from Derry was in the bishop's diocese, and said he was now convinced of our innocence. He was a lovely man who completely fitted the heroic image I had held of him since those Bloody Sunday news reports. He brought me some cigarettes and fruit, and we spent more than an hour chatting away, although it was me doing most of the talking, telling him all about our case.

An unexpected chance to proclaim my innocence publicly came after I met Kenneth Littlejohn, the bank robber who claimed to have worked for MI6, and who was the subject of strange evidence at our trial from prosecution witness Tom Watt. He had been released from prison in Ireland in 1981, but within a year was back behind bars, although he had changed his surname to Austen. He was jailed at Nottingham Crown Court for six years for armed robbery on the home of an elderly couple.

He had only been at Gartree a short while before he began pestering me, telling me he was going to write a book about the IRA and wanted me to give him information. I told him I knew nothing about them, except for the fact there were a number of their men in Gartree who would not take kindly to his snooping around. He did not take my advice to back off, and not long afterwards he was attacked by IRA men in the jail who gave him a savage beating. Several of them were charged with serious wounding and I was called as a witness.

When I told Gareth I would be appearing in court she said I should make the most of the opportunity. So when I was questioned about how Littlejohn had approached me in the first place, I made a great song and dance about being one of the Birmingham Six – the name by which we were gradually becoming known. I went on for as long as possible about our being innocent until the lawyers finally shut me up on the grounds that my speech was irrelevant to the case. The outburst won a few paragraphs in a couple of papers, which I saw as something of a success because it meant our case had at least gained some publicity.

The IRA men involved were found guilty and had years added to their already lengthy sentences. One of them, Sean Kinsella, told the court he was the senior IRA man at the prison and took full responsibility for the attack. He said he had ordered it because Littlejohn had been trying to recruit other prisoners to attack the IRA prisoners.

Littlejohn was certainly a weird character whose involvement in a great number of strange affairs has never been explained. I made a point of avoiding him in Gartree.

During the early part of the summer of 1983 the country was obsessed with a general election campaign, which culminated in a landslide second victory for Margaret Thatcher in June. Neil Kinnock became Labour Party leader in October, but political changes made no difference to my plight. I had little faith in politicians being willing or able to help us. Then later that year the governor called me into his office one morning to say he had received a phone call. It had been from Sir John Farr, who wanted to know if I was still at Gartree. On being told I was, he asked the governor to arrange for him to visit me a few days later.

Confident that Farr would give me the same old line I'd heard from so many others about not being able to do anything, I conjured up in my mind beforehand the scene that would be played out in the visiting room. As soon as he handed back my papers saying there was nothing he could do I would tear into him, letting rip with everything I felt about MPs but had never had the chance to say face to face. How they were all the same, hypocrites who were voted into power to help the very constituents they then ignored.

The visiting day came, and sure enough he took my file from under his arm and handed the papers back to me.

'The first thing I want to do is apologise for taking so long,' he said. 'But after reading it all once I was confused and concerned, so I read it again. Then I asked a friend with scientific experience to read the forensic stuff and tell me what he thought. He told me that if he were a lawyer he would seriously question the validity of the forensic evidence, because he didn't think it was worth the paper it was written on. And that is why I am here today. I want you to tell me everything that happened to you.'

It was rare for me to be speechless. But I sat there in silence trying to take in what he had said, feeling guilty that I had too quickly condemned him. Here at last after all these years was someone in a position of influence who wanted to listen. After a minute or so I thanked him for taking such interest. Then, as he had requested, I went through the whole story, with the words rushing out in a torrent. I was jubilant, and the excitement made me rush out the words even faster than normal. By the time I had finished he looked exhausted from just sitting and listening. I stressed that it was not just me who was innocent, but all six of us, and he nodded in agreement. By the time Sir John got up to leave I knew we had a magnificent new supporter and that the meeting had been a milestone in our campaign.

I felt better that Christmas than ever before in jail. Gareth had been visiting me and on one occasion had brought with her Chris Mullin, the *Tribune* editor who had expressed interest in our case. He was like a university professor with his glasses and thinning, windblown hair, but quickly won me over with his belief in our innocence and enthusiasm for our case. He had published a novel the year before, and said he was interested in doing a book about us. I thought that was a great idea, and told him I would do all I could to help. Gareth was starting to draw people in who could help on what I saw as the priority, publicity, while she concentrated her efforts on the legal aspects.

As we turned into 1984 I realised I was beginning my tenth year in prison, but I was prepared for the time ahead with a new optimism. It did not mean I got into trouble with the authorities any less, though. There were still regular clashes which resulted in me being sent to the block several times. Often it served my purposes to be on my own. It meant long spells of peace and quiet in which I could get on with my letters. Sometimes I even went out of my way to get sent to the block, which was not difficult thanks to the petty-mindedness of those in authority and their enthusiasm for punishing the slightest bending of the rules.

I was on the block when early that year came the most memorable moment in all of my time in jail. Back in 1982 I had told my daughter Tracey that I had had a dream in which she had been holding a baby, her baby. She laughed and said, 'It couldn't have been me dad, I'm not going to have any kids.' The next year, when she was seventeen, she came to see me and told me she was pregnant. We had a great laugh about what I had told her earlier, and I asked whether she wanted a boy or a girl. She said she was hoping for a boy, but I told her, 'I'm afraid you're out of luck, because the baby I saw you holding in my dream was a girl.'

One night in February 1984 I got a message from the screws that my daughter had had a baby girl, and that mother and child were fine. I was delighted. I sat down straight away and wrote her a note, congratulating her and adding, 'The dream came true.'

She arranged to come and visit me on 17 March, St Patrick's Day, with the baby and her boyfriend Mick, a young lad whom I had met and liked. Locked up for twenty-three hours a day in the block I found it difficult to concentrate on my letters because of the excitement at the thought of seeing my first grandchild. When the day came I built myself up to fever pitch, ticking off the minutes until 2 p.m., the start of visiting time. Normally before a visit a screw would come for you as soon as it was known your visitor had arrived. But I waited and waited, and nobody came. I began to get edgy, and then angry as it approached 2.30. By 3.00 I was in a rage, cursing Tracey for letting me down. I tore off my fresh T-shirt, ripping it apart and hurling it into the corner. I was about to begin smashing the cell up. And then I heard a screw approaching and the jangle of his keys. I'd got a visit after all.

In a panic I shouted out of my cell window to some lads in the exercise yard. I told them I was off to a visit but hadn't got a shirt. One of them took off his own and hurled it up to my window. As the screw opened the door I was pulling the shirt over my head and ready to go.

I approached the visiting room out of breath and still angry with Tracey for being late. But as soon as I walked in every bit of aggression evaporated. There was my eldest daughter sitting with this gorgeous little bundle in her arms. It was Charmaine, my first grandchild. Tracey stood up and passed the baby over to me. 'Here's your granddaughter, dad,' she said.

For ten years I had known nothing but the coarseness and brutality and filth of prison life. Now here in my arms was the sweetest little thing I'd ever seen. She was tiny, and clean and so innocent-looking. She had a beautiful smell, a smell that I'd never before known in prison, where the permanent odour was of boiled cabbage and cleaning fluid. I sat down in the chair, holding her as if she were some fragile, china doll. I'd missed so much of my own children growing up. And now here was the child of my child. She was the start of a new generation. I poked my finger into her curled-up hands and between her tiny toes. I rocked her gently on my lap. I looked down into her eyes, and then tears came into mine. But they were not the tears I'd cried so often, of sadness, anger and bitterness. They were tears of joy, and pride. It was the happiest moment I'd known in jail.

Outside, the big issue was the national miners' strike. Clashes between pitmen and police were shown almost nightly on the TV news, with the worst coming at the end of May with the Battle of Orgreave. Thousands of men on each side fought each other. There was terrible violence from both sides, but during scenes of cops with sticks beating miners I couldn't resist shouting out to all the other cons and screws in the television room: 'See that, look at what they're doing in front of the TV cameras and the world's press. Imagine what they could do in a room with nobody watching them.'

I met several other men in prison who had been wrongly convicted because of police brutality or lies, and it was in Gartree at this time I got to know Jimmy Robinson and Michael Hickey, who with Michael's cousin Vincent were wrongly convicted of the murder of newsboy Carl Bridgewater in 1978. Michael went on to the roof at Gartree and stayed up for nearly three months in winter to proclaim their innocence, but like us they found all their protests were to no avail.

Gareth, Chris, Sir John and the others were working away on our behalf all the time, but I had no expectation of speedy results. The knowledge that people were at last taking notice was enough to keep me beavering away on my letters. Gareth was keen to get independent scientific experts to examine the Griess test and see if Dr Skuse's results could be challenged. But she soon discovered that it would cost thousands of pounds to have the necessary work carried out. We just did not have that kind of money.

The Los Angeles Olympics were held that summer, with Carl Lewis the sprinter picking up a bundle of gold medals. Then on 12 October came the IRA bombing of the Grand Hotel in Brighton where Mrs Thatcher was staying for the Conservative

Party conference. Every time there was an IRA attack it made life difficult for our slowly growing band of supporters. In the eyes of the vast majority of the public we were IRA bombers, and so there was plenty of hostility towards our faithful campaigners.

November 21 was the tenth anniversary of the pub bombings, and I prayed for all the victims of the blasts. It was not often I prayed at that time, as too many prayers had gone unanswered in the early days. But I prayed in my cell that night, not only for those who had died, but also for the widows, the bereaved parents and all those who had lost loved ones. And I prayed for us six men, and our wives and families, for we were just as surely victims of the bombs that blew those pubs apart.

The following month it was my fortieth birthday. Life begins at forty, so they say. I had nothing to celebrate. My life had stopped at thirty.

In early 1985 Chris Mullin was commissioned by Granada Television's *World In Action* programme to investigate the case. He had some contacts at Granada and had managed to persuade them that ours was a case worth pursuing. Chris and the programme's Charles Tremayne set about tracking down every police officer who had been at Morecambe and Queen's Road stations at the relevant times. They found and spoke to many of them. Of those who were prepared to speak, all kept to the same story they had told years before. Most of those who refused to speak were the West Midlands officers who had taken part in the beatings. Many had by now risen in the force, several to senior posts. Sergeant Buckley, the Morecambe officer who almost provided us with a breakthrough at the trial, had by then retired. He refused two approaches to speak.

The programme makers also had statements from some of the Winson Green prison officers which made it clear we had been beaten before arriving at prison. The statements had been given to defence lawyers in preparation for the 1976 prison officers' trial. *World In Action* interviewed the screws to make sure they stood by them. The statements had never previously been made public.

But the real benefit in getting *World In Action* interested was that they had the money to conduct their own forensic tests. Gareth was ecstatic. The television team got two top scientists to carry out the Griess test on a range of everyday substances. The scientists contacted

Dr Skuse beforehand to make sure they conducted the tests in exactly the same way he had. They discovered that a range of products that contained harmless nitrocellulose, not nitroglycerine, also gave a positive response to the Griess test. The defence scientist at our trial, Dr Black, had been right all along. Such products included varnish and the coating used on some cigarette packets and postcards.

Then came the most dramatic moment of all. One of the *World In Action* team, Ian McBride, shuffled a pack of cards for five minutes and then had his hands swabbed and Griess-tested. The result was positive.

For all those years I had been absolutely mystified as to how I could have tested positive for explosives. One of the few truthful things Sergeant Bennett had told the court was that in an early interview, when asked how I had got nitroglycerine on my hands, I had replied: 'I don't know. Honest to God, I don't know.' Now it was clear there were all sorts of things I might have touched which could have given rise to that positive Griess test. I've no idea what it was, but I do know we played cards for hours on the train to Heysham that night. I know that the cards had been kept by the police as evidence. And I know that when we went back to the police in 1985 to ask for the cards so that they could be tested, we were told they had been lost.

The *World In Action* programme went out on 28 October 1985. It was a momentous occasion in the campaign. I did not see it on the night it was screened because it was after 'banging-up' time. But we had been allowed to set the video in the television room and myself, Hughie and a big group of inmates went in to see it in the morning. The programme particularly concentrated on the forensic case against us. While I had known generally what they had been doing because the television team kept me informed, I had not understood fully the ins and outs of the experiments they had conducted.

Suddenly it all became perfectly clear. When the Griess test sample from McBride's hand turned pink I just let out one hell of a scream which came from deep within me, a mixture of anger and joy and frustration.

'We've got the bastards,' I cried. 'At last, we've got them.'

The programme interviewed Roy Jenkins, who had been Home Secretary at the time of the bombings. He said the evidence the team had produced created 'a lurking doubt as to whether the convictions in these cases were safe'. He believed the matter should be referred back to the Court of Appeal.

Also interviewed was Joe Cahill, who had been a top IRA man at the time of the pub bombs. He made the first public admission that the IRA had been responsible. And he added, 'The volunteers who did carry out those operations are freely walking about today.'

My voice was featured several times in the programme, on a tape I had managed at some risk to smuggle out of the prison, saying: 'I am serving twenty-one life sentences for nothing. It was something I don't even know anything about. The prospect of my ever being released is very, very slim. In fact, we are all condemned to die in prison.'

As the programme ended I was close to tears; it felt as though all the years of writing letters and begging people to just listen was beginning to pay off. The rest of the cons were going mad, whistling and cheering and slapping me and Hughie on the back. All of them seemed to be shouting at the same time: 'That's it now Paddy. You'll be out by the New Year. They can't keep you now.'

The next day Sir John Farr presented a copy of all the new evidence to the Home Office with a demand the case be reopened. Everything had been passed to Gareth as it was discovered so that she could build it all into a legal case. The government announced that the Devon and Cornwall police force had been asked to conduct an inquiry into the allegations of brutality the *World In Action* special had raised. Three days after the programme, Dr Skuse, then only fifty, took early retirement as a Home Office scientist. More than a year later, on December 18th 1986, Home Office Minister David Mellor told Parliament: 'In relation to the position of Dr Skuse, it is right – and we have always made this clear – that he was retired on grounds of limited efficiency. However, it must be said, that was limited efficiency at the time he was retired, not limited efficiency in 1975.'

The programme was a watershed, for now much of the press, particularly the quality papers, were prepared to cover the story. Sir John's involvement gave vital credibility to our campaign. Many Labour MPs had started to give us support, and I was grateful for it. But while the government and tabloid press labelled them as 'loony lefties', they could not so easily dismiss such a dyed-in-the-wool Tory as Sir John.

Our case was raised several times in Parliament. Home Office Minister David Mellor was forced to concede that in Long Lartin jail John Walker, the alleged 'brigadier' who was said to be the brains behind the operation, was subject to few of the restrictions applied to every other IRA man there. Mellor did not explain why this should be. But the other five of us knew very well why. We were being treated in the same way as John, totally differently from IRA men, because the prison authorities knew we were innocent.

Now, at last, the Irish government was also taking an interest, although only under pressure from public opinion and interested members of the Dublin parliament such as Neil Blaney, David Andrews and Tony Gregory. Even so, the official Irish support was far from wholehearted. In March 1986 I had my second visit in twelve years of imprisonment from an official of the Irish embassy. It was a little more encouraging than the first. At least this time the official knew our names. The Irish ambassador in Washington, Sean Donlon, appeared to be trying to clamp down on our growing support in America when he sent a letter to Congressman Hamilton Fish. It appeared to discredit Father Ray Murray, who as joint author of *The Birmingham Framework* was a leading campaigner, as an IRA supporter. The Dublin government denied it had tried to smear Father Murray, but news of the letter caused uproar in the Irish parliament.

Chris Mullin meanwhile had been doing a lot of work. He came to see me and said he felt one of the best ways of proving we six had not carried out the bombings was to track down the real bombers. I thought he was mad, and told him so. He said he had already spoken to several of the people who were in the Birmingham IRA at the time, and he was going to go to Ireland to speak to others there.

I felt he was courageous, but a bit naïve, and told him, 'You do realise this could get very dangerous. These people don't play games. If you go poking your nose around Belfast or Dublin asking questions, especially with your English accent, you could get into serious trouble.'

He knew it was risky, but went ahead. I thought it was remarkable of him to stick his neck out for us in such a way. He got to see some people in Ireland, and by a process of elimination over several months he knew there were just a handful of key figures he needed to interview. But he finally found himself getting nowhere and returned to see me again, asking if there was anything I could do.

I knew the only way I could help was through the IRA men in Gartree with me. I went to see them and said: 'You've got to help this man Mullin. We're in prison because of what you guys have done. Surely you at least owe it to us to help us get out? You've got to put him in touch with the right people, and you've got to make sure nothing happens to him over there.'

A few weeks later one of the IRA men approached me. He said there had been a lot of discussions, not just at Gartree but in other prisons and outside. They had decided to give Chris a telephone number and he would have to take it from there. I was not to ask for any further help. Chris got the message and made several more visits to Ireland over the following months.

So much was happening in 1985 in terms of our case that I had little time to take notice of major events that year. President Gorbachev became leader of the Soviet Union and began his programme of reforms; Liverpool soccer fans were involved in a riot at the European Cup Final at Heysel stadium in which more than forty people died; and an IRA plot to bomb British seaside resorts was uncovered. The only development I paid attention to was the signing of the Anglo-Irish Agreement in November between Mrs Thatcher and the Irish prime minister, Garret FitzGerald. I saw it as a possible way to have our case raised at a political level if we could only get the Irish government interested.

In July 1986 Chris Mullin published his magnificent book *Error of Judgement*, which went even further than the demolition of the case against us by the *World in Action* television programme. He had tracked down some of the IRA team responsible for the pub bombings, including one of the two men who had planted the bombs. None of those he spoke to had ever heard of us before our arrests. He would not identify those involved, but he said several had been known to the police as IRA suspects and had actually been questioned but released after the bombings.

All of these developments caused the climate to change considerably, and I felt it was time for a renewed round of letters, particularly to the press. Now I discovered several were being printed rather than dumped in the bin. The standard letter I wrote began as follows:

I am Paddy Hill, one of the six innocent Irishmen who were tortured and framed for the Birmingham pub bombings of 1974. Since then we have been trying to get people to listen to us. We do not expect everyone to support us when we say we are innocent. What we do expect is that we be given a chance to prove that we are innocent.

I would go on to say how I was prepared to take a lie-detector test, undergo hypnosis or be given a truth drug, and then be questioned about that day in 1974. I challenged those cops who had beaten us to take similar tests.

In October 1986 Hughie and I achieved a minor sensation when, as a result of our letters, the *Birmingham Post* devoted two full pages to our case, detailing the case for and against us. It was a great victory in that it was the first time the paper in our city, the city where the bombs went off, was prepared to give us space to put our case. An editorial accompanying the piece called for an inquiry to be held, and copies of the paper were sent to every MP in Britain.

Shortly after it appeared Chris Mullin had a letter published in the *Post*, congratulating it for the article and urging any former or serving cops who might be able to help with his investigation to contact him. A few days later he had an approach. Tom Clarke had been in Queen's Road police station while we were there. He was later sacked from the force for stealing £5 from a prisoner and spent two months in jail, and so was not the best of witnesses. But he confirmed many of our claims about the way we had been treated. Preparation of another *World In Action* programme got underway.

At about this time Pat, who was now my ex-wife, came back on the scene. She had remarried in 1983, but there had never been any bitterness between us. I even sent them a card for their wedding, wishing them the best of luck. Pat arranged a visit because of a problem with one of our daughters, and I was pleased to see her when she arrived at Gartree. I knew there was never any question of us getting back together, but we both realised we had to keep in touch at some level because of the kids. We had a good long chat, and after that Pat would write a letter now and then and occasionally visit.

Bishop Daly of Derry had become an active campaigner on our behalf. He issued a statement:

I have no doubt these men are completely innocent, and I partially base that belief on almost thirty years' experience of visiting men in prisons. During that period I have corresponded with and visited hundreds of prisoners and you quickly develop a way of sorting out the genuinely innocent. These men should be released immediately.

We had a London campaign group led by people such as Paul May and Sally Mulready, while Father Joe Taaffe was spearheading the group in Birmingham. Father Bobby Gilmore, who was head of the Irish Chaplaincy scheme in Britain and was to become chairman of our national campaign, told the press, 'Foreign countries set their standards of justice against the British system. It's incredible to quote British justice when you have these mistakes. I believe it would benefit justice worldwide if the mistakes were admitted.'

As the *World in Action* team pushed ahead on their second programme, the authorities tried to throw another spanner in the works. The Home Office had carried out a detailed investigation into the Griess tests shown on the first programme. Now, more than a year later, it suddenly claimed the television tests were invalid because of a mistake in the recipe of the chemicals used by the programme makers, even though it had been supplied by government scientists. They claimed Skuse had actually used a different recipe, despite the fact that the one used by *World in Action* was that given by Skuse to our Dr Black at the time of the trial and never before disputed. The new recipe, they said, would indeed give a positive result only for nitroglycerine.

*World in Action* demolished that nonsense with a powerful new programme which went out on 1 December 1986. They reinterviewed Dr David Baldock, a former Home Office forensic scientist, who had conducted the tests for the first programme. He said: 'I think they are clutching at straws to avoid reopening the whole case. I specifically wrote to the Home Office to ask them what recipe was in use at the time in order to avoid exactly the situation we're now in. They're throwing up a smokescreen to avoid having the case reopened.'

*World in Action* also interviewed at length the ex-policeman Tom Clarke. Of the attitude among the cops at Queen's Road police station after our arrest he said: 'Everybody was over the moon, delighted.

Every police officer throughout the country believed that they were guilty.'

That was why he had gone along with the way we had been treated, the guns and the dogs and the lack of sleep, even though he knew it was wrong. 'I think the object was to get them as tired as possible, to get them at their lowest ebb,' he said. 'We were told there were instructions not to let the prisoners sleep at all. I've never seen men so frightened in my life. They were petrified.'

It all finally proved too much for the government. On the afternoon of 20 January 1987, Home Secretary Douglas Hurd rose to address a packed House of Commons. He told MPs: 'I have examined all the material with great care. I am satisfied that there is new evidence to justify my returning this case to the Court of Appeal.'

# 24

## Back to court

As Douglas Hurd was making his announcement to the House of Commons I was being taken to the less glamorous setting of the governor's office at Gartree Prison to be given the news.

I had known the pressure of our campaign meant a return to the courts was inevitable. But it was nevertheless one hell of a feeling when I was told. I punched the air and yelled in celebration. The screws told me to calm down as they escorted me back to the workshop from which I'd been taken. As I walked in there was a hush and everybody looked towards me. The cons all knew an appeal was possible. But rejection was not out of the question. I broke into a wide grin and shouted out at the top of my voice: 'Yeeeeeeeesssss!'

The lads in the workshop went crazy, screaming and shouting and banging on the machines. When you are in prison, good news such as mine gives everybody a boost.

The grounds on which Hurd had referred the case were new evidence relating to the forensic evidence presented at our trial and Tom Clarke's allegations. In addition, he had instructed the Devon and Cornwall police force to investigate Clarke's claims. The only bad news of the day was that Hurd refused to reopen the case of the Guildford Four. I had already met one of them, Paul Hill, years earlier, and another, Paddy Armstrong, was in Gartree with me. I knew and liked him, and felt sorry for him that their case had been knocked back.

I knew it would be months before we would actually get back to court, but there was plenty to do in the meantime. Out came the pen and paper again as I wrote off to influential people, not just in Britain, but in Europe and America too. I wanted to get as many big names as possible along to our appeal because I was not at all confident, despite the new evidence, that we would win. We had gone down for life at Lancaster without an outside voice raised in dissent. I was determined that if we lost this time there would be observers from around the world to see what British justice was doing to us.

By now there was a big campaign for us in the United States, which had started in a small way a few years before. Sister Sarah Clarke had been contacted by an American woman, Kathleen Lisowski, who had heard about us and wanted to help. Over the years Kathleen was responsible for bringing our plight to the attention of all sorts of people. She highlighted the fact that the Irish government was doing nothing to help us, and managed to bring aboard the force of the powerful Irish-American political lobby. She enlisted the support of Mayor Ray Flynn of Boston; William Bolger, who was then serving as Governor of Massachusetts; members of the Kennedy family; Senator Fran Doris; Congressman Brian Donnelly; Tip O'Neill, the Speaker of the House of Representatives; and many, many more. There was also intensive lobbying within the European Community. Christine Crawley, who was a European Member of Parliament for Birmingham, came to visit me after I wrote to her. She later successfully proposed a resolution in the European Parliament that the British government should reconsider our case.

There was going to be another significant difference this time around in court. We now had a great legal team, led by Lord Gifford QC, Michael Mansfield QC, and Richard Ferguson QC, who was an Ulster Protestant and a former Unionist member of the disbanded Stormont parliament for Northern Ireland. It was ironic that a man of his background should be working so strongly on behalf of six Irish Catholics. These barristers were well used to tackling the most difficult of cases, particularly ones which proved embarrassing for the authorities. Gareth Peirce was now acting as solicitor to four of us, Gerry and Richard having decided to stick with the lawyers they'd had for some years. But there was a lot of co-operation between the legal teams.

As we were all going to stand or fall as one we had to be brought together to work on the case. So in February 1987 Hughie and I were taken to Long Lartin and placed on A-wing. John was there, now looking very old and having problems with stomach ulcers. The next day Gerry arrived from Wakefield and was put on C-wing. Then they brought Richard and Billy from Wormwood Scrubs in

London, and put them on F-wing. We all got to meet the following day at the entrance lobby to our wing.

It was an emotional moment, the first time the six of us had been together since being convicted at Lancaster. I had not seen Gerry or John since 1981; Billy since 1976; and Richard since we were in Bristol together straight after the trial, other than a glimpse at the prison officers' trial. We had not been close friends when we went down, but now we felt like brothers, bound together in a common cause.

We just stood there for a while, shaking hands and slapping each other's backs. I felt choked up seeing them all again, but we were soon back into our old ways of slagging each other and cracking jokes.

'Hey John,' I shouted out. 'You're meant to be the brigadier and in charge. Where's the tea?'

A few days after that Gareth came to see us and we got down to a lot of hard work on the case. We were given one of the prison classrooms to meet in for a couple of hours each day, and for several weeks we went over the papers of the case. The barristers came to see us for the first time and their enthusiasm and confidence gave us a great boost.

It was at that time in Long Lartin that I met Gerry Conlon, one of the Guildford Four, whose own bid for a return to the appeal court had been rejected. We took to each other on meeting for the first time, but I couldn't help feeling a little sad that we were going back to court while this young lad had had his hopes dashed. I told him that if we six were released, we'd do everything we could to ensure they got their freedom too.

At the end of March we had our first meeting with a delegation of members of the Irish parliament, who came with some staff from the Irish embassy. Some of them, particularly David Andrews, had been working hard on our behalf, but I had been angry for years with the lack of help generally from the Irish government. By now there was massive public support in Ireland for our case, with huge interest in the media, and I felt the government was only acting because of that. I told them to go back home with the message that it was time for the Dublin government to declare publicly its full backing for us. The meeting lasted only about thirty minutes and then they said they had to go.

I was astonished. 'What about other innocent Irishmen in this prison? Aren't you going to see them?' I asked. I told them that Gerry

Conlon was there, and that it was disgraceful they were planning to head off home without having the decency to see him. I told them I would start wrecking the visiting room unless they saw him. They knew I meant it and eventually relented, and Gerry was called up to see them after we left.

The six of us were together for several weeks until we had done as much as we could on the case, and then some of us were returned to our own jails. I went back to Gartree, but Hughie stayed on at Lartin. Then we were all brought together again in October at the Scrubs to await the appeal. Britain had its so-called 'storm of the century' that month when a hurricane swept across the South-east. Stuck inside the formidable fortress of Wormwood Scrubs the weather meant little to me. But as a keen punter on the horses I was much more interested at the end of the month when the great jockey Lester Piggott was jailed for three years for tax evasion. Much as I would have loved to have met him, there was no chance he would end up in a maximum security jail.

It had been announced that the Lord Chief Justice himself, Lord Lane, would preside over the appeal and I saw that as a bad omen. I was not too impressed with his track record on other cases, many of which I had studied over the years in the hope of finding something relevant to our own circumstances. I also felt that as head of the judiciary he would not take kindly to having a case referred back to the courts by politicians. Judges like to think they have a monopoly on the ability to get things right, and get upset at anything they feel could be classed as interference in their affairs.

But despite that I still had that glimmer of hope that perhaps this time the judges would do the decent thing and let us go home. I knew the only way we could possibly lose was for all six of us to be again dismissed as liars, and for the issue of the forensic evidence to be completely ignored. If Lane and the two judges sitting with him were to do that, there would surely be a storm of protest, not just in Britain, but across the world. Observers from around the globe were making arrangements to attend.

The appeal opened in court 12 of the Old Bailey on 2 November 1987. We were brought to court with all the usual security precautions of armed cops, dogs, vans and motorbikes. There was a rigorous security check for all those entering the public gallery, with people having to give their names and addresses and be searched. Most of them were our families and friends, and I have no doubt the procedure was designed just to give them a hard time. For everybody in authority knew by now we six were no more of a security threat than kids who pinched apples.

The courtroom had none of the judicial majesty of Lancaster. It was a modern, compact arena with us in the dock at the back of the court opposite the three judges. The lawyers all sat in their finery in the middle, with the press bench to the left of us and beside that the jury box, which had been set aside for observers. In the coming weeks they would include Chris Mullin, who by now had been elected an MP, Sir John Farr MP, a delegation from the European Parliament, other British, Irish and American politicians, Bishop Daly of Derry, the Cardinal of Ireland Tomás O Fiaich, observers from the Vatican, the Soviet Union and Amnesty International, and the author and broadcaster Ludovic Kennedy.

The public gallery was up above us, to our right. As we were brought into court, a few minutes before the judges, the place went mad. There were cheers and waves from our families in the gallery, and the observers poured out of their seats to greet us and shake hands. The same thing happened at the end of the day, after the judges had left the courtroom. Lord Lane got to hear of it and ordered that in future, to avoid such scenes which tarnished the dignity of his courtroom, we would be brought in last and taken out first.

It was the first time we had been seen together in public for thirteen years. And how different we looked from the pictures taken while we had been in police custody, those staring, vacant faces that seemed to reinforce public opinion that we were indeed a gang of heartless bombers. We were all neat and tidy in collar and tie and suit, Billy with his hair now almost white, Hughie and John having the appearance of benevolent grandfathers, Richard earnest in his gold-rimmed spectacles; and Gerry and myself looking quite dapper.

The rosy-cheeked Lord Lane presided in his half-moon glasses, flanked by the bulky Lord Justice O'Connor and the pinched face of Lord Justice Stephen Brown. The Crown case was led by Igor Judge QC, who had acted for the prosecution in the infamous Carl Bridgewater trial.

When the case began a hush fell over the courtroom; the atmosphere seemed to suggest that all those present might be about to

216

witness historic events. Mr Mansfield began with our application for a retrial. He said the central issues of the case would not be affected by the fact there had been a lengthy gap since the original trial.

'Thirteen years have not tarnished the ability of people to remember what happened in various police stations at the time. The material is still ripe for jury trial.'

The judges ruled that a retrial was 'not appropriate', and the appeal proper began with a lengthy opening speech by Lord Gifford outlining our case. In it he said the original forensic and confessions evidence was now so flawed that the question had to be asked whether we were just as much victims of the pub bombings as those who died, were injured, and were bereaved. 'If that is so, the miscarriage of justice will have been one of the gravest in recent times,' he said.

His speech spilled over into the second day and contained a wealth of interesting information, much of it a surprise to us. There was for instance the fact that two thousand witness statements taken by the police at the time of the bombings had, contrary to normal procedure, never been given to the defence. It may be that there was nothing in them that would have helped anyway. But our original lawyers should have been given an opportunity to study them. Now they could not be found.

Several new witnesses were presented to the court. There was Bill Bailey, who had been head cleaner at Morecambe police station when we were held there. He testified that the cells area had been declared out of bounds to him on that Friday, and it was the following Monday afternoon before he could gain access. He found blood on the walls and door of one of the cells. 'I saw this blood, and I had not seen anything like it before during my five years of cleaning the cells out,' he said. 'I did not comment on it. I did not concern myself with police business.'

An ex-policeman, John Berry, told how he had gone to Queen's Road station on the Friday night on a routine inquiry. In the cell block he saw a man he understood to be one of the pub bombers. The man had a swollen eye and lips. Two Winson Green prison officers testified we had injuries when admitted to the prison on the Monday morning. It was the first time any court had heard such witnesses.

Despite the impression this sort of evidence would make on an unbiased listener, I knew after the first few days that we had little chance of success. My initial fears about the attitude the Lord Chief

Justice and his colleagues might take was justified again and again. They seemed angry at even having to hear the case, as though they saw the Home Secretary's referral as a slight on the entire judiciary, which I suppose it was. Certainly the man who had sent us down for life, by now Lord Bridge, was one of their esteemed brothers on the bench.

There was a palpable atmosphere of enmity towards our legal team. Almost every time the judges spoke to our barristers it was with a dismissive or wearisome tone, and sometimes outright hostility. Our witnesses were treated in a manner bordering on contempt, while the learned judges bent over backwards to help Crown witnesses out of the sticky situations in which they frequently found themselves.

Essentially the appeal hinged on the evidence of just a handful of people, and once again on the two issues of confessions and forensics, in both of which I had a key part.

The Devon and Cornwall inquiry had discovered a document which came to be known as 'the Reade schedule', after Detective Superintendent George Reade, the man who led the police team that travelled from Birmingham to Morecambe. The schedule consisted of notes he had made about interviews conducted and the police officers involved. This schedule, unheard of until now, was for me a tremendous step forward, because it supported something I had been claiming for thirteen years – namely that I had been interviewed three times on the Saturday at Queen's Road. The police had always denied this on oath. They said I had been seen in the morning and evening, but categorically dismissed at the trial my claim that I had also been interviewed in the afternoon.

Now suddenly here it was, in Reade's own handwriting, a note of an interview with Hill said to have started at 3.45 p.m. It referred to things I had always maintained happened during that interview. And then it had all been crossed out, with the word 'OUT' in Reade's handwriting alongside. It obviously had not fitted the scheme of things in the way the police had wanted to present it. Reade said he had prepared the schedule in mid-1975 to help the prosecution at the trial. Why then, he was asked, had he told the Devon and Cornwall inquiry he had drawn it up as we were being interviewed in November 1974? He couldn't explain. Nor could he explain why it was that if indeed it had been prepared for the trial, he had not included any references to the interviews with Hugh Callaghan at

Sutton Coldfield. It referred only to events at Queen's Road and five of us. And he couldn't explain why a lot of interview times had been crossed out and others inserted.

Mr Mansfield described the Reade schedule as a blueprint for perjury, saying: 'You have to have a schedule like this if you are being dishonest.'

Lord Lane was not impressed. 'So this was a blueprint for a completely false case to be put forward by the police witnesses at the trial?' he asked.

'That is right,' said Mr Mansfield.

'And it successfully hoodwinked everybody?' said the Lord Chief Justice, sighing with disbelief.

Reade's answer to almost every question he was asked was that he couldn't remember, or he wasn't sure, or he didn't know, or he couldn't explain. He did, though, give a straight answer on one other issue. He agreed that in 1975 he had led a team of detectives in a raid on the house of a man who later sued and won damages after a court ruled the man had been punched by police and kicked down a staircase. When asked if he had given evidence in that case, denying that his men took part in any assaults, he put his head down and replied in a low voice: 'I did.'

Tom Clarke, the ex-policeman who had come forward, told his story. But the cloud under which he had left the police force for alleged theft meant he was never going to be an impressive witness.

In contrast, a witness who proved to be amazingly impressive was Joyce Lynas, a former policewoman who had been a cadet at Queen's Road on the night we were taken there. She gave evidence during the first week of the appeal, with evident reluctance admitting only that she had seen us roughly pushed around. Despite probing from our lawyers she would not go further and say that we had been assaulted. When the court resumed on the Monday of the second week, Mr Ferguson caused something of a sensation when he asked that she be recalled. He explained that she had been in touch with lawyers over the weekend to say she wanted to add to her evidence.

She now told the court that in July 1987, after she had left the force, she was contacted by Devon and Cornwall police who were tracing everybody who had been in the police station at the time. She rang

Queen's Road to check the identity of the Devon officer, and then asked what the feeling was there about the inquiry. She was told, 'You know what you saw, but remember, we've got families.' About a week later she received an anonymous phone call from somebody who said, 'Don't forget, you have got children.'

Mrs Lynas said that over the weekend after giving her evidence she had seen a TV programme about bullying in the army which focused on victims and witnesses afraid to speak out. She was unhappy that she had not told the full truth about us in court and after talking it over with her husband had rung Gareth Peirce to say she wanted to return to the witness box. She then went on to tell how she saw one of us being assaulted and the cops involved shouting, 'This is what we do to fucking murdering bastards.'

I felt she was a very brave woman to come back to a courtroom which had discharged her. After her first spell in the witness box, she could have walked away and forgotten about the whole thing. She knew full well that having denied seeing ill-treatment in her original evidence, she had now opened herself to a charge of perjury. And her new evidence was perhaps all the more remarkable because of another event that weekend. The IRA exploded a bomb at a Remembrance Day service in the Northern Ireland town of Enniskillen, murdering eleven people. That would have been enough to convince a less brave person than Joyce Lynas that she should not help out men accused of being IRA bombers.

The forensic evidence was again complicated, but this time around Skuse fell far short of the status of sainthood that Bridge had bestowed on him at the original trial. Like Reade, he evaded much with pleas of not remembering or being unable to explain.

He was asked about the recipe for the Griess test. Could he explain why it was the Home Office was now claiming the *World in Action* scientists had been given the wrong recipe for the combination of chemicals he had used on us? Those scientists had got their information from Skuse's boss, Mr George Walker, who had already testified he got the recipe from Skuse. Walker had said he was sure Skuse knew his inquiry related to the Birmingham case.

Skuse said he had not realised Walker's inquiry referred to the Birmingham case, and so he had simply gone to check the standard formula for a Griess test in a textbook. But he insisted the recipe he had used to test our hands was one he had developed himself to prevent any confusion between nitroglycerine and other substances. When asked why he had made no mention of his own special recipe at the original trial he said it had been 'an oversight'.

Skuse admitted changing some of the times in his original notes; the effect was that, remarkably, they tied in precisely with times in the Reade schedule. But he denied any collusion with the police over this.

The only other forensic evidence of substance against us was the laboratory test on a special machine of a sample from my left hand which Skuse had claimed proved positive for nitroglycerine. He said he had no record of the test, but that it had been witnessed by Dr Janet Drayton. This was the first we had ever heard of her. But it now appeared she had been alongside Skuse for the whole test. It turned out that on viewing the result of this crucial test, Dr Drayton, who was far more experienced on the equipment than Skuse, had thought it only 'possible nitroglycerine'.

Dr Drayton was then called, and with her evidence came a few more shocks. Several pages had disappeared from her notebook covering the relevant time. Those pages recorded the way she had prepared the machine involved for testing the sample from my hand. Normal procedure was for samples known to contain nitroglycerine to be passed through the machine to check it was working properly. Then the machine would be completely cleaned before a sample was tested. Otherwise the machine might still be contaminated by nitroglycerine. Dr Drayton was confident her notes would have shown exactly what she had done before finding a 'possible nitroglycerine' for me.

She had not got the faintest idea what had happened to those missing pages. She agreed under questioning that she had never, as a scientist, made a habit of ripping pages from her notebooks. She did say that she would have taken a printout from the machine doing the testing, and that she would have given that to Skuse. He had already told the court he could not recall having any such printout.

Our scientist, Dr Black, had testified at our trial that the sample from my hand should have been machine-checked at least three times before it could be said confidently that nitroglycerine was present. Skuse had settled for one test. Dr Drayton confirmed that samples from the hands of Billy and Gerry, which proved negative, had been tested two or three times. She agreed that was normal practice. Then what of the sample from my hand? She couldn't remember. And, of course, she had no notes to remind her.

Mr Judge, in trying to answer our case on behalf of the Crown, said there had been an 'orchestrated campaign' to try to have us freed, but the campaigners had been selective in the material they were willing to air publicly. 'The outside world hears only what the media chooses to present to it,' he said.

I had to agree with him there. In every single court action we had been associated with up to that point, the media had stressed the prosecution case almost to the exclusion of any reference to our defence.

While Widgery, who had refused us leave to appeal against conviction, had disagreed with Bridge on the importance of the forensic evidence, Mr Judge took issue with him over the circumstantial evidence. Bridge believed it fell 'a long way short' of proof. Judge, however, was confident it was enough for a conviction even if both the forensic and confessions evidence was ignored.

'Our submission is that it would have been virtually impossible to find stronger evidence, except perhaps a film of the actual planting of the bombs. And even if there had been such a film that too would have been disposed of as a police conspiracy,' he said.

The hearing ended on 9 December after thirty-two days, which made it at the time the longest appeal hearing in British history. The decision was to be given in the new year. In the meantime we would be sent back to jail. That meant another Christmas inside, our fourteenth.

I was put in a van with Gerry and we were taken to Gartree. As we arrived in the reception area there were loads of screws milling around in a panic. I presumed a con was being transferred and there had been a problem.

'Somebody on the move then?' I asked innocently.

A tight-lipped screw replied with a scowl, 'Yes, two just went by helicopter.'

At this Gerry Hunter went crazy, shouting: 'Bloody marvellous, isn't it. Here's me, an innocent man and been in prison for thirteen years and I still get taken all round the country in a freezing old van. Yet some blokes get a bloody helicopter!'

It was not until we got back on to the wing and spoke to the other cons that we realised the reception screw had been economical with the truth. The helicopter had been used by a London gang to pick up two guys from the exercise yard and fly them to freedom.

We returned to the Old Bailey on 28 January 1988 for the judgment. For some reason it was to be delivered in a different court, number 2, which was much more old-fashioned and in keeping with the image of a place for dealing with major criminals. We'd seen and heard enough during the hearing to realise we had no chance, but still we had to go through the motions, sitting through five hours as the three judges took it in turns to defend the ludicrous decision they were to make. At one point Billy told me he was going to walk out. But I told him to sit tight. If people who had come from around the world could sit through this rubbish, so could we.

The judges supported everything the Crown had said in preserving their case against us. Those who had spoken in our favour were castigated as liars or wrong; those against us were good, honest people making valid points. The cleaner at Morecambe might have seen blood on the walls of a cell, but it couldn't have been from any of us because none of us had claimed we had smeared a cell wall with blood. The prison officers were obviously trying to minimise the part played by prison staff in causing our injuries. The cop who saw one of us at Queen's Road looking battered must have been mistaken. Tom Clarke was a bitter man and an unconvincing witness. It had been clear his motive was to make money and blacken the reputation of the West Midlands Police. The view taken of Joyce Lynas was most ridiculous of all. Anybody could see she was a brave woman who had risked a great deal by returning to court to tell the truth. But to the judges she was a witness 'not worthy of belief'. The remarks made to her over the phone about her family could not be viewed as a threat which would worry her. She had admitted lying the first time she gave evidence, so she was a liar and that was the end of the matter. They felt she could not be believed whatever the circumstances.

But Skuse and Reade were decent guys who had been doing an honest job, and it was hardly surprising that they could not remember details about things that had happened thirteen years before. Reade had been an appalling witness in the box, but they saw that as being in his favour. 'With no disrespect,' they said, 'he was quite clearly not a person capable of carrying through such a huge and complicated conspiracy.' Of the Reade schedule they said, 'This court is quite satisfied the original purpose of this document cannot sensibly or seriously be a blueprint for perjury.' Skuse was ticked off on a few points, but it was irrelevant now because Dr Drayton, who had only appeared on the scene at this appeal, was now the expert. Ignoring the fact she had marked the sample from my hand as only 'possible nitroglycerine', the judges said she had convinced them that: 'Hill's left hand is proven to have nitroglycerine on it, for which there is, and can be, no innocent explanation. That conclusion is fatal to the appellants.'

Then as if to bear out what I had thought right at the start, that they were annoyed the case had even been sent back to them, they said: 'As has happened before in references by the Home Secretary to this court, the longer this hearing has gone on, the more convinced this court has become that the verdict of the jury was correct. We have no doubt that these convictions are both safe and satisfactory.

'The appeals are dismissed.'

# 25

# My father dies

We stood up in the dock, gave half-hearted waves to our families in the public gallery, and then in dignified silence trooped down the stairs from the courtroom.

We walked along a corridor below the court, mumbling a bit to each other, but there were no shouts of anger or outrage. We had all expected the decision. I was just surprised the judges had been so blatant. I had not been able to see how they were going to be able to reconcile all the new evidence with a conviction, but in the event they didn't even try. They simply went over it with a steamroller. We were taken into a cell and the legal team and secretaries began arriving, telling us how sorry they were. A lot of people in the crowded room were in tears, men as well as women.

Then Richard Ferguson, one of the QCs, walked in. I grabbed him and asked: 'Just tell me one thing, Dickie. Why the hell wasn't I born a Protestant like you?'

Everybody laughed and it eased the tension. He looked at me and said he couldn't express in words how bad he felt about what had been done to us.

'Don't worry, Dickie,' I told him. 'We'll be back.'

We were eventually taken off to our various prisons, and back at Gartree I was met with nothing but sympathy from the cons and screws. They couldn't believe it. I found it difficult to sleep that night, replaying the events of the previous few weeks in my mind. I eventually nodded off, cursing the judges and the system they ran.

The following morning I awoke with that same depressed feeling I'd had every single day for more than thirteen years as I opened my eyes to find myself still locked in a prison cell. But the depression soon lifted. As soon as I saw the daily papers I knew the tide had changed. As I listened to commentators on the radio it became obvious we had reached a crucial watershed. It was clear things would be different from now on. While some people had thought – and hoped – that Lane's judgment would be the last they would hear of the Birmingham Six, as we were by then known by everybody, I saw light shining at the end of the tunnel more brightly than ever before. There was widespread shock at the decision, with columnists suggesting that while we had suffered terrible injustice in the past, this latest bout of judicial gymnastics was the most blatant of all. It was not a view shared by all the papers, of course.

The tabloid press talked of how justice had been done yet again and that this time it really should be the end of the matter. There were headlines such as: 'JOY AS IRA BOMBERS ARE KEPT IN PRISON'. Most vicious of all was the editorial which read: 'If the *Sun* had its way, we would have been tempted to string 'em up years ago.'

It didn't worry me too much. I skimmed quickly through the *Sun*'s racing pages, the only part worth reading, and then took away the editorial to use as toilet paper.

A few people too were still expressing their blinkered views, most memorable among them being Lord 'appalling vista' Denning. Shortly after the appeal judgment he declared on TV how he would rather ignore possible miscarriages of justice than do anything that might undermine the criminal justice system. He was stating publicly something I had known for a long time: some sections of the Establishment were adamant that the reputations of the police and courts were more important than the question of whether somebody was innocent or not.

Far from being laid to rest, our campaign now really began to roll. Within days more than one hundred MPs had signed a motion at Westminster expressing concern over the 'widespread disquiet' at the result. The motion said an independent tribunal should be set up to look at the case, and in particular the claim by Chris Mullin in his book that he had traced and interviewed some of the men really responsible for the bombings. Bishop Daly wrote a great piece about our appeal in the Irish magazine *Magill*, part of which read: 'The judges displayed an inability to grasp the difficulties and behaviour of poor people who are unemployed. There was an unbridgeable cultural gap between the judges and the appellants.' Chris Mullin,

Gareth Peirce and the *World in Action* team were still working away on our behalf, discovering more and more evidence of dirty work that had gone on behind the scenes, and of how the authorities had conspired to keep us inside. Their work forced the Director of Public Prosecutions to order an inquiry two months after our appeal into allegations that Skuse and Reade had been in contact with each other throughout it. The Attorney General later told Parliament that the police inquiry had thrown up no evidence of criminal conduct. When Chris, as a Labour MP, pressed the matter in Parliament he was denigrated by Tories such as Birmingham MP Anthony Beaumont Dark who said: 'No-one had a fairer trial, no-one had a fairer appeal. Is it not time the Opposition looked at the IRA instead of being its greatest supporters?'

In April 1988 we were refused leave to appeal further to the House of Lords, but that hardly bothered me. We were on the way now and I knew we were unstoppable. The move to get international observers to attend the appeal had proved a great success and now almost every week there were supportive stories appearing in newspapers around the world. There was also a lot of criticism of Lord Lane. At home the press and TV were clamouring for interviews with us in prison. What a difference from those early days when we really needed them.

But then came an event which brought everything to an abrupt halt for me. It was the death of my father.

As a boy in Belfast and a young man in Birmingham I'd always been close to my dad. Even though he was quite strict, being a former army man, and I had often felt the power of his big hand on my backside, we had a great relationship. And if ever he asked if I had done something, I would always tell him the truth. It might mean one hell of a belting, but I used to dread to think what the consequences might be if I were ever to lie to him and he found out.

The day he came to see me in Winson Green after the pub bombings changed that relationship forever. He had asked me if I had been involved and I had told him the truth. But for the first time in our lives I knew from the look in his eyes that he doubted my word. He simply could not contemplate that the police could do what they had done.

Shortly after that he was badly beaten up at work for being a 'bomber's father', and he never worked again. He visited me only a handful of times over the years that followed, and never wrote. When he did come, always with my mum or brothers, the strain was unbearable. We knew our relationship had changed forever, but neither of us wanted to raise the issue. We would exchange a few pleasantries, but then he would sit in silence, neither of us willing to look at the other straight in the face. He could only take twenty or thirty minutes and then would have to leave.

So many times before one of those rare visits I would spend days planning how I would challenge dad, forcing him to admit that he had not believed my word. But when it came to the moment I could not face the confrontation. I finally blew up during one of my mum's visits, shouting at her that dad blamed me for everything that had happened, that he had never really believed me. She tried to tell me that that was not true, that was not how he felt. But I knew it was.

Then came *World In Action* and Chris Mullin's book, and mum told me they had had a profound effect on dad. In September 1987, shortly before the appeal, he came to see me at Gartree for the first time in years. He sat opposite me, alongside mum, and after a few minutes he looked straight at me, as he had done that day in Winson Green. I knew he wanted to say something. As I looked back into his eyes I'm sure he wanted to tell me that he was sorry for the doubts he had held. But the words would not come. Tears welled in his eyes, and mine too. Then he got up and walked out without saying a word.

Almost a year later, in June 1988 after our appeal had failed, dad was taken into hospital. My brother Sammy came to see me with his wife, and as soon as I saw his face I knew something was wrong. We shook hands and sat down and Sammy told me he had bad news. Dad had cancer and had less than a month to live. He was lapsing in and out of consciousness, and could go at any time. Sammy said the family wanted to know if I would be able to visit dad, or go to the funeral. I asked one of the screws to get whoever was in charge to come over to our table.

A Principal Officer came across and explained that as a Cat. A prisoner I was unlikely to be allowed out more than once, although the final decision would rest with the Home Office. He asked whether I would rather go to the hospital and see dad while he was still alive, or go to the funeral. I told him that if dad were conscious, I would like to go to the hospital to speak to him.

I made the formal application and waited. Over the next few days I heard from the family that dad was deteriorating rapidly. Eventually I was told one morning to get ready to go.

I got showered and shaved and went to reception where we went through the procedure for going out. I was handcuffed to a screw called Big Taffy and put in the Cat. A van. The Principal Officer travelling with us said there would have to be the usual police car escort for a Cat. A prisoner, but because of the circumstances there would be no sirens or flashing lights.

Nobody spoke in the van on the way. I was trying to prepare myself mentally to see dad for the first time since that September visit. I sat chain smoking, and memories of me and my dad went through my mind. I recalled how as a kid back in Belfast he would put me up alongside him as he drove his big army lorry; sitting on the handlebars of his motorbike as he cruised slowly up and down the street; the belting he gave me for taking mum's money box; and how he would come looking for me in the snooker halls I sneaked into as a young teenager.

I remembered how happy I'd been to be reunited with him when we moved to Birmingham, and how not long after that I would go out to pubs with him where we would play darts and dominoes together. How he would drag me out of bed at four in the morning to go fishing with him. The times we'd been together, at family weddings and other parties.

I was lost in these thoughts when one of the screws, who knew I was from Birmingham, asked if I recognised the area we were going through.

'I sure do,' I told him as we started to go through familiar streets. 'My mum and dad live there.' And I pointed out the house as we flew by.

We were soon at Good Hope Hospital and pulled up at an entrance. We were about to get out when loads of armed policemen suddenly surrounded the van. We all froze and you could touch the tension in the air. An older cop, in plain clothes, came to the door and shouted, 'Don't come out until you're told to.'

The PO turned to me and said with a guilty face: 'Paddy, don't ask me what's going on here. I swear we didn't know anything like this was going to happen. I'm as surprised about this as you are.

229

Don't start losing your temper. You're here to see your father, so just keep cool.'

After a few minutes the older cop came back and told us to get out. I could not believe what I saw around me. There must have been more than a dozen policemen with guns and radios, and wearing flak jackets. Me and Taffy got out and two cops stood in front of us with their guns pointing at us. They walked backwards as we moved, with another pair with guns walking in front of them. Four others did the same behind us.

We walked into the hospital and along a corridor, where there were lots more armed cops. There was lots of shouting, and they were pushing people back inside doors so that the corridor was kept clear. They marched me around a corner and into a lift. Me and Big Taffy stood cuffed to each other with our backs against the lift and the cops training their guns on us. Taffy was as white as a sheet and I told him, 'For God's sake take it easy. Don't do anything stupid, because I'm the one they'll shoot.'

I felt so angry about the way this was all being done, it was so pointless. But I kept telling myself, Don't let them get you upset, keep cool. You're going to see your old man, don't let these bastards bother you. I was determined not to give them the pleasure of seeing me boil over.

We got out of the lift and went along another corridor, and as I walked I was praying inside: Please God, let him be conscious, let me be able to speak to him.

We came to a room and stopped outside. Then one of the cops pushed the door open and waved his gun, telling us to go inside. I went in with Taffy and found myself at the foot of a bed with the body of an old man sprawled across it.

This isn't my da, I thought. They've brought me to the wrong room.

And then I noticed at the head of the bed yet another cop, standing there with a scowl and his gun at his side. I knew this must be the right room. But I couldn't understand why nobody from my family was there. They had told me somebody was with dad all the time.

I looked down again at the bed. Nothing could have prepared me to see him in such a state. He had been such a big man, over six feet tall and hefty. That was the way he'd been when I last saw him. Now he was like a skeleton, with skin hanging off him. He was seventy-two, but looked far older. I just burst into tears. I touched him on the leg and said: 'Da, can you hear me. Wake up da, its me, Paddy.'

He didn't stir. I stood there for a few minutes, shaking his leg and calling to him, and crying. But it was obvious he was not going to wake up. I turned to Taffy and told him to pass on the word that we were going, and to ask the cops if any of my family were there. He spoke to someone and then I went to kiss my dad at the head of the bed. The cop who was standing there put his hand on his gun and told me not to move. I stood glaring at him for a few seconds, then turned and walked out of the room. The plainclothes cop was outside and told me my mother and brother Sammy were in the hospital, and that he would bring them to see me. They came after a few minutes and there were more tears. My mother looked awful. Sammy said they had been down in a room below under armed guard. I told them I was going back to prison, that I did not want to stay any longer. I asked Sammy to phone me and let me know when dad died. He said he would, and told me: 'We didn't know it was going to be like this. When I spoke to the police about what would happen they said it would be low-profile. Look at them, they're all over the place.'

I was taken back to the van with the cops all around me again, and we headed back to Gartree. Not a word was said during the drive. Back at the prison I went through the reception in a blur. I just wanted to get back into my cell on my own, and for once was pleased when that door slammed shut behind me. Three nights later one of my brothers called to say dad had died. Mum later told me that he had regained consciousness for a short time and said to her: 'Paddy was here. Now I can die in peace.'

My brother Bobby came to see me to discuss the funeral. After what had happened at the hospital I had no intention of seeking permission to go. I was not going to let them make a mockery of my father's funeral.

# 26

# On the way

My dad's death left me in a deep depression for weeks. I did not want to do anything, never mind continue with the campaign. I just wanted to be left alone in my cell, sitting and smoking, and regretting the fact dad and I had not had a chance to talk before he died.

But gradually, with the help of some of the lads inside and the support of letters from people outside, I picked myself up. I got a big boost in August when the human rights organisation, Amnesty International, which I had written to several times, gave us their full backing. They presented to the government a paper outlining their concerns, with the conclusion:

Grave doubts remain about official denials that these six prisoners were ill-treated while in police custody, and therefore about the safeness of their convictions based on confessions. Amnesty International believes that the case should not be closed and that the allegations of ill-treatment must be subject to further review.

Chris and Gareth were now turning up new information with almost incredible frequency. They discovered papers in the files of Lancashire County Council (which covered Morecambe police station) which suggested background collusion between that council and the West Midlands over our efforts to sue their police forces for injuries inflicted in custody. One note, documenting a phone conversation between the two parties, read:

The chief purpose (of the conversation) was to ensure that both police forces are in step and do not fall out with one another in the slightest respect.

It was important to agree that neither force would try to blame the other. And it was 'essential' that they should agree on the exact time we had been handed over from the Lancashire police to the West Midlands. These papers were from 1977. Yet officers from both forces had sworn on oath at our trial two years earlier that the handover was at 9.30 a.m., a time we strongly disputed. Why was it at that late stage being deemed essential to establish the time?

The note documented that there had been an agreement during the telephone call that such matters should be discussed over the phone rather than in writing.

If these matters were to be in correspondence there might be a danger of our not being able to claim privilege, and if the plaintiffs were to get hold of the correspondence they would of course seek to show that there was deliberate collusion between the two forces in order to present a common front.

The note went on to say both sides had agreed to co-operate as there was a common interest.

This is to make sure that the plaintiffs' case against the police officers utterly fails because of the serious implications that would arise, if by some mischance the plaintiffs were to succeed.

There were further notes in the files up to the time of the police appeal against the Cantley decision which had allowed us to sue them – the appeal that was heard in November 1979 by Lord Denning. One of the notes from shortly before that date pointed out the appeal would be heard by Denning, 'who it is thought will be sympathetic to our case'. How right they were.

Late that summer the Olympics were held in South Korea, and the events from there were among the few things I had time to watch on television. Ben Johnson won his gold medal for winning the 100 metres, and then had it taken away for using drugs. George Bush was elected President of the United States in November. A few days later Margaret Thatcher was in Poland, congratulating Lech Walesa and his Solidarity union on their great 'struggle for freedom'. She didn't seem to be taking much notice of my struggle for freedom. Just before Christmas, PanAm flight 103 was blown up over Lockerbie in Scotland, killing all 259 aboard and 11 people on the ground. It took from the Birmingham pub bombings the mantle of being the biggest mass murder in British history.

As we moved into 1989 my old friend Lord Denning was back in the spotlight. Apparently he was upset over the fuss being caused by people supporting ourselves and the Guildford Four. He told the *Spectator* magazine: 'We wouldn't have all these campaigns to have the Birmingham Six released if they'd been hanged. They'd have been forgotten, and the whole community would be satisfied.' This from a man whom many believed was the ultimate dispenser of common sense on judicial matters. A man who for many decades held the power to grant or deny life and liberty to other men.

The following month I was sitting in my cell reading a paper when a headline about Prince Philip, the Duke of Edinburgh, caught my eye. He was off to Japan, to attend the funeral of Emperor Hirohito, a war criminal if ever there was one. As I read through the story my mind went back to our trial almost fourteen years earlier. We had been ridiculed when we tried to explain that in going to James McDade's funeral we were not honouring an IRA bomber. It was just the way people from our community did things, it was tradition.

The newspaper story said there was sure to be some criticism of Prince Philip's trip, because of the evil deeds Hirohito had been responsible for during his lifetime. But, it pointed out, Philip would not be honouring the man. It was simply convention for dignitaries to attend such a funeral. It was the way things were done. It was tradition.

Later that year the West Midlands Police found themselves having a hard time. Case after case involving the Serious Crime Squad was thrown out of court because of irregularities in the evidence, or the manner in which confessions had been obtained. Eventually they could take no more embarrassment, and in August 1989 the Chief Constable of the force, Geoffrey Dear, took the sensational step of disbanding the squad and ordering an inquiry into its activities. And who was head of the squad at the time? None other than Ray Bennett, my 'interviewer', who by then had been promoted to Detective Chief Inspector.

Some officers retired, and dozens were demoted to desk jobs. However, the inquiry was to stretch back only to 1984, neatly avoiding the need to investigate the most infamous case with which the squad was associated.

The police were by now changing tack dramatically on the part we were supposed to have played in the pub bombings. While we had been described at our trial as senior IRA men, with John a brigadier and Hunter a captain, we were now being reduced to the ranks of 'foot soldiers' or 'labourers'. Mr Dear, who it must be said was not part of the force at the time, was saying, 'From the early days it was recognised that the six were not the only ones involved.'

That was odd. After the confident assertion of his predecessors that the police had caught 'those primarily responsible', there was never any suggestion the police were looking for others. The public was given the very firm impression at the time that the whole gang had been rounded up through brilliant police work. But if it were believed now that we were just 'labourers' what were the police doing about capturing those responsible? Not much, it seemed.

In October 1989 one of the few decent policemen I came across in this whole saga decided to go public with his doubts about our guilt. Fred Willoughby, who was by then retired, was the cop who had questioned me at Heysham and taken me to Morecambe. He said he was deeply concerned that we could spend the rest of our lives in prison when there was so much doubt surrounding the case. He pointed out that I had answered his questions honestly when he first quizzed me, and went with him happily when he took me off the boat. It was not a major step forward. But it was yet another revelation casting doubt on the case against us.

That same month came freedom for the Guildford Four. The government, after originally knocking them back in January 1987, on the same day our appeal was announced, had been forced to take action. Earlier in 1989, the Home Secretary finally ordered a new appeal. But come October the hearing was not expected to start until the following year.

I was with Gerry Conlon, one of the four, when the news came through that he was to be transferred to London for an unexpected hearing. When the screws came for Gerry it was clear something was happening, but nobody knew what was going on behind the scenes. I helped him pack his things. I gave him a hug and told him, 'Be lucky, Gerry.' Then he was gone.

The Guildford Four went into court on 19 October, when Chief Justice Lane and two colleagues were told by a Crown lawyer that there was so much doubt about the integrity and honesty of the police officers involved in their case that the Crown could no longer sustain the conviction. They were free to go. That night on television I watched the scenes as Gerry walked into the street outside the Old Bailey. He stormed up to a microphone and told angrily how he had spent fifteen years in prison for something he hadn't done, and how he'd watched his father die in prison for something that he hadn't done. Then he shouted: 'He's innocent, the Maguires are innocent, the Birmingham Six are innocent. Let's hope they're next.'

Gerry's father, Guiseppe, had died in prison, one of seven other innocent Irish people jailed on bombing charges who became known as the Maguires. It would be nearly another year before the government accepted that those convictions too were 'unsafe'. Back in the Gartree TV room there was pandemonium, with the other cons clapping and cheering and telling me they were sure that I would be next. Gerry's freedom was a moment of incredibly mixed emotions for me. I was so happy for him and the others, but was obviously left wondering just when our time would come. In a statement to Parliament, Home Secretary Douglas Hurd said he would not be referring our case back to the courts because the appeal judges had considered the matter fully earlier that year. It didn't bother me too much though; I saw it as just another hurdle that would be cleared. We had been struggling uphill for years, but now I had not the slightest doubt we were on the downhill slope to freedom. Gareth put in a new submission to the Home Secretary in December, urging him to look not just at new evidence, but at how the police had treated us from the start.

By 1990 the campaign was in full swing, with support groups being set up everywhere in Britain and abroad. 'FREE THE BIRMINGHAM SIX' became a slogan printed on badges, T-shirts and sweaters; an information pack was produced; a campaign newsletter was printed every three months and public meetings were held regularly.

Songs were recorded about us by popular Irish artistes Christy

Moore, Brush Shiels and the Pogues (the Pogues' song was banned by the Independent Broadcasting Authority in 1988 on the grounds that it appeared to suggest support for convicted terrorists!). Thousands of ordinary people we had never known sent letters and cards to us in prison. I received a poem from a girl of sixteen called Sarah Hardy. The words read:

> For so long
> You have been crying out.
> Unlike liberty,
> Dignity cannot be denied.
> At times it must feel
> That no one is on your side.
> Is it because they cannot hear,
> Or will they just not listen?
>
> For so long,
> Injustice has been triumphant,
> While staring them in the face
> Have been six innocent men.
> When will this nightmare end?
>
> They use the word justice.
> This cannot be.
> If justice had been declared
> You would be free.

The government was put under pressure on a variety of fronts. There were pickets at British embassies around the world; the Gorbachev-led government of the Soviet Union invited campaign representatives to attend a human rights meeting in Moscow; and families and campaigners went to a major human rights conference in Copenhagen, Denmark, at which the case was given massive publicity.

The Irish government was at last taking a more active role, raising the case at meetings with the British government under the Anglo-Irish Agreement. There was a spectacular 'Parade of Innocence' in Dublin during a summit meeting of European leaders. Catholic cardinals and bishops, and churchmen of other denominations, began to speak out in far more strident tones than ever before.

In February 1990 Nelson Mandela was released after twenty-seven years of captivity in South Africa. As I watched him walk from the gates of his prison in the TV room of mine, I couldn't help but wonder if my ordeal would last as long. Within a few months of his release he was in Ireland, where he was presented with books and posters about us, and he sent a message of support.

There were more television specials on our case in 1990. The first, in March, was *Who Bombed Birmingham* by Granada Television in conjunction with *World In Action*. It was a drama documentary which had actors playing our parts. At the end the programme named four of the people said to have been actually responsible. I was unhappy about that. On one hand it gave added impetus to the view that the police knew who the real bombers were and should be trying to get hold of them. But I felt it wrong for TV to accuse people in that way. I certainly don't know whether those people named are the real bombers. Having been a victim of injustice for so many years, I'm now a strong believer in the view that everything should be done correctly. I don't think that tossing out names on a television drama does anything for our system of justice.

But the programme certainly added to the pressure our campaign was exerting. Shortly after it was shown, the Home Secretary, David Waddington, announced he had ordered a new inquiry into the case, again to be conducted by the Devon and Cornwall police. Chris Mullin had been actively investigating further leads, and in the summer of 1990 produced a revised and updated version of his *Error of Judgement*. In it he said he had now identified and tracked down both men who planted the pub bombs, as well as the bomb makers and those who gave the orders. Again he refused to name them on the grounds that he had only got to speak to them after giving an assurance of anonymity. He also pointed out that the police knew who they were anyway, having interviewed them at various stages after the bombings.

The *World In Action* team were also busy and had obtained a file from the archives of the West Midlands Special Branch. It included a report of an interview with a member of the Birmingham IRA who had been arrested quite some time after the pub bombings. He had co-operated with the police, naming a whole string of other members. Needless to say, not one of us six appeared on his list. Specifically he named the men he believed were the leaders of the group responsible for the pub bombings. The names were the same as those Mullin had obtained through his own inquiries.

But there was more. The informer had told the police that six weeks after the bombings he met one of his IRA colleagues in a pub in Birmingham. The man told him he had planted the bombs.

In July another *World In Action* special went out which featured an interview with a man, disguised in front of the camera, who was said to be one of the men who planted the bombs. He said: 'There were only two of us. These six people are innocent. I have never met these guys in my life. The first I ever saw of them was when I saw photographs of them in the papers.'

The interview caused something of a controversy, with some right-wing MPs demanding that the programme makers be prosecuted for refusing to reveal the man's identity. Strangely, their voices were quickly silenced. Perhaps it was because any official acknowledgement that this was indeed one of the real bombers would lead to the inescapable conclusion that we six were innocent.

By the middle of that year even the staunchly pro-government *Daily Mail* was declaring: 'Justice so long delayed is justice denied. How much longer before the re-opening of the case of the Birmingham Six?' Shortly after that, United States Congressman Joe Kennedy announced he was coming to Britain and hoped to visit all six of us. But we were Category A prisoners. Anybody who wished to visit us but was not immediate family would have to go through the ritual of Special Branch investigation and interview. One night after I had been banged up a screw came to my door and said I was to go to the office of a new assistant governor, a woman, who was the first of her sex to hold such a high position at Gartree.

'I have been told to inform you that when you wake up in the morning you will no longer be a Category A prisoner,' she said with a smile.

It didn't mean a great deal to me. It was years since I had been treated as a cat. A man, but at least now that I was no longer officially a highly dangerous threat to society I could get whoever I wanted to come and see me. I certainly did not feel I had any reason to be grateful.

'Oh really,' I told her. 'And how different will I be tomorrow morning from the man I have been for the past fifteen years? Why will I be less of a danger? You know and I know why I'm coming off Cat. A. It's because the government does not want to have an embarrassing row with an American politician.'

Joe Kennedy saw me shortly after that and told me of the massive interest in our case in America and how the number of US politicians getting involved was growing by the day.

It was also at about that time that a fellow Belfast man, Brian Keenan, was released in Lebanon where he had been held as a hostage for several years. I watched him on the television news shortly after he was freed. He described what it was like being a hostage, saying, 'It's a silent, screaming slide into the bowels of ultimate despair.'

I knew just what he meant.

# 27

## 'Apparent discrepancies'

The beginning of the end came in August 1990, when the then Home Secretary, David Waddington, told Parliament he was referring our case back to the Court of Appeal because the latest police investigation had found 'apparent discrepancies in the record of an interview with one of the six men'.

'Apparent discrepancies', and only concerning one of us? It didn't matter; at last, more than two and a half years after the rejection of our first appeal, we were heading back to court, and this time we knew it would be different.

As with the announcement of our first appeal, I was told the news in the governor's office at Gartree.

'You won't be coming back this time Hill,' he said.

I felt great. At long, long last, we would be going home. But the joy was quickly snuffed out.

Earlier that year my daughter Sharon, who was twenty, had told me she was pregnant. She was over the moon about it, but it didn't mean a lot to me, to be honest. By now three of my daughters had children, and although this would be Sharon's first baby, to me it was just another grandchild coming along. During the year she had to go into hospital a couple of times for high blood pressure, or something like that, but there was no real concern.

Then on a Friday afternoon in September, shortly after the Home Secretary's announcement, Sharon was rushed into hospital. I was given a message that night that she had had a baby girl, but that the baby was in an incubator. I presumed it was nothing more serious than the baby having come along a little early. On the Saturday evening I got a call from my ex-wife Pat, who was crying and telling me there was something seriously wrong with the baby. I asked what

241

it was, but she didn't know. She said the doctors were carrying out tests, and I asked her for the name of the doctor in charge.

The next morning I got permission to phone the hospital in Birmingham and I spoke to the doctor, explaining who and where I was. He told me that the baby had some rare syndrome which they knew little about. All they could do was take her out of the incubator in a couple of days and see how she did. But he didn't think there was much hope for her. I said I was going to put in a request to go to the hospital and see Sharon and the baby, and he said he would see me there.

As I was no longer a Cat. A prisoner I knew getting permission would be just a formality. I got approval a couple of days later and was taken over to reception to go out. I went through the normal procedure and was cuffed to a screw. But then I saw some police cars, the sign of a Cat. A prisoner escort. The memories of what had happened when I went to the hospital to see my dying father came flooding back. I exploded, telling the screws, 'Listen, I'm not an A man, so I'm not going to travel as an A man. What the hell's going on?'

The screws calmed me down, explaining the only reason for the escort was to ensure I got to the hospital without hold-ups. There would be no sirens or flashing lights unless there was a problem on the road. I accepted their word and got in the van.

It didn't take long to get to the hospital and when I arrived the cops kept a very low profile. I have nothing but praise for the way they handled things on this occasion, so differently to the experience of two years before. I went into the hospital and saw the doctor, who asked for Sharon to be brought in. As we waited, the screw put on the long-chain handcuffs, so that we could move up to ten feet apart, but still be connected securely. I knew the aim was to allow me more freedom, but that did nothing to ease the feeling that I was being treated like a dog. The doctor began to explain the situation and the screw went to wait outside the room. But of course, we couldn't close the door because of the chain.

The doctor said the baby's defect was a chance in a million. They would be taking the baby out of the incubator later that night.

'And I'm afraid, Mr Hill, that it's my professional opinion she won't last more than thirty minutes,' he said. 'I'm sorry, but there's nothing we can do.'

Then Sharon came in. She just fell into my arms crying her eyes out. When I saw the state she was in, my heart went out to her and I ended up breaking down myself and crying, telling her I was so sorry. What can you say to your daughter to comfort her when she knows she's going to lose her child?

Between sobs Sharon asked if I had seen the baby, who she had called Sade. She took my hand and led me into another room, with the screw following behind at the end of the chain. On a table there was a small glass case with two little holes in the side of it. And inside lay this helpless little thing. Sharon put one hand through and I did the same, and we both gently stroked the baby. She looked so beautiful, so perfect that you would never know there was something wrong. Sharon had her free arm around me and just kept repeating, 'She's not going to die, dad, is she? Tell me she's not going to die.'

And as I stood there, trying to be strong for Sharon's sake, I was asking, Dear God, hasn't this family suffered enough?

I don't know how long we were there, but eventually the doctor came and took us into his office. He explained to Sharon what he had told me earlier, but I could see his words were not getting through to her. He left us alone and I sat with her for a while. I'd got myself under some sort of control, and told her: 'It's all in God's hands now. There's nothing anybody can do. If he wants her, then he'll come to take her.'

After a short time Pat and my daughter Michelle arrived, and they were in a terrible state too. Pat explained through the tears that a priest was coming that night to baptise the baby as soon as she was taken out of the incubator. She said one of the family would phone me that night to let me know what happened. After a few minutes I felt I couldn't take any more. I told the screw at the end of my chain I wanted to go back. He was very kind, and said I could stay a lot longer, but I had had enough. Pat had told me the rest of the family were coming up and I couldn't face seeing each of them under these circumstances. I just wanted to get out. He put the regular handcuffs on and I said my goodbyes and went out to the van.

There was silence all the way back to Gartree, and after I'd changed into my prison gear I went back to my cell. Later that night a screw passed a note through the door saying that one of the family had called. Little Sade had died. I sat on the bed and cried what few tears were left.

The next day I applied for permission to go to the funeral. It was the same routine as with the journey to the hospital, and again the police kept a discreet low profile. We went straight to the church, where there were lots of family members I had not seen for years. But it was no happy reunion. I had got permission to go to the cemetery too, but during the funeral service I decided I couldn't take it. When the priest finished, I told the screws to take me back.

A week before Christmas there was a preliminary hearing in our appeal at which it became clear the Crown case was collapsing. The Director of Public Prosecutions revealed that evidence had been available at the time of our trial fifteen years earlier which would have 'cast grave doubt' on Skuse's forensic testimony. It should have been passed on to our lawyers at that time, but was not. It should have been passed to our lawyers for our 1987 appeal, but was not. It had been given to them just two weeks before this hearing. The court was told that details of the evidence would be revealed at the full appeal. The DPP said the Devon and Cornwall inquiry was continuing, and that it would be wrong to begin an appeal until it was complete, probably within a month or two. In the meantime, the judges would have a lot of paperwork to study before the appeal itself began. Lord Justice Lloyd said he and his colleagues would not allow that to 'spoil our Christmas'.

I was facing my seventeenth Christmas in prison as an innocent man, but I was delighted to hear that our case would not spoil the festive season for the good judges and their families. He was castigated in a leading article in *The Times* the next day for conjuring up an image out of Dickens rather than that of a modern judiciary. It was a notable piece, for the headline on it read, 'Free the Birmingham Six'.

Never in my wildest dreams had I ever expected to see such a call from the mouthpiece of the Establishment. Now it really was just a matter of time.

The appeal date was set for Monday 4 March. In early February there was another preliminary hearing at which the DPP said he would no longer rely on the scientific evidence against us. A week before the appeal was to open there was a final preliminary hearing. This time the DPP said he would not rely on the evidence of any of the policemen who had interviewed us. The decision followed a ten-hour interview with George Reade by John Evans, the Chief Constable of Devon and Cornwall, who had flown to Australia, where Reade was living, to conduct it.

So the two 'absolutely critical' planks against us, as Bridge had put it, had now disintegrated. The DPP said he would no longer try to support the convictions as safe and satisfactory.

As with the earlier preliminary hearings we were not in court, but I heard of the DPP's decision on the news headlines on the radio. Surely this meant it was all over? It was a similar decision that had led to the immediate release of the Guildford Four. But there seemed to be a determination not to let us go so easily. It appears that after the Guildford case Lord Lane had decided never again would such major decisions be taken out of the hands of the judiciary. Later in the hearing the judges said it didn't matter that the DPP had thrown in the towel. It would be 'quite wrong' for him to decide whether verdicts made by a jury were unsafe and unsatisfactory, the grounds on which we could be freed. That was a task for the Appeal Court alone. A few more days meant nothing to me, as I was consumed by an overwhelming sense of anticipation.

Lord Denning was dug up again by the media to pontificate on the collapse of the Crown case. Without the slightest hint of embarrassment or regret over his 'appalling vista' judgment of 1980, or any other judicial decisions in our case over the years, he said he felt 'let down' by the police.

'I've always thought, and thought at the time, that our police were splendid and first class,' he said. 'I am very sorry that in this case it appears the contrary. My opinion has changed. I still hope and believe the ordinary people of England will rely on the police. It grieves me very much they should have let us all down in this case.'

I was moved down to London, to Wormwood Scrubs, where the six of us were brought together again. I said my goodbyes to the lads at Gartree and gave to Ronnie what few possessions I had. For I knew without a shadow of a doubt that this time I would not be going back.

It's impossible to capture in words the difference in atmosphere between the 1987 appeal and that of 1991. At the first we were still regarded as a ruthless gang of terrorists, held and escorted by armed guards, our families subject to searches every time they entered court. This time it was like a carnival.

Everybody was happy. The screws at the Scrubs and the cops on the escorts couldn't have been nicer. Handshakes, smiles, jokes. It was a different world. When we walked into the court, we were treated as old friends while our families waved and blew kisses to us from the gallery. The place was packed with journalists, campaigners and observers including Bishop Daly, Chris Mullin, and Sister Sarah Clarke, the little nun who had been a saint over the years. Also there was Sir Allan Green, the Director of Public Prosecutions himself, who was later to resign over allegations of involvement with a prostitute.

The three judges presiding were lords Lloyd, Mustill and Farquharson. Our barrister Mike Mansfield opened up by asking that the convictions be set aside because they constituted a 'grave and abiding' miscarriage of justice.

'They were brought about in the wake of the emotional turmoil after these bombings,' he said.

'Once the die was cast, it has proved very difficult indeed to unravel the twists, the turns and the contortions of evidence that arose at source in 1974 when these men were arrested. It has only been possible in the past twelve months to accomplish the task of unravelling. It has been accomplished with the help of fresh discoveries and techniques in the field of science. One of them, dramatic in its own fashion, happened barely a month ago.

'A discovery was made that the constituents of soap could also give rise to the same positive results as the tests used by Dr Frank Skuse in 1974.'

Soap! I almost had a heart attack. Skuse had told our trial that he was 'ninety-nine per cent certain' that nitroglycerine was on my hands. What he told Bennett had caused Bennett to kick me all round the room and tell me I was covered in 'gelly'. Now here I was, having been locked up for more than sixteen years, being told that the same result could have been caused by soap. It meant, as Mr Mansfield explained, that Skuse could have even contaminated the results himself when he washed his own hands and equipment.

Then Mr Mansfield turned to the new evidence which had been referred to at the first preliminary hearing in December, information which should have been available to our lawyers in 1974, as well as at the 1987 appeal but which had only been passed to them weeks before that hearing. It now transpired that on the night of the bombing we were not the only people travelling to Belfast who were subjected to the Griess test.

Two fancy goods salesmen travelling to Ireland from Liverpool had been stopped at the docks and tested by a scientist other than Skuse. He also got some positive results. But where Skuse plumped immediately for explosives as the cause and told the police, this other scientist looked to see if there could be a more innocent explanation. He made a few inquiries, and quickly came to the conclusion the positive results were caused by the handling of . . . adhesive tape.

Mr Mansfield said it was 'inexplicable' that the defence had never been provided with that information until November 1990. The Griess test, even in 1974, was regarded by most decent scientists as nothing more than a screening test which showed nitroglycerine could be present. No conclusions should have been drawn until the results of further sophisticated tests were known. But the flawed scientific 'evidence' had blinded everybody involved. 'Police, lawyers, the judge and the jury had been contaminated by the certainty of Doctor Skuse's conclusions that two of the men had handled explosives,' Mansfield said.

Next came the reconsideration of the evidence of Dr Janet Drayton, who on viewing the result of laboratory testing of the sample from my left hand had noted 'possible nitroglycerine'. At the 1987 appeal Lord Lane and his colleagues had gleefully latched onto her evidence describing it as pointing 'fair and square to the presence of nitroglycerine' and 'fatal' to our case. They had felt that even if Skuse's tests were not convincing, her evidence was.

She now gave evidence that she had never said the result obtained from my hand could only indicate nitroglycerine. The 1987 appeal judges had misinterpreted her views. Further, she accepted that two top government scientists, Dr John Lloyd and Dr Alan Scaplehorn, had showed that a random swab from a smoker's hand could produce the same result she had witnessed. So too could other substances, such as food preservatives.

It was beginning to sound as though there were very few things around that would not produce a positive Griess test. I don't know what it actually was that produced those fatal positive results from my hand. But I was a smoker. And I had played cards for hours on the train to Heysham. And I had bought a meat pie that night when we changed trains at Crewe. It probably contained food preservatives. And it had broken apart in my hands.

Whatever the real cause of the test result, Lloyd and Scaplehorn said Drayton should never have put down even a 'possible positive'.

Drayton's laboratory test using a machine was the subject of yet another revelation. A record had been found of the operation of that machine on the day Drayton had used it to test my sample. For some reason there was no mention of my sample. But that aside, the record showed that, during the day, test samples of nitroglycerine had been run through the machine to ensure it was working properly. So it was possible that traces of nitroglycerine were still in the machine when my sample was tested.

The record had been discovered before our 1987 appeal and should have been handed to our lawyers. Like so much crucial evidence, it was not.

The court was still reeling from all this new evidence on the forensic front – as was I – when Mr Mansfield dramatically exposed to the world what had gone on in the police operation to convict us. Revolutionary new scientific testing of police notes of the alleged confessions had shown that at least some of the notes could not have been compiled as the interviews took place. The police had sworn on oath that they were.

A process called ESDA (Electrostatic Document Analysis) had been used on the notes concerning Richard, and it had proved beyond doubt that great chunks had been written in later, that pages had been swopped around, and other versions of pages had been prepared. An examination of the ink showed parts had been written in out of sequence.

The scientist who did the work, Dr David Baxendale, gave evidence as to the alterations he had discovered. Dates when interviews were said to have taken place had been altered in police notebooks. Notes said to have been compiled in 1974 had actually been written up in 1975. So this was what the Home Secretary had meant when he referred to 'apparent discrepancies'.

Mr Mansfield was ruthless in his condemnation. 'A very grave shadow has been cast over the honesty and integrity of the officers conducting the interrogations,' he said. 'Without mincing words, effectively it means that the officers particularly involved in McIlkenny's case, Reade, Morris, Woodwiss and Langford, have been complicit in the fabrication of these notes and consequently have committed perjury in court.'

John Evans, the Chief Constable of Devon and Cornwall, told the court that he and his investigating team had prepared a dossier of questions for the detectives who had interrogated us. Reade had provided some replies. But, said Mr Evans, 'most questions in most cases were completely unanswered'.

The case dragged on with more and more detail of what had been done to put us in prison and then to keep us there. Each night I was taken back to the Scrubs, and as I set off each morning the cons would wish me well, both them and I wondering if I would return. At the end of the seventh day there was a great feeling of expectation that by the following afternoon it could be finished. But it was an anti-climax, and the legal speeches continued. The next morning the cons at the Scrubs gave us a wonderful send-off. This surely had to be the day, they said. The screws felt the same, and as we left that old place you would have thought we were the best of pals, not prisoner and jailer.

But on that ninth day in court there was a surprise. Mr Graham Boal, counsel for the Crown, seemed to strike out on his own. After accepting the forensic evidence and the confessions were no longer valid, he launched into one last-ditch effort to claim we were guilty. He conceded that John Walker, who had ludicrously been described as a brigadier in the IRA, might not have been of that rank, but claimed, without giving any details, that there was 'powerful evidence' he was at least a quartermaster. And in any new trial we would all be seen to be so closely bound to John we would all be found guilty. Then he came up with the astonishing proposition that the convictions were unsatisfactory, but not unsafe. I must get him to explain that one to me some time.

Mr Mansfield gave him short shrift. If the case were to begin again tomorrow, the prosecution would never even get into court, never mind get a conviction, he declared. Mr Boal was like an emperor without clothes. He was trying to suggest that rather than be found 'guilty' or 'not guilty' we should be found 'not very guilty'. A deflated Mr Boal rose to try to defend his position.

And suddenly it was all over.

249

# 28

# Free to go

It was 3.30 p.m. on Thursday 14 March 1991.

Lord Justice Lloyd interrupted Mr Boal, telling him to sit down. Lord Gifford, one of our team, started to rise, but the judge waved him down too, saying, 'We have heard enough.'

The whole court fell silent. Then he looked at the six of us in the dock, told us to stand, and said, 'In the light of fresh evidence which has become available since the last hearing in this court, your appeal will be allowed and you will be free to go as soon as the usual formalities have been discharged.'

And that was it. The nightmare that had lasted 16 years, 3 months and 23 days was finally over. The place went crazy. I was stunned at first, trying to take it in, telling myself, We've done it, at last we've done it.

Then I erupted with the fury of a volcano that has been bubbling away for so long, just waiting for its moment. As the judges left the court I banged the sides of the dock in triumph and screamed, 'Now it's our turn.'

But the flash of anger subsided quickly as I was caught up in the tide of joy that flooded through the courtroom, the mayhem sweeping respect for the staid majesty of the Old Bailey out of the windows. We six were throwing our arms around each other. People were crying, laughing, kissing, jumping up and down, yelling. The campaigners and observers and even some of the reporters rushed over to shake our hands. It was the most magnificent moment of my life. Our families and friends up in the public gallery were going wild. And as our barristers and solicitors celebrated, Gareth Peirce, the woman who had done so much to make it all possible, was in tears. It was ironic that on the day I'd met her nearly ten years before I'd told

250

her I didn't need her legal skills. Now I realised how important they had been.

I don't know how long we were in that dock savouring it all. But after a while a cop or a screw told us we would have to go downstairs and collect our property. We shouted up to our families that we would see them outside in a few minutes, and with their cheers ringing in our ears we went down the stairs from a dock for one last time. We were floating, walking on air. We each had only a few things to sign for, and as we stood waiting we were still laughing and joking, but nobody was speaking the words we all felt in our hearts: At last, it's over.

We couldn't wait to get outside. A young cop came and politely told us that there were big crowds on the street, and if we wanted we could slip quietly out the back where the police had laid on some cars.

'Get stuffed,' I told him. 'You brought us in the back door. We're going out the front with our heads held high.'

We had been dressed in casual clothes when we were stopped that night in 1974. Now we were resplendent in the collars and ties and smart suits our families had brought in for us to wear during the appeal. The cops showed us the door and I stopped and turned and said to the others, 'Are you ready lads?'

Were we ready? After nearly seventeen years dreaming of this moment? We went through a revolving door and as we came out into the street all I could see in front of me was a sea of faces. Then I was hit by a huge, deafening roar. There were people everywhere, cheering and clapping, waving banners, shouting out our names and reaching out to us. The crush barriers erected by the police to keep the crowds back were pushed aside by members of our families who rushed over to hug and kiss us. My brother Sammy, my sister Josie, and my ex-wife Pat were all there. So too was Paul Hill, one of the Guildford Four. He'd been putting a bet on a horse in the Cheltenham Gold Cup when he heard the roar and had rushed out into the street to see us emerge. He got through the barriers and threw his arms around me. He knew, in a way few others could, exactly how I felt.

We had been told some microphones had been set up in the street in case we wanted to say anything. I certainly did. And this time I wanted to be heard, after all those years of nobody listening. Chris Mullin was there with us, and he started ushering us forward.

Richard, with a folder of papers under one arm, took the microphone with the other. The noise of the crowd subsided as he began.

'It's good to see you all,' he said.

That brought a massive roar of delight. He went on.

'We have waited a long time for this. Sixteen years because of hypocrisy and brutality. But every dog has his day, and we're going to have ours.'

I was standing alongside Richard. And as I took in the scene, I felt that anger and bitterness I'd known every single day in prison rising in me like an unstoppable force. I looked around at the families, the women and the children. Yes, they were weeping with joy now. But I remembered all the tears of sorrow and pain that had been shed over the years. There'd. been too many tears. Richard finished, and in a rage I pulled the microphone towards me. With my right arm stretched out behind me and my finger jabbing at the Old Bailey, I shouted, 'Ladies and gentlemen, for sixteen and a half years we have been used as political scapegoats for people in there at the highest level. The police told us from the start they didn't care if we'd done it. They told us they were going to frame us. Just to keep the people in there happy. That's what it's all been about, saving face.' I was determined the world should know that the happiness I felt at being released could not extinguish the fires of bitterness raging inside. Arching around to look at the court building, with my eyes blazing and my finger still stabbing the air, I spat out the words that came from deep in my heart: 'Justice? I don't think those people in there have got the intelligence or the honesty to even spell the word, never mind dispense it. They are rotten.'

The crowds cheered, and I was going to say more, but something told me I'd said enough, that I'd got the message across. Then Hughie stepped forward.

'I have done sixteen years in prison, and that's a long time. Justice has been done today – but it's taken sixteen years,' he said.

It was Billy's turn. He wanted to know why Judith Ward (convicted of the M62 bombing) was still in prison; why three innocent men known as the Tottenham Three were still inside; and why the innocent men jailed for murdering newsboy Carl Bridgewater were not out too.

'There are many people behind prison bars wrongly convicted, and they're not all Irish. English people too,' he said.

The six of us lined up with Chris Mullin between us, our arms held aloft and our hands linked. I couldn't resist grabbing the microphone just one more time. 'Now we are going to show the world, prove to everybody what they did to us,' I shouted.

Richard stepped up again on behalf of us all to thank everybody who had turned up to see us freed, and the families and campaigners who had made this moment possible. I broke away to go over to the crowd behind the barriers, shaking hands and kissing complete strangers who were there to share the joy of our freedom. Somebody grabbed me by the arm at one barrier and started pulling me over it, and as I struggled happily to keep my feet I suddenly found myself looking across at the courtroom door through which we had walked to freedom. Standing there, framed in the doorway, was Gareth Peirce. And on her face was the biggest, broadest smile I've ever seen.

We strolled around for the next few minutes, stopping now and then to link hands and raise our arms so that the photographers could get the shots they wanted for the next day's front pages. And then we were told that transport was waiting for us and we moved off, with the crowds still cheering and waving goodbye.

The campaign had arranged for some limousines to take us off to a mansion in north London, and I squeezed into one with Sammy, Josie, Pat and several other people. The car was packed, but I didn't care. It was just such a tremendous feeling to be travelling in something other than a prison van, with my wrist no longer cuffed to a screw. Everyone was talking at once and trying to grab hold of me, but I managed to shout to my brother Sammy in the front to stop at a phone box so that I could call my mother. I knew she was at home in Birmingham waiting to see what happened.

Sammy said, 'There's a phone here,' and pushed a piece of plastic towards me. It looked like the sort of toy phone I'd bought for the kids years before and I threw it back at him, telling him not to be stupid. But then he tapped it a few times and passed it back to me, telling me to hold it against my ear. I heard a phone ringing. And then I heard my mother's voice. My heart nearly stopped. She was asking who was on the line.

'Hello ma, it's me. Paddy.'

She burst into tears, and I couldn't control the lump swelling in my throat. We had some sort of conversation, but I can't remember much of it because we were both in such a state. I can recall her saying: 'It's the happiest day of my life, son. I only wish your dad was here to share it.'

'So do I, ma,' I told her.

The car headed up through north London and as I gazed out the window, past the houses and beautiful trees, I saw a man walking his dog. And I thought how marvellous it was going to be now that I too had the freedom to walk where I pleased.

We arrived at the house and standing at the door welcoming us was Father Bobby Gilmore, who had chaired our national campaign. Inside it was bedlam, with all the families and the campaigners who had worked so hard for us. Tables were weighed down with food and drink. It had been arranged that we would give a press conference there, and a little later dozens of reporters and cameramen descended on us. We each said just a few words, mainly on the lines of what we'd said outside the court. We were all still too excited to say much beyond that. Then we posed for countless pictures before getting back to the party. It was a tremendous occasion, as though the joy of every party I'd ever been to was rolled into one. Sammy and Josie were the only family members with me at that time. One of my cousins, Billy, who lived in London, had hired a minibus and gone to Birmingham to pick up my mother, my children and grandchildren. He was to take them to a house in West Wickham, just south of London, where the campaign had arranged for us all to stay for a few days. But they were not expected to get there until very late. During the evening, as some of the other lads started moving off with their families, Billy Power asked if I fancied going to the Irish Centre in Camden, where another celebration was being held to mark our release. I was keen to go, but was not sure about the position regarding transport. I spoke to the limousine driver who had brought us to the house, to see if there was any chance of getting a lift to Camden.

'I'll take you wherever you want, mate. I'm yours for the night,' he said.

So we went off and had another great couple of hours, singing and dancing, and just feeling very, very good. But I was really looking forward to later on and being reunited with the rest of my family. So shortly after midnight we left the party and my driver took us to West Wickham. There I met my mother, the girls, Sean and the grandchildren. It was such an emotional moment. To see my mother as a free man for the first time in so long gave me a feeling I could never describe. We hugged and kissed and cried, and sat chatting until about 5 a.m. She could hardly believe I was really out, and neither could I. We had a lot to talk about, an awful lot, but eventually we both needed to sleep. I had been running on adrenalin since 3.30 the previous afternoon and finally the excitement and celebrations caught up with me. I gave mum a kiss goodnight, and went off to one of the bedrooms. I slumped on a bed beside one of my little grandsons and fell asleep, exhausted but happy.

A few hours later I woke up with bright spring sunshine blazing in through the window. That awful feeling I'd known every morning in prison was gone. I must have looked like something out of a children's fairy story as I lay rubbing my eyes to check that it really was true and not just a dream. I swung my legs over the edge of the bed and sat there, with the little boy asleep beside me, staring around the room. And when my eyes came to the door I got a real shock. It had a handle. On the inside! For more than sixteen years I'd never known what it was like to wake up in a room with a door handle you could see. In prison all the handles are on the outside, and inside there's just a big steel plate. Only somebody who has spent years in jail would understand how something as mundane as a door handle could send a surge of excitement through my body. That handle symbolised the fact that I was now a free man. I could just get up, turn the handle and walk out if I wanted to. There was nothing and nobody to stop me. I sat staring at it, hypnotised by it, until I heard my mother calling me. That broke the spell. So I got up and I did it. I put my fingers firmly around the wooden handle and I turned it. The door opened and I walked out.

I had breakfast – what a meal that was – and spent some time playing with the grandchildren and getting to know my own children again. I knew so little of them as people that I felt strangely uneasy speaking with them individually. I feared that building relationships with them was likely to be a long, difficult process. After a while I decided to exercise my newly restored right to take fresh air whenever I wanted.

I strolled off to the nearby shops with my daughter Tracey and her little Charmaine. I wanted to buy some shampoo so that I could try to wash the feeling of prison out of my hair for good. We came to one of those giant supermarkets, the sort that didn't even exist when I was put away. As we walked in I could see there were a dozen or more aisles stacked with goods, but I was completely taken aback by the sight that met me as we went down the first of them. There was nothing but bottles of booze. Whisky, brandy, vodka, gin, wine – every form of alcohol you could think of. And after the bottles came stack after stack of tins of beer. I'd never seen anything like it. At the time I was locked up you could only get booze in a pub or in an off-licence, one of those small corner shops. I was glad I had given up drink, because otherwise I would have been tempted to go crazy and buy a bottle of everything.

We wandered around into the next aisle, and then the next. Each was crammed with hundreds of different types of food. There were massive freezer cabinets stacked with all sorts of exotic-sounding meals I could never have dreamt of. And everything was in bright colours; there were splashes of reds and yellows and blues and orange everywhere. After the drabness of prison it was hard to take in.

I had told Tracey that I wanted to buy a bottle of shampoo, which I thought would be an easy enough task. She brought me to the toiletries aisle and when I saw what was laid out there I nearly collapsed. Row after row of bottles and tubes and sachets sent my head spinning. There were shampoos for dry hair, greasy hair, thick hair, fine hair, 'normal' hair, whatever that was, and hundreds more. There were conditioners and dyes and rinses. They were in all shapes and sizes and in every colour you could imagine. I was dumbfounded. All I wanted to do was wash my hair. Tracey laughed and said to me, 'Hurry up dad, or we'll be here all day.'

But I was confused and felt off-balance. Every time I went to pick one bottle another would suddenly catch my eye. I must have taken and put back twenty or more different shampoos. Eventually Tracey, seeing the look on my face, said, 'Here dad, this is what you need,' and dropped a bottle into her wire shopping basket.

What to many people would be no more than a comical experience had a deeper effect on me. I had had my first hint of a panic attack. In prison you don't make decisions, everything is decided for you.

If this was what my new world was going to be like, would I be able to cope?

We bought all the newspapers and walked back to the house to read them. They were full of stories and pictures of our release. Inevitably the *Sun* did not share our joy. It ran a piece saying we would probably become millionaires overnight through compensation. It certainly got that wrong. Alongside the stories about us was news that I had missed in the excitement of the previous day. Within minutes of our being freed, yet another Home Secretary, Kenneth Baker, was telling Parliament he was setting up a Royal Commission into the entire criminal justice system. He said its brief was to make recommendations to ensure no such miscarriage of justice ever occurred again.

Baker said the Royal Commission, the first for twelve years, would embrace all aspects of the criminal process, from investigation to appeal. There would be particular emphasis on the handling of initial inquiries by the police and the reliability of scientific evidence. But he rejected calls for a specific inquiry into our case.

I spent the next few days at the house with my family, but then they all returned to Birmingham. I moved to London to stay with my cousin Billy and his family for a while. I had a lot of things to consider, and needed time to think straight. I didn't feel I could do so in the emotional pressure-cooker atmosphere of my mother's house or in the homes of the children I hardly knew. I wanted to think about where I would live in the future. Belfast was never a real possibility. I had never wanted to go back in all the time I was in England, so why should I now? My second fifteen years had been spent in Birmingham. But could I return there after all that had happened? I needed time and space to decide.

I also needed time to acclimatise to everyday life again. One of the biggest problems I had at first was just getting used to the massive amount of traffic. It felt as though every car in the world was there in London. And I couldn't believe they were in so many different colours – in 1974 there were just a few colours to choose from for a car. Now, the volume of traffic made crossing a road a major challenge. I would wait nervously on the pavement for several minutes before dashing across.

It was the little things like that which made me realise that adjusting to life on the outside would be a lengthy process. Having to remember to carry a key with me all the time so that I could get into the house; sorting out the right money to buy something at the shops; buying clothes, because I would no longer be able to rely on a wardrobe that consisted of nothing but jeans and T-shirts; using a remote control unit to change channels on the television set. And there was food. It was not something I ever gave much thought to in jail. They gave it to you, you ate it. Simple. Now suddenly I was faced with all sorts of decisions about food. Should you choose Chinese, or Indian, or a pizza, or settle for fish and chips?

Luckily, drink was not a problem. It had got me into trouble before I went into jail and while I was inside. I had no intention of letting it bother me again. Three days after my release I went to a St Patrick's Night party with my family and, as at the other parties, drank nothing but orange or lemonade. But when one of my brothers went to buy the final round of drinks at the end of the night I said I would have a brandy. I raised it and toasted my father, drank it, and turned the glass upside down on the table. That symbolised for me the fact that I was going to stay away from drink.

There were a lot of press interviews in the first few days and then I went over to Ireland with Gerry and Richard to appear on the Gay Byrne chat show. We were put up in a beautiful hotel on the outskirts of Dublin, the first luxury hotel I'd ever stayed in. It was superb, with an *en suite* bathroom, a television, a telephone, a huge bed and, of course, a handle on the inside of the door. I was still revelling in the novelty of that. The American singer Tammy Wynette was also on the show, and she and her husband told us backstage how they had watched us coming out of the Old Bailey on American television news. They said that any time we were in Nashville we should look them up!

We flew back to England, and then a day or two later I was off again, this time on my own to appear on a chat show in Germany. I was picked up at Hamburg airport by a chauffeur in a stretch limousine and taken to the television studios where the show went out live, with me wearing headphones through which I got an immediate translation of what was being said. There was a phone-in after I was interviewed, which apparently drew the biggest response the show had ever had.

Thirteen days after our release I was back in court again. This time, though, I was in the public gallery, not the dock, to hear the three judges who had freed us give their reasons for doing so.

They took two and a half hours. Lord Justice Lloyd reviewed the history of the case. He said it was not surprising our trial judge, Bridge, accepted that the confessions were made voluntarily, because we had not looked injured on our first court appearance. Even so, Bridge had made it clear to the jury it was up to them to decide, both on the matter of confessions and the forensic evidence.

The appeal judges dismissed the once-crucial forensic evidence in a few brief lines, saying there was now no satisfactory proof I or Billy had ever handled nitroglycerine. There was no significant condemnation of Skuse, whom they felt overall, was a diligent scientist. Any problems with the Griess test were due to lack of knowledge about it at the time. Weaknesses in his evidence were not due to incompetence but were matters our lawyers had failed to expose. But the judges had far more to say on the 'confessions'. They said Reade had been unable to offer any convincing explanation for the ESDA results on the notes of one of the McIlkenny interviews. 'At best, officers were lying when they said the noting of the interviews was contemporaneous,' said Lord Justice Farquharson. 'At worst, they must have put their heads together to fabricate part, or the whole, of the interview.'

He said it was curious that McIlkenny was not alleged to have made any admissions during that particular interview. 'What was the purpose of fabricating? Perhaps we shall never know,' he said. 'But in the absence of an honest explanation, the impact of such evidence on the jury at the trial would have been very great.'

I can understand the judges finding that point curious. I had always been baffled by a similar mystery, over why the Birmingham police had all along insisted they had had no contact with us until after 9.30 on the Friday morning after the bombing. The contact actually began much earlier, but for some reason they stuck to that time and would not budge from it, even though it had little relevance to what they did to us. If we had just been able to prove they were lying about the time, it would have let the jury see they were capable of lying about other things.

Farquharson said the matter of whether notes had been written up during or after interviews was probably not crucial in itself. 'It may be said that even if notebooks are not made up until much later, even as late as 1975, it does not mean that the evidence cannot be relied on,' he said. 'The difficulty is that this is not what the officers said at the trial.'

What they had said of course, on oath, was that they had written up the notes as they went along – a lie which science had now laid bare.

He said that the 'most puzzling' part of the Reade schedule was the interview with me which had been crossed out. Reade's only explanation was that he must have been misinformed. The judges at the 1987 appeal had been confident Reade had not tried to deceive them. Nor had they thought him capable of organising such a complicated conspiracy.

'We are now three years on,' said Farquharson. 'We know now that Superintendent Reade, whether or not he is capable of organising a conspiracy, is at least capable of deceiving the court with regard to the McIlkenny interview.' While Reade might have used the schedule as an aide-memoire, he could not explain why my interview had been crossed out. That cast doubt on his honesty and reliability.

In drawing to a close, the judges appeared to be going out of their way to clear the Chief Justice, Lord Lane, of any blame for the way he handled our 1987 appeal, saying much of the evidence now available had not been around then. But some of it had. It was just that Lane failed to take any of it into account.

Lord Justice Lloyd said that it was clear the fresh evidence would have had a 'considerable impact' on the jury at our trial, and added, 'We would say that in the light of the fresh scientific evidence, which at least throws grave doubt on Dr Skuse's evidence if it does not destroy it altogether, these convictions are both unsafe and unsatisfactory.

'The fresh investigation carried out by the Devon and Cornwall police renders the police evidence at the trial so unreliable that again we would say that the convictions are both unsafe and unsatisfactory. Adding the two together, our conclusion was inevitable. It was for these reasons that we allowed the appeals.'

I was not impressed with the judgment. Nor was Gareth Peirce. She said afterwards the judges had failed to grapple with the crucial question of the failure of the prosecution to disclose vital evidence to our lawyers. Nobody had explained why that had happened. 'It just isn't good enough to say it's a mystery,' she said.

The broadcaster Ludovic Kennedy, famous for his work on other miscarriages of justice, felt the judgment was unsatisfactory because it gave a 'clean bill of health' to the trial judge and the earlier appeal judges.

John Evans, the Devon and Cornwall chief constable, said it was sad that police irregularities had occurred, but it had happened in 1974 and it was now 1991. 'One has to keep the whole thing in perspective,' he said. 'It is very, very unlikely it could happen again.' I wish I shared his confidence.

With the judgment over I left the courtroom for the last time in connection with our case. As far as the judicial process went, the Birmingham Six were now history. But as I walked out into a chill March wind, I felt cheated. For I suddenly realised something.

Despite everything that had happened to us, not one policeman, not one prosecution lawyer, not one judge, had turned to the Birmingham Six and said: 'We're sorry.'

# 29

## Stranger in the family

A few hours after leaving the courtroom I was squeezing my way into Wembley Stadium with my son Sean and 80,000 other people to watch an England–Ireland soccer international.

Sean had been just twenty-three months old when I was sent to jail. His knowledge of me as a father consisted of prison visits lasting an hour or two every few months. Now he was eighteen. It was not a question of rebuilding a relationship with my son, but building one that had never existed. The injustice done to me had robbed me of the strong bond I'd had with my father. I was determined to try to ensure it did not steal my son too.

When Sean was born I had dreamed of the things we would do together. But as he grew up there was nothing we could share. I was prevented from doing any of the things a father naturally wants to do with his only son – such as taking him to a football match. Perhaps, I thought, it was not too late to start.

Gerry Hunter no doubt felt the same way about the sons from whom he had been torn apart. Sean and I met Gerry and his boys at the ground, and together we watched a great match, ending in a 1–1 draw. But by the time the final whistle blew I knew there was hard work ahead if I was to have the relationship I wanted with the son I didn't know.

My children and my mother lived in Birmingham, so to see them I would have to go back there. I was not afraid of returning. I had nothing to be ashamed of. But I did feel a strange sensation the first time I got off the train from London at New Street station.

As I made my way from the platform to the concourse I began churning inside with an odd mixture of emotions. This was where the nightmare had started. The station had changed a lot since that

Thursday night when the six of us gathered there. But the memory of it all came flooding back in brilliant detail. I stood and looked across at where the Taurus bar had been, and recalled how I had met the other five lads just inside the entrance. How they had told me it was too late to buy a drink, so I took a swig from Billy's glass. How we joked and laughed as we ran down the stairs to board. How Hughie stood on the platform waving to us all as the train to Heysham pulled out.

I stared down at the platform for a while, then quickly made my way out, wanting to put it all behind me. The station had changed, and so too had the city around it, but the landmarks I'd known, such as the Rotunda and the Bull Ring shopping centre, were still there. It was good to see them again after so long.

I went to my mother's house and spent some time with her before going to see some of my daughters. They are all grown up now and live happily in the city with young families of their own. Seeing them and my grandchildren that day really brought home just what I had lost. My six kids had been aged between nine and two when I was taken from them. No words can describe how a father feels at not being around for his children's early years. At the start it was mainly concern for their welfare, especially when Pat had to put them into care. Then in later years came the heartbreak each time they reached the milestones that every dad wants to share – the birthdays, the Christmases, the first day at school, the school concerts. My little boy's first kick of a football. These were all things that could never be brought back. Like so much in the previous sixteen and a half years they were lost for ever, gone for ever.

I did not meet anybody other than my family that first day back in Birmingham, but I've met plenty of people on my many subsequent visits. I have never been treated with anything but kindness, never had any unpleasantness from people who once hated me so much. But I knew as I returned to London that night there was no point in trying to pick up the shattered pieces of my life in Birmingham, a city with its constant reminders of what had happened to me. How could I ever go past my old home, or the Crossways, or Queen's Road police station, without everything coming back? I decided then that I would settle in London for the time being and try to build a future there.

Within a few weeks of being released I received an interim compensation payment of £50,000 from the government, while my solicitors negotiated with the Home Office over an acceptable total figure. The first thing I did was to give a lump sum to each of my children. I suppose the gesture was a combination of feeling guilty at not having been around as they grew up, and a desire to buy the love I had never known. By giving them money to get things for their own children and their homes I felt I was doing something I had not been able to do in the past – providing for them.

I took one of my daughters and her children to Oxford Street in London. I told her just to wander in and out of the shops and pick whatever she wanted for herself and her kids. I found somewhere to sit and read some newspapers for an hour or two, and then went back into the shops with her. We picked up the dresses, coats, shoes, other clothes and stacks of toys she had chosen, and I mechanically paid as we went from store to store. But I didn't get any sense of happiness, of celebration, out of it. The feeling was of nothing more than performing a duty.

It was the same when I bought things for the other girls and for Sean. I felt as if I were buying for people I did not know, and emotionally that was indeed the case. These were my children, but I felt more like some long-lost uncle who had returned after years abroad. When I went to their homes I found I had very little to say to them, and could never feel relaxed. Conversation was an effort; it felt as if there was no common ground between us, no shared experiences to talk over. I had lived in a world totally alien to theirs, and now that I was in their world I could not feel part of it. After the first few minutes with any of them I began to feel awkward, as though I were an outsider intruding in their lives. I would come up with some lame excuse about why I could not stay long, and would feel a great sense of relief when I was able to get out of the door and into the street.

For years I had promised my little grandchildren that when I got out of prison I would take them to Disney World in Florida. Now I decided that when further compensation came through I would take them all, children and grandchildren, to Florida for a long holiday. Perhaps if it was just me and them, away from it all, I could get to know my kids properly and overcome this feeling of being an outsider.

It was particularly painful being uncomfortable with my children, but in those first weeks of freedom it was not just with them that I felt uneasy. I found there were few places where I could relax completely.

I began to suffer frequent panic attacks. I would be walking along a street and suddenly hear the sound of sirens. Then a police car would come into view and I would freeze. It was a totally irrational fear. My head knew that they were not coming for me; but my body felt differently. My mouth would go dry and my legs weak, and I would be unable to continue walking until the car was long gone. I was caught up in one or two bomb scares in London, and the sight of lots of policemen shouting out orders would bring on another attack, even though I knew the cops were no threat to me. Sometimes when just standing in a shop queue, waiting to buy a newspaper, I would feel a panic attack coming on and would have to get out.

Every day I felt under pressure to some degree. The anger I had felt in prison did not seem to be receding. I began to wonder if it ever would. Often I would explode in an unexplained rage and shout at people who were just trying to help. At other times I would find myself sitting alone in a room having a cup of tea when suddenly, without reason or warning, some incident from those awful years inside would pop up in my mind. I would sit back and gaze at a blank wall as a jumble of thoughts tumbled through my head: words, names, faces, pictures. Each flashing past, each competing for attention. It would go on until some noise outside or knock at the door would bring me back to reality with a jolt. I would curse myself for daydreaming, thinking I had been lost in thought for several minutes. But then I would find my tea was cold. And when I looked at my watch I would realise I had been sitting there for hours.

I didn't seek medical help for any of these problems at the time, none of which I could explain. I presumed they were part of returning to normality and that I would just have to live with them.

Ironically, the one place where I did not feel at all awkward or under pressure was back inside a prison. I had promised plenty of the lads I had left behind that I would not forget them when free, and I was determined to keep those vows. I spent an enormous amount of time and money travelling the country to various jails to see old friends. You might think that after all those years locked up I would never want to see a prison again. But not once did I ever feel daunted in walking in through the prison gates. In a perverse way this place that had been my home for years was now the only place where I actually felt at home. I would bounce into visiting rooms, greeting the cons and screws alike with raucous hellos. I knew the people, the language, the procedure; the whole atmosphere was familiar and made me feel relaxed. I would not admit it at the time, but those visits provided an escape from the pressures of the outside world.

People who have never been inside for a long spell cannot possibly understand how prison moulds you to live within prison conditions, which are abnormal. You eventually accept the abnormal as normal. Then when you are thrown out into what is supposed to be the normal world, you find life there to be abnormal. It is not easy to come to terms with.

At the end of April I went to Crete for a holiday with my son Sean and a few friends, including Gerry Conlon and Paddy Armstrong. It was the first holiday I'd ever taken with Sean. The weather was superb, and we had a great time driving around on mopeds or just lounging around the hotel swimming pool. We went out each evening for a meal, but then I would usually go back to the hotel while Sean and the other lads went off to nightclubs. Sean and I were not like father and son, but more like two men who were becoming friends . . . men who liked each other but were not entirely comfortable in each other's company. I wanted it to go beyond that, for us to have a deeper relationship, and I'm sure Sean did too. But neither of us knew where to start.

The holiday came to an abrupt end when I went down with a severe bout of food poisoning and had to fly back to Britain early. Sean flew back with me, but as I recovered at home and thought back over the holiday I realised I would have to accept that there could never be a normal father-son relationship between us. That hurt, particularly when I thought of how Pat and I had desperately wanted a son after five little girls. And it hurt knowing that I had had such a great relationship with my own father until I was held for the pub bombings. Sean will never have that special something that I had with my father, and I will never have with Sean what my father had with me.

In early summer there was a massive thank-you party for our campaign supporters in Britain at the Camden Irish Centre in north London. It was a tremendous night, with the lawyers, the politicians and the media people who had helped us all there, along with hundreds of campaigners. I found it very moving to meet the faces behind names I knew only as a signature on a letter or card. There were other thank-you nights held in several cities around the country, and each time the biggest pleasure I got was in meeting face to face for the first time the people who had supported us. I then went off alone to America to thank people there on our behalf. I particularly wanted to meet Kathleen Lisowski, who had done so much for us in making Americans aware of our case. She had personally sent me an enormous amount of money over the years to help with the postage costs for all the letters I was sending.

I flew to Boston and stayed for ten days, having a marvellous time meeting campaigners and being hosted at receptions by people such as the Mayor of Boston and the Governor of Massachusetts. Meeting the dignitaries was an honour, but I got even more pleasure from meeting those ordinary Americans whose names would mean nothing to most people, but meant a great deal to me. They were the hundreds of people who for years had sent me letters of support while I was in jail. There was Kathleen of course, and meeting her was a very emotional moment. And among the many others was Katy O'Sullivan, who had begun writing to me when she was a child of just eight or nine, having read about me in some campaign literature. It was marvellous to meet her in person ten years later, by then a young woman of eighteen.

While I was there I was asked if I would be willing to take part later in the year in a speaking tour across the States, organised by the Irish-American Unity Conference, a group which supports the unification of Ireland through peaceful means. I readily agreed.

Shortly after returning from the States I was on the move again, this time joining the other five lads on a four-day trip to Dublin for a massive thank-you to our Irish supporters. I was honoured to meet Dr Mary Robinson, the President of Ireland, who immediately made us all feel relaxed with her warmth and easy-going manner. We made a tour through the centre of Dublin on an open-top bus, with thousands of people lining the streets and cheering. The other lads had their wives and families with them on the bus, and I had my daughters Tracey and Maxine and son Sean alongside me.

A platform had been set up for us in front of the GPO building in the city centre to address the crowds, and I wondered whether I should just say a few words of thanks and no more. But I felt it would be dishonest not to let these people who had turned out to greet us know how hopeless their successive governments had been in failing to help us. So I told them that while I felt gratitude at being in Dublin and getting such a reception from the people, I did not feel in any way grateful to Irish governments which for years had regarded us as nothing but an embarrassment. The crowd roared their approval.

The Dublin visit ended with a stirring concert on the final night with singers, bands playing traditional music and girls performing Irish dancing. The six of us were each called on stage to be presented with pieces of crystal. It was a marvellous ending to a marvellous few days.

Back in England I had received another interim compensation payment and decided to splash out on one big effort to build a proper relationship with my children. To keep that promise made in jail to the grandchildren, I said I would take everybody on a fifteen-day holiday to Disney World in Florida.

So at the end of August I set off from Gatwick airport with my mother, four daughters, my son, and seven grandchildren. Maxine could not travel as she was unwell. I had booked three apartments for us at Orlando, and for the first two or three days all was well. The weather was superb, and we simply spent time together lazing around the swimming pool, acclimatising to the ninety-degree temperatures. I think the kids knew I saw this as an opportunity to bring us all together as one big, happy family, and initially were on their best behaviour. But then the petty arguments began. The girls would have rows with each other and with Sean over what seemed to me the most trivial of matters. It appeared they could not be in the same room together for more than a few minutes without an argument breaking out.

I was horrified. Here I was paying for everything on a dream holiday and it seemed all they could do was fight. I had come from a large family, but we had not fought like this. Was it because I had been missing from their lives when they were growing up as brother and sisters? Would it have been different if I had been there to enforce some fatherly control over them? Whatever the reasons, I could not stand the arguing and at every opportunity I would take off with some of the grandchildren for hours at a time. But the tension was unbearable and eventually I snapped. I laid into each of them, telling them I could not put up with any more of it. I told them that our lives had been ruined in the past because of other people pulling us apart. Now they were tearing the family apart themselves. If I could have got a plane home that night I would have done so.

Tracey, being the eldest, had a word with them all and things improved over the final days of the holiday, but I knew I couldn't hide from myself any longer the truth of the situation. I didn't know my children, and they didn't know me. Too many years had been spent apart for us ever to really change things. I had become a stranger in my own family.

As I flew home from Florida I realised how naïve I had been in thinking that buying presents and holidays could somehow make up for the years of loss. It just can't be done. My children never had a proper childhood, and I never got to enjoy proper fatherhood. I was not there to hold them when they were frightened. I was not there to pick them up when they fell over. They call me 'dad', but for me the word is empty of the joy and sense of shared happiness it should conjure up. I know I'll be able to pull some parts of my life together again in the coming years, but I have no way of experiencing those precious moments I've missed.

After the emotional turmoil of Florida I needed a proper, stress-free holiday. Shortly after being released I had met a beautiful young woman called Alison. With all the pressures I had to deal with on being freed I felt the last thing I needed was any kind of romantic relationship or long-term commitment. But I immediately felt at ease in her company. Not only was she beautiful, but she was intelligent and had a great sense of humour. The more I was with her, the more I felt I would like us to be together. During the summer I met her several times and eventually we began going out together.

I found I could talk to her about things I would not dream of discussing with other people, and could confide in her with complete confidence. I also discovered she had an amazing ability to make me feel calm when I began to get angry, or at times of stress, so I felt she would be the ideal companion for a quiet break.

Before going to Florida I had raised with Alison the possibility of us going to Ireland together when I returned, and she said she would like to join me. As the Florida holiday became more and more of a disaster I could not wait for it to be over so that I could head for Ireland with her. When I got back from the States we set off almost immediately and had a wonderful week, which came to an end all too quickly.

I returned refreshed and ready to take on another round of travelling. Since being released I had been in constant touch with Mrs Anne Whelan, the mother of Michael Hickey, one of the men wrongly convicted of murdering newsboy Carl Bridgewater. She has for years led the campaign for the release of her son and the men convicted with him, Michael's cousin Vincent Hickey, and Jimmy Robertson. She was organising a nationwide series of meetings with Sharon Raghip, the wife of Engin Raghip, one of the men known as the Tottenham Three who had been convicted of the brutal murder of a policeman. They were also wrongly convicted of murder, and Anne's and Sharon's campaign was to draw attention to their respective cases. I had met all of the men involved at one time or another in prison, and had promised that I would offer whatever help I could when I got out. Anne was keen for me to speak at each venue, and I was delighted to help.

We set off for a twelve-day tour of Britain, holding meetings in a different town each day. Other members of the Six joined us on the platform on occasions, and we had various lawyers and campaigners addressing the meetings. I spoke briefly about our own case, the battle we had fought to be freed, and how I knew the other men to be innocent having met them inside. It was encouraging that so many people turned up to the meetings, but depressing to hear so many other tales of miscarriages of justice from families of jailed men who came along for advice on what they could do. I could see there was a great need to help these people, who were in the same position I and my family had been in.

As soon as that was finished I was off again to the States for the speaking tour I had been asked to take on earlier in the year. It was a packed programme, taking in fifteen states during the two months of crisscrossing the country. I was interviewed on radio stations, spoke to high schools and colleges, addressed conventions of lawyers and human rights activists, and gave talks to a wide range of clubs and organisations. The talks were all generally on the theme of miscarriages of justice, but often broadened out to other related issues during question-and-answer sessions. It was a tremendous trip, and I had a great time visiting exciting places, but it was exhausting.

I returned home shortly before Christmas 1991, physically and mentally shattered. It had been nine months since I had been freed. I had done so much in that time that the weeks had flown by. After so many years of knowing nothing but the drabness of a prison cell I had suddenly experienced the luxury of hotel suites. I had swopped the indignities of the prison van for the comfort of a chauffeured limousine. I had been to places I had only dreamt of previously and been treated like a celebrity. But now the parties and the travelling were over.

# 30

# Facing the future

For nearly seventeen years there was only one driving force in my life – the determination to be set free. Everything I did and everything I felt in those years was geared towards the day when I would no longer be Prisoner 509496. Suddenly it came. But when the euphoria and the celebrations and the travelling ended, I had to face the harsh facts of life. I was forty-six, with no wife or family, no home, no job, no income and no prospects.

I was locked up for a major part of my life through no fault of my own, spending large chunks of that time in solitary confinement. Then one day they opened the door and told me that I was free to go back into a world I knew nothing of. What kind of freedom is that? There was no offer of counselling to help me find my feet again in this strange new world without bars; no offer of medical help to deal with the demons of anger and bitterness raging inside my head; no offer of financial advice to help me to cope with a world where the currency was pounds and pence, rather than tobacco and weed.

The result was a succession of violent swings of mood, from great happiness to overpowering depression.

I knew that readjustment to life outside of prison would be a long and difficult process. In the early days of freedom I was completely disoriented by not being locked up. Trying to establish new relationships with strangers, or re-establish relationships with old friends, was a painful experience. In jail, everything is controlled and regimented. You don't have to work at relationships, they are forced on you. There is very little self-responsibility. Outside you have to make decisions yourself. And it's not easy. It leads to further depression, and the stoking of that all-consuming anger that cries out: This shouldn't have happened to me.

When the rushing around ended and I found myself spending more time alone, the bouts of depression grew deeper and more frequent. The question I could never get out of my head was: What do I do now? A major problem in trying to map out a future was that I had not received a full compensation settlement. The government was wrangling with our lawyers over what it should be. That meant I was suspended in a sort of limbo, not able to put the past behind me or look to the future because I did not know where I stood financially.

I set up home with Alison and she was a great help in getting me through some of my blackest moods. But she had a full-time job, so I spent lengthy periods on my own, just sinking further into troughs of despair.

Eventually I knew I needed help and began receiving counselling, fixed up through Gareth Peirce who was, as always, remarkably supportive. I started regular sessions with two doctors, James McKeith and Gisli Gudjonsson, to talk through the problems I was experiencing. I was diagnosed as having post-traumatic stress disorder, which basically meant I was paying mentally, and had been for years, for what had happened to me. The long spells in solitary confinement had particularly left their mark, even though at the time I had no idea of the damage they were doing.

I seemed to spend much of the next three years doing nothing other than receiving counselling and working on this book, which in itself has been a therapy, helping me come to terms with all that has gone on. But it was difficult. I found it impossible to concentrate for more than a short time. Then I would go for weeks doing nothing. The lowest point came when my mother was diagnosed as having cancer. She had been my one permanent pillar of strength through all those years. I was devastated. It was so unfair that she should now have to face this ordeal after everything she had already suffered.

I was prescribed anti-depressants, but did not take them for long. I did not want to become dependent on drugs, and knew in my heart that ultimately it was down to me to overcome the problems I faced. Gradually, I began to benefit from the counselling and the solid support of Alison, and started to take a more positive attitude to life. I confronted the fact that gaining my freedom was not some pot of gold at the end of the rainbow. I had spent so long in jail thinking only of the day I would be freed that I had never looked beyond it, to consider what I would do with the rest of my life.

I was also able to confront the fact that my years in jail had actually left me missing aspects of prison life: the friendships, the jokes, the absence of having to make decisions. I know now that is why in my first couple of years of freedom I went back to prison so often; I felt part of me was still there. I still do.

Such visits led to one of the fiercest rows I've had with any of my children. One day in the summer of 1993 I was at Tracey's home in Birmingham and Maxine called around. As usual, after a short time I said that I would have to leave, explaining that I was off to see an old friend in jail. Maxine exploded.

'All you seem to do is keep going back to jail,' she said. 'You come up here and spend twenty minutes with us, and then off you go to a prison and spend hours there.

'When I was growing up all I ever used to wish for was that my dad could be around. I've waited sixteen and a half years while you were in jail, and two years since you've been out for you to be around. And you're still not with us. I don't think we'll ever get you back.'

She was right to be angry, and there was nothing I could say to her in reply. I could not explain to her why it was I felt more comfortable back at a jail than I did with my own children. I could not explain it to myself at that time.

Since confronting the fact that I was escaping from reality by returning to prison, I have learned to cope with the situation. I have cut down the number of times I now return, although I've no intention of stopping completely. I know all too well the value of a visit to a prisoner. But I also know I have to focus on my future as much as on the needs of my friends.

An important part of that future involves my claim for compensation for the ordeal I suffered, because until it is settled I cannot get on with the rest of my life. I have not received anything since those two interim payments shortly after my release. Half of the money went on buying a house so that I would always at least have a roof over my head. A fair amount of the rest was spent on my family, but the bulk has gone on day-to-day living.

I'm keen to work again, but even if there were not millions already unemployed, what hope would I have?

I believe that I and the other five are entitled to far more than what we have received so far. We and our families were devastated by the experience of arrest, trial and imprisonment. We were simple, working men who had our lives and families ripped apart. I lost the middle years of my life, I lost my wife and I lost my children. I was brutally beaten and intimidated, and neither the physical nor the mental scars will ever heal.

I have suffered the most serious defamation in recent history, being labelled as one of the perpetrators of the worst IRA bombing Britain has seen. At every step of the fight for freedom the case was back in the public eye, which brought renewed abuse and contempt from the outside world. And I was convicted because of the greatest of failings of the authorities involved.

Money will never be able to compensate me adequately for my life being destroyed. But I believe I have a right to a payment which would reflect the injustice done to me, and would help to alleviate the problems I will clearly face in the future. I would want to invest the bulk of the money to provide a regular income. It's not for me to put a figure on how much it should be. But a case settled in March 1991, the month I was released, makes interesting reading.

It involved a Mr George Lunt of Liverpool who was wrongly imprisoned for non-payment of rates. He was held in Walton jail for forty-two days. There was no suggestion of ill-treatment, but he suffered humiliation and distress. A court awarded him £13,500 for his ordeal, but Mr Lunt appealed that it was insufficient. A higher court subsequently awarded him £25,000, with three senior judges unanimously agreeing that it was not excessive, considering the 'horrific experience' Mr Lunt had undergone.

If £25,000 for six weeks was a 'proper award in all the circumstances', as the judges put it, how much should I get for everything I suffered? The truth of the matter is that not even the Queen, the richest woman in the world, has enough money to compensate me for what I have lost.

There are those who get incredibly angry at the thought of the Birmingham Six receiving a penny in compensation, and who for their own motives seek through innuendo to undermine our innocence whenever possible. They claim we 'got off on a technicality'. There have even been absurd suggestions in some newspapers that there is 'new evidence' that nitroglycerine was indeed on our hands.

Not me and Billy though, as originally alleged, but some of the others. Absolute nonsense, but it is enough to keep a suspicion in the minds of the public who do not know the whole story, that maybe we did have something to do with it after all. I challenge the people who spread this rubbish to bring into the open any such 'new evidence'. We have nothing to fear.

Such adverse publicity in the media reinforces my view that I will remain a figure of notoriety for the rest of my life. I am acutely aware that there is a sizeable body of people, especially among the more rabid of the press, ready to pounce on any failing on the part of any one of us six. The implicit suggestion would then be that if we were guilty of some unrelated indiscretion, we were probably also guilty of the pub bombings. It's as though they desperately need to believe we were indeed guilty and that the system did not get it badly wrong.

Two incidents have already thrust me into the headlines again since my release. In one I was completely blameless. The other, to my shame, was of my own making, and I bitterly regret it. The first involved a front-page story in the *Sun*, Britain's biggest-selling tabloid, about the holiday I had taken in Crete. The story claimed I had been involved in drunken and unruly behaviour. It was completely untrue. An editorial suggested that any sympathy for me over my wrongful imprisonment was misplaced. I sued and received an apology and damages.

The second incident occurred at a rally in Derry in January 1993 to mark the twenty-first anniversary of Bloody Sunday, the day on which British troops shot dead thirteen civilians in the city. I had been invited to speak, and really should have refused. I had enough problems of my own at the time in trying to come to terms with the anger I felt at what the British authorities had done to me. The last thing I needed was to get caught up in the whirlwind of emotion that surrounds this particularly black day in Irish history. But I went and spoke about how over the years many innocent Irish men and women had been killed by British soldiers, not just those who had died on Bloody Sunday. I said that British rule over a people who did not want it would have to come to an end at some time. But then I got carried away and, pointing at the soldiers on duty on the edge of the crowds, said, 'There is only one way to send them back, and that is in boxes, because that is what they do to us.'

I was foolish to have said such a thing and have regretted it ever since. Not because of the inevitable condemnation it brought, but because I did not mean it. How could I possibly have meant it when my father and brother Bobby were both in the British Army, and indeed Bobby served several times in Northern Ireland? I don't want to see any more deaths there, on either side. I apologised afterwards, especially to those thousands of people, both British and Irish, who had supported our campaign for freedom and were completely opposed to violence and such talk of violence. I felt that after all they had done for me, I had let them down badly. But I realised the harm had been done. I also realised I would have to be very careful in future about failing to control my emotions and the risk of blurting out things I did not mean.

I doubt, though, whether I will ever be able to control my emotions when it comes to the people who played a part in locking me away. The anger and bitterness towards them is still there in large doses. Skuse, I'm happy to say, was forced to retire several years ago. He began libel proceedings against *World In Action*, but later dropped them. By January of 1996 he was suing the libel lawyers who represented him for £1 million in damages over their handling of the case. The lawyers countersued for more than £130,000 they claimed was still outstanding on his bill. One of his lawyers was reported to have told him he had not "a cat's chance in hell' of winning the libel case. He is now said to be financially ruined, having spent his life savings on legal costs, and his home is said to have been burgled many times.

Some of the Winson Green prison officers who beat us have gone up in the service, but obviously there's no question of any of them being brought to justice now. I noticed, though, as recently as 1993 a report concerning a prisoner who was suing the Home Office on the grounds that he was beaten up within an hour of arriving at the prison. In his case the court believed him and amazingly he won £3,000 in damages.

My original defence barrister, Field Evans, was made a judge, as was the prosecutor, Mr Harry Skinner. The judge at the trial, Mr Justice Bridge, is now Lord Bridge, one of the country's most senior legal figures. The man who presided over our 1987 appeal, Chief Justice Lane, retired shortly afterwards, and many believed his decision to go was influenced by the storm of criticism directed at him over his handling of our case.

And then, of course, there are the police. Just days after our first appeal began, the IRA bombed a Remembrance Day service in Enniskillen in Northern Ireland, killing eleven people including a young nurse called Marie Wilson. I well remember watching her father, Gordon, who had lain in the rubble with her as she died, appear on television after the blast. He was heartbroken, but was somehow able to forgive the murderers who had taken his daughter's life.

I wish I could find it within me to forgive the policemen who ruined my life, and the lives of my wife and children. But I cannot. Not yet, and I doubt whether the day will ever come. George Reade, the man who led the police inquiry, and two of his colleagues with whom he interviewed Richard McIlkenny were charged after we were released. They were accused of perjury and conspiracy to pervert the course of justice in relation to interviews with Richard. They had by then all retired from the police. They went on trial in October 1993, but after three days of legal arguments Mr Justice Garland halted the case and said they were free to go. He said it would not be possible for them to receive a fair trial because of the publicity surrounding the whole matter of the Birmingham Six. And he felt that it would be difficult to isolate the precise charges against the men from the overall case of the Six.

I was angry at the decision, but not surprised. I had felt all along that the Crown had shown little enthusiasm in pursuing the matter. The prosecution did not even interview Richard about what had happened. And as for the suggestion that the men would not have received a fair trial because of adverse publicity, I can only say that I doubt whether we would have received such a generous response to that argument back in 1975. As *The Times* said of that part of the ruling, 'It seems to offer a bizarre incentive to defendants to whip up adverse pre-trial publicity about themselves.'

With the collapse of that trial, the country was left with two unresolved scandals. The authorities had failed to convict either those responsible for the pub bombings, or those responsible for a massive miscarriage of justice. I believe it is a scandal in itself that a public inquiry has not been held into what went wrong.

The end of the case against Reade and colleagues saw Lord Denning rolled out yet again to pontificate on matters concerning us six. He even managed to remember his 'appalling vista' expression, using it this time to say, 'the appalling vista is that the Birmingham Six have been acquitted and the police have been acquitted. What is the public to think of our system of law? It would have been most unfair to continue this case against the police officers. I have always supported the police. The judge was right to stop it.'

What of the other police officers involved in the case against us? It appears no action is to be taken against any of them. The infamous squad from which they came, the West Midlands Serious Crime Squad was disbanded in August 1989. Ray Bennett, the man who had dealt with me, was by then the head of the squad, and had been promoted to Detective Chief Inspector. He was still serving at that rank when in December 1992 he was stopped for speeding in his car in the early evening. The cops who stopped him smelt alcohol on his breath, and he was found to be well over the drink-drive limit. He retired shortly afterwards, and in January 1993 was fined £440 for drink-driving.

When I last heard of John Brand, Bennett's sidekick, he was still serving in the force. John Moore was later promoted to Detective Superintendent. He retired in the early 1980s and went to live in the United States, but I've been told he returned to Britain and was living in the Midlands.

When the squad was disbanded, an inquiry was ordered into its activities of the previous few years, although not of course stretching back to 1974. The authorities had to do something because the courts were beginning to throw out with embarrassing regularity cases where defendants alleged that members of the squad had fabricated confessions. In 1993 a man who had been jailed for a jewellery robbery became the fourteenth person to be cleared because of concern over evidence from the discredited squad. Gary Binham claimed his confession had been made up. When efforts were made to get his original statement so it could be subjected to ESDA examination, the police said it could not be found. Several other similar cases are still in the pipeline. The inquiry into the squad investigated 66 former members, and recommended that 16 be charged with criminal offences. The Director of Public Prosecutions, Barbara Mills, rejected that advice. A report then went to the Police Complaints Authority which decided 7 detectives should face internal disciplinary proceedings. A further 10 would have faced disciplinary charges if they had not retired, and another 102 serving officers were to be given 'informal advice'.

I find it almost beyond belief that not one policeman in the Birmingham Six case is to be punished. What those men did was evil. But I believe there was incompetence among the police too – if they had done their job properly the pub bombings need never have occurred, and the lives of so many people need never have been lost or blighted.

According to the police, they knew on the morning of 12 November 1974 that James McDade's thumbprint was on a bag that had probably carried an incendiary device that had gone off at an office in Birmingham several days earlier. Why then was he not immediately pulled in for questioning? I suppose it could be argued that he was allowed to remain free and put under surveillance in the hope he would lead the police to other IRA men. But if that was the case, they failed to watch him closely enough and it became a gamble that failed. For he was not under surveillance when he blew himself up in Coventry. And if he had not blown himself up, his colleagues would not have blown up those two Birmingham pubs in a twisted form of revenge for his death.

The police have escaped punishment, and so too have the real pub bombers. I don't know for certain who they are, but I do know that if a fraction of the effort invested in convicting us and keeping us in prison for nearly seventeen years had been channelled towards catching the real bombers, they would have been put behind bars years ago. My sympathies go out to the parents and families of those 21 people who died in the pubs, and those 162 who were injured. For so many years the only consolation they could have had in their grief was a belief that the men who did it were in jail. To discover that's not the case can only have compounded their agony. I can understand the feelings of bitterness and hatred they must have felt towards us for so long. I would have felt the same had it been any of my children in one of those pubs. But I hope now they can see that we and our families were all victims too.

If the TV programme which named the alleged bombers got it right, then the police should be pursuing them with a view to bringing them to justice. Of the two said to have planted the bombs, one is now reputed to be a high-ranking member of the

IRA in Ireland, while the other lives alone with his secret on a housing estate in Dublin. The man said to have been the head of the Birmingham IRA and to have ordered the pub bombings left on the plane with McDade's body and is now an alcoholic living in Dublin. Also in Ireland are said to be the two men reputed to have made the bombs, one of whom phoned the warning to the *Birmingham Post* and *Mail*.

But in April 1994 the Chief Constable of the West Midlands Police, Ron Hadfield, announced that the file on the pub bombings was closed, saying, 'There are no more lines of inquiry.' He said that a three-year investigation which began after our release had not found sufficient evidence to support further criminal proceedings. 'We have done everything we could have possibly done to bring the perpetrators to justice,' he said.

I was angry, but not surprised. The police have always had a vested interest in keeping the belief going that they had caught the guilty men in the first place. When pressed by reporters about the acquittal of the Birmingham Six, Hadfield said pointedly, 'They were innocent so far as the courts were concerned.'

Whether or not any of the truly guilty men are still members of the IRA, the organisation's bloody war against Britain continued with no sign of peace until the ceasefire called by the IRA in late summer 1994. I pray that the ceasefire will be a lasting one, but I fear the troubles will never truly be at an end until Britain pulls out of Ireland altogether. But that could well be followed by a bloodbath of terrifying proportions. The British government has pledged that the North of Ireland will remain part of the United Kingdom so long as the majority of the people there so desire. To withdraw otherwise would be seen as a major victory for terrorism.

Despite that, opinion polls in Britain consistently show a majority of people in favour of withdrawal. Many ordinary English people take the view that the Irish should be left to fight it out themselves. They know that their sons are being killed in Ireland, but they know very little of what it's all about. I do know what it's about, and while I would like to see a united Ireland, I want to see the killing and suffering on both sides brought to an end. The question is how? I, like so many others, do not have any simple answers.

Nor, I am sorry to say, do I have the foolproof answer to how future miscarriages of justice can be prevented.

The Royal Commission into the criminal justice system, which was set up under Lord Runciman on the day we were released, reported to the government in July 1993 with a total of 352 recommendations. One of the most important, and it has since been accepted by the government, was that there should be a new independent review body, made up of lawyers and laymen, to oversee the investigation of alleged miscarriages of justice. It will be able to order fresh inquiries and, where suitable, refer cases to the Appeal Court, removing the Home Secretary's power of referral. It will not make a recommendation to the court, but will give the reason for referral and pass on any new evidence.

The trouble is that the new body, to be called the Criminal Cases Review Commission, will not have its own investigation team. It will continue to rely on the police to make new inquiries. The Royal Commission felt there was no practical alternative to using the police, but I disagree. I believe a team of independent lawyers and other suitable people could conduct the necessary inquiries without the risk of bias that is almost inevitable when policemen have to question the behaviour of fellow officers.

The Royal Commission also called for the creation of an advisory council to oversee forensic science services and ensure high standards; the retention of the adversarial system in courts, in which prosecution and defence lawyers fight it out; and the abolition of the right to trial by jury for relatively minor cases. As for judges, the Commission said there should be substantially more resources for training, and proper monitoring of performance. The government has yet to give its view on many of these other recommendations, but I can give them only a qualified welcome. I firmly believe the entire criminal justice system needs a more drastic overhaul. There has to be a better way. I make no claims to being an expert on the subject, but as somebody who has suffered at the sharp end of the system, I think I have a right to express thoughts on certain reforms I believe are essential.

There should be an entirely independent forensic science service, not just an advisory council. It should be funded by the government and be open for use by both prosecution and defence. At present the forensic scientists are tied too closely to the prosecution, which in real terms means the police. I would also like to see a mechanism which would allow a cooling-off period after arrests have been made, so that some independent body could then step in and look at things at an early stage. Perhaps something like the examining magistrate system used in France. I believe that in our case the early intervention of an independent body would have established pretty quickly that we were not a gang of bombers.

Obviously I am disappointed the Commission recommended that unsupported confessions should remain as a basis for conviction. And while I welcome the recommendation of a new body to consider possible miscarriages of justice, I don't think it goes far enough. Under the Commission's plan the final decision would still rest with the Court of Appeal. The court has proved so reluctant in the past to overturn convictions, even in the face of the most compelling evidence, that I think the new body should have the ultimate power to make decisions. Other suggestions, such as video recordings in police stations and training for officers in interviewing, should all help.

Miscarriages of justice undermine the confidence of society in the judicial system, and I don't just mean the jailing of the innocent. In the week the Birmingham Six were freed, a jury at the Old Bailey acquitted a young Irishman, Kevin Barry O'Donnell, of IRA-related charges after guns and ammunition were found in his car. Not long afterwards O'Donnell was shot dead in Northern Ireland and it became clear he was an IRA man. I don't know whether he was guilty or not of the charges against him in Britain. But it could be said that the members of his jury, influenced by all the publicity surrounding such a case of injustice as ours, were reluctant to convict in case they got it wrong.

There are many, many cases of people in jail who should not be there. The case with which I am most familiar, and which I will continue to campaign on until they are freed, is that of the Bridgewater Four, Jimmy Robinson, Michael and Vincent Hickey, and Patrick Molloy (who died in jail). As in our case, almost the entire population of the British prison system, both screws and cons, knows these men are innocent. Getting them out is another matter. The Home Secretary has consistently refused to reopen the case. I fear it may be that because there have been so many high-profile examples of miscarriages of justice in recent years, so many high-profile examples of convictions that have finally been quashed, that the powers-that-be now feel enough is enough, whatever the merits of individual cases. The Guildford Four, the Birmingham Six, the Maguire Seven (whose convictions were quashed only in 1991, after they had completed their sentences), Judith Ward (freed in 1992, after eighteen years) the Broadwater Three (convictions quashed in 1991), the Cardiff Three (freed in 1992) – I suspect that with those major, political cases out of the way the prison gates may have been slammed shut. I hope and pray that's not so.

Prison doesn't work as a means to reducing crime in society. We have more prisons than ever before in Britain, but crime continues to rise. The figures show that anybody who has been in once stands a very good chance of returning. I saw it at first hand. Guys who were finishing a sentence when I was first jailed were soon back in to serve another seven- or nine-year stretch. They completed that and were released, and before I was freed they were back in once more. Surely that is just the opposite of what society is trying to achieve in sending somebody to jail in the first place. The former Home Secretary, Douglas Hurd, said on a visit to Long Lartin Prison in the 1980s: 'People are sent to prison, and that is their punishment. They are not sent to prison to be additionally punished.'

But they are additionally punished, from the pettiness of the regime and the psychological intimidation of the prison officers with their boots and uniforms, to the incarceration of men in jails hundreds of miles from their families and friends. The deprivation of liberty is punishment enough; all the rest simply serves to breed resentment, which simmers constantly and occasionally boils to the surface in the form of prison riots. It's all very well hardliners spouting about prisons being full of warm cells and colour televisions, and demanding an ever more Draconian regime. But that rhetoric won't solve any of the problems. I believe that certain sweeping steps should be taken to bring about a massive change in the way prisons are run. Then there might be some hope of success for the programmes aimed at rehabilitating prisoners. At present the vast majority of cons just get increasingly bitter, and leave jail ready to be more anti-social than when they went in.

I think there should be a minimum standard of rights for prisoners, accompanied by a realistic grievance procedure, so that men do not see themselves as being in a system which views them as worthless. Recognition that prisoners are individuals who must be accountable for their actions would in itself encourage prisoners to adopt a measure of self-responsibility. Such a sense of responsibility would be further enhanced by introducing some form of meaningful work at more realistic rates of pay. At present prisoners are forced to work at soul-destroying, pointless tasks for pitiful amounts of money. Earning money which could be used to help to support a wife and children on the outside would be a great boost to a prisoner's self-esteem, the lack of which is at the root of so many problems. Allowing a prisoner to make some form of useful input on a whole range of issues within prison would be an improved preparation for eventual release into society.

Prisoners should be housed in jails near their families. Forcing a man's wife and children to travel hundreds of miles for a visit, with all that entails, simply breeds destructive resentment. A prison ombudsman should be appointed to oversee the operation of prison policy. And the Boards of Visitors, which could carry out some good work, should be reformed. At present they are too closely identified with disciplinary processes within prisons. Cons see them as nothing more than a rubber-stamping body for the governor's decisions. That undermines everything they do, and complete independence is the only answer.

Prison is a brutal place, ordained by a system which too often leaves it in the hands of brutal people to run. They try to grind you down and break your spirit, because then they can mould you to do their will. They have a saying in prison: Plan for the worst, hope for the best, and take what comes. It's the only way to survive.

Surviving in prison as an innocent man and winning freedom are really the only subjects I'm qualified to talk about with authority. I'm hoping to use that as a basis for my future life. I believe I'm now over the worst of the depression and difficulties that followed my release, and with the help of counselling have come to terms with the reality of my situation. Which is that, at fifty, I'm unlikely to be offered any meaningful employment and therefore it will be up to me to find something worthwhile to do.

So I have given a lot of thought to putting to good use the only valuable experience I've gained in what should have been a major part of my working life – how a victim of a miscarriage of justice can be set free. I hope to play a leading role in the formation of a national organisation to co-ordinate the efforts of the numerous, but separate, small groups fighting to highlight such miscarriages. It would provide a comprehensive support structure for innocent men and women serving life sentences. And it would offer that vital commodity – hope – to those who feel abandoned.

I have become well aware of the magnitude of the problem, both from my own years in prison and through meetings with families of prisoners since I was freed. The general public might not want to face the fact, but there really are an awful lot of innocent people behind bars. Many do not fight back at all because they believe there is no way out. For those who do fight, and their families, it is a lonely, uphill struggle. They have to battle alone because there is no organisation around specifically to help them.

I had not got a clue where to start when I was first locked up. But by the time I was released I was something of an expert on the appeals process and the formation of a campaign. It would be such a waste not to pass on the benefit of that expertise to those who desperately need it, and who should not have to spend years acquiring it in the way I did. And helping to do so would bring some real meaning to my own life.

What I foresee is a group made up of just a small core of full-time workers, who while few in number would have access to a broad range of key people in crucial areas: experienced campaigners, lawyers, journalists, and lobby groups. A convicted prisoner proclaiming his innocence could contact the group for help, either directly or through his family. His case would be studied, and an assessment made as to whether he was indeed a victim of a miscarriage of justice. I don't believe there is a serious danger of the group being fooled into taking up the cases of guilty men. The people making the assessment would be well experienced in separating those who have a case from those simply trying it on. It is nothing like as difficult as the authorities often try to make out.

Once a case was accepted, the group would swing into action on behalf of the prisoner, bringing pressure to bear in the appropriate quarters. The expertise of people who had led previous campaigns would be used; lawyers with the right experience for the particular case would be approached; the media would be presented with details and lobbied to take an interests, as would MPs. The family and friends of the convicted man would not have to feel they were alone in the wilderness, as happened to us and still happens today.

One of the most depressing handicaps for our original tiny band of supporters was that they had nobody to turn to, nobody who was willing even to listen. The group I envisage would provide that vital 'ear' that is so important in keeping hope alive.

The ultimate aim would be to get the innocent person back into court quickly, and once he or she was there to ensure that all the facts be presented to the court and public so that freedom would be the only outcome.

All of this is not some pipe dream floating around my head. It is something I have discussed at length with lawyers, prisoners and their families, campaigners and various other groups all around the country. There has been a great deal of enthusiasm for it. We have considered financing and the other logistics of founding such a group. I have already earmarked a proportion of my compensation to go towards its formation, and I am confident that others in the same position as myself will make generous donations. There is no doubt that it can be done. As soon as my claim is settled I intend to throw myself into setting it up with the same single-minded determination that got me out of prison.

As for other aspects of my life, I realise that I've still a long way to go on the hard road back to a normal existence. I take each day as it comes, knowing that slowly but surely I'm getting there. I still receive regular counselling, and I know that I shall need that sort of help for many years to come. I've accepted that my relationship with my children is not what I had hoped it would be, and never will be. But that does not mean I love them any less or, I hope, that they love me any less. I still keep in contact with them all, and still get a great kick out of playing with my grandchildren.

I go back to prison from time to time to see friends who are still inside, but I no longer feel that I must go back to escape the pressures of the outside world. I have passed my driving test and that has given a new freedom of another kind. I'm planning to take a computer course, which I think will prove invaluable in the work I plan to do in the years ahead.

I'm very happy and settled in my relationship with Alison, who has been and continues to be the finest stabilising influence I've known. I don't suffer those unexplained rages as much as I did in my early days of freedom, but they do still occur from time to time. Alison knows intuitively when the anger is about to erupt, and she seems

287

to have found the key to restoring my calmness. But I don't want to rush things. I learned through bitter experience in prison not to set my heart on anything. So I'm being cautious, enjoying our time together and taking the view that if things are meant to work out for us in the future, they will.

I see the other five lads from time to time. Like me they have all had, and will continue to have, problems arising from our shared experience. The fact that we were not close friends in the past and probably won't be in the future will never be able to break that special bond that now exists between us.

So I look to the future with optimism and confidence. I have something positive to aim for; I've a small group of friends I know I can rely on; I've a great lawyer; and I've got Alison. But most of all I've got the knowledge that I fought and struggled against the highest powers in the land for nearly seventeen years without ever letting them grind me down. I knew that one day I would beat them, that I would win. Now that I'm free I don't intend to let things go wrong.

In the years ahead I would like to lose the tag of being 'one of the Birmingham Six', although I doubt whether I'll ever again be known simply as Paddy Joe Hill. Whenever I am introduced to strangers they inevitably want to know about our ordeal and I accept that. I'm happy to talk about it. But to those people who offer me their sympathy I always say this.

Don't be sorry for me. Be angry.

Because everything that happened to me was done in your name.

# Postscript

Five years after being released from prison in March 1991, I and my fellow members of the Birmingham Six have still not reached an agreed settlement with the government on compensation for our ordeal.

Two interim payments have been made while our lawyers continue to negotiate on our behalf. The Home Office appointed an independent assessor whose task was to come up with a figure of fair compensation for all those seeking redress for years of imprisonment for crimes of which they were innocent. These included the high-profile cases – the Birmingham Six, the Guildford Four, the Maguire Seven, Judith Ward and so on – as well as some lesser-known victims of miscarriages of justice.

In my case, an offer of final compensation was made in March 1995. It was in my opinion a derisory amount, an insult to add to the injury of sixteen and a half years of wrongful imprisonment. My lawyers rejected it and pushed ahead with efforts to obtain a fair and realistic award.

Why on earth is it taking so long to finally resolve this matter? I know such things take time. I had expected it might take up to eighteen months after our release for the whole thing to be sorted out. But it has been five years. And there's still no end in sight to the wrangling. I can't help but think that perhaps the government has decided to set a certain amount of money aside to cover compensation to all the various claimants, leaving the assessor with the task of deciding how to slice the 'cake'. And if his starting point is a very small cake, it is no surprise that some of the slices he offers are thin indeed.

I don't believe that I am a greedy person, stubbornly holding out with a bitter determination for every penny I can get. I simply want to receive a fair and equitable payment that reflects the suffering I have endured. Until I do I cannot put it all behind me and get on with my life. The constant waiting for a final resolution, dragging on month after month, is like another form of imprisonment in itself. Until this is all settled I still don't have the freedom to plan what I will do in the years ahead. Luckily, I lead a fairly simple life and manage to survive on what remains of the interim compensation payments without any other significant form of income. I still have my home in North London and, I am delighted to say, Alison still shares it with me. I don't drink, or go to night clubs, or eat out very often. Occasionally the two of us go to the cinema, or to the theatre.

Most of my life is taken up with campaigning on behalf of others who have been wrongfully jailed, and in particular trying to win freedom for the three surviving members of the Bridgewater Four, whose case I have mentioned earlier. It remains a stain on British justice that these men are still locked up for a crime they did not commit. I travel to meetings and rallies around the country to speak about this case and other sad examples of miscarriages of justice. I generally receive expenses for my petrol or other travelling costs, and an evening meal. But it is all done on the basis of fairly loose arrangements and not as part of the co-ordinated system I would like to see set up through a properly-funded national organisation, as I have described in this book. That still remains my life's ambition. But until that compensation issue is resolved I am afraid all of those plans will have to stay on the back burner.

Relations with my children have improved slowly but surely over the past couple of years. I don't see them very frequently, but when we do get together I find that our conversations are becoming less and less strained. My son Sean has recently left Britain to build a new life for himself in South Africa where he has a job as a chef, so I don't expect to see him too much in the years to come. But when we parted it was on good terms; I took him to the airport to see him off.

I return to Birmingham regularly, mainly to see my mother who has been in poor health. It is on those trips that I occasionally call in to see my daughters. They are all busy with their own families, and with jobs or studying. But I can sense that there is a gradual thawing of the ice that had built up between us.

I still have problems with bouts of deep depression. But then, I was told long ago that the psychological damage inflicted by the experience I have been through would not be waved away with a magic wand on the day I left prison. I was examined by one of the top psychiatrists in the country who declared I would probably need to continue treatment for up to ten years – and possibly longer. At the time I thought he was talking nonsense. Now, halfway through that ten-year period, I can see how right he was. I still fly into fierce rages or sink into black moods without knowing why. I feel very mixed up and and cannot understand the conflicting emotions that often clog up my mind.

I am truly lucky to have the support of Alison, who has told me she can see the onset of a depressive mood as clearly as watching a black cloud beginning to obscure the sun.

These mood swings have given me a Jekyll and Hyde personality. I can be warm and loving and attentive. But I can also be cold and bitter, and almost evil. When I get like that nobody can get through to me.

I still dislike the idea of taking medication to help me over these problems, but I know that I must. So every now and then I take a short course of anti-depressants, and I find they help a great deal, although not to the extent that I have become hooked. My regular sessions with psychiatrist Dr McKeith are also a great help. It is such a relief just to be able to talk completely openly to someone who is used to dealing with people suffering from a similar kind of anguish. Each time I come away from a session I have a feeling of huge confidence that I am going to be able to cope for quite a while. Those are the problems I face on a personal level. On a much broader front, the conflict which led to my being jailed – Northern Ireland – has a crisis of its own.

The ceasefire called by the IRA in September 1994 came to an abrupt and bloody end on February 9, 1996, when a massive lorry bomb exploded in the Docklands area of London's East End. Two people died, scores were injured, and millions of pounds' worth of damage was caused. After seventeen months of peace, the spectre of the return of the bomb became reality. It was a devastating blow to the overwhelming majority of us who want to see the problems resolved by peaceful means.

But it was not unexpected. Despite what were no doubt acute differences of opinion within the hierarchy of the IRA, it announced a ceasefire on the expectation that such a move would lead to all-party talks – including the IRA's political wing Sinn Fein – on the future of Northern Ireland. Those talks never came about, mainly because of the British government's insistence that the IRA should give up at least some of its weaponry beforehand. Anybody with a passing knowledge of Irish history knew the IRA would never take such a step. And while I don't claim to be an expert on international political history, I've not heard of a similar conflict being resolved by talks after one side agreed to hand over its arms. The Middle East peace process was not dependent on the Palestinians' handing in their guns; the ANC did not give up their weapons before South Africa's peaceful transition to democracy; the Bosnian peace deal, fragile as it is, was not drawn up on the basis that any of the combatants would have to surrender their arms. So why has the so-called 'decommissioning of arms' issue taken on so much importance in the Northern Ireland peace process?

I think the British government was taken completely by surprise by the IRA ceasefire. Believing that it would never come about, Prime Minister John Major and his colleagues had no policy to put into effect once it did in fact happen. That vacuum was filled by Ulster Unionist and right-wing Tory MPs then demanding that talks could not take place unless weapons were handed in – a demand that Major took up and made his own. That led to the lengthy stalemate and the eventual, predictable return to violence.

I hold no brief for the IRA – the group, remember, whose activities led directly to my loss of liberty for more than sixteen years. But I do want to see an end to all violence in the north of Ireland, and I find it appalling that the prospect that was withing our grasp has been ripped away by short-sighted politicians and self-serving factions. At the time of writing (mid-February 1996) there is still a slim chance that people who treasured that seventeen-month period free of the bomb and the bullet can yet rescue it and turn it into a permanent peace.

I hope and pray that they do.